'Tis the Season for Murder

I grabbed my bathrobe and cocooned it around me, threw the door open, and gave Amber my best glare. "I can see I'm going to have to have another talk with Aunt Ginny about letting the police in without a warrant."

She sailed past me and pushed her sunglasses up to her blond cop bun. "I guess you're not entertaining right now, or you would have zhuzhed up a little. At least I hope."

"What could you possibly want at seven a.m.?"

Amber pulled a cell phone from her uniform pocket. "You'll want to sit down."

"I won't."

"You'll at least want to get changed."

"Not doin' it."

Amber sighed. "I need you to come with me."

"Why?"

"A body was found in a walk-in freezer."

"None of my business."

Amber tapped something on her phone. "It's a little bit your business."

"Why do I have to be involved? Can't I just revel in the glory that for once I didn't find it?"

"There was a note taped to the victim's shirt." She held up the screen so I could see the message. It said, "Get Poppy . . ."

Books by Libby Klein

Class Reunions Are Murder

Midnight Snacks Are Murder

Restaurant Weeks Are Murder

Theater Weeks Are Murder

Wine Tastings Are Murder

Beauty Expos Are Murder

Antiques Auctions Are Murder

Mischief Nights Are Murder

Silent Nights Are Murder

Published by Kensington Publishing Corp.

Silent Nights
Are
MURDER

LIBBY KLEIN

Kensington Publishing Corp.
www.kensingtonbooks.com

KENSINGTON BOOKS are published by

Kensington Publishing Corp.
900 Third Avenue
New York, NY 10022

All Kensington titles, imprints, and distributed lines are available at special quantity discounts for bulk purchases for sales promotion, premiums, fund-raising, educational, or institutional use.

Special book excerpts or customized printings can also be created to fit specific needs. For details, write or phone the office of the Kensington Sales Manager: Attn.: Sales Department. Kensington Publishing Corp., 900 Third Avenue, New York, NY 10022. Phone: 1-800-221-2647.

KENSINGTON and the KENSINGTON COZIES teapot logo Reg US Pat. & TM Off.

First Printing: October 2024
ISBN: 978-1-4967-4442-5

ISBN: 978-1-4967-4443-2 (ebook)

10 9 8 7 6 5 4 3 2 1

Printed in the United States of America

For my mother. Who wasn't impressed that I was a published author until Alexa knew my name.

And for my readers. Thank you for going on this amazing journey with me. I'm so thrilled that you love Poppy and Aunt Ginny as much as I do.

CHAPTER 1

"Who wrapped Figaro like the baby Jesus and stuffed him in the manger?"

Aunt Ginny called to me from the dining room, where she was putting away the breakfast china. "He likes it."

My black-smoke Persian stared at me, his wide, orange eyes unblinking.

"Do you really want to be part of the Nativity scene? 'Cause I can have Smitty take you out to the yard as soon as he arrives to put the lights up."

Figaro's eyes bore into mine, and he squirmed.

"I didn't think so." I extracted my fluffy cat from the wooden trough and unswaddled him. Fig fled the sitting room, to enact his vengeance upon the next victim who wandered across his path.

Aunt Ginny marched in with a plate of cherry Christmas cookies and placed them on the coffee table for our guests. "You would think a missing engagement ring would strike terror in the heart of the man who suddenly finds his pocket ten grand lighter, but our men are as tight-lipped as a Russian spy in the suburbs."

"I'm sure someone is just waiting for the right moment." *Or in Royce's case, he's forgotten he bought a ring.*

Aunt Ginny huffed. "Well, Royce had better hurry up and get to asking me before the Senior Center Christmas party. I'm a hot ticket as a holiday date."

"That's because you carry peppermint schnapps in a flask for emergencies."

She gave me some side-eye. "It protects against the flu." Aunt Ginny threw her hands into the air. "I'm calling an emergency meeting."

"I don't have time for an emergency meeting. You wanted me to read your great-great-grandfather's diary today to see if this family was cursed." *So far, my experience points to yes.*

"That curse is a hundred years old. A couple more days won't kill us. I need to know if Royce is going to propose before I put on my holiday weight. Get the girls assembled while I make some cocoa."

I sent my best friend Sawyer a 911 text.

You were right. Aunt Ginny was the first to crack. Get over here.

OMW.

Sawyer had discovered the ring box three nights ago after Thanksgiving dinner, while we sat in the wood-paneled library with my Great Aunt Ginny and Georgina, the woman I used to call my monster-in-law.

Actually, it was Figaro who'd discovered the blue velvet box and swatted it to our attention. That was the last time a male had been helpful in this situation. We'd waited for nearly two hours to see which man would return in a panic, giggling over what possible excuse he would come up with as to why he was back so soon. Lost wallet? Missing cell phone? And my personal favorite—intense candied yam craving. We were prepared to act clueless. Something women had been doing to preserve the male ego since the Garden of Eden.

All night, I kept checking my cell phone, sure that Officer Ben Consuelos would call me any minute and ask about the ring, swearing me to secrecy from Sawyer. Or Smitty would appear at the back door and make some excuse about a creaky hinge that needed to be oiled that Georgina couldn't know about. But not even Aunt Ginny's eighty-year-old boyfriend showed up with no idea of what he was looking for, but sure it was here.

Nothing.

After three days of strategic hints and cleverly placed engagement innuendos, we'd learned exactly Jack Diddly.

Now Aunt Ginny was herding Georgina into the library so we could discuss our fellas and their irritating sneakiness.

I had just got the logs in the fireplace to catch when Sawyer brought in a silver tray carrying four hot cocoas and gingerbread biscotti. "I thought for sure Royce would crack by now."

Aunt Ginny took her seat and blew across a steamy cocoa. I caught a peppermint whiff and gave her some side-eye and a little cough. She gave me a prim look, pulled the blue-velvet ring box from the pocket of her sweater, and set it on the tray table in the midst of us. She cracked it open, and we all observed a reverential moment of silence for the one-carat diamond.

Georgina broke the spell. "Have you just been carrying that around this whole time?"

Aunt Ginny looked affronted. "Not the whole time, no. I keep it under my pillow when I go to bed."

I was a little stunned and a lot nervous. "I thought we were going to lock it in the safe until someone asks for it."

Georgina reached for the ring. "We don't know where your crazy cat found it. Smitty could have lost it in the bathroom."

Aunt Ginny smacked her hand. "Don't touch it. I'm

sure Royce would have come back to look for it by now, but he might not remember where he left it."

Royce was the front-runner in my mind for our missing groom. His dementia was the strongest argument we had for why a proposer would go silent for this long. I felt like the other three candidates would have spoken up and pulled one of us into his confidence by now.

Of course, that would mean one of the ladies in this room was a traitor and holding a secret we all agreed not to keep just three nights ago.

Figaro pranced into the library with his flat nose in the air, following the scent of drama. He jumped into Sawyer's lap and settled down like he was going for a cuddle. Sawyer rubbed him under the chin. *Sucker*. She'd have a fluffy paw in her cup before the whipped cream was gone.

Georgina nibbled the end of a biscotti. "I think we need to give them an opportunity to return to the scene of the crime. Maybe they hid the box somewhere and they don't realize the ring is missing. Your crazy cat may have ruined someone's surprise engagement. And that someone may have driven all the way up here from Waterford, and she has a big New Year's charity event to prepare for and can't afford to hang around and wait much longer."

Figaro's ears pinned down, and he lifted his back leg in Georgina's direction to start an aggressive bath from Sawyer's lap.

Sawyer had to use two hands to hold her cocoa steady. "What if we have a dinner party and invite everyone who was here on Thanksgiving, to give the man a chance to look for the missing ring?"

Aunt Ginny nodded and made mm-hmm noises with a mouthful of biscotti. "Let's have a tree-trimming party next week. Poppy can make dinner . . ."

Why does every plan include Poppy can make dinner?

"And we can invite everyone to decorate the trees for the bed and breakfast. It was going to be a lot of work for just Poppy and Kenny anyway."

I notice one name is conveniently left off that list, Ginny.

Sawyer stroked Fig's cottony fur. "That sounds like fun. But is one week enough time?"

Aunt Ginny waved her biscotti. "For a free dinner? I think we could get most of those yahoos with an hour's notice."

Sawyer grinned. "I'm sure Ben could make it as long as we can work around his shift with the police department."

Figaro agreed and plunged his paw into her cup like a furry slingshot.

Sawyer jumped. "Oh, you little brat."

Fig was vigorously licking the cream from his front paw, clearly full of regret.

After the last few days, my nerves were frayed. I was just getting used to having a boyfriend after being widowed. It was one thing to wait for Prince Charming to drop down to one knee, but these women were ready to throw down a silk pillow and give him a push. "Do you all really want to get married again? I mean, Aunt Ginny, Royce would be husband number six for you. Aren't you afraid people will talk?"

Aunt Ginny tilted her head in thought. "I don't care what people think. My life is no one's business but mine. I'd love to have the ceremony with the dress and the flowers and the cake. Plus, I'm not getting any younger. And I'm almost positive I got around to getting divorced from the last one after he disappeared for that Baby Ruth."

Georgina shot into the conversation like she hadn't heard a word Aunt Ginny just said. "There's no law about how long one needs to wait before remarrying. You need to grab happiness where you can, and I've been a widow long enough. My little Smitty is perfect. At least he will be after I throw out all those Three Stooges sweatshirts and his Eagles hat and get him to stop making those 'nyuck nyuck' noises. I'd have to return that cute little ring and replace it with the two-carat canary diamond I've had my eye on at Valkyrie's, but I don't think he would mind."

I reached for my cocoa. *He certainly wouldn't be surprised.*

"You know"—Aunt Ginny had her poke-the-bear gleam in her eye—"Smitty isn't a rich man, and you're . . ."

I cut in with, ". . . used to expensive things?"

Aunt Ginny snapped her eyes to Georgina. "Shallow. Are you sure you're ready to be a handyman's wife?"

"That's true, Georgina." Sawyer picked up a gingerbread biscotti. "Would you really leave your mansion in Virginia to move up here?"

I held my breath as fear washed over me.

Georgina tucked her feet under her and sipped her cocoa. "Definitely not."

Oh, thank God.

"Smitty would move in with me and start looking for odd jobs in neighboring towns where people don't know me. And it's not like I'd have to go to lumberyard meetings. My late husband left me very well off, so I really just want the companionship."

I whispered to Sawyer. "How long till she thinks about a prenup?"

Georgina stared wistfully at the fire. "It would be unwise to jeopardize my stocks and bonds by combining our incomes."

Sawyer gave me a wry look. "Two seconds. What about you, Poppy? Is something worrying you about marrying Gia when he asks?"

All eyes were on me, and I squirmed. "Don't you mean 'if'?"

The three of them laughed. Figaro used the distraction and shot his paw into Sawyer's whipped cream again. *Thanks, baby.*

Sawyer huffed and put him on the floor.

Aunt Ginny nudged the feline with her toe, and he ignored her. "Don't be crazy. Gia is smitten with you. I've never seen a man so twitterpated before. And that includes all five of my husbands and some of my in-between amours that you don't even know about."

Aunt Ginny had raised me from the time my mother rolled up and dropped me off right before my ninth birthday. I'd only ever met husband number five, my Uncle Danny, but some of the flings I'd seen after he disappeared seemed pretty spicy. Don't even mention the lieutenant governor to her. You'll learn way more than you want to know.

Sawyer placed her cocoa on the table. "Don't worry if things seem to be moving fast, Poppy. That's normal. You've only had one serious boyfriend before you got married. My ex-husband treated adultery like he was filling up a punch card to get his twelfth affair free. I'm ready for someone stable who makes me happy. Ben makes me very happy—and I've never seen you happier than you are with Gia."

Georgina put her hand on my knee. "My son loved you very much, but he's gone now. And you deserve to move on. If Gia proposes, I'll be thrilled for you. It'll give me more time to work on Smitty anyway."

That was the nicest thing Georgina had ever said to me. She obviously thought Smitty bought the ring.

Figaro jumped in my lap, and I covered my cocoa with my hand. *This is not my first rodeo, Bucko.* "So it's decided then. Next Sunday, we'll have a tree-trimming party and get all the men back over here to see if anyone goes on a mad search for the ring box."

Sawyer giggled. "At the end of the night, we can light up the tree and see whose finger sparkles."

Aunt Ginny dinged her teacup with her spoon. "Operation Engagement is officially a go."

CHAPTER 2

A cold December wind blew off the Atlantic Ocean, tickling the few remaining leaves on the red oak outside my bedroom window. The shadows danced above me like a flock of sparrows. My room was toasty warm, due in part to the Persian hat I was wearing against my will.

It had been five days since we'd organized the dinner-party ambush, and it was all the ladies could talk about. Each one of them had their wedding planned; all they needed now was a proposal. I was just trying to enjoy having a light schedule for a change. No more ghost tours. No more gourmet-dinner shows. No full house to cook for or restaurants to help. Of course, if it snowed, we'd be packed. Christmas in Cape May under a blanket of snow was breathtaking. It was also rare. I checked the forecast again. No snow for the next ten days.

There were three seasons to obsess about the weather. Tourist season—when guests considered it a personal failure on my part if it rained during their vacation. Hurricane season—because my creditors don't care about safety cancellations; they just want to be paid. And Christmas season—because I was delusional enough to want snow like I was living in a Bing Crosby movie. *Irving Berlin had set sixty percent of the country up for annual disappointment.*

I only had two rooms to get ready for this afternoon. A couple from Philly, and a solo guest named Doris Nightingale who should be pretty low-key. If things stayed quiet, Gia and I could bask in the romantic glow of our first Christmas together. If only I could stop being vexed by a shiny rock the size of a shirt button. *That engagement ring.*

I tried to roll over, and the fur hat's bottlebrush tail languidly dropped down to cover my face. "I'm starting to sweat, Figaro. Maybe you could move off my pillow for a while."

Figaro's tail curled back around my forehead, and he started to purr. He appreciated extravagant amounts of attention. *Don't we all?*

I checked the time and read ten after seven. It's not often I can have a lie-in like this anymore. Things had slowed down at the Butterfly Wings Bed and Breakfast. Tourists still came to the beach in the winter; they just didn't flock to it in droves, demanding all-you-can-eat crabs. I was planning on spending my afternoon baking at La Dolce Vita. I didn't really have to bake in the coffee shop anymore, but I looked forward to any chance I got to spend time with the man I was head over heels in love with.

I saw myself spending the rest of my life with Gia. I just wasn't sure I was ready to book the church right now. We were in the fun phase, where everything was exciting and new. I still got butterflies whenever Gia said my name. Once you're married, you fight over which way the toilet paper hangs and whose fault it is that the trash didn't go out. I wasn't ready to go there yet.

Plus, I'd only been a widow for eighteen months. Everyone had an opinion about whether that was too fast or too slow to be moving on.

I tried to roll over again, and Figaro batted my nose with a wet paw. *Eww.*

I wanted to tell everyone to get out of my head and take a flying leap, but years of trying to please people so they would like me had melted my backbone.

What if that ring is for me?

I loved Gia with all my heart. And I couldn't love Henry more if I'd birthed him myself. I thought motherhood was one of life's doors that had bitterly slammed in my face, and I would never get to open it again. A little blue velvet box was tempting me to think the door had cracked open.

What if that ring isn't for me?

I stretched, and Figaro slid down to the mattress. He opened one eye to glare at me.

"You can't guilt me today, Fig. I have lovely things planned. I might just lie here all morning. Do some Christmas shopping on my laptop. Work on some menus. I think I'll buy a holiday beauty mask and plan a spa day. You want me to see if Chewy has a Christmas catnip toy for you? Your crinkly chicken is one swat away from total disintegration."

A familiar flashing blue light joined the dancing leaf shadows on my wall and grabbed my good mood by the hair. I closed my eyes and thought about my happy place. La Dolce Vita, in Gia's arms, with a cappuccino. *My happy place is certainly well caffeinated.*

A light rap on the front door made me close my eyes tighter. *Go away go away go away.* My cell phone played sleigh bells. I opened one eye and looked at the screen. It was Amber.

I need to talk to you.

No.

Come on, McAllister. It's important.

I'm not home.
Aunt Ginny says you are.
Aunt Ginny drinks.

After a minute, there was a knock on my bedroom door. I nudged Fig, and he gave me a look that said, *None of my friends are up yet.*

"Who is it?"

"Aunt Ginny. Let me in."

I grabbed my bathrobe and cocooned it around me, threw the door open, and gave Amber my best glare. "I can see I'm going to have to have another talk with Aunt Ginny about letting the police in without a warrant."

She sailed past me and pushed her sunglasses up to her blond cop bun. "I guess you're not entertaining right now, or you would have zhuzhed up a little. At least I hope."

"What could you possibly want at seven a.m.?"

Amber pulled a cell phone from her uniform pocket. "You'll want to sit down."

"I won't."

"You'll at least want to get changed."

"Not doin' it."

Amber sighed. "I need you to come with me."

"Why?"

"A body was found in a walk-in freezer."

"None of my business."

Amber tapped something on her phone. "It's a little bit your business."

"Why do I have to be involved? Can't I just revel in the glory that, for once, I didn't find it?"

"There was a note taped to the victim's shirt." She held up the screen so I could see the message. It said, "Get Poppy."

CHAPTER 3

An engagement ring isn't labeled, but the dead guy is addressed to me. *What psycho knows my name and leaves it on their victim in a freezer?*

Amber clicked on her police radio and alerted someone on the other end that we were coming in. "So, any plans for the holidays?"

I opened the passenger door of her police cruiser and moved the half-empty jumbo bag of Twizzlers off the seat. "Hmm. Not yet. I mean, other than a dinner party we're having Sunday night."

Amber gave me a tight smile and pulled away from the curb. "That sounds fun. What's the party for?"

"To suss out who's getting engaged. Where is this place anyway? Do you have any leads?"

"No leads. What do you mean who's getting engaged?"

I told Amber about the ring box we found on Thanksgiving and how no one had come forward to admit they'd lost it. "So we're gonna recreate the scene with the same people and see what happens."

"What time do you want me there?"

Oh right. "Um, we're thinking five to start decorating, then seven to eat."

Amber grinned. "Then nine to corner the groom with a shotgun?"

"Something like that." It looked like we were heading off the island. That would lower the odds considerably that I knew the victim. "Are we going over the bridge?"

Amber turned down her radio. "Listen. There's something you should know."

"Let me guess. I'm a suspect."

"No. At least I think I talked Kieran down from suspect to person of interest. But if we find evidence to incriminate you, it'll blow that Armani tie right off his neck."

"Evidence to incriminate me? Who was killed?"

"I was wondering when you'd get around to asking that. And Kieran doesn't want me to tell you. He wants to gauge your reaction when you get there to give your statement."

That's sick and twisted. "Are you sure Kieran isn't from South Jersey?"

"He's not, but it looks like he may be staying indefinitely. He put in for the permanent chief position."

"What happened to Internal Affairs? Isn't this a demotion?"

Amber shrugged. "I don't know. For some reason, he wants to stay in Cape May. Maybe it's the beach and the balmy weather."

A few snow flurries lazily drifted by. "Is that what you wanted to warn me about? That Kieran is staying?"

We were approaching the marina and the Cape May bridge. Amber glanced my way. "No, I wanted you to know the suspects are not exactly on board with us bringing you on-site."

"Well yeah. Why would they be? I'm the Cape May Harbinger of Death."

"There's something else. Today is not going to be easy for you, and I'm sorry." Amber put on her blinker and made the left turn at a giant crab in a perky blond wig and pearls.

Oh my God. Please be going anywhere else. How many times had I turned in here to deliver desserts or work in the kitchen? My breath froze in my chest like I'd been stabbed by an icicle. I grabbed for the handle. "Stop the car. I'm going to be sick."

Amber slammed on the brakes, and I flung the door open and threw up in the clamshell parking lot. She handed me a couple of McDonald's napkins. "I'm sorry. I really wanted to tell you the crime scene is your ex-boyfriend's restaurant."

CHAPTER 4

Everything was swirling around me like a Van Gogh nightmare. "Is Tim dead? Is that what you aren't telling me?"

Amber rolled the car deeper into the lot. A white Seymour Veg box truck was parked next to a blue Deepwater Fisheries van that had THIEF painted across it in bright pink graffiti. She spoke softly. "I would have told you if it was Tim."

Amber got out of the cruiser, but my butt was fused to the seat.

She tapped on my window.

I shook my head no.

Amber tried the handle, but I'd locked it. "Poppy. Will you please trust me?"

Poppy? Since when doesn't she passive-aggressively call me McAllister? I rolled my eyes to hers through the window.

She softened her expression and bobbed her head towards the restaurant my former fiancé owned. "I wouldn't do that to you."

I opened the door and swung my legs out. I tried to stand. Amber put her hand under my arm and pulled.

The first thing I saw inside was Tim in a crumpled black T-shirt and jeans, backed against the workbench, locked in interrogation by Chief Kieran Dunne. Even though his brow was wrinkled and his eyes were tight with stress, a hundred pounds dropped off my shoulders, and I floated with relief that he was alive.

After breaking up with him for the second time, he didn't seem to share my sentiment. He turned at the sound of the door, and his expression fell from distress to disgust. He ran his hand through his blond hair and groaned. "I told you to bring anybody but her."

Kieran adjusted the tiny silver badge cufflink on his tailored shirt as he closely observed Tim's reaction to me.

I didn't care. I was so overwhelmed that I burst into tears. Tim and I as a couple may be a thing of the past, but a part of me would always love him. I certainly couldn't face the thought that he might have been murdered.

Tim watched me, and his eyes softened. They hardened again just as quickly, and he turned away.

Kieran opened a leather notebook and gave me a once-over as sharp as his suit.

Amber took me by the arm and faced her boss eye to eye. "I told you I didn't agree with this decision because she'd be traumatized."

His expression remained cold, calculated. "She hasn't even seen the victim yet."

Amber gently huffed and led me to the walk-in freezer. A shiny padlock hung from a latch at the top of the door, which was propped open, and a stocky white man with sandy blond hair was on the floor, crammed between an enormous box of chicken tenders and a five-pound bag of peaches that were melting to a soupy, sticky mess. The victim had Tim's custom chef knife plunged in his chest and the note taped to his sweatshirt.

Amber faced me. "Well?"

I shrugged. I was only now starting to breathe normally. "Well what?"

Amber's lips twitched. "Do you know him?"

"No. Who is he?"

"Wes Bailey, owner of Deepwater Fisheries. He supplies seafood to the restaurant."

Recognition dawned, and I called over to Tim. "Hey. Is this the fish guy you were always rushing away to call?"

Tim wouldn't look me in the eye, but the muscles in his jaw clenched. "You haven't been here for months. You have no idea who I call."

My cheeks caught fire, and I looked away.

Kieran glanced at Amber, then consulted his notes. "Mr. Bailey was discovered at six thirty a.m. by the produce vendor, Jackson Seymour of Seymour Veg, who is in the dining room going over his statement with Officer Birkwell. He has reported that the two of them did not usually cross paths."

"I'm surprised either one of them was here before the sous chefs arrived to receive the deliveries." I nervously glanced at Tim to see if he was going to bite my head off again. "At least that's what they did when I worked here."

Kieran poised his pen over his notebook. "Ms. McAllister, have you ever met the victim?"

"No."

"Are you sure?"

"Yes, of course."

"Then why does he have a note on his chest to get you?"

"Well, it's not likely he taped that note on himself, now is it?"

Kieran flicked his eyes to mine, and they were icier than those chicken fingers Wes Bailey was crushing.

"Did you check the knife for fingerprints?"

"Despite what you may believe, Ms. McAllister, the police in this town know how to do their jobs. They don't need your help or your interference."

I turned to the door. "Sounds good. I'll be going home now."

Amber grabbed my arm. "Not yet. You still have to give your statement."

I sighed loudly so they would be sure to know I was irritated. "That lock on the freezer is new. Why is that there?"

Tim crossed his arms over his hard chest and leaned against the workbench. "Gigi thinks someone has been stealing food. She put new locks on both the walk-ins and the back door."

I looked around. "I see that my chef coat is gone."

Tim snorted. "Why would I keep it when you obviously didn't want it."

"Of course, I wanted it. It wasn't right for me."

Tim's eyes flashed fire. "Then you shouldn't have strung it along for six months if it wasn't right!"

"I didn't string it along. I loved both of you, and you made me choose."

"You were supposed to choose me!"

Amber put her hand on my arm. "Okay, calm down."

I muttered to myself. "I haven't been here since April. A lot has changed."

Amber turned to face her boss. "What about the security cameras? Did they pick anything up?"

A pink blush climbed up Tim's neck, and he shoved his hands in his pockets.

Kieran shook his head. "The lenses are coated from the salt air. The picture is too blurry to make out."

That's just like Tim. The food was always his first love. "I thought you were going to upgrade the system."

Tim growled. "And I thought you were done fooling around with other men."

We faced each other in silent frustration until Kieran cleared his throat. "Mr. Maxwell, why don't we have you wait in the dining room with the others."

Tim glared at me for a few more beats, then stormed from the room.

Amber crouched down to get a better view of the body. "Was the freezer locked when the produce guy found the victim?"

Kieran nodded. "He says it was."

Amber pointed at the body. "What about the keys in his pocket there?"

Kieran squatted next to her and snapped a couple pictures. From my vantage behind them, they looked like two children playing detective.

Amber approached the body and put on a pair of latex gloves that she pulled from her pocket. Then she pulled a ring of keys from the pocket of the dead guy and tried them in the padlocks and the back door. He had one for each.

"Can I go wait in the car?"

Amber flicked her eyes to mine, then rolled her gaze across the room.

Geez, Amber. You want me to snoop right in front of the chief? Someone's getting bold. I looked around to see if anything obvious had changed. Apart from the white-board full of rules in a woman's handwriting, everything seemed in the right place.

Amber rose to her full height, which isn't saying much. "The killer could have followed the victim in here when he made his delivery, but they'd need their own key to the freezer to lock him inside."

Kieran stood and straightened his leather shoulder holster. "That narrows the suspect pool considerably."

I spotted a flash of gold partially under the victim's elbow and nudged Amber. "What's that?"

Amber picked it up and held it in the palm of her hand. It was an earring shaped like a crab. She dropped it in a plastic evidence bag.

A team of officers arrived from the forensics unit, and Amber backed away from the freezer. She took off her gloves and stuffed them in her pocket. "Alright. Let's get your statement."

Kieran puffed his chest out. "Take her in the other room, and let her give it to Birkwell."

Amber threw him a glare. "Why can't she do it in here?"

Kieran gave her a stony look back. "You know why."

Amber crossed her arms. "And you know why I think that's a bad idea."

They faced off silently until Kieran softened his expression. "This is a murder investigation. I can't protect feelings."

Amber sighed. "Come with me. You can give your statement to Officer Birkwell. How well do you know Jackson Seymour?"

We walked to the double doors that separated the kitchen from the dining room. "I've seen his truck around town, but I'm sure that's all."

Amber paused with her hand on the door. "Poppy."

"What?"

"Brace yourself."

CHAPTER 5

We pushed through the swinging door into the dimly lit formal dining room. There were a few curvy booths on the left called snugs, and white-linen-covered tables with miniature poinsettias dotted around the rest of the room. On the far right, there was a cherrywood bar decorated in white twinkle lights. The server's station, with ordering system and water pitchers, was just outside the kitchen. The nervous hum in the room went silent when we entered.

Officer Birkwell was in a snug to the left. Next to him was a rotund man shaped like Buddha, but with a full bushy head, a face of brown hair, and a T-shirt that said BODY BY SALAD.

On the right at the bar, Chuck and Tyler, the sous chefs, were sitting with Sawyer's boyfriend, Officer Ben Consuelos. Chuck gave me a tiny wave and pushed his black-rimmed glasses up his nose.

And right down the center of the dining room, Tim was standing behind his terminally perky partner Gigi, who was sitting at a table drinking some kind of green sludge.

Gigi's bouncy blond curls were pulled up into a tight

pouf. Her face couldn't decide if it was pale or pink, so it chose a blotchy mixture of both to accentuate her deepening scowl. "Get her out of here. I said I forbid it!" She struggled to her feet, revealing a baby bump that was either eleven months along or triplets.

What the Shamu! I started mentally working back to the day I told Tim I was choosing Gia. *When was that? Middle of March? Almost exactly nine months ago.* I had seen them in the baby store weeks after we broke up, but refused to believe it. I cut my eyes to Tim. "I see the mentoring's going well."

"You stopped having a say in my life the day you walked out of here."

My eyes were drawn back to Gigi's belly. She gave me a smug look and rubbed her hand over her hot-pink maternity sweater. *Well, you finally won, girl.* Tim sure didn't waste any time moving on. I was taking things much slower with Gia. A snail's pace, as Gia had pointed out, more than once.

Amber put her hand on my back. "So. Do you know him?"

"Know who?" The words came out a little more acidic than I meant them to be.

Amber leaned in so no one else could hear her. "I'm sorry you had to find out about Gigi this way. I was really hoping you already knew. You normally can't keep any secrets in this town. I just need to know if one of these people could have put the note on the victim."

I willed myself to calm down. I also willed Tim and Gigi to break out in genital rashes. "I know the chefs, but I've never met the vegetable guy."

"Maybe you could have a little chat with him and see if he admits he left the note. Let me know if he says anything useful."

"Fine. Then I want to go home."

"Of course."

I walked over to the booth to introduce myself to the produce delivery man. Officer Birkwell snapped his notebook shut and gave me a nod. I took a seat while trying not to stare at Gigi's belly, but it had its own gravitational pull. "Hi."

The man ran a hand through his beard to capture it, then let it spring back into a frizzy bush. "Jackson Seymour. Are you with the police?"

"They seem to think so. I hear you found the deceased."

He nodded. "I was putting some fruit pies in the freezer, like I do every week for Tim."

I held in a snort. *Frozen pies? How the mighty have fallen, Gigi—Miss Culinary School Snob.*

"When I opened the door, he was just lying there. I called Tim right away. Then I called 911 and waited for you guys to arrive."

The first time I found a dead person, I stuffed a pompom back in her mouth and tried to run away before anyone could spot me. I'm still mad that I wasn't faster. "That was very conscientious of you. Did you know the victim?"

Jackson eyed me warily. "I knew it was Wes Bailey. I'd seen his van outside."

"Were you friends?"

"Not as such. We have mostly different customers; a few overlap, but I do restaurant delivery all over Cape May, so we ran into each other once in a while. It's really sad to find him like this. It's a shock."

"I'm sorry. I know what that's like."

Jackson's eyes went glassy. He nodded back.

"Do you know who painted 'thief' across his van?"

"I have no idea."

"Was there anyone who might want to hurt him?"

He ran his hand back down his beard and let it spring out again. "No. Like I told the other cop, I didn't know a lot about Wes. He sells fish, and I sell produce. There's enough business in this town for everyone. We aren't the only fish and produce guys on the island."

"I see. By any chance, was that note to 'Get Poppy' already pinned on him when you first saw him?"

"Yeah. Freaky, right? I wouldn't want to be Poppy. That's for sure."

You are not alone in that. "One more thing. Was the freezer open or shut when you got here?"

"It was locked tight."

"How did you get in?"

"I used the keys Tim gave me." He pulled out a key ring and held up two keys. One was a run-of-the-mill key everyone has for their front door. The other was different. Thicker. It had DO NOT DUPLICATE stamped on the head.

I thanked him and left the booth. I crossed the room and approached Tim at the front. His expression was guarded and weary. He was massaging Gigi's shoulders like he was salting a pork shank. "How many people have keys to those new locks?"

Gigi grabbed Tim's hand and threw me a glare. "Only Tim and I have keys. Right, baby?"

I had to stifle a chuckle when Jackson Seymour overheard her and answered. "And me."

Gigi's face turned puce. "I know you didn't give out copies of our keys to the vendors when we don't know who's stealing from us, Tim. You wouldn't do that to me, would you, Tim?"

Tim held his hands up to make a shield against the crazy. "The locks came with four keys. I don't want to come in at the butt crack of dawn just because you think some filets are missing."

Gigi threw her arms across her belly in a melodramatic huff—she was pouting for two. "I said no one but us, Tim. How could you betray me like that?"

"Geeg, I can't do everything."

Gigi started to cry. "Excuse me for carrying your child."

Tim glanced at me, then away. "We'll talk about this later."

Gigi stomped her foot. "I want to talk about it now!"

Yep, that right there. That's what happens when the honeymoon is over. I'm not sure I ever want to get married again.

Officer Birkwell entered the dining room from the kitchen door and hovered around the server's station. He watched Tim and Gigi have their argument, then approached Amber and handed her a document. "This is a list of all current employees."

She called me over. "Who on this list do you know?"

I read through the names. "I only know Chuck and Tyler. And that pregnant nightmare over there. Everyone else is new."

Tim and Gigi were having a heated argument in angry whispers, so Amber made a face and nudged me to go schmooze the sous chefs at the bar while Officer Consuelos headed back into the kitchen.

I approached the boys, who I'd worked with before things had gotten ugly. Chuck was Tim's sous chef when I met him. Tim had hired him right out of culinary school. He was in his late twenties and a little goofy, with dark hair and square glasses.

Tyler was a little older than Chuck and a lot tanner. He had sexy fireman-calendar good looks except for a crooked nose from a surfboard that got the upper hand. He started at Maxine's after Tim's business picked up from the publicity over that mystery basket chef competition last winter. They were both watching me expectantly now.

I pulled out a chair, and Chuck grinned, then had to push his glasses back up his nose again. "Hey Poppy. Did you see that note?"

"Yeah." I lowered my voice to a whisper. "Which one of you wrote it?"

Tyler yawned. "Not me. I'm only here now because Tim called me at oh-dark-thirty and said to come in because a body was found in the freezer. I can't tell you how shocked I was to see your name on his chest."

Chuck nodded. "Same."

"So neither of you left a message for me on the murder victim?"

They both shook their heads.

"'Cause I don't know anyone else who works here other than Tim and Gigi. And I'm fairly certain it was neither of them."

Gigi had her head buried in Tim's chest, and he was rubbing her back. She'd apparently won the argument.

"What were you guys doing last night?"

Chuck leaned in and whispered. "I was home with my mom. She waits up for me because I have to get her medicine ready."

Tyler yawned again. "I'm sorry. I'm not used to being up this early. My girlfriend will back me up that I didn't leave the house before I got the call from Tim to come in this morning."

Chuck yawned next. "Mother will be very worried when she sees I'm not in my bed."

"You can probably call her and tell her you're okay. I'll ask officer Amber." *Now I'm yawning.*

"Thanks. If she makes my oatmeal, I have to eat it before I can have anything else. And my dog, Skippy, is real tired of cold oatmeal."

Tyler ruffled his shaggy blond hair out of his eyes. "Dude. Things have been rough since you left."

"Rough how?"

"Well, for starters, Tim was a bear that first month after you dumped him for the barista."

Chuck picked at the shoelace on his high-tops. "Then

Gigi took over like she's flippin' Gordon Ramsay, and it became a hostile work environment for everyone."

Tyler groaned. "It's so much worse now that she's a momster."

Chuck nodded along. "Yeah. If they're looking for who killed the guy in the freezer, my money's on her."

"To hear her now," Tyler lilted his voice in a Gigi impersonation, "*It's such a tragedy that poor man was killed. Where was that the other day when she was screaming at Wes that she would sue him if he didn't let them out of his 'unethical contract'?*"

Chuck yawned. "I don't trust her."

I glanced at Gigi. She was still hugging Tim, but giving me some side glare from under his arm. *I don't either, but a killer?* "Do you really think, with that belly, she could get close enough to that guy to stab him, though? Just how pregnant is she?"

Chuck shrugged, "Like, two years."

Tyler appraised Gigi like she was a car he wanted to buy. "No, I think she said she was due around New Year's Eve. That's why she made us all sign those papers that the holidays were blackout dates for taking time off because she could go into labor at any moment."

New Year's Eve minus forty weeks . . . Did she get pregnant the same day I told Tim we wouldn't work out?

"McAllister!"

"What!"

"Don't you hear me talking to you?"

"No. I'm doing . . . math."

Amber looked from me to Gigi and back. "You won't like the answer. Come on, we're ready to go."

I said goodbye to the boys and followed Amber back through the kitchen. The coroner's team was wheeling Wes Bailey's body out, and Officer Birkwell was going over every surface with chemicals and special lights.

"They found evidence of blood out here on the floor

and on the freezer door. This is probably where he was killed. No prints so far. We checked the van, and the body. The victim's wallet was in his back pocket. He had twenty-seven dollars. If he had a cell phone, it's missing."

"You think the killer has it?"

Amber shrugged. "That's one possibility. The trash was picked up before we arrived. It could have been dumped. There's no telling how much evidence we've lost."

I looked out the door. "If you were going to throw away evidence, why would you leave the knife in the body?"

"To keep the blood from getting everywhere." Amber put on another set of latex gloves and opened the back door. "What'd you find out?"

I followed Amber to the police car. "None of them are admitting to leaving the note on the body, and I think the planet would crack in half before Gigi would write my name on anything in permanent marker."

"Do you think it was Tim or Gigi who killed him?"

My stomach bottomed out at the thought of Tim in prison. "It couldn't be Tim. Come on. Can't you rule out both Tim and Gigi anyway? They'd have been together."

Amber slowly shook her head no. "Tim and Gigi spent the night in their respective apartments. They were not together."

"So neither one has an alibi?"

"Nope. No alibis, and our prime suspect is eight and a half months pregnant."

"No way I'm being your informant on this one. It's way too personal."

Amber pulled out her sunglasses and put them on. "I understand. After all, the killer only put 'Get Poppy' on the victim's chest. If you'd rather sit home and watch your Christmas-cookie-competition shows rather than find out why . . ."

Her attempt at reverse psychology was not lost on me. I pointed back at the door. "They don't want me here."

"Sure, guilty people wouldn't."

We got in the police car and put on our seat belts. I had the sinking feeling that Amber was disappointed in me, and the even sinkier feeling that I cared. "Did you notice that Gigi was wearing the other crab earring?"

Amber cranked the engine to life. "Oh yeah."

CHAPTER 6

Amber dropped me off in the alley behind the Washington Street Mall. I walked in the back door of La Dolce Vita, straight through the kitchen to the dining room, and threw myself against Gia's chest. "You will not believe what happened."

He handed a waiting customer the latte he'd just made and wrapped me in a hug. "Oh no, *cara mia*. Another one?"

I nodded against him. He smelled of coffee and vanilla, but he felt like home and safety and love.

Sierra, his part-time barista, walked to a chalkboard sign hanging by the to-go containers and erased the thirty-five and drew a zero.

Gia muttered something in Italian. He ran his hand down the back of my head. "Where did you find this one?"

I told him all the gory details, while Sierra took over the espresso machine to work the line. She gave me a tight look of pity with a shake of her cinnamon-colored hair.

Gia listened, murmuring sympathetically, while we walked back through the kitchen to his office. His eyes went wider when I told him about Gigi's new girth than they did over my name being taped to the victim. *We were clearly meant for each other.* At one point, Sierra brought back a peppermint mocha made from oat milk and handed it to me while Gia passed me tissues. "And no one there admits to leaving the note?"

"No one. But most of the staff started after I left."

"Maybe they came with Gigi."

"They could be from her restaurant. At least Amber isn't pressuring me to spy for her this time."

Gia nodded. "That is a nice change."

"Amber says Kieran doesn't want to arrest Gigi without compelling evidence because no judge wants to put away a pregnant woman."

"I can imagine. What do you need from me?"

"I need to work off some of this frustrated energy."

Gia grinned and pulled me into his lap. "I know ways to do that."

I kissed him deeply and gave his offer serious consideration.

Sierra hit the buzzer for backup out front.

"Sorry. Looks like you gotta go, sir."

Gia gave me a quick peck. "I think you love to torture me, *bella*."

The feeling was mutual. I took a moment to catch my breath, then I followed him out of the tiny room and grabbed my apron off its hook.

Christmas brought in a holiday surge of customers looking for festive treats. Today I was making gluten-free sugar cookies and iced oatmeal whoopee pies. When Henry arrived, we were going to cut out penguins and decorate them. I'd be cleaning the kitchen for hours from the fallout.

The XM Christmas station began to play Bruce Springsteen's "Santa Claus Is Coming to Town." You can't grow up in South Jersey without the Boss being a holiday staple. I hummed along as I measured the powdered sugar, ginger, cinnamon, and orange peel, and my mind wandered.

I gathered a huge ball of dough and stared at it. I wanted to punch it, but all I could think about was Gigi's stomach. I smooshed the dough and shoved it aside.

I would never be able to have children of my own. A complicated miscarriage made sure of that. It shouldn't bother me anymore, but it did. If Gia ever did want to marry me, he would never experience holding a baby again. Maybe that would be a deal breaker for him.

He came around the corner, singing with the Boss in every key but the right one. "Can I get you anything, *cara mia*?"

"You do remember that I can't get pregnant, don't you?"

He froze and then blinked. "*Si*. This I know. Why are you worried about it now?"

"I just thought that maybe it was a problem for you."

He walked over and pulled me against his chest and nuzzled my ear with his stubble. "All I need is you."

"Yeah, but you're not getting any younger."

His lip twitched. "Are you saying I am too old?"

I intended to make my point, but somewhere along the route I started to cry. "If you want another baby, you need a younger woman who can still have them."

Gia wiped a tear off my cheek. "*Bella*, the next baby I want to hold will be our grandchild from Henry."

Our grandchild. I started to cry harder.

Gia hugged me tighter and tsk'd. "Okay. You have had a rough day."

I nodded against his pinstripes. *He thinks I'm crazy. Thank God, I didn't ask about the ring.*

"It will be okay. Is there anything else you want to get off your chest?"

Nope. "Did you drop anything at my house you want to tell me about?" *Sigh.*

"I might have, actually."

My heart gave a leap. I looked into his eyes. "You did?"

"*Si.* I had a business card for a new coffee supplier. I cannot find it anywhere. Why do you look so sad? Did you throw it away? I am sure I can just google it."

The bell to the front door jingled, and Sierra poked her head around the corner. "Poppy."

Darn it. "I haven't seen it."

I went through to the dining room and stopped under the archway. Greenery tied up with red velvet bows had been looped around the polished espresso bar, and colored lights ran along the perimeter of the ceiling and the front picture window. A beautiful wreath of red-and-white gingham, clove-studded gingerbread men, and spun-sugar candies graced the inside of the front door—that was my doing. But my attention went to the tall, blue-eyed man with hunched shoulders and dark circles under his eyes. "Tim?"

His eyes darted past me to Gia and back. "Hey. I figured you'd be here."

I felt Gia's comforting presence behind me. "What are you doing here? Are the police finished?"

"I need your help, Mack."

"That's not what you said when you were backing the hostility bus over me this morning."

Tim sighed deeply. "I'm sorry. I was stressed, and I wasn't prepared for . . . you."

Gia stepped over to the espresso bar and snapped his towel. "Why don't you sit down and talk, and I will make you a coffee?"

Tim snarled. "No, I'll just be a minute, dude."

I cast my eyes to Gia, who was calm as a light breeze. "I won't say no to a gingerbread latte."

He chuckled and shook his head.

"What? That mocha is long gone."

Sierra gave me an incredulous look. "What'd you do, mainline it?"

I gave the twenty-year-old her own look right back. "Ah, yeah."

I sat at one of the espresso wood tables, and Tim pulled out the chair across from me, after casting another glare Gia's way. "Look, Mack, I know things didn't end well between us . . ."

"You threw me out."

"I know. But Amber respects you."

Since when?

"And the police seem to have decided me and Geeg are their prime suspects."

"Well sure. It's your restaurant."

Tim paled. "You can't possibly believe that I killed Wes, can you?"

"No, of course not." *Now Gigi, maybe.* "I'm just saying—the people with the keys to the locked freezer are always going to be suspects when a dead guy shows up in one."

Tim ran both hands through his blond hair. "I'm telling you, I don't know how he got in there. I don't know who killed him."

"But you know it wasn't you or Gigi, right?"

Tim's eyes shifted around the room like his head and his heart were having a disagreement.

"Because the two of you were together all night. Right?"

"Sure." Tim cleared his throat. "There is no way Gigi could kill anyone."

Liar. "Is this the same Gigi that's tried to get me run out of town since the day she met me?"

"Look, Mack, I'm not here to rehash how Gigi has treated you, okay? From her perspective, you were the enemy. I don't want my baby to be born in prison. You and I have been through a lot together. I thought . . . Can you please just help me?"

That was as persuasive as tapioca.

Gia placed my latte on the table before me and put his hand protectively on my shoulder.

Tim leaned away from me like I was on fire. "I think one of the staff she brought in might know more than they've let on. Come in and do what you do. Listen to people. People love to talk to you. You have a way of finding things out."

"They're your staff, Tim. Why can't you question them?"

"Half of them came over with Gigi when we merged restaurants. I don't have the same history with them that I do with my guys. I think they'd open up to you."

"Don't you think Gigi trying to set me on fire would send up a red flag?"

Tim stared at me and chewed the inside of his cheek like he was working up to what he really wanted. "Come work for me. I'll tell everyone you're there as extra holiday help. A cop can't pose as a chef, but you can. No one on my staff knows you but Chuck and Tyler, and they'll be sworn to secrecy."

"What are you, some kinda nut?" *When did I start channeling Aunt Ginny?* "Everyone in this town knows who Poppy McAllister is. I'm the crazy lady who finds the dead bodies."

"Come in under an alias. Everyone'll call you Mack."

"You don't expect me to bake those frozen pies, do you?"

Tim had the courtesy to let a light pink flush climb up his neck for a change. "It's the off-season."

"Uh-huh. And even if I was willing to consider coming to work with you for a few days, what about your super-pregnant girlfriend who hates me?"

"Leave Gigi to me. I need someone I can trust."

"I think you need someone who isn't me."

He crossed his arms over his chest. "I was there for you when you were the prime suspect in Barbie's murder."

Ah, guilt. My familiar foe. You appear yet again. Tim started scanning the room for something to look at when I reached up to put my hand on top of Gia's. "What do you think?"

Gia sighed and rattled off some words in Italian. "It is your call, *cara mia.* You know I will support you."

I turned to Tim. "If I do this, and that's a big if, it can only be for a few nights. Gia and Henry come first."

Tim looked at his hands, which were red and calloused from years of kitchen work. "I understand. Anyway. We have to replace everything in the walk-in, but we can open tomorrow."

"Are you sure about that?" *I wasn't allowed to make food in my kitchen for a week when someone died.* My cell phone rang, and I pulled it from my pocket. It was Kenny. I turned it facedown.

Tim stood and pushed his chair in. "That's what the police chief said. Why don't you come in for staff dinner, and I'll introduce you."

"I haven't agreed to help you yet."

Tim shoved his hands in his pockets. "I understand. It would mean a lot to me if you could work it out. If I can't prove Geeg and I are innocent, we'll lose everything." Tim turned and walked out the door, leaving a ginger-bread burst of scent in his wake.

With a sigh, I looked at Gia. He gave me a sad smile and squeezed my shoulder. Neither of us liked to see people hurting.

I clicked on my phone. "Sorry, Kenny. What's up?"

Kenny spoke in a low voice like he was hiding in the broom closet. "You need to get home right away. The weekend guest has arrived, and apparently Doris Nightingale is a false name. Aunt Ginny knows her, and she's been yelling at her for thirty minutes. She's threatened to call the cops."

"Good Lord, who is it?"

"She says she's your mother."

CHAPTER 7

My phone fell from my hand with a clatter. I must have heard Kenny wrong. Maybe he said it was the Mother Ship. That would make more sense coming from the B-movie-lovin' housekeeper slash drama queen. I hadn't seen my mother since she dumped me with Aunt Ginny and took off thirty-five years ago.

"*Bella*, what is wrong? You are white as a sheet."

I picked up my cell and stuffed it back in my pocket. "Nothing. Just a little situation at the B and B. I have to run home."

Gia pulled off his apron. "I will take you."

"No!"

His eyes grew wide.

"No, it's fine." I tried to chuckle, but I sounded more like a wheezy chicken. "I'll just pop home and be back before you know it." I headed to the kitchen and grabbed my purse.

Gia retrieved my coat from the sofa in his office. "If you are sure . . ."

"I am. Besides, it's so nice outside, and I need the walk anyway."

One of his eyebrows raised. "It is freezing outside. I think I saw snow flurries."

I whipped my coat around my shoulders and gave him a quick peck. "It's fine. I'm fine. Everything's fine."

I pushed the back door and fought it open against the wind. It slammed behind me. *If that engagement ring was for me, he's probably glad he lost it. No one wants to marry a crazy person. Except Aunt Ginny's five husbands.*

I started to run home, then I stopped myself. *Why am I in a hurry? If I was so important to her, she wouldn't have missed my entire life. Now she can wait. If it's even her.*

I changed my pace to a leisurely stroll, even though my heart was beating like I was being chased and the wind was pushing me back to safety.

There is no way. What could she possibly want after all these years?

My mother had a nervous breakdown after my father died. One of our neighbors found her wandering around Kmart in her nightgown and rain boots and brought her home. The next day, she packed all my clothes in a little yellow suitcase and dropped me off with Aunt Ginny and Grandma Emmy. She said she'd be back as soon as she got herself together. I can still see her watching me from the car, her turquoise eye shadow reflected in the rearview mirror of her Chevelle as she drove away.

I used to fantasize about her coming back for me. I expected her to show up for my birthday parties and my school plays. One year, I asked Santa to bring her home for Christmas. That's when I stopped believing.

The time I was in the hospital having my tonsils removed, my high school graduation, my wedding day? Nothing.

At first, Aunt Ginny and Grandma had made excuses for her. "She loves you, but she's not well." When I got older, something changed, and they weren't as forgiving. "I don't know what's wrong with that mother of yours,"

Aunt Ginny would say. "You can't just abandon a child when times get hard. If only your father were alive. He'd straighten her out."

Aunt Ginny had tried to toughen me up. "You just have to face facts, Poppy Blossom. She's not coming back. Iris McAllister doesn't deserve you. Unfortunately, you can't pick your mother. Now it's up to you to rise above it and do something with your life."

I had very few memories of my mother before the day she left me. A flash of sitting on her lap on our gold-velvet sofa watching *The Banana Splits* while she smoked a cigarette. A glimpse of her on her hands and knees in the backyard crying as she held a baby bird with a broken wing. The smell of rum and coke as she listened to the same Linda Ronstadt song over and over on the record player. "When Will I Be Loved?"

Good question.

The rest had been shoved aside by my first date, going to college, my miscarriage, and the doctor's announcement that my late husband was terminal. All the important moments that she had missed.

Moments a mother was supposed to be there for.

I stopped at Mr. Winston's mailbox. Aunt Ginny's house was just across the street now. A little red Ford Fiesta was parked at the curb. I'd rehearsed what I would say to her so many times I could recite it in my sleep. *Why did you leave me? Why wasn't I enough for you? Why don't you love me?*

I stared at the house like it would swallow me whole. I couldn't will my legs to cross the street. The curtain shook in the library, and I saw Joanne Junk watching me through the split. *Great.* All I needed was to give my sweet-and-sour assistant more ammunition to use against me. She'd almost stopped calling me Buttface after twenty-five years of bullying. I'd tried to casually dismiss her a couple of months ago, but she just wouldn't leave.

For a moment, I considered going back to Gia's and telling him I was ready to skip town. We could leave tonight, no looking back. But I couldn't do that to Aunt Ginny. She was family.

You don't leave family.

I took a breath and stepped off the curb. I would stay calm. Mature. Maybe this was a mistake. Maybe she'd been in a coma for thirty-five years and couldn't call. Or she'd been captured by the Russians and had been on lockdown in Siberia.

My hand reached for the doorknob, but all I got was air. It swung open to reveal Kenny and Joanne, side by side, with twin expressions of pity. I don't like pity. I'd rather be called Buttface.

Georgina sat on the couch, twisting her silk scarf into a knot, while Aunt Ginny paced the sitting room. Aunt Ginny's face was flushed, and her lips were pulled flat, creating tiny lines around her eyes and mouth. Her nostrils flared with fury and sadness.

And then there she was. On my wingback chair next to the fireplace. She was older and shorter than I remembered. Her hair was different. Darker but with streaks of gray. She'd put on weight. Different blue eye shadow. Same blue eyes. She looked bored as she lazily swiped the screen of her cell phone. Then she heard me.

Her eyes narrowed for a moment like she was nearsighted. She tapped the phone again, then tucked it into her pocket and stood to her feet, with arms outstretched. "Petal. You're home."

"Don't."

Every word I'd rehearsed, every question I wanted answered, flew at me all at once, and all I could get out was, "You don't get to call me that anymore."

Then I flew up the stairs to my room and cried.

CHAPTER 8

There are things in life that instantly transport me back in time. Aerosol deodorant and acid-wash jeans take me to Aunt Ginny's driving lessons my junior year of high school. Cracker Barrel Cheese and Aunt Ginny's pickles take me to childhood Sunday lunches. And seeing the woman who abandoned me takes me back to sitting on the front step of Aunt Ginny's wraparound porch, clutching my Holly Hobbie and sobbing, "Don't leave."

My bedroom door creaked open. Soft footfalls, followed by a gentle thud, landed on my bed. Figaro walked across the comforter, purring, and pushed his face against mine as I lay curled into a ball. A second soft rustle made me open my eyes.

Aunt Ginny lay next to me, looking up at the ceiling. "That could have gone better."

"How?"

"We should have installed a trapdoor in the front porch."

"Mmm. Hindsight."

Aunt Ginny sighed. "Kenny put Iris in the Adonis Suite."

"He should have put her back on the ferry."

"That was my suggestion."

"Good." We lay side by side in silence for a couple more minutes. "Did she say why she was here?"

"She said she just wants to see you, but my money's on she wants something."

"I hope she doesn't need a kidney because I'm saving mine for a serial killer."

"That sounds reasonable."

I rolled to my back, and Figaro climbed onto my chest in case I needed feline CPR.

Aunt Ginny tsk'd. "What did Amber want so early? She woke the whole house up."

"They found a dead guy in the freezer at Tim's restaurant. My name was on him."

"Well, there's your silver lining."

"How so?"

"For once, a murder is not the low point of your day."

I didn't leave my room until five the next morning. I'd had a fitful night with very little sleep. Gia and I talked until the wee hours. He wanted to come over and comfort me, but the last thing I needed was for him to see me with puffy eyes, wallowing like a slug with a symbiotic cat attached to my chest. I made him go to sleep around three so he could open the coffee shop for the Christmas shoppers on the mall.

Around four thirty, I figured I may as well get up. I did one downward-facing dog after ten hours of corpse pose—which I had clearly mastered—then took a long shower. I dressed in black jeggings and a plum blouse, then did my makeup to match. If I couldn't feel halfway good, at least I could look halfway good.

Fig and I went down the back stairs to the kitchen so I

could have coffee and he could practice his harassment maneuvers. He'd been so supportive of my twelve-hour anxiety attack that I opened a can of crab in lobster sauce and dumped it in his crystal pedestal bowl. "You are a very sweet boy."

He purred in ecstasy through open-mouth chomping.

I ate a piece of gluten-free toast and texted Amber an update about Tim coming by the coffee shop yesterday. Then I took out all the ingredients needed to make a white chocolate raspberry cheesecake for tomorrow's dinner party, while trying to ignore the dread churning in my stomach that Iris McAllister was upstairs sleeping in one of my beds.

I had zero excitement for this tree-trimming party, but it was too late to cancel. Sawyer's boyfriend had taken the night off just to be here, and my handyman was on his way over to get out all the decorations. Everyone was looking forward to the event. I was looking forward to Iris McAllister checking out tomorrow morning and going back under whatever rock she'd climbed out from.

I had just finished whacking a bag of chocolate cookies with a rolling pin for the crust when Joanne arrived at the back door with a basket covered in white muslin cloth. She shoved it at me. "Here. I made this last night. It's a stollen." She shrugged out of her coat. "I had some gluten-free flour lying around so, whatever."

If you'd have told me a year ago that the former thorn in my adolescent side, Joanne Junk, would not only be on my staff full-time, but would be creeping into the friendship zone, I'd say you'd been whacked with a rolling pin.

The back of my throat constricted. I knew better than to hug her and embarrass us both. I lifted the cloth and gave a sniff. "This smells amazing. I may eat the entire thing myself."

I saw a tiny grin form and disappear like the snap from a rubber band. "Good. Because no one else will want it. I'll have to make a real one later."

Kenny came down the back stairs dressed in white jeans and a white T-shirt. "You're up early. You're not planning to poison the pancakes, are you? 'Cause I was thinking maybe we use those sugar alcohol chocolates in them. Your mother will have so much gas she could fly herself home on a broom."

I snickered. "I'm not making her anything. She can eat some of the Fiber One Aunt Ginny keeps for emergencies."

Kenny's eyes softened. "She'll be gone in a little over twenty-four hours. Are you sure you don't want to talk to her? Get some things off your chest? What she did to you was horrible, but don't you want closure?"

I poured myself another cup of coffee and blew the steam into swirls above the cup. "If she's here after all this time, it's because she wants something. I don't want to give her the chance to ask for it."

Joanne took a carton of eggs from the refrigerator with a disapproving sniff. "Maybe it's taken her this long to be in a good place."

"And the first thing she does is book a room in my B and B under the fake name Doris Nightingale?"

Kenny sidled over next to Joanne and opened a pack of sausage links with his eyes on me.

Joanne shrugged. "I get it, she abandoned you. But for your own sake, maybe you should give her a chance to explain herself."

I picked up a couple of eggs and cracked them into Joanne's bowl. "This might be your first experience with empathy, so you don't know, but you're doing it wrong."

Aunt Ginny emerged from her bedroom in a karate gi. "I'm with Poppy on this one. When Iris dropped her child on my doorstep, she said she needed to go away for some mental rehab. We found out a few months later that she checked out of the facility and disappeared with the money from Poppy's father's life insurance. She called several times over the years to ask for money, but never once asked about her child."

Joanne raised her hands in surrender. "Alright. I'll drop it."

The front door opened, and Itty Bitty Smitty came down the hall whistling "Santa Claus Is Coming to Town." "Heya Boss. What's new? Gnuck gnuck."

Smitty grabbed a mug and paused halfway to pouring himself some coffee. "What? Are you all having a fight?"

"No. We're making breakfast." I took out the bread knife and hacked off a slice of the stollen appropriate for eating thirty-five years' worth of abandonment feelings.

Kenny took down a bowl and his cereal and headed for the bench seat at the table, where Figaro joined him, looking for a handout.

Someone came thudding down the main stairs and slid around the corner. Georgina appeared in a champagne silk kimono with a purple hummingbird pattern. She launched herself at Smitty, and he managed to catch her without spilling a drop of his coffee.

"There's my girl."

Kenny buried his head in the Apple Jacks cereal box to keep from laughing, but the look of horror he gave me before doing it made me snort.

Joanne was cracking eggs like she was feeding a platoon and not just one little couple from Philly and Iris. Personally, I wanted to give Iris the address to Uncle Bill's Pancake House and send her on her way.

Georgina cooed in Smitty's ear. "And why is my special man here so early? Got something you want to ask me?"

Smitty grinned and squinted his eyes. "I'm here to get the decorations out before the big shindig—and—I have a surprise for you tomorrow."

Georgina squealed.

Aunt Ginny and I caught each other's eye and passed a silent message. *So, it's Georgina.*

Georgina gave Smitty a kiss on his bald head, and he returned a gnuck gnuck and some eyebrow wiggles before heading to the garage for the plastic tubs of ancient lights.

Georgina grinned like a fool and grabbed a fruit from the bowl. She took a giant bite from it. "Look who's getting engaged tomorrow. I'm sorry it isn't you, Poppy. But you said you weren't ready anyway, and Ginny, you've already been married more than your fair share."

Joanne chuckled and whisked the life out of her pancake batter.

Aunt Ginny took a mug off the counter and poured herself some coffee. "That's a mango, Georgina. You're supposed to peel it."

Georgina spit out the thick skin and looked at the red-and-yellow fruit in her hand. "I knew that." She put it on the counter. "I'm going to get dressed and go help my soon-to-be fiancé." She flounced out of the room, her feathery pump slippers making little tippy-tap sounds down the hall.

Kenny nudged Figaro away from his cereal. "Should we go warn him?"

Joanne chuckled. "No way. He signed on for that. He knows what drama comes with the ring."

I'm fine. It's fine. I'm not even sure I want to get married again. I like things the way they are. I hacked off another chunk of stollen.

Aunt Ginny reached for the powdered-sugar-covered bread. "Are you sharing that?"

I moved it out of her reach. "Nope. Eat your Entenmann's Donuts you think you're hiding behind the Rice-A-Roni."

Her lips twisted to a pout. She opened the junk drawer

and pulled out the dirty little leather book we found in the root cellar a few weeks ago. "Here's the journal. It's your turn to give it a try. That TV-show girl who was here said my great-great-grandfather was cursed by the next-door neighbor."

"I know. I was there."

"It says his children's children. As in descendants. That means you."

"Yes. I'm aware."

"See if you can figure out what the curse is and if there's a way to reverse it. I can barely read it. It looks like it was written in chicken blood."

"Maybe that's because you refuse to wear your reading glasses."

Aunt Ginny narrowed her eyes. "The day I put on those old-lady glasses is the day I've given up."

Kenny raised his orange-caterpillar eyebrows and poured milk over a second bowl of cereal. "Maybe it will be a good distraction from your you-know-what situation upstairs."

I took the slim diary from Aunt Ginny and placed it next to my espresso machine. Then I started the kettle. "I'll take a look later. I'm making cookies with Henry this afternoon. Yesterday got hijacked."

My goals for the day were to get the cheesecake out of the oven before it cracked. Eat this entire gluten-free stollen. And avoid running into Iris before she left for another thirty-five years. I was way ahead on the stollen.

I poured juice into a carafe and went to sneak it into the dining room undetected. Iris was sitting at the table flipping through a beauty magazine. *Rats*.

"Hi, honey."

My feet were frozen by the buffet. "What would make you think I have anything to say to you?"

She flicked her eyes to me, then back to her magazine.

"I can't believe you are standing here in front of me. You look so much like your father."

"You could have been seeing me for thirty years."

"I know. I missed everything." She pulled the perfume sample out of the crease then rubbed it on her wrist and gave it a sniff.

You have no idea. "Why are you here?"

She blinked and looked around, as if somehow puzzled. "Your website says full breakfast is included."

"I mean here in Cape May. Here in my house. What do you want?"

"Nothing." She waved her hand. "Congratulations on turning this old place into something that finally makes money. Your father was sure he'd have to sell it to pay the taxes one day."

"Is that why you're here? You want money? 'Cause this well is dry."

She tilted her head and laughed. "What? No. I don't need money. Your father left me very well off."

My cheeks flamed as a blast of fury rose from my chest. "Good. I'll let Aunt Ginny know she can bring you her bill for raising me."

I stormed back into the kitchen so angry that my hands were shaking. The four of them were as still as snowmen. I'd forgotten to leave the carafe. I set it down on the counter with a thud. "Iris is up."

At my feet I felt a flop. I bent over and picked up my fluffy gray Persian with a screw loose. "I would never leave you, baby."

Joanne filled a plate of pancakes and sausage for our guest of dishonor and handed it to me.

I passed it right over to Kenny, who gave me a nod. "I got your back, Jack." He left through the swinging door.

Aunt Ginny put her hand on my arm. "She leaves tomorrow."

I nodded, and Figaro swatted at some of my hair that had escaped its headband. "We had the right to refuse to let her stay in the first place."

Kenny came back through to the kitchen drained of color and looking like the Pillsbury doughboy's Scottish cousin.

"What's wrong?"

He swallowed hard. "She wants to extend her stay a few days."

Aunt Ginny swatted Kenny's arm with every syllable. "No! Ab-so-lute-ly not! You know I could break your arm with a twist of my pinky!"

Kenny held his hands up to block her. "Don't pummel the messenger."

I grabbed Aunt Ginny's wrist. "Wait."

She turned to me mid swat. "Wait what?"

I thought for a minute. "We know she's up to something, right?"

Aunt Ginny nodded. "No question."

"I want her to leave as bad as you do, but maybe we should try to find out what it is."

The little redhead raised an eyebrow and grunted a *hmm*.

Kenny, now overly confident that he wouldn't get attacked again, foolishly let his guard down. "You don't think she's here to get the house, do you?"

Well, now I do.

Aunt Ginny smacked him again. "Do you see me standing here, boy? No one gets this house until I die, and it won't be that good-for-nothing Iris."

Kenny took a step back. "Okay. I'm sorry. I'm just thinking out loud."

Joanne, the always helpful, handed Aunt Ginny a spatula so she'd have greater reach in case Kenny had more bright ideas.

I shook my head. "No. I don't think that's it." I put Figaro on the floor and sawed off another slice of stollen. "She has no legal right to the house; it's in my name. It's got to be something else."

Joanne brought her plate of pancakes to the table and sat across from me. "You'll have a better chance of figuring out what it is if she's still here."

"That's what I'm thinking."

Aunt Ginny took a seat next to me. "But do you really want her hovering around, acting like everything's okay?"

"No. I'll only be able to handle her in small doses. Kenny, go tell her we can extend her stay until next Sunday, but she has to pay up front. That will give us a week to get her real motives out of her. And if she can't pay, we can at least narrow it down to money right now and be done."

Kenny gave me a nod. "You got it."

I grabbed a piece of sausage off of Joanne's plate. "I have a couple errands to run, then I'm baking cookies. If she leaves the house, I want to know about it."

Joanne cocked an eyebrow. "What are you going to do, search her room? Have her followed?"

"That's going to be your job."

Joanne grunted. "How are you going to do all that when you're in the middle of another murder?"

"I'm not that involved."

"Uh-huh."

Aunt Ginny pulled out her cell phone and started tapping on the screen. "Well, I'm not going to sit by and wait for her to slip up."

"What are you doing?"

"I'm assembling the troops. You will need to make another roast for tomorrow night."

"Can I assume a transactional Jell-O salad is coming?"

Aunt Ginny's phone beeped, and she checked the screen. "I can confirm one strawberry pretzel salad is in play."

"I'll prepare myself emotionally."

Kenny came back with a scowl on his face and his hand in his pocket.

"How'd that go?"

He sighed. "Well, she's not broke." He pulled out a big wad of cash. "She's paid in full for the week."

CHAPTER 9

I had more nervous energy than the day I took a pregnancy test my first year of college. It became my only year of college, so you know I failed that test. I flitted around the third floor like a bird preparing for a storm. Filling supply closets, checking email, checking reviews, checking email again because I couldn't remember what I'd read the first time. *Did I just agree to someone bringing a Doberman?*

I finally grabbed Aunt Ginny's great-great-grandfather's diary and holed up in my bedroom until it was time to head to La Dolce Vita for my lunch date.

> *May 6, 1880*
> *I have acquired a nickname.*
> *Oswald has started calling me*
> *Rooster because of my red hair. He*
> *says it's also because I like to give un-*
> *solicited advice to Brackenridge on*
> *how he makes a gimlet, but if one is*
> *to work in a tavern, they ought to*

know how to make a proper drink.
Everyone will thank me later.

May 11
Won seventeen dollars last night at
stud poker. Oswald insists I cheat.
Naturally, after he started cheating,
I had no choice but to do the same.
Everyone knows I'm gifted at both
cards and dice and Oswald is a sore
loser.

May 13
I woke with a terrible headache
this morning from Brackenridge's de-
plorable whiskey sours. He is still making them too weak, and one must
have a double to get enough whiskey
to make drinking worthwhile.

May 15
I took a new route home from
Jackson's Clubhouse last night and
cut through the field next to the
house. Had the misfortune of meeting
the kitchen maid next door. I
suggested she let the lady of the house
know the gate to the cow pen is
broken. She seemed aggrieved by my
very presence.

May 16
Apparently, that woman was not
the kitchen maid, but Bettina Meier,
the lady of the house. I offended her

by saying she has the same eyes as her cow. Truth is not the treasure of all men.

May 19
I won a donkey last night at poker. I should have known not to double down on pocket aces when Jeremiah is grinning like a fool.

May 22
I took Bettina Meier some fresh peas as a way of apology for the unfortunate liberties my donkey took with her cow. She refused my gesture and rebuffed my attempt to smooth over the grievance, stating it did not count for an apology, for the peas came from her own garden. I informed her that pettiness was not becoming on a woman of her age, and she should accept my sincerity, seeing as how I did all the work to collect the peas, saving her the trouble of doing so. The woman is quite impossible.

Oh dear. He doubles down like Aunt Ginny. It's no wonder he got himself cursed.

We had our own impossible woman on the first floor right now. Aunt Ginny was hollering that she'd run out of patience with Iris's antics years ago. Iris seemed completely confused by her stance, stating she was just asking to use the Corvette because her late husband loved it so.

I looked out my bedroom window, wondering where the field was that Grandad Rooster had mentioned. A police cruiser came down the street and pulled into my driveway. *I could get arrested right now, and it would still be less terrifying than what is happening inside the house.*

I opened my window and stuck my head out.

Amber emerged from the driver's side, shielded her eyes and called up to me. "I need cookies, and I know you always have some."

I assessed her demand for a moment—a dozen smart-alec comments flew to mind, but the fact was, I did always have cookies. "Come through the back. I'll meet you in the kitchen."

"Why don't I just go through the front door?"

Iris screeched something unintelligible, and a door slammed.

Amber's face remained passive. "Never mind. I'll find you."

She was coming in the back door when I emerged from the hidden steps in the pantry.

"Tim called me and requested you work for him, undercover, just like you said he would."

I took a can of cherry-coconut balls off the counter and opened the lid. "It's work *with* him, and I told him I'd think about it."

"What are you leaning towards?"

"I'm leaning towards changing my name and moving to Belize."

Amber picked out a cookie and gave it a sniff. "What's kept you from doing that already?"

"Aunt Ginny's on a watch list. Who is really your prime suspect?"

Amber took a nibble of the pink icing and nodded approval. "I'm afraid it's Gigi."

"Doesn't it take a lot of strength to stab someone? Gigi's pretty small—other than, you know . . ." I made a big air bump around my stomach area. "As much as I'd like to see her go down for a million little things, do you really think she'd be capable of killing that guy?"

Amber sighed. "It takes less strength than you think. And I've seen desperate people defy the laws of physics. There's a lot of evidence pointing to her, including eye-witness accounts of a verbal altercation over a contract dispute. We've subpoenaed their phone records, but it could take weeks to get them, and Kieran wants the case closed quickly. As in before thirty thousand people arrive for Victorian Christmas week. In the meantime, we could arrest her on what we've got, but it's thin. I'd hate for the killer to get away with murder because we rushed the in-vestigation and didn't have enough evidence for a convic-tion. If we can't find something to clear her, she'll be taken into custody."

Empathy and anger were having a brutal battle in my heart. I'd hurt Tim when I passed him over for another man—twice. This was my chance to make up for some of that.

But Gigi. The thought of helping that woman after all she'd done to me . . .

Then there was the baby. I felt like someone had wrapped their fingers around my heart and they were squeezing the life out of me. *Why did there have to be a baby?*

For once, Amber wasn't pressuring me. I could just walk away.

Amber leaned against the counter. "When you're done having your little meltdown there, let me know."

My emotions were frayed from the past forty-eight hours, and my temper boiled over. "Why does it have to be me! It's not my fault she's pregnant. Am I responsible for solving every murder in this town? Maybe Gigi did kill that guy!"

Then my heart betrayed me, and I felt like a soda that

had gone flat. "I can't help it if the baby will lose its mother if she goes to jail."

Amber nodded. "You're right. It's not your fault. Sometimes there's nothing we can do to stop the train wreck— no matter how badly we want to. Most of the time when I'm called in, the damage is already done. I'm just there to clean up the mess."

"How do you cope with that?"

"I turn to this know-it-all I can't seem to get rid of who keeps stumbling over the killer by accident to help me put the bad guys away so the victims can have some justice." She plucked another cookie from the tin. "And this."

"So you think I should get involved?"

"Kieran and I discussed it, and he thinks you need to stay out of it."

"Does he now?"

"He says you're too close to this one to be an informant."

"I agree with him. What do you think?"

"I think Kieran is in charge, and Kieran doesn't want you involved." Amber winked and shoved the rest of the cherry-coconut ball into her mouth.

"What was that for?"

She chewed and swallowed. "It's me letting you know to stay out of it." She winked again.

"Why do you keep doing that?"

Amber gave me a pointed look and reached for another cherry cookie. "Kieran can't tell you who to work for, but under no circumstances are you to be there at the behest of the police. Understand?"

I waited for the wink. It didn't come. "Oh-kay?"

Amber winked.

What the crap!

I took down the can of gingerbread biscotti and opened it. "What I want to know, is how can Tim open Maxine's so soon? My kitchen was closed for days when someone died at my house, and I wasn't even a suspect."

Amber shrugged. "The murder weapon at Maxine's wasn't poison, so we weren't able to get the DA to let us shut them down until the investigation is closed. We're pretty sure we got every piece of physical evidence from the kitchen."

"And after all that, Gigi is your prime suspect?"

"Everything points to her. Our biggest hurdle is alibis. The murder happened overnight, so everyone was home sleeping. No one has anyone who can prove they didn't leave in the middle of the night. At least not to any degree that will be held up in court. And then there's the problem that there are no fingerprints on the freezer door or the murder weapon."

"What about the dead guy's keys? Any fingerprints?"

Amber grabbed a gingerbread biscotti. "Only his. Do you have any chocolate milk to go with this?"

I opened the fridge and took out the milk and chocolate syrup. "If they were busy, the door would be covered in prints from everyone who works there."

I poured milk in a glass and added a hefty amount of chocolate syrup. I went to put the syrup down and Amber cleared her throat. She looked from me to the chocolate syrup. I added more, watching until she gave me the signal that it was enough. I stirred the nearly black concoction. "Next time, I'll just add the milk to the syrup bottle."

Amber took the glass from me. "If I'd known that was an option, I would have suggested it myself." She took a sip and nodded. "Gigi says they keep a meticulously clean kitchen and that's why there were no prints on the door. They wipe it down every night."

Since when? "Were there prints anywhere else?"

"Hundreds. Nothing on the workstation by the freezer, or the refrigerator on the other side of the room, but everywhere else—covered."

"Why clean the crime scene if you're going to leave the body there?"

"People in a panic don't make a lot of rational decisions. Why do you say everyone's prints would be on the freezer and not just the chefs'?"

"Because the servers plate the desserts, several of which include ice cream, when the chefs are busy. Both walk-ins are in constant use. I don't care how clean Gigi says it is; if the killer is someone on staff, they should have left things alone to incriminate everyone equally."

Amber dipped her biscotti into her milk. "Maybe the killer's not on staff."

"Then how did they get in after hours without a key?"

"Only someone on the inside could find that out." Amber winked.

CHAPTER 10

I packed three turkey sandwiches into my tote bag with some potato chips. Then Kenny took Iris a bogus guest survey to find out where she was living while she was camped out watching for me. I slipped out the back door and into the garage to crank Bessie to life. I could walk to La Dolce Vita, but the Corvette made for a faster getaway, and it seemed Iris had her eye on it.

I pulled into my spot in the alley behind the coffee shop. Gia was waiting for me with a kiss, and all was right with the world.

"Do you know how much I love you, *bella*?"

A warm glow spread through my chest. "Yeah, I know."

"How are things going with your mother?"

"Joanne has been following her around the B and B. Mostly she tries to look innocent while she waits to pounce on me."

"You know I am here for you. For all of it."

"I know." I kissed him again, and a bouncy Henry launched himself at my legs.

"You're here!"

"Hey, sweets. Are you ready for lunch?"

Henry took my hand and led me to the little table in the back corner of the dining room. It was covered with a white tablecloth, and a red rose in a bud vase sat in the center.

Gia gave me a grin. "He did this all by himself."

Henry slid out the middle chair. "That's for you." Then he climbed onto the next chair over. "Sit, Daddy."

Gia snorted as we took our seats. "Okay, Piccolo."

I unwrapped our sandwiches and some chips and set everything out. "You ready to tell me what you want for Christmas, Henry?"

Henry sniffed his sandwich. "Nope. Is this jelly?"

I tucked a napkin into his shirt collar. "It's cranberry chutney, and it's really yummy with turkey."

He gave it a little nibble. "Mmm."

Appeased that I wasn't trying to trick him, he took a bigger bite.

Gia had finished half of his sandwich before I'd gotten started. He winked at Henry. "I like the jelly." He took my hand. "I love it when you are here."

Henry nodded. "That's why we got you a new apron."

Gia cleared his throat and gave Henry a playful look.

Henry froze with his sandwich at his mouth. "Oops."

I looked from one to the other. "I smell a secret. What are you two up to?"

Henry looked at his father and put a finger to his lips. "Shh."

Gia grinned. "You shh!" He turned to me. "What are you making today?"

"We're going to start the sugar penguins that we didn't get to do yesterday. I have all the icing ready in squeeze bottles. Then if there's time, we have a pan of Hello Dollys to make."

"It sounds like you have a fun day planned."

I grinned at Henry. "We do. Are you ready to get messy?"

He gave me a serious nod.

My cell phone chimed sleigh bells. It was Tim.

The police just left. They've been here all day questioning me and Gigi. I need help.

I turned the screen to show Gia. He leaned towards me and put his arm around the back of my chair. "Have you made a decision on whether or not you will help?"

"I don't want to miss out on all the fun with my special boys."

Henry stuck his finger inside his sandwich and licked the cranberry sauce off it.

Gia nodded. "*Si.* I understand. But you will not regret that later?"

"How would I regret it later?"

"Are you okay with Gigi going . . . away, and the baby growing up without its mother?"

Henry's eyes were the size of quarters behind his glasses. "Like I growed up without my mother?"

Gia tousled Henry's hair. "You are not grown up, Piccolo." He turned his eyes back to mine. "But isn't that how you grew up, *bella*?"

"Why did there have to be a baby? That makes the decision so much harder."

"You are generous and kind. Those are some of the things I love about you."

My phone chimed again. It was Joanne.

I just caught Iris digging through the silver drawer. She says she's looking for your baby spoon. Please tell me you don't actually have a silver baby spoon.

I texted Tim back.

Fine. I'll be there at four. Please keep Gigi from attacking me.

You don't have to worry about a thing. She'll be on her best behavior.

A lump caught in my throat. Apparently, regret had arrived early.

CHAPTER 11

I drove to Maxine's for my first dinner shift as an off-the-books police spy. Chatter from the kitchen met me as I approached the back door. Everything went silent when I entered, and seven sets of eyes watched me anxiously.

Tim and Gigi stood at the head of the center worktable with three live, banded lobsters in front of them. Chuck and Tyler were to their right. To the left were three staff members I'd never met. The room smelled of garlic and hostility. *It's colder in here than it is outside.*

Tim waved his hand in my direction. "Everyone, this is the new pastry chef I've been telling you about. Mack will be joining us as extra help for the holidays, since Gigi needs to be off her feet more with the baby coming."

Gigi picked up a cleaver and hacked the head off a lobster with her eyes locked on mine.

Tim looked from the lobsters to Gigi to me. "Mack, this is Chuck and Tyler, my line chefs."

In keeping with the ruse that we'd never met, the boys waved hello. I nodded at each of them. "Hi."

Moving to the left, "This is Chelle Cleveland. She's our front-end hostess."

A large black woman with a straight bob and an amazing smile gave me a wave. "Hello. I don't come back to the kitchen very often. I'm mostly in the dining room, but let me know if you need anything."

Gigi hacked the head off the other lobster, and Chelle jumped. She gave me an apologetic grimace, which I mirrored back to her.

Tim moved the introductions down the table to a woman who could be the next contestant for a Jersey Shore reality show and a boy who looked like a recent graduate of juvenile detention. "This is Nikki Bonatti and Andrew Jessup, two of our servers."

Nikki was a beautiful woman with long, wavy dark hair that had professionally applied golden highlights. She had big brown eyes and Gwen Stefani lips. She waved hello and flashed a set of very long, perfect fingernails painted like tuxedos. "Hey."

Andrew was slim, of medium height. His frosted hair had grown out to show dark brown roots, and he had a gold hoop in one eyebrow. He caught my eye and gave me a smile and a wave.

I raised my hand. "It's nice to meet all of you."

"Our bartender comes in at five, and I have another server who hasn't arrived yet . . ."

Chelle rolled her eyes. "Big surprise."

Tim nodded. "Yeah. Well. Let's go over tonight's specials."

Nikki drawled in a Brooklyn accent, "Lobster, I presume."

Gigi waved the cleaver. "No. This is my dinner. The special is shrimp Fra Diavolo."

"I'm here!" A young woman with a mass of strawberry-blond hair down to her waist flew into the kitchen while shedding a gold parka. "I'm sorry I'm late. I told my mother I needed her to take me to work by three, but, of course, she was late getting home from dialysis anyway."

She disappeared down the hall by Tim's office to put her things away while chattering the whole time. She entered the kitchen, tying a black apron around the tiny waist of her white angora sweater. "So it's really not my fault. Oh . . ." She finally spotted me for the first time. "Who are you?"

Tim took a breath. "Teela, this is Mack, our temporary pastry chef for the holidays. Mack, this is Teela."

I gave the girl a smile. "Hello."

She appraised me for a moment, then put her hand on Tim's arm. "I need to talk to you later."

"Okay. Find me when it slows down."

She grinned and held his eyes a few seconds too long. "What'd you make for us tonight, chef?"

Gigi whacked off another lobster head.

Tim brought out a huge skillet and removed the lid. The servers took out their pads and jotted notes while he spoke. "Linguini and shrimp Fra Diavolo. Make sure you tell the customers the special has a little heat to it. Fra Diavolo is a silky tomato sauce kicked up with garlic, white wine, and cayenne. I toss the shrimp with fresh linguine, then finish it off with buttery toasted panko, a squirt of lemon, and some parsley for freshness."

The staff grabbed plates, and Tim served them, while I took my purse to his office and grabbed a white apron off a hook by the lockers. I turned around to find Gigi standing behind me with the cleaver. "What the!"

"If you disrupt my kitchen or get in my way, you're outta here. Understood?"

"You know you're only wearing one crab earring, right?"

Gigi reached for her earlobe. "So?"

"What happened to the other one?"

"I don't know. Is this the kind of crack detective work we can expect out of you tonight? I'll just call the news and tell them you're the new Sherlock Holmes. Criminals beware."

"I could leave now and let the police come to their own conclusions."

The blood drained from Gigi's face. She spun on her heel and waddled back to the kitchen.

I followed her from a safe distance, stopping at the walk-in to see what I had to work with tonight. The padlock was dangling from the hook at the top of the unit.

Chelle was in the refrigerator gathering heavy cream. "I need to go stock the bar fridge for Gabriel. You haven't met him yet, but let me just tell you, he is *fine.*"

"Do you need help? I want to look at the current menu to see what desserts are listed before I get started."

"Oh, sure." She handed me a quart of cream and a gallon of orange juice. "Follow me."

We went out to the dining room and crossed over to the polished bar at the front right corner. There were only six barstools wrapped around the modest L-shaped counter, but about a hundred pieces of stemware in every size and shape hung from a metal rack overhead.

Chelle stored the cocktail ingredients in the mini-fridge underneath, then grabbed a menu off the hostess stand. "If you want to make something off-menu for tonight, just let me know, and the servers can add it to the list of specials. We used to have seasonal desserts all the time before Gigi got so far along. And I heard we used to offer several gluten-free options, which were very popular."

"Is that right?" I perused the basic desserts you could find on just about every mid-range restaurant menu in America. Chocolate cake—unoriginal. Pies—apple and cherry, courtesy of Seymour Veg, I suspected. Crème brûlée—the ubiquitous gluten-free option I was usually saddled with when I went out to eat. I had some ideas for what to make, but I'd have to check what was in the storage room first.

"I heard there was a tragedy here the other day."

Chelle's eyes grew twice their size. "You don't know the half of it. They found the fish supplier dead in the freezer. No idea who did it."

"Did you know him?"

She pressed her lips together and shook her head. "Not well. He came in as a customer sometimes, but the chefs are the ones who had all the business dealings with him."

I returned the menu and went back to the kitchen. Gigi's eyes glared at me wherever I went, like one of those oil paintings in a haunted house. I gathered my ingredients while she made herself busy with those lobsters behind the grill.

The busboy eventually arrived. He was a fifteen-year-old kid who worked part-time after school and was afraid of everyone on staff. Gigi yelled at him to load the dishwasher faster, and he may have wet his pants.

For the next couple of hours, I baked four dozen ramekins of gluten-free apple, pear, and cranberry crisp. Then I made a batch of chocolate-chip cookie dough to be baked on demand for warm milk and cookies. I started a batch of yeast rolls for tomorrow and put them in the walk-in to rise overnight. It took that long for Gigi and Tim to leave the kitchen on a shared break.

I had just measured some gingersnaps for the crusts of two candied ginger cheesecakes, but I left my workstation to check in with Chuck and Tyler while we were alone. "Alright, tell me more about this fight Gigi had with Wes Bailey."

Chuck turned four filets and tossed a pan of scallops sizzling in butter. "Which one?"

"You said the other day that she threatened to sue him if he didn't let Maxine's out of a bad contract."

Tyler was working a huge sauté pan of shrimp Fra Diavolo. "It's hard to narrow down the momster's melt-downs, but last week she chased Wes out of the office, screaming about Deepwater Fisheries raising their rates three times in six months. Always citing some vague loophole."

Chuck plated the scallops and added a spoonful of browned butter. "That was the big one. She said what Wes was doing was illegal and he should be reported to NOAA, but Tim said they couldn't report him."

"Why not?"

Chuck shrugged. "He wouldn't say."

Tyler dumped the finished pasta into a waiting strainer, then added it to the pan of shrimp. "Tim said it was Gigi's fault for signing a contract that got them into this mess."

"*A contract with who?*" *Because I knew for a fact that Tim used Deepwater Fisheries before he and Gigi merged.*

Both Tyler and Chuck shrugged.

"What's NOAA?"

Tyler turned one of the burners down. "Government fisheries enforcement. National Oceanic and Atmospheric Administration. We call them the fish police."

"I see."

Chuck dolloped four plates with mashed potato and plated the filets on top, each with a sprig of rosemary. "All I know is Tim doesn't usually go all DEFCON 1 at Gigi, but he did last Thursday."

Andrew came into the kitchen with a tray. "You got my filets?"

Chuck moved the finished plates down the line, and Andrew loaded them and took them out.

Teela entered the kitchen and looked around. "Where's Chef Tim?"

Chuck bent down to face her under the grill hood. "In his office. What do you need?"

She glanced at me. "I'll find him." Then she took off down the hall. A few seconds later, we heard Tim and Gigi's voices carry an argument out to the kitchen, then it got quiet again.

Teela walked back through to the swinging door. "I'll ask him later. I put through two of the specials for table one."

She went back through to the dining room, and I asked Chuck, "Where did the new employees come from?"

"Teela, Chelle, and Gabe came over with Gigi. Most of our regular staff quit when Gigi took over. A couple seasonal employees stayed for a while, but they've been gone for weeks."

Tyler started a new pot of water and added linguine to the ready pot. "Nikki's a direct hire. She's only been with us a couple of months. And Andrew came at the beginning of the summer. He can get really angry, really fast, but he seems unfazed by Gigi's rants."

Tim came back into the kitchen red-faced and tight-lipped. Gigi stormed down the hall behind him and walked out the back door. I moved out of the crossfire and retrieved some eggs for my cheesecake.

I placed the eggs next to the upright mixer and cautiously approached Tim as he was starting a new sauté pan of shrimp. "Hey, who unlocked the walk-ins today?"

Tim gave me a stony look.

"What?" *Geez, you asked me to come help.*

Tim closed his eyes and took a breath. "I did. And I have to lock them back up when we close at the end of the night because Gigi is convinced the homeless man down at the marina is stealing food after we leave."

"How does she think he's getting in?"

Tim snorted. "I have no idea."

Teela ran back into the kitchen to pick up a large order for six. "Can we talk now?"

Tim nodded.

Teela loaded her tray and hoisted it to her shoulder. "Okay, I'll be right back."

She returned a few minutes later and motioned him towards his office. A cryptic look passed between Tyler and Chuck. I unwrapped two huge blocks of cream cheese and dropped them into the industrial mixer while trying to eavesdrop. All I picked up over the sizzle of the grill and the quiet hum of the exhaust fan was the faint sound of Teela crying.

I thought I should maybe make a syrup from ginger ale for tomorrow's cheesecake, so I quietly made my way to the stockroom next to Tim's office. Quietly, so as not to disturb the ginger ale, which can be temperamental.

I stood in front of the rack of bottles and strained to hear.

Teela's voice was high and quivery. "Chef Gigi said it was my fault. I left here so upset that I forgot my cell phone. I can't not have my cell phone for twelve hours. So I came back to get it at six, thinking you'd be here taking a delivery, and the back door was open. I saw the light inside the walk-in was on, but the door was locked."

Tim reassured her, "It's okay."

She started crying harder, with great hiccups of anguish. "I turned the light off because I know how money is tight and you don't want us to waste electricity. So I think my prints were on the switch, and the cops will think I did it. They said my parents can't alibi me because they were asleep when I came home. I mean, all they do is work and sleep. How is that my fault?"

A sharp icepick of a voice drove through my skull. "What are you doing in here!"

I see Lady Marmalade has returned.

I made a big show of scanning the shelves until I found the green glass bottles in front of me. "Ah. Here it is. I need this for a dessert."

Gigi stepped closer to me with the intention of getting in my face, but between my height and her girth, our faces were a good four feet apart. "I don't trust you, and I don't want you here. If Tim wasn't so sure you had that woman police officer in your back pocket, I'd never allow this."

In my pocket? What am I, a Kennedy?

Tim murmured again, "That's okay, Teela. I'll take care of it."

Gigi's eyes bugged out a little and she fast-waddled for the office. I followed because I was nosy, and in this case, I had been asked to be.

Gigi threw the office door open, surprising both Tim and Teela. It's not like Tim was doing anything inappropriate, but the way Teela convulsed at seeing Gigi standing there like a puffy little rhinoceros in a maternity muumuu made her look mighty suss. Gigi pointed down the hall. "Get out front and help Andrew and Nikki."

Teela scuttled from the room and wiggled her size-four behind all the way to the dining room.

Gigi threw the office door shut in my face.

I returned to the kitchen and turned on the mixer for the cheesecakes. Once they were in the oven, I baked a few cookies and warmed some of the winter crisps for the dessert orders. The servers entered the kitchen at different times and let themselves into the freezer to top my desserts with ice cream, as I knew they would. I cleaned up my station and still had about forty-five minutes before the cheesecakes were done, so I stepped outside to check the messages on my phone and get some air.

A flicker of orange light about forty feet away caught my attention. A scruffy man with wild hair was sitting on an old lawn chair down by the dock. He was dressed in a long, olive-green parka, and he'd built a small fire next to his cardboard box to keep warm. He wasn't watching the water, as you'd expect. He'd angled his lawn chair to face Maxine's, and in the moonlight, it was clear that he was watching me.

CHAPTER 12

I returned to find the kitchen was a hive of activity. All three men were working the line for the final push. Teela and Nikki were plating desserts, and the busboy was loading dishes as fast as he could, afraid that Gigi would bite his head off again. The Queen herself had never emerged from the office after her last fight with Tim.

I sidled up to Chuck and Tyler and lowered my voice. "How long has the homeless guy been here?"

Tyler did a wrist toss on his pan of shrimp and linguini. "A few weeks."

Chuck had four more filets and two pork chops on the grill. He did a texture check on the steaks. "I think he's crazy."

Tim was seasoning a couple pans of scallops and letting them brown. "It's mentally ill, Chuck. Either that or he's a drug addict. I tried talking to him once, and he didn't make any sense. Sometimes we catch him looking in the windows. Gabe, he's the bartender—did you meet him?"

"No, I've been in the kitchen all night."

"Well, he's had to chase him off a few times. I feel sorry for the guy, but he scares the guests. It's not good for business."

Nikki entered the kitchen with a plate of shrimp Fra Diavolo. "Chef. The guy at table five is sending this back. He says it's too spicy."

Tim took the plate and set it down by the sink with a thud. "It's Fra Diavolo! It means the devil's brother. What the *fudge* did he think it would be!"

Only he didn't say fudge.

Tim left for the dining room to do a customer-service run, and Chuck took over his scallops.

I checked the timer for my cheesecakes and slipped the little device into the pocket of my apron. Then I grabbed the sent-back plate of shrimp and linguine and dumped it into an aluminum takeout container. "I'm taking this out to him."

Chuck and Tyler and even the busboy turned to me in a panic. Chuck's glasses were steamed up from the heat coming off the grill. "If Gigi finds out, she'll kill you."

Tyler tried to gently take the aluminum dish from me. "We've all tried to send him the throwbacks. Gigi says it's an automatic dismissal for the next person she catches sending food down to the dock."

I took the pan back from Tyler. "Well, I'm going to go talk to him. Maybe he saw something. Gigi can take it out on me if she doesn't like it. What's she gonna do? Fire me?"

Tyler let go of the pan and raised his hands in surrender.

I grabbed a pack of plastic cutlery and walked down to the fire. The man was very scruffy and had a bushy, wiry beard like he'd been living rough for a while, but his eyes were alert, and his parka looked brand-new. "I brought you some food. It's a bit spicy, though. Do you like shrimp?"

I offered him the takeout container, and he stared at it. Then his gaze shifted to Maxine's back door.

"I know. It's okay this time."

He gingerly took the container and the fork. He lifted the lid and sniffed. He must have liked the aroma because he ripped the plastic covering the fork and napkin with his teeth and dove in.

He attacked the shrimp, while I tried to ask him a few questions. "What's your name?"

Nothing.

"Where did you come from?"

Nothing.

"Do you want me to call a local shelter to see if they have a place for you?"

His eyes flicked to mine, and he shook his head in such a way that he reminded me slightly of a terrified woodchuck.

"Okay, okay." I sat on my heels and watched him for a minute. "I was wondering, did you see the police here the other day?"

His eating slowed, but he didn't look at me.

"Do you know what happened?"

He closed his eyes and rocked back and forth like he was in an invisible rocking chair. I had a friend when I was in grade school who did the same thing whenever she knew she had done something wrong.

"You can trust me. If you saw something, you can tell me."

"Rats."

His voice startled me. "What?"

After a long pause, he repeated it. "Beware of rats in the kitchen." He returned his focus to the food.

I tried to gently push him to tell me more, but he blocked me out.

"I will bring you something else the next time I'm here."

I walked back to the restaurant, pondering over what he could have meant by rats in the kitchen. Everything that came to mind made me uncomfortable, and I tried to come up with something that would allow me to sleep at night.

Through the window, I watched Tim, Tyler, and Chuck wrap up food and clean the grill. The busboy was scrubbing stock pans. I opened the back door, and everything stopped. Gigi stood with her hands on her hips, waiting for me. She was about to launch a verbal missile attack when my apron started to beep.

"That'll be my cheesecakes."

The guys all watched me walk past her and grab the potholders. I took the candied ginger cheesecakes from the oven, gave them a jiggle, and set them on a baker's rack to cool. I leveled a stare at Gigi. Her nostrils were flaring, but the dark circles under her eyes told me she didn't have as much fight in her as she had the will to fight. "Just remember why I'm here."

She gritted her teeth and looked at the busboy, who whimpered.

"When that's over, I'll be gone."

She didn't have a reply. She disappeared down the hall, then reappeared wearing her coat and carrying a bright pink tote bag. "I'll see you at home, Tim." Then she was out the door with a slam.

We spent the next hour cleaning the kitchen and getting ready for tomorrow. The servers came through and picked at the leftovers, chitchatting with the chefs, then moving out to the bar for end-of-shift drinks before heading out.

Chelle came in and invited me to join them. "It's kind of our thing at the end of the night. Gabriel makes us all a drink, and we gripe about who had the worst customer of the evening. Smart money for tonight is on Teela. She had one guy who complained about everything, then left her a three percent tip."

"That sounds like fun, but maybe another night. I need to finish closing back here."

"Sure thing. See you tomorrow. And hey, those winter crisps were da bomb. We don't normally sell that many desserts."

When she'd gone back out front, Tim called over to me. "You really don't have to help close, Mack."

"I know. I don't mind for tonight. Aunt Ginny doesn't need me." *Plus I'm avoiding the B and B.*

He nodded, but he wouldn't look at me. "Okay, if you're sure."

I was sure.

I was sure I didn't trust Gigi not to ambush me in the parking lot. I was sure I didn't want to go home and deal with Iris McAllister. Mostly I was sure I was going to watch the cleanup to see who fastidiously wiped off the doors and handles of the walk-ins to keep a "meticulously clean kitchen."

And as sure as I was tired of finding murder victims, no one did.

CHAPTER 13

My back was still sore the next morning. Restaurant work was a lot more demanding than people realized. I cracked my neck and tried to loosen a knot on my shoulder blade. I'd spent one night spying on Tim's staff, and so far, no other suspects had risen to the top. I was carrying the sick feeling that Tim was hiding something.

I tried to center myself for the day ahead. Tonight was the big dinner party where Aunt Ginny was determined to force a proposal out of one of the men. I checked my email again to see if a guest had reported losing an engagement ring. *Boy, wouldn't that suck.*

Nope, we were still all clear. Now if I could just keep Iris McAllister from ruining everything.

I'd spent so much of my childhood wondering why she didn't want me. Just when I'd finally made peace with it, she appeared, and all my fears were stirred up again. I had a sudden overwhelming desire for Pop-Tarts.

I needed to shift my mind to something else. I picked up my great-great-great-great-grandfather Rooster's diary off the nightstand and began to read.

May 25
Now the shrew across the field has accused me of turning the cow's milk sour. It was probably her shrill voice calling the poor thing to the barn that made it so, and I told her as such. Upon reflection, the ensuing fracas may have been in some small way partly my fault for suggesting she hire a bar wench to call the beast and spare it from distemper.

May 27
The constable was here again last night. We are soon to be on a first-name basis. That woman has reported me for carousing. I do not believe she would recognize carousing if it bit her on the nose. One is allowed to sit on one's own front porch and drink ale when the heat is too oppressive to stay indoors. That is not a crime. I received a warning not to put her name into bawdy drinking songs no matter how well they rhyme.

May 31
I may have killed the neighbor's cow. I did not know fireworks could scare livestock to death.

There was a strong family resemblance between Rooster and Aunt Ginny. Self-awareness must not be carried in the McAllister DNA.

I got myself together and went down to the kitchen to

bake some cookies before the dinner party. Kenny was washing the dishes from breakfast, and Joanne was getting out ingredients to make oatmeal butterscotch cookies for the afternoon. Aunt Ginny paced between them on her cell phone, and from the sounds of it, something very distressing was happening.

"When did they decide that? Why didn't you tell me sooner? You know I've been swamped with running the bed and breakfast."

Kenny and I glanced at each other and snorted.

Aunt Ginny hadn't noticed us. "I'll be darned if I'm beaten out of first place because of Edith's whiskey fudge again. Put me down for a secret entry. You'll know which one is mine when I bring it in."

She hung up her phone and went to the corner cabinet and started digging around.

I assembled the ingredients for cherry-coconut cookies while ducking flying Tupperware. "What are you looking for?"

Aunt Ginny pulled out an old yellow box from the back of the cabinet. "I just found out the Senior Center Christmas party is next weekend instead of the third Saturday, like it usually is. All because Neil has tickets to see the Hip Hop Nutcracker in Newark on the nineteenth."

"Okay." I measured the dry ingredients into my mixing bowl. "What does that have to do with your grandmother's recipes?"

She flipped through the box, squinting at the ancient cards. "I've got to beat Edith's fudge. She wins every year because the judges are a bunch of lushes. They may as well serve it in shot glasses."

Joanne and I caught each other's eye across the kitchen island. She dumped a cup of oats into her cookie dough. "Beat it in what?"

Aunt Ginny gave Joanne one of her peeved looks. "The

recipe contest. They have it at every Christmas party. I think it's just Neil's sneaky way to get a bunch of donations, so the Senior Center doesn't have to pay for all the food."

Kenny snorted. "Is this the same whiskey fudge that you refused to share with anyone at Thanksgiving?"

Aunt Ginny blew her bangs off her face. "I didn't say it isn't good. I said it isn't unbeatable. I've got a plan for this year that will knock the judges' socks off. And that was my personal fudge."

I ran a whisk through the dry ingredients, then placed the butter and sugar in my KitchenAid. "And how do you plan to do that when you know as well as I do that your special talents don't exactly involve kitchen skills."

Joanne chuckled and slid a look to Aunt Ginny. "Do you want some help?"

Aunt Ginny plucked a card from her box and held it up. "Aha! No, I do not want help, Judge Judy and Miss Know-it-all. I may not bake as good as you two do, but I have my grandmother's recipe, and I know it will win over Edith's hooch candy."

Kenny dried his hands on a tea towel and lowered his voice. "Hooch candy that you ate a pound of at Thanksgiving."

I sighed and chopped my maraschino cherries. "So, what is this award-winning recipe of Great Grandma's?"

Aunt Ginny pursed her lips, and her eyes half-closed. "I can't tell you. It's a secret."

I turned on the mixer and flicked my eyes to Joanne. "How afraid should we be?"

Joanne was stirring butterscotch chips into her cookie dough. "You don't have to set anything on fire, do you? 'Cause I've got a tenner riding on Poppy burning the place down first."

Aunt Ginny gave a sniff of disdain. "You'll see. Prepare to eat crow."

Kenny grabbed a bottle of water before heading to clean the guest rooms. "Eww. It has crow in it?"

Aunt Ginny picked up a dish towel and slung it at him. "No, you silly fool. It doesn't have anything weird. But I do need to order a special ingredient on the internets."

I measured out my coconut. "What could you possibly need to buy on the internet if Great Grandma used to bake with it?"

Aunt Ginny gave me a snarky look. "You just get ready for tonight. Make sure you're quick with that video doohickey when Royce pops the question. I want to capture the moment in case I have to remind him he proposed later."

She flounced from the room. I punched in the XM Christmas station on the kitchen iPad, and it started to play Bruce Springsteen's "Santa Claus Is Coming to Town." "Okay, Joanne. Report. What has Iris been up to?"

Joanne shrugged. "She doesn't leave the house. She only leaves her room for breakfast and sneaking around, and she's doing plenty of that. I caught her taking photos of that Louis the Sixteenth armoire in the Scarlet Peacock. She said she's an antiques expert."

Kenny grabbed a package of paper towels from the mudroom. "Really? 'Cause she asked me if it was Art Deco when she cornered me in the hallway. I haven't even cleaned her room. She keeps answering the door and telling me to come back later."

"Well, that's not good. How are we supposed to rifle through her trash?"

Joanne tasted her cookie dough. "You may need to give her a reason to get out."

"Like setting a small fire?"

She looked at me like I'd gone insane. "Like invite her for coffee. You and Sawyer drink a ton of it."

Kenny snickered. "You know, you and Aunt Ginny are a lot more alike than you realize."

I pointed a rubber spatula at his head. "That's how you get fired, buddy."

Joanne tsk'd and started dropping mounds of cookie dough onto the parchment-lined sheet. "Maybe we can get Georgina to take her shopping for the B and B since you just used my butter for tonight's mashed potatoes."

When Joanne saw the look I'd given her, she moved a step away from me and changed the subject. "How did it go last night? Gigi try to poison you yet?"

I snorted. "Gigi tried to fire me twice, and I don't even work for her."

Joanne chuckled. "Yeah, demanding bosses are the worst."

Kenny laughed and choked on his water.

I threw him some side-eye. "Serves you right. I'm a delight."

He made a face of mock seriousness. "Oh, I know."

"Gigi had a fit when I took food out to a homeless man who's camping by the docks behind them."

Joanne slid two trays of cookies into one of the ovens. "Why?"

"She said it's like feeding a stray cat. If we give him food, he'll never leave."

"I see."

"She also thinks he's been breaking in and stealing steaks out of the freezer."

Kenny made a face. "How is he cooking the steaks if he's homeless?"

I mixed my cherries and coconut into the buttery dough. "I guess he could cook them over his fire out there after he thaws them. But stealing bread and cake would be a lot easier. At least they're ready to eat."

Joanne put her mixing bowl in the sink. "What do you think?"

"I think it's more likely Gigi's imagination, caused by pregnancy brain."

"No, I mean do you think the homeless man killed the fish guy?"

"I'd like to say no. But if he's mentally unstable, it's possible. I didn't get much chance to talk to the staff. The ones I don't know work in the front of the house, and I was stuck in the kitchen all night."

Joanne snickered. "You're gonna have to waitress."

I dropped my dough by teaspoons onto the cookie sheet. "You're right. I'll have to tell Tim. The only thing I learned last night was that everyone touched the walk-ins, and no one wiped them off, which means the killer wiped them down."

Joanne shrugged. "So whoever killed Wes Bailey didn't work in that kitchen."

"Or they want the police to think that."

CHAPTER 14

"Until Figaro can walk down the aisle without attacking these ribbons, he's fired as my ring bearer." Aunt Ginny untied the silk pillow from my fluffy gray feline, who was currently face-planting into the blue oriental rug under the weight of his unwanted responsibility.

I picked up the black smoke Persian, who had gone boneless, and kissed him on top of his head. "I'm not sure he intended to apply for the job. Not to mention, you aren't engaged yet. None of us are."

"Well, that's a situation I think will be rectified before this party is over. Right now, I've got Royce lining up my nutcrackers on the buffet in the dining room."

Iris called from the top of the steps. "Are you going to put that glass angel on top of the tree? That was always your favorite."

"That angel fell and shattered ages ago, just like your credibility."

Iris whined. "What'd I do?"

"Go home and decorate your own house. Wherever that is." I took the ceramic sweet shop for my holiday Dickens village out of its Styrofoam encasement and placed it in the bay window on a tuft of cotton snow, in between the bakery and the butcher shop. I plugged in the new addition and hit the switch. Every building lit up from within. The lampposts bedecked with festive wreaths and the skating rink filled with Victorian holiday revelers cast a magical glow in the room. The lovely scene was my favorite part of the Christmas decorations, and right now I could use all the Christmas spirit I could get my hands on.

The box of ornaments tinkled, and we caught Figaro's tail sticking out of a web of silver. Aunt Ginny clapped her hands and shouted, "Zzzst!" Figaro shot from the room with his ears pinned. Footfalls heavy enough for a toddler galloped up the steps. A moment later, we heard Iris shout, "Ack!" and Figaro flew back down with his tail dragging the floor.

"Don't worry, Fig. She won't be here long." *Not if history repeats itself.*

Aunt Ginny rolled her eyes. She squeezed my hand, then went back to the dining room to micromanage Royce.

Kenny and I had spent the afternoon setting up three live Christmas trees around the bed and breakfast in preparation for this tree-trimming party. A few calls had come in from reporters looking for a quote about my involvement in the recent homicide—no comment. And Tim had texted me three times asking if I'd figured out how to clear his name before Aunt Ginny hid my cell phone from me.

Iris crept down the stairs and plunged her hand into the ornaments. "Do you still have those German blown-glass ornaments of your father's?"

Kenny appeared at my side and took her by the arm. "Ma'am. We talked about this. This floor is off-limits for a private party."

Iris protested. "But I don't want to go to the Peter Shields.

I want to help decorate the tree. It's my favorite part of Christmas."

Aunt Ginny rounded the corner and pointed up the stairs. "You had your chance to be here for the last thirty Christmases, and you weren't interested. Now git."

Iris stomped up a few steps before stomping in place and sitting down.

Sawyer walked through the foyer, scowling at the stairs. "How you holding up in here, hon?"

"Fine. If I can get the Dickens church to light up."

"You know Iris is camped out on the steps, eating a box of Douglass Fudge."

"Yep."

"You want me to take her to her room?" Sawyer lowered her voice. "Take her out back and beat her with a sack of potatoes?"

"She'll just come back to raid the heirlooms when she thinks the coast is clear. Just act normal and ignore the delusional woman on the stairs."

Sawyer sighed. "Okay. Well, I'm back to the library to move Amber's ornaments up past the middle of the tree. Why you assigned a five-foot-tall cheerleader to put glass ornaments on the nine-foot-tall Douglas fir I'll never know."

I gave Sawyer an evil grin, and she snickered.

The Biddies were decorating the Victorian tree in the sunroom. Mostly they were rearranging the pink-and-lace ornaments one of the others had already hung, then coming to me to tattle about it. It was all a ploy to sneak peeks at Iris.

Mrs. Davis slow-walked around the corner past the steps into the sitting room and whispered. "She was playing on her cell phone until she spotted me. Then she shoved it under her butt, covered her face, and pretended to be crying."

I whispered back, "Okay."

She raised a fist of solidarity and walked back through to report to the others.

The blue spruce next to me was ready to be festooned with the sparkly birds and frosted pinecones my father had loved putting on our Christmas tree when I was little. I opened the box of antique ornaments and dug around for my favorite.

"Ow! What is wrong with you?" Gia came around the corner holding two mugs of hot cider and handed me one. "That crazy cat just leapt off the steps and attacked me, then ran off."

I took the Grinch mug and kissed him. "He's been all frisked up since Iris tried to sneak onto the love seat and sat on him."

"I wish you had let me come over when she arrived. You have seen my family. You cannot scare me."

Henry ran through the room dragging a brown-velvet garland of sleigh bells, Figaro on his heels. I caught the five-year-old and gave him a kiss on top of his head. "This is what I need to make everything better. You ready to tell me what you want for Christmas, sweet boy?"

Henry pushed his glasses back up the bridge of his nose and giggled. "Still a secret." He ran through the dining room, jingling all the way.

Gia shook his head. "We will have to bribe Santa."

"He's gonna make me work for it, isn't he?"

Aunt Ginny swept through the room and shook a matching garland of reindeer bells with her fist. "I want understated elegance. This isn't the Magic Kingdom."

I gave Gia a glittery blue jay and chose for myself the pheasant with the three-foot tail feathers. It was my father's favorite.

Aunt Ginny spun the dial on the intercom radio, and Bruce Springsteen began to belt out his iconic rendition of "Santa Claus Is Coming to Town."

I gave her a wry look as I set the pheasant front and center on a high branch. "You know, we do have satellite now. There are no commercials."

"It's nostalgia. I've been decorating for Christmas while listening to the local station since before you were born." She wrapped the sleigh-bell garland as high as she could around the bottom half of the sitting-room spruce.

Gia gave her a sly grin. "You want me to get a step-stool so you can reach the middle?"

"You better watch it, boy." Aunt Ginny made two fists and waved one at him. "This one's six months in the hospital, and the other is sudden death."

Gia, through much inner strength, managed to wipe most of the glee off his face and attached a mourning dove with gray feathers to the tree. His eyes shifted to mine as he bit his lower lip.

Amber appeared by my side. "Joanne said to tell you that you're out of mayonnaise for the horseradish sauce."

"Tell her to use sour cream. No one will know the difference."

Amber nodded and headed back to the kitchen.

A voice floated down the stairs. "Something smells real good."

Aunt Ginny called up to answer, "The Peter Shields is still available."

Silence.

A few minutes later, Kenny trudged over and rolled his eyes to mine. "The kitchen scrooge who still thinks she's the boss of me has ordered you to call everyone to dinner. She says the potatoes will only be perfect for a few minutes and you're not to complain about them. Just take a Benadryl." I blinked at Kenny, and he ducked his chin lower and raised his eyebrows.

I walked to the intercom and pressed the "all" button. "Dinner is served." I grabbed Iris by the arm and spun her back towards the foyer. "Not you."

Iris frowned. "I have a stomachache anyway." She stomped up the stairs.

A tyrant cleared her throat behind me. "Peas can't be reheated."

"I'm coming now, Joanne." *And yes, they can.*

The dining room looked like a Hallmark movie set. Twinkle lights were strung around the perimeter of the tray ceiling, and fresh evergreen boughs dotted with sprigs of holly and red velvet bows hung above every window and doorway. The room smelled of fresh balsam and pine. The coffee cups and tea chest had been removed from the buffet to make room for Aunt Ginny's nut-cracker collection, some of which one of her five hus-bands had sent home from Germany a long time ago. Kenny lit the tapers on both tables, and Aunt Ginny low-ered the lights.

Everything was perfect except for Mommie Dearest at the top of the stairs humming "Blue Christmas" as loud as possible. *She missed thirty-five years of events. One more isn't going to kill her.*

Joanne had set an elaborate table like this was a state dinner at Buckingham Palace. Kenny got a weird look on his face when he realized he was across from Amber, but he quickly recovered when Joanne brought in the stand-ing rib roast. She placed it at the head table, gave a look around the room, and retreated to the kitchen.

I excused myself and followed Joanne. "What are you doing?"

She flounced down at the Formica table, where there was a place setting for one. "Getting ready to eat dinner. What do you think?"

"I think you'd better move your butt into the dining room, that's what I think."

"Staff eats in the kitchen."

"Then I'd have to eat in here, and I'm not doing that. Now get out there."

"You only want me because you have an empty seat."

"You set the table. Like it or not, you're one of us, Joanne. Now get out there. Everyone knows you can't re-heat peas."

She huffed as she got up from the vinyl seat, but I saw the crack of a smile before she went through the door. It was almost a lovely moment, until everyone at the table started yelling.

I threw the door open to find Figaro galloping around the edge of the room with Daddy's stuffed pheasant in his jaws. Sawyer tried to trap him by the china hutch, but he slipped through her fingers. He wound through the legs of the chairs down the men's side of the main table like he was running the obstacle course on Feline Ninja Warrior. First Royce, then Gia, then Smitty. Kenny grabbed him around the middle, but he was too wild. Fig knows when he's got something he isn't allowed to have, and the forbidden treasure is more delicious than sardines. He wriggled free and landed on Smitty's plate.

Smitty stabbed a piece of roast and held it in front of the feline, who was momentarily dazed. In a move Figaro had obviously been practicing, he dropped the feather-encrusted Styrofoam in Georgina's lap, causing her to scream, and used his paw to bring the meat to his mouth. I grabbed him around the pudgy middle and held him over my face.

"Naughty boy!"

I sensed from his rampant purring through the lippy-smacky sounds that regret was not forthcoming.

I returned from stashing the furry villain in Aunt Ginny's boudoir off the kitchen after taking a reassuring hug in his smooshy belly. "Just a few more days and Iris will be gone, and we can get everything back to normal."

The Jell-O salad was unveiled, the plates were passed, and Joanne was beaming from the praise over her home-made dinner rolls.

I took my seat next to Sawyer and whispered. "None of them have asked me if I found a ring box. You?"

She whispered back. "Not a peep. And I'm so nervous, my stomach's in knots."

Aunt Ginny leaned to whisper behind Sawyer. "If it's Royce, I don't think we'll ever get a confession."

Georgina was looking at Smitty like he was a teen idol. "When do I get my surprise?"

He wiped his mouth with a napkin. "You want it now?"

She clapped her hands. "Yes, please."

Sawyer reached under the table and grabbed my hand. I looked across the table at Gia, and he grinned in that way that made me feel special and gooey inside all at the same time. A ring and a piece of paper didn't matter.

Smitty got up to look behind the buffet, and my breath caught in my throat. He pulled out a big box.

That's a shirt box, not a ring box.

Aunt Ginny jabbed me in the side.

The room went silent.

Iris called from what sounded like the bottom step. "What's happening?"

Georgina blinked and looked very confused. "What's this?"

Smitty grinned. "It's your surprise. Open it."

Georgina pulled the lid off the box and lifted out an Eagles jersey to match the one Smitty was wearing. Her eyebrows plummeted. "An engagement shirt?"

Now Smitty's eyebrows took a dive. "What?"

Georgina looked down at the green-and-white jersey in her hands. "I don't get it."

Aunt Ginny threw her napkin on the table. "Oh, fer Pete's sake!" She pulled the blue velvet ring box out of her pocket, opened it, and placed it on the table. "Which one of you left an engagement ring at our house on Thanksgiving?"

No one moved.

Royce pushed his chair back and stood to his feet. He came over to Aunt Ginny's side and dropped to one knee, taking her hand.

Aunt Ginny's other hand flew up to her chest. "Uh, Royce. What are you doing?"

"Ginger, my love. Will you marry me?"

Aunt Ginny sputtered. "Um. Well . . ."

It's Aunt Ginny. My heart gave up. It stopped beating altogether. *It's not me.* I knew I had to flee to the safety of the kitchen before I embarrassed myself. "I'll get the champagne."

I ran through the swinging door and brushed the tears from my eyes. *Why am I upset? I didn't even want to get married.* I took two champagne bottles from the wine fridge and stopped to catch my breath.

This doesn't change anything.

I was thrilled for Aunt Ginny, but I'd been lying to myself that I didn't want this. All that talk about not being ready, and here I was, devastated.

"*Bella.*"

I wiped my eyes. I hadn't heard Gia follow me in. "Can you believe that?" I turned to face him with a brave smile and found him down on one knee. Henry was down on one knee next to him, holding the ring.

I started shaking.

Gia grinned. "Royce may have stolen some of my thunder, but, baby, you are the best thing to ever happen to me. I love you more every day. You are my happily ever after."

He nudged Henry. "Will you be my momma and tuck me in at night and read me stories and play dinosaurs with me?"

Gia grinned. "Will you marry us, *cara mia*?"

My hands shook, and the words got stuck in my throat. I nodded like an idiot, and the word "yes" came out in a sob.

Gia stood and slipped the ring on my finger, then pulled me into a kiss while Henry bounced around us, chanting, "I'm getting married."

A cheer erupted from the doorway, where most everyone else was crammed together to watch. Aunt Ginny was front and center with an evil gleam in her eye. "We knew you'd need a little time to work through your feelings, so we concocted this little ruse to get you started."

I looked at them one by one. "You were all in on it?"

Sawyer pointed to Aunt Ginny. "She's the ringleader, but I'm sure you guessed that."

Aunt Ginny grinned. "You know how hard it was to get that naughty cat of yours to play with the ring box?"

Georgina gave me a smile. She was wearing the Eagles jersey. "It's time for you to move on, dear."

Aunt Ginny took Royce by the hand. "Everyone knew except for Royce, who forgot."

Royce gave me a sheepish shrug. "I panicked."

Sawyer couldn't take it any longer and pushed through the door to wrap me in a hug, followed by Kenny and then, the shock of my life, Amber.

Smitty called out, "I'm going to eat my dinner before it gets cold. You'll be looking at that ring on your hand all night anyway."

The Biddies grabbed the champagne and the glasses. "We'll take care of this. You two go eat your supper."

I looked at my hand, and my heart gave a little flip. *It is me. I'm getting married.*

Everyone trickled back out to the dining room after giving us hugs and congratulations. Nothing could ruin the moment.

Except Iris McAllister, falling out of the pantry closet into the kitchen.

CHAPTER 15

"Have you ever seen anything so beautiful in all your life, Fig? That's a one-carat diamond in a halo setting. See all the little diamonds circled around the big one?" I tilted my hand to let the morning sun sparkle off my ring.

Figaro gave my hand a sniff. Once he'd determined that I wasn't offering him a treat, he turned his back to me and showed a disappointing lack of appreciation for the stunning engagement ring. Until a reflection played across the bedroom wall, and he lunged to swat it. He thought he'd caught the light under his fluffy bedroom-slipper paws, then lifted one for a peek. I shifted my hand, and the light moved down the wall, with him swinging like Serena Williams every few inches.

Let's face it, I could sit here and look at my hand all day. Or I could look at my hand at La Dolce Vita and show it off to strangers. *Oh this. Why, yes, I am engaged.*

I picked up the framed photo of my late husband, John. "I'm getting married again. Gia asked me last night. I know you'd be happy for me because you are the most generous man I've ever met." I blew him a kiss and re-placed the photograph on my nightstand.

I dressed in black jeans and a flowy black blouse—not because my ring would pop against the contrast—but because everything goes with black. *Especially diamonds*.

After doing my hair and makeup, I went down the spiral stairs to enjoy my first day of being a fiancée with no rush to set a date. I pushed through the double doors into the dining room and was flattened by a shock wave from event-planning Normandy.

Aunt Ginny and the Biddies were spread across the mahogany table with a dozen bridal magazines. Georgina laid down a multicolor array of index cards listing restaurants and banquet halls, and Mrs. Dodson was sliding the salt and pepper shakers across the landscape of potential allies and enemies in a well-seasoned invasion of Cape May's florists, printers, and caterers.

Mother Gibson had her cell phone to her ear. "That's too far out, Vincent. Our girl doesn't have that kind of time to wait."

I approached the table. "What you all doin'?"

Mother Gibson held up a finger. "No, she isn't pregnant, you fool. She's middle-aged. Time is not on her side."

I walked to the buffet and grabbed a coffee cup and the carafe from the Nutcracker Battalion. *Middle-aged?* "Who are you talking about?"

Aunt Ginny shushed me.

Mrs. Davis had fluorescent-green reading glasses perched on the bridge of her nose. She held a tablet at arm's length. "I found a site that sells those English cabbage roses at a discount, but we'll have to make the bouquets ourselves."

Georgina handed her a green index card. "Write it down."

Bloomin heck! They're planning my wedding, aren't they?

I poured creamer in my coffee, and Mother Gibson clicked off her phone. "The Trellis is a no. They don't have an opening for two years . . ."

I sipped my coffee and heard the angels singing when the caffeine hit my bloodstream. "Opening for what exactly?"

Mrs. Dodson huffed a sigh and moved a pink index card to the discard stack. "We should have started this weeks ago when we knew it was afoot."

Sawyer pushed through the double doors carrying a quiche. "Hot out of the oven. Joanne is right behind me with plates. She says not to discuss the cake until she gets here. And since I'm obviously the maid of honor, I think she should make some samples before anything is decided."

Kenny pushed through the door carrying what I assumed was a pitcher of mimosas, since orange juice isn't usually bubbly. "Do they have male bridesmaids? Groomsmaids?"

Joanne came in behind him and put a stack of plates on the table, then started to cut the quiche. "White cake with a raspberry filling is always a classy option. But I think she should do a mocha cream covered in milk chocolate ganache for the groom's cake."

"How are you planning already? I've only been engaged twelve hours. And we still have a B and B to run."

Aunt Ginny shrugged. "The Philly couple left early when the reporters showed up asking questions about a body in the freezer at Maxine's."

"We still have three sets of guests arriving for Victorian Christmas week who are hopefully blissfully ignorant."

Iris came around the corner in a vintage kimono. She

brazenly approached the table and helped herself to a slice of quiche. "Can I see the ring?"

Everyone stopped talking at once. Aunt Ginny growled at her. "Where did you get that?"

Iris ran her free hand down the front of the dress. "I found it in the attic, just hanging there. Don't I look slim?"

"That's hand-painted silk, Iris. I brought that home from Okinawa. Go put it back at once!"

Iris pouted and removed the delicate wrap. "What's the big deal? You obviously weren't wearing it." She dropped it over the back of Mother Gibson's chair and reached for a fork.

Aunt Ginny smacked her hand. "You're not welcome in here. You could have planned the girl's first wedding, which you refused to even attend because she was pregnant."

Georgina piped in, "Thank God I was there for her. She was as nervous as a debutante at her first ball. Speaking of which . . ." She flipped her issue of *Modern Bride* to show the ladies the center photo. "What do you ladies think of these veils?"

The Biddies gushed over the photograph, and Mrs. Dodson ripped it from the magazine and taped it to a posterboard she was filling with wedding ideas.

I was so busy trying to come up with a way to stop the speeding train before me that I didn't even register what was happening when Iris took my hand. I spoke to the squadron passing around champagne flutes of breakfast booze. "Don't you think you're getting a little ahead of things? Gia and I haven't even discussed what we want to do yet."

Aunt Ginny ignored me and passed a plate of quiche to Georgina, the Stalin to her Churchill. "This is a family-only event, Iris. You can eat on the side porch after you put my kimono back. And stay out of my storage room."

Iris pulled me into an awkward choke hold. "When is the big day? And when can I meet my future son-in-law?"

My insides recoiled, and I backed away from her. *Maybe it's not too late to enter witness protection and disappear.*

The front door opened, and Gia called to me. "Good morning, *cara mia.*"

The ladies around the table let out a cheer, which made me feel a little bit like a shriveled pear that some church agreed to take as a pity donation for their Christmas fruit basket. I rushed to the foyer to get him the heck out of there before they could tie him to a chair and make him look at centerpieces. "Hey, we gotta go. Now."

Gia shut the door from the inside and pulled me into an embrace. He whispered tightly into my ear. "Not yet. Remember, I love you. And eloping is one hundred percent on the table."

I pulled back and looked into his eyes. "What's wrong?"

He rubbed the back of my hand with his thumb. "I should have seen this coming."

"Seen what coming?"

The doorbell rang.

"Do not answer it."

"You're scaring me. What is it? If it's another wife, I'm going to punch you in the throat right now."

The door opened, and like Pandora's box, Gia's mother, aka Momma, aka Mussolini, stomped into the foyer, followed by Gia's sour sister Teresa, aka Mussolini junior. I steeled my spine and prepared for the usual onslaught of insults.

Momma's eyes crinkled at the sides, making the loose flyaways from her gray bun sway like a black widow spider weaving a web. She rushed me with her arms out. *"Mia dolce figlia.* Come to Momma." She grabbed my face in her hands and kissed me on both cheeks, while Teresa grappled my arm in what could have been misconstrued as a hug.

What fresh nightmare is this?

Teresa took me by the hand. "You'll have to start catechism classes right away if you're going to convert in time for the spring wedding season."

"Convert to what?"

Teresa laughed, a sound I had never heard from her before. I did not care for it.

"Convert to Catholicism, silly. You can't get married at Our Lady Star of the Sea if you're not Catholic."

I looked at Gia and saw that his pained and confused expression matched my own.

Momma said something in Italian, and Teresa translated for me. "Momma want you to wear her wedding dress. It need to be let out very much, and half meter added to the hem. Madalena, Francesca, and I all wear it. Stefania refuse, and now she is divorce so . . .."

Iris had followed me out to the foyer like toilet paper stuck to my shoe. "Is this the groom? Poppy, oh my heavens. He's gorgeous! Why is he with you? Men who look like that don't usually fall for chubby girls." She turned to Gia's mother. "Poppy gets her weight from her father. She was such a chubby baby. I had her on a diet when she was five, but it just didn't take. I think she would sneak cookies."

"So that's where my self-esteem issues come from." *Self-loathing, party of one.*

Gia's eyes narrowed at Iris, and his neck flushed red. "Poppy is the most beautiful woman I have ever met. Inside and out. I do not deserve her." He pulled me against himself and kissed me, hard.

Momma said something in a chastising tone and swatted Gia.

Gia started throwing some rapid-fire Italian in his mother's direction. She shooed him away like a moth and took my arm to drag me into the library.

I looked over my shoulder to Gia. "Isn't she still on house arrest for racketeering?"

Teresa answered me. "We told the parole officer you were getting married, so he gave permission for Momma to come here as often as she wants."

I'm pretty sure that's when I started to black out.

I was brought back to the unfortunate present when Iris introduced herself to Momma as mother of the bride. "Nope. That is not happening, Iris. Aunt Ginny is mother of the bride."

Iris pouted. "Then what am I?"

Georgina appeared in the doorway. "Not invited."

Momma was still prattling on when Figaro galloped across the hall with a bedazzled blue jay in his mouth. Momma screamed, and Fig slid to a stop, then hit the floor.

Aunt Ginny came flying out of the sitting room with the spray bottle of water she used on the ferns. "I told you to stay out of that tree, you rascal."

I snapped my fingers at the damp cat. "Fig. Drop it!"

He took one more look at Momma and dropped the stuffed bird. He sprang to his feet and shot down the hall with his tail dragging the floor. *Coward.*

Aunt Ginny stopped in front of Gia's mother and smoothed her hair back with her free hand. "Whatever you're doing, you're too late. He's already put a ring on it. I've got witnesses."

Momma started mumbling like she was putting a curse on Aunt Ginny.

Aunt Ginny held her own, blatantly telling Gia's mother she always knew this day would come and the old bat had made her bed.

Iris tapped me on the arm. "Hey, Petal. Do you have a minute? I want to talk about my role in the wedding."

"You just called me too fat for my fiancé. What do you think?"

She gave a wide-eyed look to Gia. "I didn't mean it as an insult."

Gia stared at Iris with narrowed eyes. He took me by the hand and led me outside to the front porch. He kissed me while muffled arguments beat against the windows, like bats trying to escape a hat box. "I am sorry about Momma. Do you still want to marry me?"

I grinned and took his hand. "You know it." I was silent for a moment, then I asked, "Your mother won't expect to live with us, will she?"

Gia flinched. "I have bribed six sisters for thirty years to make sure that will never happen."

My shoulders relaxed, and I laid my head against his shoulder.

He ran his hands down my back. "I do not like your mother."

"Join the club."

He started to rub tiny little circles into my back, and I felt warmth radiate down my body. We stood in the crisp quiet of a December morning, contemplating elopement.

The front door opened, and the Italian delegation marched out. "*Dove sei?*"

"There you are, new sister. We have much to plan. Momma want you to look at china pattern this afternoon. There is nothing good enough on the island, so we go to Vineland. Momma is not allowed to go that far, so she will be on the FaceTime."

Ice churned through my veins like I'd been hooked into a 7-Eleven Slurpee machine. All my life I had been a good person, but I wasn't a brave person. And right now, I'd rather face a killer than spend the day with Gia's mother. "I'm sorry, I can't go. I'm filling in as extra holiday help at a friend's restaurant."

Teresa checked her watch. "It is early yet. Can you not spare a few hours this morning?"

Gia looked into my eyes. "No, she cannot. In fact, she was just leaving."

I was left with the choice between facing the chaos inside the house or the human rights violation out here on the porch. Being the strong, independent woman that I was, I ran for my life.

CHAPTER 16

Since just about everyone I knew was inside my house yelling, I got in Aunt Ginny's Corvette and headed for the Laughing Gull Winery in West Cape May to see Kim. I hadn't been there in months since one of my Wine Tour guests had the nerve to get himself killed during a wine-and-cheese flight. If Kim hadn't been one of my high school best friends, I would have refused to jump through the hoops she put me through to clear her business partner's name. Sawyer still hasn't gotten over our climb to break into the second-floor window. She shudders every time we pass a dumpster.

I pulled the car around the back to the service entrance and knocked. The winery didn't open for two more hours, but Kim had said she would be in the office doing paperwork. The heavy metal door opened, and a hand came out and pulled me inside. "Let me see the ring!"

News traveled fast around Cape May.

I held out my hand, and Kim squealed. "It's gorgeous! I bet the single women on this island are in mourning right now. And you really didn't suspect a thing?"

My butterflies started a kickline. I shook my head. "I had no idea. I hoped, but I didn't know."

Kim wrapped me into a hug. "I'm so thrilled for you. Every few years or so, Rick and I talk about getting married. Then we sober up and order Al's hot wings instead. It's still a gamble, but we know with the wings the pain will only last for a few days."

Kim and Rick had been together almost as long as my first marriage. But where mine had started with a shotgun, hers was with a kiss at the drop of a New Year's ball in Times Square.

She led me through the kitchen out to the tasting room. A fire blazed in the hearth, and she had two mugs set up with coffee on the table in front of the leather sofa. "I want to hear all about it."

I recounted the ruse everyone had put me through over the past week, and I gushed about the proposal—especially the part with Henry down on one knee.

Kim wiped a tear and smudged her blue-glitter eyeliner. Which was a shame because it matched the blue glitter in her hair perfectly. "That is . . . the sweetest thing . . . I have ever heard."

I looked at my ring for the millionth time.

Kim played with the fringe on her fuchsia suede skirt. "And have you thought about who you want to be your bridesmaids by any chance?"

I took a sip of my coffee. "Not at all, why?"

She threw me some shade. "You mean to tell me you haven't considered this possibility at least once in the past year?"

I snorted. "Kimberly, will you please be a bridesmaid?"

She squealed. "Yes! Can I pick the dress?"

Visions of Lady Gaga passed through my mind. "Not a chance."

"Oh, come on. What if I promise it will only have feathers or sequins, but not both?"

"You know, I might just elope."

"Okay, fine. But picture this. A *Twilight*-themed wedding."

"As in nighttime?"

"As in vampires. It could be awesome. Everything could be bloodred, and we could hold the ceremony in the woods in the moonlight."

"I was thinking more like we hold it in the church in the normal light."

"You're right. *Twilight* is so over. What about a *Hamilton*-themed wedding. Gia could wear a powdered wig, and you could rap your vows?"

"Uh . . ."

"Oh! With your red hair, you should have a *Little Mermaid* wedding. You could do it on the beach and wear a wedding dress made of seashells. Ooh! Or *Brave*! Gia could wear a kilt."

Is ten a.m. too early for wine? "I've really just been looking forward to wearing a dress that didn't come from the maternity department this time."

She squeezed my hand. "You're finally going to be a mom. But speaking of moms . . . What's the deal with yours?"

"Ugh."

"Sawyer said she just showed up after she abandoned you at—what? Seven years old?"

"Nine."

"Where has she been?"

"No idea. She told Aunt Ginny she needed some time to grieve when my father died, then she'd be back."

"And that was the last you heard from her?"

I nodded and stared at my engagement ring. "A few times she called Aunt Ginny for money over the years.

Then a couple of days ago, she checked in to my B and B under a false name, acting like nothing had happened."

Kim shook her head. "That is unreal. What does she want?"

"I dunno. She hasn't worked up to asking for it yet. But she keeps rifling through our possessions."

"Do you think she came because she heard about you in the news or saw that viral video with Aunt Ginny?"

Nausea curled in my stomach. *How far did that news travel?* "What would she have to gain from that?"

"Maybe she's one of those people who are drawn to drama because it makes them feel alive."

"If that were true, she would have never left Aunt Ginny in the first place."

Kim sipped her coffee and nodded. "Maybe she's digging for dirt about you to sell to a tabloid."

"She wouldn't be the first. At least I have a murder investigation to distract me." *Whoa. Now there's something I never thought I'd hear come out of my mouth.*

"Do the police have any suspects?"

"Yep."

"That's good."

"It's Tim and Gigi."

Her mouth dropped open. "Can you imagine what conspiracy theorists would say about the Murder Magnet's high school boyfriend committing murder?"

Holy crap. Now that's all I'm going to think about. "You don't think the police would hold that against him, do you?"

Kim cocked an eyebrow. "Lawyers have built cases on less. And Wes Bailey wasn't exactly beloved in this town."

"What do you mean?"

"We lost some of our wholesale contracts to supply wine to local restaurants last summer. When the owners were asked why they were switching to Cape Vineyards, they said it was to avoid penalties."

"Penalties from who?"

Kim shrugged. "They wouldn't say, but there was a lot of grousing behind closed doors, and no one would talk about it. The one name that kept coming up was Wes Bailey. Around the same time, Jackson Seymour tried to spearhead a campaign on behalf of local businesses to shut Deepwater Fisheries down. He said they were ruining business equity around town. It's a shame he didn't get anywhere with it. Of course, Wes is dead now, so I guess Jackson wins after all."

CHAPTER 17

I texted Gia to see if it was safe for me to come by La Dolce Vita for coffee and kisses before I went to Maxine's. He responded with a photo of his mother sitting in the wing chair by the front window crocheting, followed by the message, **Please don't stop loving me.**

To which I replied. **Never.** And then thought, *but we might have to move away.*

So I did some Christmas shopping and had my nails done. I was under the UV lights when a text came in from Joanne.

Did you tell Iris she could use your laptop? She's asking for the password.

Absolutely not.

A few minutes later, a text came in from Kenny.

Joanne sent Iris to the library to use their computer, so I'm finally getting into her bedroom. I'll let you know what I find.

I can't wait.

I paid Pearl for my manicure and headed out to the car to go into Maxine's for the night. As I pulled into the parking lot, my phone played sleigh bells again.

Um. Your mom has a bunch of parenting books in her room.
Okay. Whatev.
And Aunt Ginny's fur coat.

"I don't want your ex-girlfriend in my kitchen, Tim. Is it too much for you to respect that?" Gigi held her belly with both hands like she was afraid the baby would fall out.

I kept my eyes down on the workbench while forming tonight's dinner rolls and sighed. Why was I working at Maxine's again? Oh yeah, so Tim's baby mama wouldn't have his baby in lockdown. *For the baby.* Of course, I was avoiding Gia's mother too, so there was that. And I needed to get one of those airport security scanners installed before Iris checked out and robbed me blind.

"What do you think, Poppy?" Tim was staring at me across the stainless-steel workbench, Gigi at his side with a smirk that could cut glass.

"What do I think about what?"

Gigi huffed, "Haven't you been listening?"

"No. I tuned out your argument somewhere around your swollen ankles and Tim's lack of commitment. Let me know when you want to talk about the actual murder."

Gigi closed her eyes and rubbed her belly like she was hoping a genie would pop out.

Tim cleared his throat and studied a bowl of onions. "It's usually pretty slow on Mondays . . . and we don't have a lot of reservations tonight . . . and we do already have a lot of chefs on the line. Plus, you loaded us up on desserts with the crisps and those two fabulous cheesecakes."

I formed my last roll and placed it on the baking sheet. "Riiiight?"

He gave me a hopeful look. "Do you think you could fill in as a waitress instead of working the pastry station—just tonight?"

Gigi's eyes flashed fire and brimstone. "Why just tonight?"

Tim rolled his eyes. "A couple nights, tops."

This was as big a demotion as you could get in the kitchen. The only rung lower was dishwasher, and that kid looked like he might burst into tears if I stepped towards him. Chuck and Tyler wouldn't even look at me. Chuck might have been having a panic attack. His black-rimmed glasses were fogged up to the Band-Aids holding them together at the bridge.

They didn't know Joanne and I had talked about this just a few hours ago. I washed the flour off my hands and dried them. Then I reached into my apron pocket, took out my engagement ring, and slipped it back on my finger. "Yeah, sure."

Tim's eyes followed my hand, and his brow furrowed ever so slightly. I fought the urge to plunge my hand back into my pocket.

"I need to talk to the front-end staff anyway. The sooner we can find out what really happened, the sooner I can get back to my life."

Gigi's sour look slid off, took a bounce on the workbench, and hopped onto Tim's face. "Fine. Good. Then it works for everyone."

Tim walked back to the storage room outside his office and returned with a black server's apron that he threw at me. "Let Chelle know that you'll be out front tonight. She'll tell you where to go."

Gigi muttered something very un-mom-like about where I could go, and I considered calling Amber and confirming—yep, Gigi did it. Send the black-and-white.

My eyes were drawn to Gigi's belly. I pictured Henry

growing up without his mom, wondering where she was, and my heart broke a little. I tied my apron around my waist and pushed through the dining room door.

Chelle wasn't at the hostess station. She was behind the bar with a gorgeous dark-skinned man. A flat-screen TV was playing college basketball on the back wall.

Chelle looked up from her close examination of the man's pecs. Her eyes lit up, and she flashed a thousand-watt smile. "Hey Mack, you're back. We had a bet on you being a one-and-done. You wouldn't believe how many employees don't make it past their first night here."

I heard the distant sound of Gigi yelling that someone had chopped the onions too large and a metal pan hitting the floor. "I'd believe it."

Chelle grinned at the large black man. "You two haven't met yet, have you? This is Gabriel, like the archangel. Gabriel, the new pastry chef, Mack."

Gabriel was about six foot two and built like a line-backer. He had piercing blue eyes and close-cropped hair. When he flashed me a brilliant smile, dimples appeared on his cheeks. "You can call me Gabe. Only Chelle and my momma use my whole name."

She gave me a look that said, *Well, wouldn't you—just look at him.*

"It's very nice to meet you, Gabe."

Gabe looked at my left hand. He put his hand out to me. "Are you engaged? Let me see the ring."

His genial disposition was infectious, and I placed my hand in his without hesitation.

He squeezed my hand. "It's beautiful. How wonderful for you." He let me go, and his eyes turned sad and intro-spective. "Hang on to it. Love can be fickle and fleeting."

"I will do my best."

Chelle nudged me. "What you doing out here wearing a server's apron, girl?"

"I overdid it on the desserts, and the kitchen is full, so it's either go home or waitress for tips."

Chelle and Gabe passed a look between them. Gabe took a highball glass from a plastic tray and polished it with a cloth. "I've never heard of a chef working the front end."

I smiled. "It's better than being off the clock."

Chelle shook her head and tsk'd. "Well, you'll need to get an order pad and a folio from the storage room. Have you ever waitressed before?"

"In October, I helped out at the Southern Mansion for their ghost tour. Before that, I waited tables when my late husband was in law school."

The basketball game went to commercial, and the New Jersey Lotto came on. I wasn't a player myself, but with my odds of finding murder victims, I might want to start.

Chelle snatched up the remote and pointed it at the television. "Nobody got time for that. Alright, let me give you the tour. This, of course, is the bar, with the most amazing bartender in South Jersey. Gabriel can make anything."

Gabe grinned. "Girl, you're too much."

Chelle took a long drink of him. "He's even got some special Christmas cocktails on the menu. I'll give you a cheat sheet in your order pad, so you'll know what they are when someone asks."

"Great." I turned my face to Gabe. "Where'd you learn to bartend?"

His expression clouded over like a squall was approaching. "The Marines."

"Really?"

He nodded.

I waited, but he did not expound upon the thought.

"Well, that's fascinating. How long were you in the Marines?"

"Long enough."

Another long pause.

Okay then.

Chelle walked out from behind the bar. "Follow me, and I'll go over the dining room."

Nikki and Andrew were rolling silverware in napkins at the back table by the server station.

Chelle walked me around and showed me how the tables were numbered. Then she assigned me to a section. "Subject to change based on any groups that come in without reservations, and when or if Teela comes to work tonight."

"I noticed she was late last night too."

Chelle made a face. "That girl thinks the schedule is a suggestion open to her consideration."

"She's young."

"She's a train wreck, with more family drama than Britney Spears."

"As strict a boss as Gigi seems to be, I'm surprised Teela gets away with it."

Chelle lowered her voice. "She's crafty. She knows which boss gives in to crocodile tears, and she uses it, and her tight sweaters, to her advantage."

"Everyone seems to like Chef Tim a lot more than Chef Gigi."

Chelle's lips rolled in, and she tipped her head in thought. "Mostly. I'd be careful with what I say to Gabe, though. He's Team Gigi all the way. Don't tell him anything you don't want Gigi to find out."

"Good to know."

I glanced back at the booth where Andrew and Nikki were laughing. Nikki looked up, and her eyes caught mine. She looked away. "What about Nikki? Is she Team Tim or Team Gigi?"

Chelle shrugged, and I followed her up to the hostess

stand. "It's hard to tell with that one. She's the newest one here, and she don't really make friends. Most of us hang at the bar after work to chill before going home. Gabriel tries out his new cocktail ideas on us while the kitchen closes down. Nikki don't stay. She's always in a rush to get home to her grandmother."

"Was anyone friends with the guy from the freezer?"

Chelle snorted. "I doubt it. Everyone knows Tim and Gigi were trying to get him off their backs for months."

"Get him off their backs for what?"

She glanced at the kitchen door. "Business in this town can be cutthroat. Everyone here knew Wes was shaking them down for more money."

"Is that what Wes and Gigi argued about a couple days ago?"

"Girl, that wasn't no argument. I heard it was a death threat. Teela said that Tyler told her that Gigi screamed at Wes that if he didn't let them out of his contract, she'd bury him. And you don't know Gigi very well, but she isn't the forgiving sort."

"Is that right?"

The front door opened, and Teela ran through the dining room like she was chasing a bus. "I know. I'm late. It's not my fault. My stupid brother said I could use his car, and then he changed his mind because his wife wanted to go food shopping. Like it's my fault she can't take the twins during the day."

Chelle tsk'd. "You better thank your higher power that Gigi don't know you're late." Chelle watched Teela run through the rows of tables to the kitchen and grunted. "Wes only started being a nuisance after he met Teela. He was obsessed with her."

"Did she return his interest?"

"She seemed to at first. Then something changed her mind, and she threatened to quit if Tim didn't get rid of him."

"Chelle!" Tim stood in the doorway to the kitchen. "How many reservations tonight?"

"Gotta go. We'll talk later."

She went over to the hostess stand to check an iPad, and I started back for the storage room to get an order pad. I tried to walk slow so Tim could move out of the way before I got there, but he'd turned into a statue. He and Chelle hollered to each other about the seating for the night, and when I was about to edge past him, he turned his face to me and lowered his voice.

"When did you get engaged?"

Eight months after you knocked up Gigi. "Last night."

He looked away and gave a single nod.

"When you have a chance, I need to speak with you about the desserts for the rest of the week."

His voice came out tight. "Just do what you think is best. You're not here for that anyway."

CHAPTER 18

I sat alone by the server station and finished rolling the napkins. I watched first Nikki, then Andrew go over to the bar to talk about me with Gabe. I knew they were talking about me because they kept huddling up and glancing my way.

My cell phone buzzed in my back pocket. It was Aunt Ginny.

When are you coming home?

Later.

I put my phone away as Teela emerged from the kitchen and looked around the dining room.

"What are you doing up here?"

"Working front end tonight."

"I thought you were a pastry chef."

"I am."

She nodded. "Ah. Got it. Well, you better not take any tables from my section. I barely make enough money to survive now."

"I thought you lived at home with your parents."

Her lip curled. "Yeah, so?"

I shrugged. "Nothing."

Teela adjusted the tie around her waist. "I only live at home until I can make enough money for my own place. I had a roommate, but she kicked me out because she's getting back together with her lame husband. I need better friends I can rely on."

"I'm sorry."

She shrugged. "I would have been able to move by the end of the year if I didn't have to pay my stupid parents rent. Can you believe they charge me two hundred dollars a month? They should let me live at home for free. Isn't that what parents are supposed to do? Help their kids get started?"

Teela tossed her strawberry-blonde hair and caught it together into a ponytail. "They don't know how hard it is out here. My dad's a plumber, and my mom doesn't even have to work. She just goes to doctor's appointments."

I grimaced and tried to cover it with a sympathetic nod.

Teela interpreted the expression as solidarity. "Yeah. I go to community college three times a week for an acting class. My 'rents won't pay for it because I changed my major a few times. I wish they were more understanding. I'm still finding myself. And God knows there aren't a lot of jobs in this town in the winter."

"Sure."

"Also, I don't know what's going on here, but I should be making more tips than I'm getting. I think someone is stealing them. I know it isn't you because you just got here and all, but if you see someone taking money out of my folders, let me know, okay?"

"I'll keep my eyes open."

She looked to the front, where Chelle was leading a group of four to the fireplace room past the snugs. Teela pulled her order pad from her apron, and we both started heading for the water station at the same time. She looked at me, and I looked at her. We paused, then we both took another step.

"Did Chelle give you the fireplace room?"

I took a shallow breath. "Yes."

Teela let out a string of creative profanity and slammed her order pad on the table, knocking over the pile of napkins I'd just rolled. She marched towards the kitchen, complaining about all the reasons her life wasn't fair.

I picked up the black folio, and a torn scrap of paper fell out and floated to the tabletop. It was a note that said, *Meet me in the kitchen after closing.*

A sharp pain started forming behind my eyes. Is this from Teela or for Teela? Is Tim fooling around with Teela after hours? Or could this be from Wes Bailey?

I snapped a photo with my cell phone and tucked the note and my phone into my apron pocket. Then I grabbed the pitcher of water and hurried to the side room, trying to eavesdrop while looking like I was minding my own business. A few minutes later, Tim came out of the kitchen and called Chelle over. He glanced my way just as I finished taking the order.

I started towards the server station, and Chelle caught me. She sighed and gave me a tired look. "I'm pulling you off the fireplace room and putting you in the back section by the kitchen."

My cell phone buzzed again. "Teela really has a lot of pull with Chef Tim, doesn't she?" What are you doing, Tim?

Chelle rolled her eyes. "You don't want to know what I think. I'm just really sorry to do this to you."

"I'm a pastry chef sent out to Siberia. Don't worry about it."

She let out a breath and noticeably relaxed. "Thank you. Put in their order, but Teela will pick it up when it's ready."

I keyed my order into the computer, checked my texts—Aunt Ginny, again—then pushed through the kitchen door. Gigi was at the head of the line, next to Tyler and Chuck. I looked around and didn't see Tim anywhere. Chuck made eyes at me and nodded towards the office.

Andrew entered the kitchen with a tray as Tyler was cleaning the edge of a plate of scampi. "I'm finishing the shrimp now."

"Alright. And I'm gonna grab two winter crisps for table ten. Let me take this out for Nikki, and I'll be right back for the specials." Andrew picked up Nikki's tray and left the kitchen.

I helped load the four plates of shrimp for when he returned. "Does he always carry her trays?"

Tyler handed me a plate finished with parsley. "If they're too heavy for her."

Andrew returned and took his next tray. The guys started adding food to the grill to fill the new orders that were coming through the electronic ordering system.

I headed down the hall, aware that Gigi would follow behind me any minute.

Tim was at his desk, checking the computer screen. "Hey."

He glanced up. "What?"

"I wanted to ask you something real quick."

"Shoot."

"What's up with you and Teela?"

"What? Nothing!"

"It doesn't look like nothing."

"She's a nice kid, and she's got a lot of problems at home. I'm just trying to be supportive."

I showed Tim the note that had fallen out of Teela's order pad. "Is this from you?"

He looked at it. "Never seen it before."

"Uh-huh. And what's the deal with Gigi threatening to bury Wes Bailey over a contract dispute?"

Tim wouldn't look at me. He kept his eyes on the screen. "That wasn't a big deal. Don't worry about it."

"Wasn't a big deal? At least three people have told me about it. You don't think they won't tell the police?"

"It was a misunderstanding." His face reddened. "Just drop it, Poppy. It isn't relevant."

"If you aren't going to let me help you, I may as well just go home."

A blond beach ball threw the door open and crashed into my hip. She looked from me to Tim, nostrils flaring. "You're needed on the line. You know scallops make me nauseous right now."

She backed into the hall, and Tim pushed past me. Gigi stood in the doorway, glaring. "Have you learned anything yet?"

"I've learned a lot. None of it will help you."

Gigi's eyes narrowed. "Then you might as well go home and quit wasting our time."

I don't know what made me do it, but to answer her, I flashed my engagement ring.

Her face went through four out of five stages of grief before she responded. It was embarrassingly satisfying.

She speed-shuffled back to the kitchen.

My cell phone buzzed again. I took it out and texted Aunt Ginny.

I'm busy.

Tim and Gigi were out back having a moment. Nikki was in the kitchen picking up her order, Andrew right behind her to carry the tray. Once she followed him out to the dining room, I turned to Chuck and Tyler. "Hey, what do you guys know about Nikki?"

Chuck shrugged. "Not much."

Tyler checked the ticketing system and put a steak on the grill. "She hasn't been here long."

Chuck turned to Tyler. "Didn't she move down from New York?"

Tyler gave a half shrug. "I think so. We've only talked like twice. She's always running home to give her grandma insulin or something."

I nodded. "Hmm. Okay." I followed Andrew and Nikki out to the dining room to casually observe them together. Nikki ran her hand down Andrew's back while he placed the tray on a stand for her.

Chelle caught my eye as she led a group to my section. I had a table of four arrive, and they each ordered one of Gabriel's seasonal cocktails, giving me a chance to make a trip to the bar.

Gabe was shaking up a white-chocolate martini for one of Teela's tables, while she rested on the barstool like a battle-worn soldier. They were deep in conversation until they saw me headed their way.

Teela pushed away from the bar. "No offense about the side room, Mack. Chelle should never have put you over there. That's the room with the fireplace, and Tim said it could be my section because it gets reservations first."

I forced a friendly smile. "It's no problem."

"Good. I can't take any more stress tonight. I am so done."

I pulled the note that had fallen from her folio out of my apron pocket. "Oh here, before I forget. You dropped this earlier."

Teela held the note like it was laced with anthrax. "That's not mine."

"Are you sure?"

She looked away. "I've never seen that before in my life."

Gabe stuck a tiny candy cane in the martini and passed it to her with a wink. She patted his hand and left to deliver it. I turned in my order and tried to make small talk.

"How's your night going?"

"Fine."

"That white-chocolate martini looks delicious."

"It is."

I watched him measure and dump four kinds of alcohol into a shaker.

"I made up a drink once. It was really good."

"Yeah?"

"We called it a ghost story."

"Cool." He added ice to the canister and shook it. I sat in silence until he passed me the finished cocktails.

"Okay. Well, thank you." Was it something I said? Is he just not a talker, or did that little confab earlier sour him against me? What did Andrew and Nikki say about me?

I delivered the cocktails to my table and went to the back to wait for their food.

Andrew approached me with a grin. "Hey. Chelle said to give you snug number five in my section since Teela threw a hissy to Tim about the front."

"You don't have to do that."

His eyebrows scrunched. "I don't care. You can get good tips from anyone if you're nice. That's Teela's problem. She thinks everyone owes her. She flirts with the men to get bigger tips, and then their wives end up paying the bill and stiff her for revenge."

"Is it my imagination, or is Teela after Chef Tim?"

Andrew inched closer. He was shorter than me and had to crane his neck a little. "Gigi is horrible, but she doesn't deserve what Teela is doing. She is the worst employee here, and she gets away with murder."

I laughed quietly. "Be careful saying that to the police unless you mean it."

He shook his head. "I know everyone thinks Chef Gigi killed the fish guy, but just between you and me, I don't trust Chef Tyler."

My head jerked to the side so fast I pulled my neck. "Tyler? How come?"

"I used to work for the guy in high school."

"Chef Tyler? Doin' what?"

"Waiting tables. Tyler used to own Devon's Steaks and Seafood over in Margate."

"I didn't know that."

"Food was pretty good, but business was slow. Payroll was always late. A bunch of us showed up one night to work, and the place was locked and dark. It was a shock to find him working in the kitchen here when I started."

"Did Tyler use Deepwater Fisheries at his restaurant?"

Andrew shrugged. "I have no idea, but a buddy of mine works at the Seafood Hut, and they use Deepwater Fisheries. Word of advice—don't order the scallops."

"Why not?"

"Just trust me."

"I'll take your word for it. You must have known Wes pretty well. I hear he used to hang out at the bar here."

Andrew's lip curled. "The guy was a jerk. He started showing up a few weeks ago to hang with the staff. We tried to get him to take the hint that no one wanted him here after we'd closed, but he was sprung for Teela, and he just wouldn't give up. I'm sorry he's dead, but I'm glad he's gone. We're hanging out tonight after closing, if you want to join us."

My cell phone buzzed again, and I pulled it out to check it.

I want to show you a wedding dress.

I slid it back into my pocket and sighed. "I can't tonight. I have to take care of a small problem at home." *Named Aunt Ginny.*

CHAPTER 19

I'd returned home to find that Smitty had added lights to the garage and around the mailbox. That was new. Maybe Georgina had convinced him to hang around yesterday while she was busy controlling—I mean planning—my wedding with Cape May's finest busybodies.

I'd found a note in my room that one of the new guests had brought a surprise pet with them. The word "pet" was in quotes, which made me very nervous. I really hoped it wasn't the kind that slithered or lived in a cage. I could not be held responsible for what Figaro would do under those circumstances.

Aunt Ginny had left a stack of wedding-dress pictures from magazines on my bed. I flipped through them out of morbid curiosity. There was a tight mermaid gown that would make me look like a snowman in a bed skirt. A backless number that I'm sure would work great with my double Ds. A gown that Princess Diana would have said was too fussy. And one with a pleated lace skirt that would make me look like I was wearing a giant cupcake liner upside down.

Fig sat on the bed, judging the pictures with me. I could tell he thought they were horrible too.

"Everyone has a lot of opinions about my wedding, Fig. I don't even know what I want yet." *Ooh, what's this?*

My frustration fizzled as I looked at the photo on the back side of one of the pages. It was a beautiful empire-waist satin gown with clean lines. It had an illusion neckline like a strapless dress, but the décolleté and sleeves were made out of tulle beaded with crystals.

I removed the page from the stack and pinned it on my corkboard. I was afraid to tell Aunt Ginny I loved it in case it meant I'd be drowning in magazine pages every night, but it was perfect.

I flopped on the bed, and Figaro snuggled against me in an obvious plot to steal my heat. He nuzzled into my neck, purring, with his paws kneading my shoulder. *Little opportunist.* I fell asleep instantly and woke up the next morning when my cell phone made a weird chime.

I grabbed it off the nightstand and checked the screen. I had a Google alert that Poppy McAllister was mentioned in a press release. My spirit slumped. It had been several weeks since my name was in the news. Usually, it was associated with death threats and crime scenes. Today I was sure I would find someone had leaked to the paper that my name was discovered on the deceased body of Wes Bailey. CAPE MAY'S MURDER MAGNET, POPPY MCALLISTER, NAMED BY KILLER IN LOCAL RESTAURANT SLAYING.

I followed the link to the report in the *Herald*. It was so much worse than I could ever have imagined, and I shot straight up in bed with my heart pounding. There, on the society page, was my senior prom photo, complete with eighties hair and blue-carnation corsage, the engagement announcement of Virginia McAllister Frankowski's grand-niece to local café owner Giampaolo Larusso.

An inset picture of Gia looked like he had been taken

by surprise when he handed a customer a coffee—his expression a mixture of confusion and annoyance. I had really hoped my family wouldn't start to irritate Gia until after the ceremony, when it was too late for him to back out.

I texted him. **Don't check the paper.**

Too late.

I'm sorry.

He replied with a photo of his mother holding up a pleated wedding dress that looked like it was made from a lace tablecloth. The female Larussos were a tiny people.

I take it back. You deserve that picture.

He sent me a selfie shot with the most pitiful expression.

LOL. Now I see where Henry gets it.

Henry is the master of the sad face. XOXO

I'll try to stop in soon so I can collect those kisses in person.

I got ready for the day, but I was still full of nervous energy and irritation over that announcement. I grabbed Great Grandpa's diary to give myself a few minutes before I had to descend the steps and face my own feisty rooster.

June 3

I have tried to make polite conversation with that woman, but she is completely unreasonable. I cut through her field on my way to the clubhouse and enquired as to what smell was emanating from her home. I assumed she was attempting to cook again. She does not seem especially domestic, and all early indications point to her not being knowledgeable in the kitchen. I suggested she contact my sister Elizabeth and take some lessons because she has no chance of getting a husband on her appearance alone. She turned contemplative at the suggestion, so I assume she is taking it under advisement.

June 5

I won twelve dollars from the dice last night. Hazard is my new favorite pastime. Oswald has nearly caused my death once again. He will insist upon the toddies when the heat is oppressive.

June 12

The crazy lady delivered a peace offering today. I am not sure what it is. I believe it is a brick. I will find a use for it somewhere.

June 13

So much for peace offerings. Much to my surprise, the doorstop was supposed to be a pound cake. I was aghast. It is surely ten pounds. The woman showed up on my porch very early and caught me while I was still at my breakfast. I did not have time to come up with a suitable lie, so I found myself confessing that I'd placed the item by the library door to prop it open in an attempt to garner a cross breeze. I think she tried to cast *some sort of voodoo magic on me. I have only read of such a thing in nature magazines.*

I was beginning to think that McAllisters had a special talent for creating chaos. I gathered myself and went down the back stairs to face my own ball of terror.

Joanne and Kenny were in the kitchen getting ready to serve French toast to the guests. Neither one would look me in the eye as I stood there silently holding up my cell phone showing the engagement announcement. "Where is she?"

Kenny pointed towards the sitting room. "I told her not to do it."

I went through to the sitting room. Aunt Ginny was staring out the front window with an enigmatic glare at Nell Belanger's house. Nell was participating in the Victorian Christmas Homes Tour and was hanging a gorgeous wreath of white gardenias and red berries on her front door.

"I saw the announcement."

Aunt Ginny flinched. "You didn't give me any choice—with your 'no-picture' policy. I always said if you were kidnapped, I didn't have a current photo to use for your milk carton."

"Who took the candid of Gia?"

"Edith. Thelma tried, but she couldn't figure out how to use the camera on her cell phone."

"Why does he look so annoyed?"

"I might have just knocked over that display of cake pops you made."

I sighed. "If I'd known it was that important to you, Gia and I would have done a professional photo shoot for the announcement."

"Really?"

"No."

"Then big hair and blue taffeta it is."

I was about to launch a formal complaint that could not be ignored, when I looked down at my Dickens Christmas village. Someone had turned the butcher shop into a crime scene. The townspeople were gathered around the butcher lying prone, a toy Jeep racing from the scene of a hit-and-run. Miniature crime-scene tape had been strung up between the Victorian light poles. "Hey!"

Aunt Ginny followed my gaze and snickered.

"Who did this?"

She shrugged. "Probably your mother."

That thought sent a shiver down my spine.

I set the village back to the festive happy scene that I had created the night of the tree-trimming party and stuck the toy Jeep on the bookshelf.

The Christmas tree shook, and a tinkle of bells sounded. A cardinal jumped off the tree, clenched in Figaro's mouth, and he shot from the room. "Fig! Get back here with my bird! That's older than I am." I sighed.

Aunt Ginny cackled, then looked back across the street with a grunt.

"What are you looking at?"

She had a cryptic tone to her words. "Nothing."

"That's the kind of nothing that usually ends with me posting your bail."

"Focus on your crime scene."

Georgina called to me, and I looked around to see where the voice had come from. She waved from the dining room, where she sat at the head of the table with the guests, like the lady of the manor. Her syrup-smeared plate had been moved aside for a three-ring binder.

"Now, I want you to keep an open mind."

I heard my mind snap shut like a trap. "Uh-huh."

I looked around the room and greeted our new guests. A little old couple in their eighties from Long Island, a fiftyish pair of sisters from Maryland with matching feathered hairdos, and an Indian couple I estimated to be in their thirties; the woman sneezed. None of them looked like the kind of people who would kill the baker in the Dickens village, but you never could tell. "Hello, everyone. Are you all having a good time?"

The young woman sneezed again, her eyes were red and puffy. "I'm allergic to cats."

"Oh no. You didn't see that we have a cat on the website?"

She shook her head. "My husband booked the trip to surprise me."

Her husband hung his head and sighed.

I forced myself not to say, *We have a cat, surprise!* "Aww. That was sweet."

Iris wedged herself between the Indian lady and Georgina. She grabbed a chocolate muffin. "Isn't my daughter's little inn just adorable? She gets her decorating skills from me."

I clamped down my expression to hide my irritation from the guests.

The guests complimented Iris for my good taste, which she took credit for. They said some stuff I didn't catch after that because I'd temporarily gone deaf from anger, but I did catch their rave over the breakfast and praise for the chef.

"Joanne is fabulous. I'll have her come out and . . ." I completely lost my train of thought because while I was talking, a giant ball of tan fur with a snout poked its head over the table from one of the sister's laps. There was so much hair I couldn't see any eyes. *What am I looking at?*

The woman sneezed again. "I'm allergic to that too."

The puff kind of looked in my direction, and a blue tongue came out from the center of it under the snout. *Is it a baby bear?* It looked a little like a naked Paddington.

Georgina lurched in her seat. "My lord, has that thing been in here the entire time?"

The sister without a bear in her lap nudged her partner in crime. "I told you he wasn't allowed in the dining room."

The one with the now-guilty look on her face shifted the bear and immediately started to apologize. "I'm sorry. I should have known animals weren't allowed around the food."

Kenny entered from the kitchen with the juice pitcher to offer refills. Figaro pushed himself through the door on Kenny's heels and trotted at his side to beg for scraps from the table.

"No, it's fine. God knows we can't keep the cat out of here. But what exactly is that in your lap?"

Kenny laughed at me. "Poppy. It's a mini chow chow, and his name is General Tso."

The puff looked at me—I think—and even he seemed to be dubious about Kenny's answer. A paw touched the table, making the china rattle, and Figaro jumped with his back arched and hissed. He looked at the puff, and I swear his eyes narrowed.

Iris tittered. "Oh dear. It looks like your little kitty is afraid. You might want to get her out of here to someplace safe."

"You clearly don't know Fig." *Or me.* "Plus, he's a he."

Georgina gave her most ladylike snort. "Trust me, that cat is anything but helpless. He's a little con man, if you ask me."

Yep. Georgina knows Fig.

The allergic woman blew her nose and excused herself from the table. Her husband followed meekly behind her. I apologized and offered to get them some allergy medicine.

The lady holding the ball of fluff set him on the floor. "General Tso really is a very sweet boy. Chows are gentle."

The dog wobbled on his feet, then fell to his butt like standing was a new experience for him. The blue tongue came out again, and I saw the hint of eyes in the fur. Figaro approached tentatively and gave him a pat on the black button at the end of the pup's snout, then ran from the room for all he was worth. The dog didn't react.

His owner cooed. "See how good my boy is? He's so smart. He knows your kitty is harmless."

That stuffed cardinal didn't think so.

The chow chow leaned into the leg of the table until his face was buried in the tablecloth.

Kenny chuckled. "He's clearly very bright."

I suspected General Tso was about as smart as a potato.

Georgina flipped through the book until she found what she was looking for. "Poppy. Come here. I want you to see these bridesmaids' dresses I've saved for you."

Iris refolded her napkin and spoke in a singsongy voice. "If I'd known you were getting engaged, I could have brought my wedding album."

I tried to bite back my words, but they slipped out between my teeth. "If you'd have been involved in my life, Aunt Ginny would have told you I'd be getting engaged."

The couples at the table gave each other looks confirming that I'd just made things awkward. Or exciting. Depends on how exciting things were for them at home, I guess.

I ignored the delusional woman and sidled over to the pushy one. "Where did you get that binder?"

Georgina blinked and smacked her lips. "I've been putting it together for months now. I've saved every idea I thought was right for you."

I spotted the line of bridesmaids in frothy orange-sherbet gowns on the page. *Oh dear God.*

Iris sat with her hands in her lap, staring at the photo. "That color, with her orange hair?"

Excuse me. I had so much to say and too many guests present to be able to say it. "My hair is auburn."

Georgina gave a withering look to Iris. "You are not planning this wedding. You had your chance with the last one, and as I recall, you declined. I'm the only mother this girl has known her entire adult life."

The pit of my stomach gave me a shake. *Oh God, that's not true, is it?*

Georgina slammed the binder shut. "I think I would know what colors are best for her wedding." She gave me a pleading look. "Isn't that right, Poppy?"

I didn't hesitate. "Why, yes you would, Georgina."

Georgina glowed like a supernova. "We'll go over my ideas later when it's just us family."

The doorbell rang, and I'd never been so fast to answer it in my life. "Sorry. Let me just see who that is."

I opened it to find Teresa's husband, Angelo, holding a pink pastry box. "Good morning, new sister."

"What do you want?"

He moved the pink pastry box closer to me. "Momma sends some Italian wedding cookies for you to try for your reception. She says they will be perfect in little boxes to give away as favors."

"Is that right?"

Angelo looked down and pointed at my feet. "Did you get a puppy?"

I followed his gaze. The mini chow chow was tugging my shoelace. "No, he belongs to a guest."

He nodded. "Well, send Momma your guest list, and she'll add it to hers so she can make enough for every-one."

"Momma has a guest list?"

"Oh yes. Momma has already sent word to the old country that Giampaolo is to be married. She wants to bring everyone over for the coming nuptials and has requested I get a date from you so she can book your counseling with the priest."

I looked back at Iris. *If I book the wedding, maybe I can get a deal on the exorcism.*

CHAPTER 20

I headed down the hall to escape the dining room and do some research on Deepwater Fisheries at my desk. General Tso tried to follow me, but he got distracted by the metal wastebasket next to my desk. Not the contents, mind you. The actual wastebasket. He stopped to stare at his reflection. Then he face-planted into the side of the can, and that's where he stayed while I looked up how long Wes Bailey had been in business and what kind of reviews the company had. I found nothing on their website or Yelp to indicate there was a problem.

Figaro jumped on my desk to stare over the edge at the mini chow. He looked from the dog to me, and I thought I saw concern in his eyes.

Nope, I was wrong. Figaro lifted his paw and nudged a plastic box of paper clips off the desk onto the puff we were assuming was General Tso's head. I opened my mouth to scold him, but the dog didn't seem to notice. The box of paper clips rested right on top of the pouf of tan fur.

He was still face-planting into the wastebasket.

He may have fallen asleep.

Now Figaro looked genuinely concerned.

I picked the box off the chow's head and put it back on my desk. Figaro lifted his paw again, and I said, "No." So he lay down and watched the dog to see if it would move instead.

I looked up Wes Bailey on Facebook and found a sparsely used account with just a few posts. A few videos of Wes fishing from his YouTube account, and a lot of Wes reposting memes.

There was very little personal information, so I closed Facebook and went to the Deepwater Fisheries website. It was a simple page with contact information and several photos of Wes Bailey and his crewmates posing with various catches. I called the phone number, but got an answering machine message. *Due to a death at the company, the office will be closed until the end of the week. There will be no grace period on your invoices.*

Fig shot his paw out and knocked the box back on General Tso.

"Fig!" I retrieved the box and sent an email requesting more information when they returned, then made my way to the kitchen to bake some gluten-free muffins.

Aunt Ginny was butt-in-the-air, elbow deep, in the baking cabinet, muttering angrily that she could never find anything.

"What are you looking for?"

"Nunya!"

I caught Joanne's narrowed eyes and replied, "Nunya business."

I bent over to speak into the cabinet. "Is this for your super-secret dessert entry?"

"Don't worry about what I'm doing. Maybe you should just stick to picking a wedding date."

Joanne stared at me openmouthed. "You don't have a date yet?"

"I've been engaged for all of forty-eight hours, and half of them I've been at a crime scene. No, we don't have a date yet. And Angelo sitting out there on the front porch won't make it happen any faster either."

I started taking out ingredients for candied ginger-bread muffins when Kenny flew into the kitchen with his hand stuffed in his shirt. He looked left and right before whispering, "You will not believe what I found in Iris's room."

Aunt Ginny dropped a tube pan on her rapid ascent from under the island. "What? What is it?"

Kenny pulled his hand out and held up a ziplock bag-gie full of white powder.

Joanne dropped her mixing bowl. "Oh my God! Is that what I think it is?"

Kenny was a symphony of panic. He held the bag out and danced around. "Whatdowedo? Whatdowedo? I'm too pretty to go to jail."

Joanne was also a little breathless. "Should we call Amber? Maybe we should just flush it."

I could barely think straight myself. "Why did you touch it, Kenny? Now your fingerprints are on the bag."

Kenny turned puce and hissed. "It was under her pil-low. I was just trying to make the bed while she was out."

Joanne waved her arms around. "She's not out. Her car is still here. She must be snooping around the house again."

Aunt Ginny had been strangely calm this whole time. She took the bag from Kenny, plunged her finger into the powder, and tasted it.

Ten years fell off my life. "Why in God's name would you do that?"

Her eyes narrowed as she assessed. "Talcum."

Kenny's eyebrows stopped dancing around. "What?"

"It's talcum powder." She smacked her lips, and her eyes narrowed. She stuck her nose in the bag and took a deep inhale.

My heart fluttered in my chest. "You are going to kill me. You know that?"

Aunt Ginny ran from the kitchen into her bedroom. A few seconds later, we heard her swear—something that was very unusual for Aunt Ginny. Then she marched back into the kitchen with a small round cardboard container. She made a face, turned it upside-down, then smacked the empty container down on the counter. "It's my Evening in Paris dusting talc. She has to go."

Joanne and I talked Aunt Ginny off the ledge. Mostly Joanne. I was on board with making Iris leave until Joanne made the point that Iris hadn't tried to leave the house with anything yet. If she did, we could press charges. Until she did, she could make the argument that she was just borrowing the items from family.

That wasn't good enough for me. I called Amber. "Hey. How long does a background check take?"

"An hour or so."

"Can you run one for me?"

I gave Amber my mother's details with help from Aunt Ginny and a storage box of old records. Then I finished baking and cooling six dozen gluten-free muffins, and Joanne put some aside for the bed and breakfast. I boxed up the remaining muffins for La Dolce Vita.

I texted Gia that I was on my way and carted four pastry boxes out to Bessie. I had to park at the curb last night because a little red Ford Fiesta was blocking the driveway. I'd considered "accidentally" pushing Iris's car down the street, but I didn't want to scratch Aunt Ginny's paint.

I put the boxes on the passenger seat and waved to Nell. She was hanging green-and-white wreaths on the vintage post lights on either side of her driveway.

She waved a pink velvet bow. "Ginny's house looks beautiful."

"Thank you. So does yours. Very elegant. When is the tour?"

"This weekend. I hope I'm ready in time."

"I'm sure you will be."

A movement to my right caught my attention, and I spied Aunt Ginny, grimacing at Nell's house from the sitting-room window. I didn't like the wild gleam in her eye. I looked around the yard to see what had gotten her so riled up and noticed we now had a festive igloo bird feeder at the front of the property.

I walked closer to get a better look at it, and it lit up and started to play "Winter Wonderland." *That's gonna scare the bejeezus outta some birds.*

I caught Aunt Ginny's eyes and pointed to the bird feeder. She grinned and gave me a thumbs-up. In retrospect, it was less of a grin and more of a maniacal red flag that I failed to pick up on in time.

The next-door neighbor called to me from her front porch. "Poppy dear?"

I gave her a little wave. "Hello, Mrs. Pritchard. How are you?"

"My rheumatoid arthritis is acting up something fierce. It's this cold weather. Could you be a darling and bring me my mail? I'm in my housecoat."

I walked over to her mailbox and pulled out a mountain of junk mail. I carried the haul up to her front porch.

Mrs. Pritchard reached for the stack of store circulars and catalogs and started taking them from me one piece at a time. "Thank you, honey. I used to get a lot of Christ-

mas cards this time of year. Of course, nowadays, the
kids—they don't send cards. They want me to look everything up on Instagram. I don't even remember how to log
in to the thing."

I loved Mrs. Pritchard. She'd lived next door to Aunt
Ginny my entire life. But those muffins for the coffee
shop would be stale by the time she collected all the mail
in my arms. "Why don't I put this inside for you?"

Her face brightened, and she edged towards the screen
door. "How sweet of you. I'm not as fast as I used to be."

I chuckled to myself. *It would be impossible to be
slower.* I followed her into the front parlor and put her
mail on the credenza, where she'd indicated. She had one
of those ceramic light-up Christmas trees on the edge of
her desk next to a sepia-toned photograph of a man standing in front of the house. "Who is this?"

She picked up the picture. "That's my late husband's
grandad. That's the day they moved in here."

"What year was that?"

Mrs. Pritchard pressed her lips together and looked at
the ceiling. "Turn of the century? They had just finished
building the house, and the inspector said everything
passed with flying colors, so it was a momentous occasion." She picked up the picture and took it out of the
frame. Turning it over, it had *Ernest, September 1902*
written on the back.

"He built the house himself?"

She nodded and flipped it back to the front. "With his
brothers. It was a source of pride that the family built this
house with their own hands. When I go, the house passes
to my son, Michael."

"What was here before the house was built?"

Mrs. Pritchard shrugged, and her papery cheeks quivered. "I don't think anything was. The house on the other
side was a farm, so . . . maybe a cornfield."

I looked through the front-parlor window on the north side of the house. We were in a long row of Victorian homes. Which one of those was the infamous neighbor Grandpa Rooster was at war with? Or could it be on the other side of us?

"Have you ever heard about Aunt Ginny's great-great-grandfather Callum?"

Her brow knit for a moment. "No. I don't believe I have. I only know about my husband's family. They built several of the buildings on the island."

I gave her a smile. "That is very impressive. It seems my ancestor was just known for creating scandals."

She patted my arm. "We can't choose our family, can we? Speaking of scandals. I heard about that incident down at Maxine's. Isn't that chef the fella you used to go with?"

"Yes, but he isn't responsible for what happened."

She gave me a coy look. "Are you sure?"

I looked into those innocent blue eyes and couldn't lie. "I'm mostly sure."

She grinned. "Well, I might not know anything about Ginny's people, but I do know that Wes Bailey was a bad egg."

"How do you know about Wes?"

"I'm pretty sure it was on the front page of the *Herald*. You can't sling mud and not get dirty yourself."

"Who was he slinging mud at?"

"Honey, it was all over town. The produce supplier wrote a letter to the Chamber of Commerce complaining that Wes was involved in illegal and unethical business practices. He sent copies to every newspaper in South Jersey. It got very ugly."

"Do you have a copy of the article?"

She shook her head, and her cheeks gave a little jiggle. "No. That went out in the recycling ages ago. The library might have a copy, though. Do they still keep papers and magazines, or did that practice go away with the Christmas cards?"

I stifled a giggle. "I'll check." *And by check . . . I meant google.*

She patted my hand. "Good girl. And best wishes on your pending nuptials. There are a lot of broken hearts around Cape May. If you didn't have enemies before, there are a few new ones today."

CHAPTER 21

I walked in the back door of the coffee shop and set the boxes of muffins on the counter. Gia came back, whistling, to greet me and broke into a grin. "There is my love."

My stomach did a little flip, and I walked into his arms. *I hope this never gets old.*

He kissed me until I forgot all the drama of the morning. Well, almost all. "Do you know anything about shady business practices in this town?"

His lip twitched into a smirk. "Not firsthand, no."

"Could you ask that secret syndicate of yours and see what you can find out?"

He murmured against my neck. "I thought we settled this last spring. I am not in the mafia."

"What mafia? I'm talking about the Chamber of Commerce."

Gia threw his head back and laughed. "You got me. What is bringing all this on?"

The buzzer calling for backup rang in Gia's office.

I picked up the boxes of muffins. "Something happened on my way over here."

"That could be good or bad."

Gia took two of the boxes from my hands. I followed him to the front, where his sister Karla was working the espresso bar. She stopped mid-froth to give me a hug. "I'm so excited for you." She grabbed my ring hand. "It's gorgeous! Could you just die?"

I gave her a smile. "I love it."

I tried to put out the candied gingerbread muffins and sold four before getting them into the pastry case. Once Gia had worked through the line of customers, he took me by the hand and looked to his sister. "Make me that drink we talked about earlier." With a nod to her, he led me to the back room.

"Ooh, what drink? Is it a surprise?"

Gia grinned. "*Si*. It is special surprise just for you. Now tell me everything."

I grabbed my apron and pulled the recipe cards from my purse. "Mrs. Pritchard said something as I was leaving. She said Jackson Seymour wrote a letter to the Chamber complaining about Wes Bailey. He supposedly sent copies to all the newspapers. Do you know anything about that?"

Gia folded his arms across his chest. "No. But I usually read the news on my phone."

"Yeah. Me too." *If by news you mean celebrity gossip and reality-show recaps.*

"Which newspaper? It should be on their website." Gia pulled out his phone and started typing, while I assembled ingredients to make gingerbread biscotti.

"She mentioned the *Herald* specifically."

By the time I had everything set up, he held his phone out. "The *Herald* had a letter to the editor over the summer from Jackson Seymour, but it reads like one man who is complaining business is bad. It does not mention Wes Bailey by name, and he is pretty vague about the business in question."

I scanned the letter. "He calls them 'a local fish sup-plier with a blue van who has turned seafood delivery into organized crime.' This can't be the whole thing. Mrs. Pritchard thought it was on the front page. This is one paragraph. If you were angry enough to report him to the Chamber of Commerce, wouldn't you write more than this?"

Gia slipped his phone back in his pocket. "*Si*. Or leave a horse head in his bed."

I snickered. "I need to find a way to ask him about it that won't spook him."

Gia thought for a minute. "What if we set up a meeting with Seymour Veg to discuss a contract for Mia Famiglia? Momma is doing better from her broken hip, but she won't be able to open the kitchen until after the holidays."

I grabbed his arm. "That's perfect. You are so smart."

Gia beamed. "*Si*. It is because of you, *cara mia*. Your sneakiness is rubbing off."

"There is one problem, though."

"What is that?"

"He thinks I'm a police officer. I never actually cor-rected him."

Gia gave me half a shrug. "That is no problem. You can tell me what to ask and listen from the kitchen."

"I love it. Call him now."

Before we could look up the number for Seymour Veg, my cell phone rang. It was Amber. "Bad news on the background check, McAllister."

"I knew it. She's a domestic terrorist, isn't she?"

Amber snickered. "That would be Aunt Ginny. Appar-ently, your mother has spent considerable time overseas. An international background check will take longer."

I sighed. "How much longer? I think she's slowly rob-bing us."

"A few days to a week. I'll keep you posted."

As soon as I clicked off, a small delegation from the Italian wedding coalition burst through the door. Momma came hobbling in with her cane, flanked by Teresa, who was carrying another pink pastry box.

"Hello, sister. We are here to discuss bridesmaid dresses. And Momma brought three more cookies for you to taste for your wedding dessert table."

I had a brick of butter poised over my KitchenAid. "My what?"

Karla peeked around the corner and held out a latte like a white flag. "This is a special surprise for a special sister."

Gia said something rough sounding in Italian, and Karla answered. "Yes, I called them! Momma owns my house. She said she'd change the locks."

Gia's mother linked her arm in mine and started to monologue. Not that I understood any of it.

Teresa took the butter from my hand and translated. "There are eight of us plus Giampaolo. Six girls and two boys. Do you have three male cousins who could be groomsmen? If not, Zio Alfio could fill in, but his gout is acting up, so he will need to use the walker. And our cousin Zeppo is coming from Roma. He is only four feet tall, but Daniella could wear flats and hunch."

I looked over my shoulder to Gia. He mirrored a look of horror back to me. His mother reached for him, and he pretended he was on a call on his cell.

Teresa took my hand and pulled me towards the door. "Momma have to sit by front window close to her restaurant, so she no set off her ankle alarm."

She led me out to the dining room and backed me into a leather club chair. Teresa was going on and on about spring weddings and spaghetti straps. I got all the information overlapping in two languages like I was watching a UN debate on C-SPAN. My head was swimming.

Sawyer ran past the picture window and into the coffee shop. "Poppy! Thank God you're here. I need you to come with me now. It's an emergency."

My heart began to race. I grabbed my latte and popped out of the club chair. "What's wrong? It's not another murder victim with my name on them, is it?"

The room went silent.

Teresa translated for Momma.

Sawyer grabbed my wrist and led me to the door. "Now."

I called over my shoulder, "I'm so sorry. I have to go."

Once outside, Sawyer fast-walked me down the brick lane. "Shh. Just follow me."

I held my latte out to the side to keep from spilling it on myself. "What's the matter? Is it Aunt Ginny? Is someone hurt?"

I jogged after her around the block to the back of her bookstore. She unlocked the door and pulled it open, looking around to see if we'd been followed. "In here."

We were in the stockroom just outside her little office. "Sawyer, what are we doing?"

She grinned and held up her cell phone. "Gia texted me to come rescue you."

My heart warmed. "Aww."

"I thought we could talk wedding stuff while my staff restocks."

I followed her into her office, and we sank down onto the pullout sofa. She tucked her feet up under her.

I took my first sip of the latte. "Whoa! This is good! I think it has rum syrup in it."

Sawyer took it from me and gave it a taste. Her nose wrinkled. "That's disgusting. It tastes like a fork."

"It does not, you weirdo."

She handed it back. "Well, you can have it. So, how is everything? How are the wedding plans coming?"

I snorted. "About as well as everything else in my life goes."

"Do you have a date set?"

"We haven't even narrowed down a language for the ceremony."

Sawyer cocked her head to the side and raised an eyebrow. "Gia's mother being a thorn in your side?"

"She's more of an ice pick in the temple. Today she tried to lock down his sisters as my bridesmaids."

"What does Gia think about that?"

"I believe you got his text."

She laughed, then stopped mid-chuckle. "Who does she think is the maid of honor?"

"I'm pretty sure Teresa is campaigning for the position."

Sawyer's mouth opened, and she looked around the room, at a loss for words.

"Don't worry. You are the only one who could ever be my maid of honor."

She breathed a sigh. "Oh good. I think I still have my maid-of-honor sash from your first wedding."

"Really? All I have left is the mother-in-law. And I gotta say, between Gia's family and Iris sneaking around the house, Georgina is looking pretty normal right now."

CHAPTER 22

Sawyer and I had spent an hour browsing wedding bouquets on Pinterest. I found a gorgeous picture of cream-and-blush cabbage roses, burgundy ranunculus, and orchids, with sprigs of eucalyptus that I pinned for later.

Once the coast was clear, I was able to sneak back into La Dolce Vita to finish several batches of cookies. That was after Gia sent Karla home early because the fink sang like a canary the moment I'd arrived the first time. It was all self-preservation with this family.

As much as I wanted to laze about in the joy of being engaged, Gia and I needed to get everyone we were not marrying off our backs. I was not about to go into another marriage with a meddling mother-in-law, and I didn't have twenty-five years to wait for this one to mellow.

I kissed my fiancé goodbye and headed over to Maxine's, not sure of which of Gigi's personalities I would find tonight.

She was sitting in the kitchen at the work island in a maternity jumpsuit, eating a family-sized casserole of rigatoni. She didn't speak, but her eyes said they would slit my throat in the parking lot later. Tim, Tyler, and Chuck all worked the line in complete silence. I don't think they were allowed to talk.

That right there is the reason I can't find another suspect.

I collected my apron and order pad and made my way out to the dining room. Chelle grabbed me right away. "I'm so glad you're here. I've only got Nikki right now, and there's a big group coming in."

"Teela late again?"

Chelle rolled her eyes and smoothed her sleek bob. "I'm on my last nerve with that girl."

"Where's Andrew?"

"Tuesday's his night off. Can you do the snugs tonight? They're all booked after six."

"Yeah. Of course. Hey, I wanted to ask you something."

"Shoot."

"Did you ever hear about the fight the Seymour Veg guy was having with Wes Bailey?"

"That's old news. Everyone knows Wes was making enemies outta all the vendors."

"Do you think maybe another one of Tim's suppliers would kill Wes at Maxine's right before the vegetable delivery to frame Jackson Seymour?"

Chelle shrugged. "As far as I know, Wes and Jackson were the only locals Tim used. I think everything else comes on a big truck, but you'd have to ask the kitchen."

The front door opened, and a reservation of four came in. Chelle took them to a snug, and I joined Nikki at the back table, refilling the salt and pepper shakers to give them a couple minutes with the menus.

She looked up and frowned. "Hey."

"Hey." I stretched my arm across my chest. "Those trays are so heavy."

"I guess."

"It's really nice of Andrew to carry yours for you when he's here."

"I guess."

"I hear you're from New York. How long ago did you move down?"

"Couple months. My grandmother's sick. She needed someone to take care of her, and I'm all she's got . . . so here I am."

"She's lucky to have you."

Nikki looked at me, but didn't smile. "I thought wait-ressing last night was a one-time thing for you."

"Looks like I'm helping the front of the house again tonight."

"Who'd you piss off? Mr. or Mrs.?"

I gave her a wry grin. "Mrs."

She nodded. "Been there, done that. Don't worry, she'll either be on maternity leave or in jail soon. Either way, things will be a lot friendlier around here."

"You think she killed the fish guy?"

Nikki shrugged. "Everyone thinks she killed him. She's a hothead. I mind my own business. I'm not here to make friends. I'm just here to work."

"You were home with your grandma when it hap-pened?"

"Yep."

"Lucky you—a solid alibi."

Nikki screwed the lid on the last saltshaker. "I didn't even know the guy. He delivered straight to the kitchen."

"It's a shame you moved all the way down here just to get caught up in this."

"Yeah, well. Gram's upset, so . . . she wants me to get another job."

"When will you do that?"

"After the holidays, when things settle down here.

Everyone's up in arms over this fish guy. People get murdered in New York all the time. Nobody gives a—"

"Nikki!" Chelle was on her way over to the bar. "You got a table."

Nikki stood. "Well, anyway. I should probably be more respectful to the guy, but I heard he was a jerk, so . . ." She grabbed a water pitcher and approached the couple in her section.

I checked in on my snug and took their drink orders.

I had just put in an order with Gabe for two martinis when Teela flew past me. "It's not my fault."

Chelle caught my eye and nodded to two ladies she was leading to a snug. They'd brought in a dozen shopping bags, claiming they were afraid to leave them in the car because of the vagrant behind the parking lot. I suggested they try the white-chocolate martinis, on the house, to make their experience more pleasant.

As I crossed the room to the bar, Nikki walked past me carrying a tray with six drinks and a raw bar tower.

I had just finished giving the shopping ladies' order to Gabe when the front door opened, and two uniformed officers entered.

Gabe groaned.

"What's happening?"

"It looks like Gigi called the cops on the homeless guy again."

CHAPTER 23

Shane Birkwell gave me some side-eye while his partner took Gigi's report.

"I'm sorry, ma'am, but we can't arrest him."

Gigi was breathing hard, and her cheeks were crimson. "Why not? He's scaring away our business."

Officer Birkwell's radio squawked, and he reached up to his shoulder and turned it down. "Because he's not on your property. The owner of the marina said he could be there."

Tim took Gigi's hand in his. "Just breathe. I'm sure it's not his fault. Tuesdays are always slow in the off-season."

Gigi's nostrils flared. "Two women were almost too afraid to come in tonight because they thought the bum would break into their car. Just ask Mack there." She flung her arm in my direction.

Shane looked at me, and his eyebrows shot up to his sandy-blond hair. "Mack?"

"Yes, I um . . ." I cleared my throat. *Who told Gigi about that?*

Chelle stood at my side to support my testimony. She had no idea I was on really thin ice here. And the other officer was looking at me weird. He nudged Shane. "Isn't that . . ."

Shane cut him off. "That's fine, Miss Mack. What can you tell us?"

"Well, the ladies *were* afraid to leave their packages in the car."

Gigi harrumphed and pointed at me while looking at Officer Birkwell.

"But I don't think the homeless man had threatened them in any way. If they were really afraid, they could have gone somewhere else to eat, but they came inside."

Tim quickly escorted Gigi from the room. Chuck sent Chelle back out front, so I could talk to the police in private. Once they were gone, Officer Birkwell turned to me and asked, "Are you doing what I think you're doing?"

"Not . . . officially."

He sighed. "I should take you in for your own safety."

"From the homeless man?"

"No, from the pregnant woman. She looks like a tick about to pop, and she wants to twist your head off."

"Well, you're not wrong there."

"Okay." He looked at his partner. "Let's go. We'll give the man a warning to stay away from the cars and the building, but that's all we can do."

I looked across the grill at Chuck. "I think we can do a little bit more, can't we?"

Chuck's eyes darted to the office. He pushed up his glasses, and he pointed to the aluminum takeout container by the sink.

I picked up the container and a set of plastic cutlery and told Officer Birkwell, "I'll go with you."

I followed the officers out back to the man's lawn chair by the little fire. He had a new box today, and a little plastic Acme bag with a crumpled hoagie wrapper. I waited while the officers questioned him about his doings and tried to convince him to go to a shelter. The man wouldn't make eye contact or speak for himself, but he hunkered down inside his coat.

Shane spoke into his radio, saying that they were finishing up with no action against the complaint. As he was leaving, he turned to me. "Have you at least learned anything useful?"

"Lots of things. But I'm still sorting through them."

He nodded. "Be safe . . . Mack."

The homeless man turtled out of his parka and watched the cops walk away. He looked expectantly at the takeout container in my hands.

"I brought you something warm." I looked through the plastic lid. "I think it's scallops and grits with some spicy greens."

He grinned, then took the container and the fork and dug in.

The wind blew off the ocean and cut through me. I rubbed my arms to warm them. "Are you sure you're okay out here? It's going to get very cold. I think I have an old pop-up tent in my garage. Could you use that?"

He stopped eating and nodded.

I dug my cell phone out of my back pocket and called Smitty. "Hey. Tomorrow, I want you to get the orange tent out of the garage and bring it down to the marina behind Maxine's. Give it to the man you'll find on the shore."

"You got it, boss."

"Thanks." I put my cell phone away. "It's all set. A little bald man wearing an Eagles jacket will bring it in the morning, but you really should consider a shelter for the winter."

The homeless man grinned at me, showing teeth that were even and white.

I gestured to the restaurant. "Have you ever been inside?"

He shook his head no. He was back to avoiding my eyes. "Stay away."

"They told you to stay away?"

He didn't answer.

I can't really blame them for that. Gigi's crazy, but this is a no-win situation. "Did you know the fisherman? The one who died?"

He kept on eating. Slower and more thoughtful now. "He baited the snakes."

"He baited the snakes?"

"Dangled the baby snake."

"I'll keep that in mind. Try to stay warm tonight."

I started back towards the kitchen, but I heard him say, so softly, "The snakes are coming."

CHAPTER 24

I drifted off and woke up to the sound of a yipping dog. My eyes cracked open, and I peeked at my cell phone. *How is it six a.m. already? It was just midnight fifteen minutes ago.*

Figaro was stretched out to his full length, flanking me. I pushed myself up and turned over, trying not to disturb him. One orange eye cracked open to a slit, assessing how long until I'd be ready to go to the kitchen and open a can.

I looked at my left hand and smiled. I texted Gia.

Good morning, handsome. I love you.

I love you too, my bella. I am tired of waiting. I want to be together.

So do I.

Did you get your lazy butt out of bed yet? We have work to do!

I guess the honeymoon's over. Oh. Joanne's text notification had hijacked my screen. I texted back. **Leave me alone!**

What is wrong, bella?

Sorry. I thought you were Joanne.

Did you get the magazine pages I left you?

I blinked at the screen. *Oh, good Lord. Now I'm being bombarded by Aunt Ginny.* **Can we talk about this when I come down?**

I don't have all day, Buttface!

Joanne again. I dropped my phone on the other side of the bed. I wouldn't be able to do that much longer. I wouldn't be alone in here much longer. Would I still be here at all? *Where are we gonna live?*

I sat bolt upright, and Figaro rolled to his back. I could feel my heart rate picking up speed. I'd always been a big chicken with important life decisions. What if I made the wrong one—as per usual? What if it ended in disaster—as per usual? People could get hurt.

My cell phone was flashing like a disco from all the texts coming in. One was a Google alert for the phrase "Murder Magnet."

I clicked the link and found myself on a website called The Mommies Blog. The blogger was a self-proclaimed "Jersey Girl with the best kids in the world." Her latest entry was a rant about a single dad, "sexy barista," and his engagement to "the Cape May Murder Magnet."

My heart caught in my throat when I read, "That poor little boy. Can you imagine her being his mom? What if he's with her when she finds the next one? I'd never let my son go to her house for a playdate in a million years. He'll need therapy before he's an adult."

I burst into tears and threw the phone across the room. People could be so ugly on social media. Everyone thinks they have the right to express their opinion about everything. Even when they have no idea what they're talking about or who they're hurting.

I was angry, but so much more than that, my heart was broken. *How could I do this to Henry?* He would never have a normal life if I was his mom.

I crossed the room and grabbed my cell phone, making

sure I was on Gia's screen, and tried to type through the tears.

We need to talk.

Uh-oh.

We shouldn't get married.

Why not?

I don't want Henry to be in therapy.

What?

When I said yes, I was only thinking about myself and how happy I would be. But what about Henry? How will it affect him when people point at me and run the other way? What if the other kids tease him that the Cape May Murder Magnet is his stepmother? Not to mention where are we gonna live? What about Aunt Ginny? I can't just leave her.

I am coming over.

NO! I'm a wreck. I don't want you to see me like this.

Three dots appeared, then disappeared a couple times. Finally, Gia responded to my rant. **I love you. We will work everything out. I promise. Come and see me and we will talk.**

My neck relaxed a fraction, but my stomach was still in knots. I trusted Gia more than anyone. If he said we'd work it out, everything would be fine. I needed to think about something else for a while, so I grabbed the diary off my nightstand and started to read.

June 15
I spent the night in gaol. Oswald posted my bail this morning. Where are the ladies' charities to keep meddlesome women with idle hands from making false reports about honorable gentlemen peering into their windows? I told the constable that I

had not left my property, but the shrew made such a peevish ruckus that he had no choice but to put me in the cells overnight. The unpleasantness is making my gout act up.

June 18
Had a most pleasant time at Jackson's Clubhouse last night. Breckenridge has acquired a lovely rum. Even Oswald was in an agreeable mood, and he is usually sour about everything unless he is winning at the tables. On an unrelated issue, I must call the doctor later to acquire an analgesic. These constant headaches are quite bothersome.

June 19
The delusional woman is threatening to put a curse on me. What utter nonsense. She insists I trampled her strawberries and sabotaged her chicken coop. I deny both allegations most emphatically. Oswald is coming over shortly to watch her chase the brood around the field. We've made bets on how many chickens she will be able to catch by supper.

June 22
Apparently, I am forbidden to pass through her yard now. It is my best

shortcut to the Clubhouse. Going around the farm will add several minutes on my route. Maybe I should get a horse.

Good Lord. How much damage could he do with a horse? And where was Jackson's Clubhouse?

I put the diary back on the nightstand and got my laptop from my desk. I tried looking up the neighbors' houses on Zillow to see when they were each built. Many were newer than ours, but two houses nearby were old enough to be the enemy's.

I couldn't imagine Rooster sitting on my front porch bothering any neighbor farther away than those with his "caterwauling," as the diary called it, so it had to be one of these two. I wrote the addresses down so I could do a little digging later.

I had to put on a brave face to get through the morning. I took a shower and got dressed in black jeans and a turquoise blouse. Then I dried my hair and used a straightening iron and put on a dusting of makeup. Enough to cover the freckles and dark circles, and to make my eyelashes show up, but not so much that I looked like I was in a burlesque show.

I added a little more mascara. Slightly burlesque.

I grabbed my purse and took the front stairs past the guest bedrooms, with Figaro trotting beside me. I stopped in front of the Adonis Suite, where Iris was staying, planning to give a little listen. General Tso was lying flat on his back with all four paws straight up in the air outside the Purple Emperor Suite. The door was wide open, and the sisters were sitting on the bed, eating breakfast on trays.

"Good morning, ladies. What happened here?"

One sister gave me a wave. "We took him for a walk on

the beach this morning. That's as far as he made it when we got back."

Figaro swatted the puff of fur, then ran for his life down the stairs just in case it woke up.

"Fig says hello."

The ladies laughed. "Tell the chef, the eggs benedict is delicious."

A series of sneezes erupted from the Monarch Suite. Mental note to add a checkbox to acknowledge *Cat in residence* on our online reservations page.

I made it to the sitting room, where there had been another violent crime at the Dickens village. The constable was on-site at the butcher shop, where there had been a toothpick stabbing, complete with ketchup and crime-scene tape. I looked at the ceiling and considered the lovely sisters with the mini chow. They didn't seem like homicidal maniacs. The older couple was so sweet, and the poor allergy lady was so sick. Was Iris trying to not-so-subtly shame me? Did everyone feel like the Mommie Blogger?

The bells on the Christmas tree jingled. "That had better not be you, Fig." The bells silenced. Then a ceramic ball painted with cardinals and pinecones fell to the floor with a thud. I picked it up and hung it back on the branch. A bejeweled blue jay flew out of the tree, with a crazed Persian attached to his back, and flew into the dining room.

"Figaro! Stay out of this tree!"

I followed the trail of feathers to the dining room, where the sweet little older couple was enjoying breakfast next to the allergy woman's husband. Iris was at the table, reading a baby-name book. It was on the tip of my tongue to say, "Isn't it too late for that?" but the older couple were grinning with pleasure, and I didn't have the heart to ruin their moment.

"Good morning. Did you see a cat run through here?"

They both pointed at the kitchen door. "I think he caught a bird," the lady said.

I passed through the swinging door on the warpath. The warpath ended at the island, with Joanne holding the damp bird and Kenny holding a wiggly cat. Aunt Ginny looked up from the business laptop that was supposed to be on my desk. "How do you spell bitter?"

Kenny put Figaro down on the floor. "J. O. A. N. N. E."

I held in a laugh. "Aunt Ginny, what are you trying to do?"

"A recipe."

"Of something bitter?"

"Don't question my methods."

"Is this for the Senior Center Bake-Off?"

"That's on a need-to-know basis."

"Don't I need to know?"

"Not if you plan on blabbing to that nosy Edith."

"When am I going to see Mrs. Dodson?"

"She has ears everywhere."

"Okay. Well, thank you for the dress pages. I'm running to La Dolce Vita. I'll be back later. Text me if you need anything."

Joanne protested. "I've been waiting all morning for you to come down here and talk about cake."

"Why?"

Joanne huffed. "Because I'm making your wedding cake, and I need to know what you like."

"Well, I'm not getting married today. Can't we talk about it later?"

She groaned like I'd pronounced I was going vegan. "Fine. I also wanted to tell you that Iris was trying to pick the lock on your bedroom door yesterday."

My head snapped up so fast I heard my neck crack. "Next time lead with that. What was she looking for?"

Joanne dropped the ruined bird ornament in the trash. "I don't know. She spotted me before she got the door open and acted like she was lost."

Aunt Ginny snorted. "She lived here when she was first married to Poppy's father. I doubt she was lost."

"Keep watching her, Joanne. If you catch her trying to get into my room again, text me right away. Wes Bailey won't be the only murder I'm involved in this week."

I left through the back door and walked down the driveway. My phone buzzed. It was Aunt Ginny.

Remember. Snitches get stitches.

My lips are sealed.

There were antlers coming out of the front windows on either side of the Corvette, and a giant red ball stuck out of the grill. *That's new.* I turned around to look at my house and saw an enormous wreath on our front door and one on every window. Red bunting had been draped across the porch with pine greens. *What in the world?*

I backed out of the driveway. Nell had added two light-up snowmen to her yard. She gave me a tight smile and a wave.

I waved back, but a bad feeling was inching its way up my spine.

CHAPTER 25

I passed the potential home of the infamous enemy. I'd seen it many times. A pink-and-green monstrosity with a wooden plaque in the yard that read THE HORSE-SHOE CRAB. *What a terrible name.* Why anyone would want to associate their home with something so rank and ugly was a mystery to me.

The house was completely bare of holiday decorations. Considering the abundance of weeds, I figured the owners had the house on the rental market. There was a little driftwood coffee table on the porch in front of a chipped gray love seat. On top of the table sat a hurricane vase full of wine corks and bottlecaps. There was a fine line between statement piece and garbage can.

"What are you looking at!"

I startled. I was so busy taking in the state of the yard that I'd missed a man lounging on a plastic chair. He was shaped like a barrel and had a metal coffee can on the ground in front of him and he spit something into the can.

"I'm your neighbor from a couple doors down. I was just wondering if anyone lived here."

He spit into the can again. "What's it to ya?"

I made my voice light and easy. "Just wondering in case we want to go caroling later tonight."

"Don't you come messing around my house with that noise. I'll get my air rifle if I hear one note of 'Jingle Bells.'"

Well, I found the Grinch. I'll be sure to lock up my Who Hash. I tipped my hand and let my foot off the brake. I sure hope he's not the owner. I'd hate to have to come back and ask for his help.

I did a U-turn at the next intersection and went back down my street. I passed Nell again. She was watching my house. Iris was in the front-room window watching Aunt Ginny in the yard. Aunt Ginny, who I noticed had waited until she thought I was gone, was dragging a black canvas duffel bag towards Mrs. Pritchard's house. It was just the kind of bag where you'd expect to find a dead body in a Hitchcock movie.

That's not gonna help our reputation.

She spied the Corvette and ducked behind the tree. I didn't stop. Not because I wasn't curious, but because I was already over my limit on weirdos, and it was only eleven a.m.

I drove down to potential enemy number two. It was a gorgeous blue-and-gray Victorian with white icicle lights hanging from the roof and the porch; it had been turned into a bed and breakfast called the Crow's Nest. I'd met the owner at community meetings. She was nice. A bit odd, but I was technically the competition. Still, she had to be better than the Horseshoe Crab guy. *Which, now that I think about it, is a perfect name for that house.*

I'd have to come back later and see if she'd be willing to talk to me. I turned at the corner and drove down to the Washington Street Mall. All the Victorian Christmas events began this weekend, and things would start getting busy tomorrow.

As soon as I saw Gia, I burst into tears again.

He stroked my hair. "Now, calm down. Everything will be fine. I refuse to let you call the wedding off. There is nothing we can't work out."

I sniffled and nodded against his neck.

I followed him to the front, where Sierra, his part-time barista, was working the bar. "Hey, Poppy. Let me see that rock on your hand."

I held it out, and she whistled. "It's about time. You two have been drooling over each other for a year."

Gia came up behind me and wrapped his arms around my waist. "I had to be sure she loved me back."

I snuggled into him, and Sierra made a face. "Okay, eww. People in love are the worst."

I giggled.

Gia went behind the bar and started making some Christmas concoction. He glanced at me and grinned.

"Hey, do you know of a website where I can find out about the history of a house? I've narrowed down who my ancestor was feuding with to two different addresses on our street, but I can't find any information on the people who lived in either one."

Sierra took out a bottle of Godiva chocolate syrup from the cabinet under the bar and swapped it with an empty bottle on the counter. "Have you tried the Historical Society? They might have records about the previous owners that you won't find online."

"I feel kind of silly that I didn't think of that myself."

Sierra grinned. "Your head is stuffed full of mushy thoughts right now. It's to be expected. You know, they're just down the street. My little sister had a local history project last year, and she interviewed one of the docents for extra credit."

"I'll stop in before I go to my hostile, unpaid side job."

Gia came around the bar and handed me a latte. "Now, come tell me what is bothering you." He took my hand and led me to the couch in his office.

I sipped the latte and recognized the flavors from yesterday. Cherry, rum, orange, and something else. Ginger? "This is the new latte?"

"Fruitcake. Do you like it?"

"I love it. Sawyer thought it was gross. What do other people think?"

"Same. They either love it or hate it. Like fruitcake."

"Well, I love it."

He took my hands. "*Cara mia*, I love you. There is nothing we cannot get through together. We will live wherever you want. You can move in with me, or Henry and I can move in with you. And Henry is so excited to have you for his mommy he can barely sleep at night. If he is teased, we will teach him how to rise above it. Besides, his nonna is on house arrest with a half-mile radius. I think that is a bigger deal than his mother helping the police with a few murder investigations."

I felt like a brick house had been lifted off my shoulders. "You're right. I let a blogger get in my head. And I'm overwhelmed with my mother showing up—wondering what her agenda is. And trying to help Tim clear his and Gigi's names in Wes's Bailey's murder. I'm getting smothered with everyone's wedding ideas. They mean well, but they are so excited for me that I can barely think about what I want. Are you worried about anything?"

Gia breathed out a laugh. "Only that you would be happy."

I snuggled into him. "I am happy. Do you know when you want to get married?"

He ran his fingers down my arm and took my hand. "How about yesterday?"

I giggled. "What do you think about the spring? Maybe April?"

He groaned. "What about next weekend?"

"I'll have to see if Tim will give me the night off."

Gia laughed. "April is so far away, but if you are happy, I am happy."

"Okay. Hey, this is our first Christmas as a couple. What do you want?"

He kissed my neck. "I already have you."

My cell phone rang the Chipmunks Christmas song. It was Brenda from the Teen Center. "Hey, lady. Just checking in to make sure you're still coming tomorrow to teach the cooking class."

I looked at Gia, and my eyes grew to the size of Ferrero Rocher balls. "Of course I am. I'm looking forward to it." That was a total lie. I had forgotten all about it. "How many kids do you expect?"

"Eighteen have signed up. Six will most likely chicken out because it isn't cool. At least one will wander in unannounced and say they hadn't heard about it, but want to participate."

"I'll come prepared to make cookies for twenty, and you can keep the leftovers for the Christmas party."

"Yeah, we don't have a Christmas party. This is a government-run program. We have a Winter Hannu-KwanzaaMas Festival."

"I need to diversify my cookie cutters. I'll see you tomorrow afternoon." I hung up and answered Gia's eyebrow raise.

"I forgot I promised to teach a baking class at the Teen Center."

"Being the town Murder Magnet keeps you busy."

"You think you're funny, don't you?"

He snickered. "*Si*, I do."

He leaned in to kiss me, and the front bell went off. Sierra called back to us. "The lady cop is here to see Poppy."

I frowned at Gia. "She probably wants an unofficial update."

We both stood to go out to the dining room. Amber

was sitting at the bar, staring ahead. Kieran sat next to her, doing his best impression of a well-dressed angry elf, wearing a three-piece suit, with a badge hanging around his neck and a leather shoulder holster peeking out of his tailored jacket.

I looked from him to Amber, and she made a face that I interpreted as *shush.* "Hey. What's up?"

Amber smiled. "Just here for coffee."

I stopped behind the counter and gave her a long look. "*You* want coffee?"

Her eyes grew bigger. "Of course I do."

I turned to Gia. "Make her a triple chocolate mocha with extra whipped cream and only one shot of espresso." And to Kieran. "What can we get you?"

Kieran appraised the menu. "I'll have what Officer Amber is having." He pulled out a leather wallet and put a twenty on the counter.

I took two sugar cookies from the case and put them on napkins, then slid them to the officers, who looked like a swat team from the Lollipop Guild. "On the house."

Amber shoved her cookie in her mouth while keeping her eyes straight ahead. I made myself busy cleaning the counter and restocking the cups, while Sierra wiped tables and Gia made the mochas. No one spoke. Overhead, the Rat Pack Christmas CD started another loop.

Amber studied the blackboard, while Kieran stole glances at her. He cleared his throat and she said, "Hmm?"

He replied, "I didn't say anything."

To which she said, "Oh. I thought you did."

Gia passed them their drinks, and I tried to cut the tension. "So, what's new?"

Amber shook her head. "Nothing."

Kieran shrugged. "Just another day in law enforcement."

Amber slid off the stool. "Where's the ladies' room?"

I nodded towards the back.

"Thanks." She headed in that direction, and Kieran focused all his attention on his coffee.

Gia, the smartest, most wonderful man in the world, opened the door to the pastry case and looked inside. "Poppy. Please see if we have more blueberry muffins in the back."

"Can do." We didn't have any blueberry muffins, and he knew that.

I slipped into the kitchen and overheard Gia ask Kieran what his plans for the holidays were. The ladies' room door cracked open, and Amber hissed, "Psst."

I kept one eye on the dining room and slipped inside to join her. "What is going on?"

Amber smoothed her hands down her slacks. "First of all, the coroner's report is back. Wes Bailey was in a fight just hours before he died. The bruising on his face was not from the murder."

"So he took a punch?"

"Most likely."

"Okay, well, no way Gigi did that. She couldn't even reach his face unless he was sitting down."

"But Tim could."

"Oh. Yeah, I guess that's true."

"Also, we pulled a print off the light switch to the freezer."

"It's Teela's."

Amber frowned. "How'd you know that?"

"I overheard her telling Tim that she was there to get her phone shortly before Jackson Seymour arrived and she turned off the freezer light from outside."

"Interesting. That was not in her statement."

"Did you find any prints on the back door?"

"None."

"Wes's keys?"

"Only his own."

"Someone went to a lot of trouble to clean up that crime scene."

Amber nodded.

"If Jackson isn't the killer and he just showed up at six to deliver produce, why aren't his prints on anything?"

"He was wearing work gloves."

"So how do we know he wasn't wearing those gloves when he killed Wes?"

"Then why would he wipe down a bunch of other people's fingerprints? Besides, we collected his gloves at the crime scene. No blood evidence anywhere on them."

"So you're not considering him a suspect?"

"I didn't say that. Because Wes was in the freezer for hours, we don't know the exact time of death. Jackson could have killed him, cleaned the crime scene, then returned later to 'discover' the body. You got anything yet?"

I filled her in with bullet points on what I had learned. Wes hanging out at the bar with the staff at Maxine's; Nikki moving to the area recently; Teela leading Wes on, then turning cold overnight; and Gigi threatening to bury Wes because of a contract dispute that Tim refused to talk about. "And, of course, Jackson Seymour's public battle to take Deepwater Fisheries down."

"Wow. You got all that already?"

"That, and the homeless man knows something, but he doesn't trust me enough to tell me yet."

Amber pressed her lips together and nodded. "Alright. Keep me posted."

"You got anything else for me?"

"There is one thing."

"Yeah?"

"Kieran kissed me."

CHAPTER 26

I peppered Amber for details, but she was still a little dazed and gave me a muttering jumble of answers. Apparently, Kieran had kissed her in the middle of a rant on proper police procedure while they were in the bushes staking out a package thief. I'd often wanted Amber to stop harassing me, but that method of silencing her had never crossed my mind.

I know she wanted to say more, but they got a call for a domestic dispute and had to leave in a hurry.

Gia and I snickered about it in the kitchen, while I drizzled pink icing on a batch of candy-cane brownies.

"I've never seen her so pale and nervous, and I've seen her right before taking a chemistry final that she was definitely gonna fail."

Gia handed me the brownie cutter, and I plunged it into the sheet pan of swirled, pepperminty chocolate and cut it into perfect rectangles. "Do you think she likes him back?"

"I don't think she knows. She didn't seem repulsed, but I don't think she ever thought about him like that either."

"I guess technically, he is her boss."

I chuckled. "Technically, you're my boss."

Gia snorted. "That is not true."

"Sure, it is. I work for you."

Gia took my hand and looked into my eyes. "No, *bella*, you work *with* me."

The afternoon was over way too quickly, and I wanted to make a stop at the Historical Society Museum before going into Maxine's for the night. I grabbed an eggnog latte for the road, kissed my fiancé goodbye, and went to my car. There was a used bingo card slipped under my windshield wiper, with a note scrawled across it in green marker.

I'll give you ten dollars to tell me what Ginny is making for the bake-off. Edith.

"Ten whole dollars." I dropped the card in my purse, Aunt Ginny's threat of stitches still ringing in my ears.

I drove over to a tiny white clapboard house on Washington Street. Formerly a tavern and home of Revolutionary War patriot Memucan Hughes, it was the oldest house on the island, dating back to the late seventeen hundreds.

I gave a tentative knock on the museum door, and a kindly gentleman welcomed me in. His hair was fluffy and white, the front strip pasted to his forehead, the back pointing in every direction at once, like it had gotten away from him. A bit stooped in the shoulders and wearing an oversized Christmas sweater that was buttoned askew, he perked up when I pulled out the bag of peppermint brownies and chocolate-dipped shortbread cookies I'd brought with me as a bribe—I mean gift.

"Well now, thank you, missy. Thank you very much." He patted his stomach. "Yes, I'll put these to good use." He held out a gnarled hand. "Albert. Nice to meet you, Miss . . . ?"

"Poppy." I grasped his hand in mine.

He shuffled back behind a modern desk and stashed the treats in a bottom drawer. "Gotta hide them from Lionel. He steals."

"I'm sorry to hear that."

He waved me off. "That's alright. I steal his stuff too. Unless it's cabbage day." He wrinkled his nose. "Ugh. Life's too short. Now what can I do for you?"

I looked around the museum of colonial life on the island. There was a spinning wheel and a butter churn in the dining room. A uniform from a Revolutionary War soldier in the living room. A bed warmer hung on the wall like a prized piece of art. Over the fireplace was a cross-stitch sampler, and I swore I'd seen an identical one in our mudroom. There was also a portrait of George Washington because I'm sure he slept here. I didn't ask.

"I have some questions about an ancestor of mine and some problematic neighbors."

"Problematic neighbors?" He reached over to a large book on the desk and began to flip through it. "What's your ancestor's name?"

"Callum McAllister, but his friends called him Rooster."

Albert stopped flipping and paused with his hand on the page. "Callum McAllister, you said?"

"Yes, that's right."

"Haven't heard that name in a while." His hand shook as he started turning pages again. "I got some stuff on a Virginia McAllister from the nineteen fifties."

You better believe I want that. "I'll come back for that, but first I need some details on my great-great-great-great-grandfather to figure out . . . some stuff."

"Some stuff? That's the most pathetic excuse I've ever heard. You wanna narrow that down for me a bit?"

How do I say I need to see if he brought a generational

curse on me? Correction, how do I say that and not sound like a whackadoo?

I decided to go with the bed-and-breakfast cover story. "Callum McAllister was the original owner of our home, which is now the Butterfly Wings Bed and Breakfast. I'd like to be able to tell guests about the history of the house."

He glanced at me, then back at the book. "Right. For the bed and breakfast. No other reason?"

"Nope."

He sighed. "Okay then . . . I'll do some digging and see what I can find."

"Let me give you my address."

"No need. I know who you are."

Oh. Right. Murder Magnet. "Our house was built in 1879. All that I know from his diary so far is that he loved drinking and gambling, and he had a big mouth. But he also seemed to have a lot of friends on the island."

Albert chuckled. "And what was that you said about the neighbors?"

"It seems he had offended the next-door neighbor and her cow."

Albert nodded thoughtfully. "Do you know who the neighbor was?"

"Bettina something. According to the diary, she was right next-door to us, but newer houses have been added since then."

I was looking around at the period furniture and antiques and happened to spot a familiar face pass by the window outside. "Plus, I don't know in which direction the lady's home would have been. But I do think I've narrowed it down to one of two addresses."

I peered through the glass. *That's Teela. Why isn't she at work?*

Albert closed the book. "Okay, which two?"

"A private residence that goes by the Horseshoe Crab and the Crow's Nest Bed and Breakfast. I really hope it's not the Horseshoe Crab."

Albert chuckled. "Willie's harmless. His bark is worse than his bite."

"I can write down the house numbers for you."

"Mm-hmm. I'll check the land records and get back to you. You got a cell phone?"

"I really appreciate any help you can give me." I wrote my cell number on the back of my business card, along with the addresses, and thanked him. Then I darted out the door to see where Teela had gone.

I looked down the block towards the shops. Teela had disappeared.

CHAPTER 27

I scanned the direction Teela had headed. There was a cluster of shops on a brick courtyard, including a fancy kitchen store with gourmet foods, a women's boutique called Rosie's Posies, a funky T-shirt shop, a children's store, and an art gallery. They were all bedecked with lights and wreaths on their doors.

Going straight for the women's boutique, I looked in the window. My stomach dropped when I saw the racks of frilly lingerie. I hoped this wasn't for Tim's benefit.

I went inside and looked around. Unless she was in the fitting room, Teela wasn't in here. I started to leave when a little voice went off in my head. *You know . . . you are getting married.* The voice sounded a lot like Sawyer nagging me.

I hadn't bought lingerie in years. Hanes everyday, six-pairs-for-ten-dollars probably did not count. I held up a gauzy film of sheer pink that would hide as much as a sheet of Saran Wrap.

A crackly voice startled me from behind. "The feather trim on the bottom hem is to keep your neck warm." I turned to see who was speaking, and it was a little old lady of about Aunt Ginny's age. She gave me a knowing grin.

I felt my cheeks heat up and replaced the nightie on the rack. "I was just looking."

"'Tis the season to get frisky."

I think I just died a little. "Actually, I was looking for someone. Did you see an attractive strawberry blonde come in here about five minutes ago?"

"She's gone already. Picked up her special order. Are you sure you aren't looking for anything for yourself? A little Christmas gift for your fella maybe?"

I looked back at the rack of lacy gowns. "Well, I do need a few things for my honeymoon."

She grabbed my hand and gawked at the diamond. "Would you look at that. You're engaged."

A giggle escaped my throat against my will. "Yeah. I am."

"When's the big day?"

"We're thinking next spring."

She tsk'd. "Well, honey, there's no time to lose. You need everything."

She dragged me through the store, pulling out a whole lingerie catalog worth of supplies. Lace baby-doll nighties the size of lampshades, mesh teddies, and bikinis covered in sequins. When she pulled out a red leather cat suit, I nearly lost my nerve and told her I'd changed my mind; I was converting to Amish for the ceremony.

She shoved it back on the rack. "Okay, calm down. We'll save leather for your first anniversary. How about this?"

She held up something made of ribbons that looked like a spiderweb. "Now I know it's a little risqué, but trust me, the men love it. What do you think?" She held it against me.

"I don't even know what it is."

The doorbell chimed, and we both turned to look. Teresa stood in the entryway, clutching a red bag with ROSIE'S POSIES written across it in black. She gave a long look down the spiderweb.

"That is not for your wedding night, I hope."

I pushed the spiderweb away from me. "What? No. Of course not." I looked around frantically and grabbed a high-necked flannel gown off the clearance rack.

"I was just getting this." I took twenty dollars from my purse and stuffed it in the shopkeeper's hand. "Thank you for your help."

I started to go, paused, leaned in closer to the shopkeeper, and whispered. "Hold everything. I'll be back."

I walked back to where I'd parked in front of the Historical Society. The sun had gone down, and the temperature had dropped to the upper forties, but I was a little overheated after my lingerie fail. I tossed my coat on the passenger seat to drive over to Maxine's.

Gia texted me just as I pulled into the clamshell parking lot. He'd set up an interview with Jackson Seymour at Momma's restaurant for tomorrow. We were all set to interrogate the veg man.

Two police cruisers pulled into the lot after me and rolled up alongside my car. I didn't know either officer, which could be good or bad, depending on why they were there. We got out of our cars, and all three of us stepped towards the kitchen door at the back of the restaurant.

Gigi thundered out of the building with her curls shooting out of a flowered bandana in reckless abandon. "It's about time. I have a business to run."

I looked from the cops to her belly. "What's going on? Are you in labor?"

Gigi flailed her arm in the direction of the homeless

man down by the dock. He was hunkered down in his chair facing Maxine's. "Two different groups of customers left as soon as they saw him. He's trespassing, and he might have killed my seafood vendor. I'm going to call every day until you do something."

I gave the homeless man a little wave. He held up two fingers and wiggled them back.

The first officer leaned against his police car. "Ma'am. We've already told you, until you have proof that the man has done something illegal, we can't arrest him. He's not on your property."

I left Gigi to her rant and went inside. Teela had already arrived, and apparently, Tim was showing her how to flip a pan of shrimp by letting her lean against him.

She held the handle of the sauté pan, while Tim covered her hand and snapped it back. "Oh, Chef Tim, you're so good at that."

I don't know why that irritated me so much. He wasn't my man. Maybe it was phantom emotions from back when we were in a relationship. I knew I should keep my mouth shut since I needed Teela to like me, but Aunt-Ginny-attitude slipped out. "He should be good at it. He's been practicing since you were a baby."

Tim cleared his throat and put the pan on the burner. "Your table is waiting for their lamb chops."

"Didn't I just see you down by the mall?"

Teela shook her head. "Wasn't me."

"Do you have a twin? 'Cause she had your hair and your gold parka."

"Oh yeah. That was me. I was late because I was picking up medicine for my mother."

Not from down there you weren't.

Teela shifted a look to Tim, took two plates from under the warming lights, and left the kitchen after throwing me some stink eye.

I gave Tim a look that said, *What are you doing with her?* He returned my look with one that said, *I don't know what you're talking about.*

I stashed my purse and checked supplies in the storage room. I ran into Nikki skulking out of the office on my way back to the kitchen.

She snapped an old flip phone closed and shoved it into her back pocket. "Just checking on Grandma."

The back door slammed shut, and Nikki picked up the pace down the hall. "Forget you saw me." She slipped through the door into the dining room.

Gigi didn't say a word to anyone. Red faced, she puffed her way past me and shut herself in the office.

That baby is gonna come out hard-boiled.

Tim groaned. He turned the grill over to Chuck and slowly made his way down the hall to the office and disappeared inside to take his punishment.

"Psst."

I looked behind me.

"Psst."

Chuck was motioning to me from behind the grill. His eyes met mine, and he jerked his head for me to join him at his station.

I inched over. "What is it?"

He pushed his glasses up the bridge of his nose with his knuckle. "I should have told you the day the cops were here, but I didn't think it was important until last night when Tyler reminded me."

"Where is Tyler?"

"He's always off on Wednesday. Anyway, last week, when I was doing inventory, I overheard an argument between Tim and Wes. Wes threatened to report Tim for something."

"Something like what?"

Chuck shrugged. "I don't know. He just said . . ."

The dining room door opened, and Andrew came

through. We stood in silence while Andrew looked at us each in turn, picked up two plates of salad from the walk-in, and left without a backwards glance.

". . . that Tim was going to be in trouble, and that he didn't have an excuse because he knew what he was doing."

"Who knew what who was doing?"

"Tim knew what Tim was doing."

I nodded. "Okay."

Chuck turned some scallops in the sauté pan. "Wes said he would only back Tim up if he joined."

"Joined what?"

Chuck shrugged. "I dunno. But Tim said he wouldn't do whatever it was because it was illegal."

"What did Wes say?"

Chuck's mouth slid to a frown. "He said, 'Since when do you care about what's legal?'"

Chelle pushed through the dining-room door. "A party of ten just arrived, and I got a call for a reservation for six in an hour. Victorian Christmas week is starting early, people."

Chuck groaned.

Chelle disappeared into the walk-in and re-emerged with an armful of lemons and oranges. "Gabriel needs some whole cloves. Where can I get those?"

I stepped towards the hostess. "I can bring them out for you." I needed an excuse to get in the dining room tonight anyway.

"Thank you, darlin'." Chelle grinned and backed out through the swinging doors.

I grabbed the whole cloves and nodded at Chuck. "Keep what you told me to yourself for now, okay?"

Chuck saluted.

I walked the cloves out front. Gabe was slicing oranges on a little cutting board. He had a crock-pot set up behind the counter, with four empty bottles of red wine next to it. "Something smells good."

He put his hand out. "Just in time. I'm making mulled wine."

I handed him the cloves, and he proceeded to pierce them into the rinds of the fruit slices, like the pomanders we made at Cold Spring Village when I was a child. "Do you want some help?"

He nudged a couple of orange slices my way. "Sure."

"I hear a bunch of the staff hang out after work and you try your new cocktails on them."

Gabe nodded. "Mm-hmm. You should hang tonight. It'll be fun."

"Do you have something special planned?"

He grinned. "I've got an idea for a warm old-fashioned with maple bourbon and brown sugar."

"That does sound good. How long have you worked for Maxine's?"

Gabriel gently dropped the studded orange slices into the red wine. "I came in the spring with Gigi. I joined her a year earlier over at Le Bon Gigi."

"Is she a good boss?"

He measured brandy into the pot. "Yeah. They both are."

I waited, but he didn't say anything more. I was about to excuse myself and head back to the kitchen when Andrew appeared by my side. "When will that hot wine be ready? I have four orders for it now. Hey, Mack."

Gabe dropped in a couple of cinnamon sticks. "I need at least ten minutes for the flavors to infuse."

Andrew surveyed the dining room. "How's it goin' in the kitchen? It seemed pretty tense in there earlier."

I watched Chelle lead a group of four over to the fire-place room. "Pretty good. They're getting ready for a busy night."

"You staying after?"

"I'm gonna try. As long as I don't get any calls from home that someone is burning the place down. I'm surprised you all still want to hang out here after what happened."

Andrew picked up a swizzle stick and started absently playing with it on the bar. "Wes? He had it coming."

Gabriel placed four cocktail napkins on Andrew's tray. "Drew. Mind your business."

Andrew snapped the swizzle stick in half. "What? Everyone knows it. Wes came in to brag about what a great fisherman he was and bore everyone with those videos from his YouTube channel."

"What kind of videos?"

"Lame videos of big fishing scores. He said he was doing research to be on *Deadliest Catch* or something. Like Teela would be interested in that and let him grope her."

Gabe ladled the warm wine into glass mugs and placed them on the tray. "Okay, two minutes will have to be good enough. Time for you to go."

Andrew picked up the tray. "Dude, relax. We all cheered when you threw him out, okay? No one thinks you killed him."

Andrew headed to his table to deliver the drinks. Gabe wouldn't look at me. He busied himself polishing the spotless bar.

"He was that obnoxious that you had to throw him out?"

Gabe sighed. "Look. I don't like it when guys hurt women. And Wes was making Teela extremely uncomfortable. He kept touching her after she told him to stop. We all told him to knock it off, but he wouldn't take a hint. He had got it in his head that Teela wanted him to be aggressive."

"What makes you think that?"

"He said he knew that she wanted a real man who grabs what he wants."

"Eww."

Gabe spread his arms out and made a face like *I know.*

"So you kicked him out."

Gabe nodded. "You bet I did. Right after Andrew punched him in the face."

CHAPTER 28

Maxine's was packed with customers, and the guys were in the weeds most of the night. While Gigi threw a rainbow kaleidoscope of tantrums, I baked some bread and made a batch to rise in the fridge overnight. I ended up pitching in on the line with the boys. Mostly by grilling steaks. It wasn't my first time on the line. Chuck and Tim told me what to do, and I could follow instructions with the best of them.

When Chelle came back to announce the last guests were leaving and the front-end staff were congregating at the bar, I was more than ready to join them.

I went back to the office to tell Tim what I'd be doing and caught him handing Nikki a wad of cash. She quickly stuffed it in the front pocket of her slacks and pushed past me.

Tim looked away from me and busied himself with a stack of unopened mail. "You need something?"

"Where's Gigi?"

"She went home."

I nodded. "What's with all the money you just gave Nikki?"

"Those were her tips."

"I thought Chelle was in charge of handing out the tips."

"If I hear one more complaint about Chelle handling those tips . . ."

"Who's complaining? Teela?"

Tim dropped the mail and grabbed his jacket from the back of the chair. "Whoa. You're not my wife. What's with the forty questions?"

After assessing my expression, he took a step back and regrouped. "I'm sorry. It's been a long night."

I didn't believe for one minute that Tim was giving Nikki her tips, but I had a whale to catch. "Someone heard you tell Wes that you wouldn't do something because it was illegal. What did he want you to do?"

Tim's face remained blank, but his knuckles were white around his jacket. "They must have heard wrong. Have you learned anything out front? Anyone have a motive to kill Wes? That is why you're here. To question the staff."

"I'm here to keep your baby mama out of jail, and you aren't helping yourself or her by avoiding my questions."

"If you don't want to help, then just go."

Tim and I held each other's gaze for a beat.

His eyes softened. "I'm sorry, Mack. I'm under a lot of pressure, and I'm not handling it all well. I gotta get home and check on Geeg." He pushed past me out the door.

Of all the ungrateful . . .

I weighed staying here, where I was underappreciated, with going home, where I'd have to share the same air with Iris McAllister.

Chelle poked her head around the corner. "Come on, girl. We're waiting for you."

I fought the urge to flip a table and go home. I liked everyone who worked for Tim.

Other than Gigi.

And I wasn't too sure about Gabe yet.

And Teela was a piece of work.

Nikki was a little standoffish.

But I really did like Chelle and the guys in the kitchen. They would all be out of work if Tim and Gigi went to jail for murder. "I'll be right there."

Teela and Andrew were perched on barstools side by side, and Gabe was pouring one of them a honey-brown cocktail in a fancy glass. "Mack, you want to try my maple old-fashioned?"

I took a seat next to Andrew. "I still have to drive home, so I'd really like to try some of that spiced cider on the nonalcoholic menu."

"One kiddie cocktail coming right up." Gabe grinned, and my knees went weak on Chelle's behalf. *Wow.*

Chelle gave me a look behind Gabe's back and fanned herself as she took the seat on the other side of the bar.

Nikki walked through the dining room, pulling on a white ski jacket. She was wearing red knit gloves and a scarf, and she'd changed out of her work shoes and pulled on snow boots like she was wading home through a blizzard.

Chelle called to her over her shoulder. "Mack's staying after. You wanna join us, like old times?"

Nikki pulled a red beanie over her ears, causing her brunette hair to fan out under the hat. "Sorry. Grandma needs her shot. Another time maybe." She disappeared through the door into the night.

Chelle turned her head back around to watch Gabe. She muttered under her breath. "All we can do is ask."

I was still fuming from my run-in with Tim, but I gave Chelle a grin. "Was it a good tip night?"

Chelle shrugged. "Cash tips were low. People get Scroogey around the holidays."

"You'll deliver them yourself?"

Chelle sipped her old fashioned. "Yep. It's my job.

Tomorrow's gonna be high-season busy. Half the house is already booked with reservations." Chelle leaned past me and called down the bar. "Hey, Andrew. I'll be late tomorrow. I got my hair appointment. Can you cover for me until I get here? First reservation isn't until five thirty."

Andrew held up a Coke. "I got you."

Gabe flashed me another grin. "So, what do you think of the spiced cider?"

"Is that a hint of star anise I'm picking up?"

He tapped my arm playfully. "I knew a pastry chef would pick out the spices. I usually only get grunts and shrugs from these two, and this one only drinks soda."

I'm glad he's done with freezing me out.

Andrew slid his empty glass forward. "You can put a cherry in it, if that will make you happy."

Gabe picked up a maraschino cherry with silver tongs and dropped it into Andrew's glass. "It does, yeah."

I kept my voice casual as I asked, "Did you guys hang out like this when you worked at Le Bon Gigi?"

They all grew quiet.

Teela poked at her ice with a straw. "At first, we did. Gigi had great staff dinners where we sat around a big table in the kitchen and ate, while she told us about every special she had planned."

Chelle swirled the drink in her mug. "Once we came here, that kinda stopped."

"How come?"

Andrew pulled the cherry out of his glass and popped it in his mouth. "Gigi sucks the fun out of the room."

Teela nodded. "Gigi's not been herself since she got pregnant. It's turned her into a psycho."

Gabe's lips flattened, and he walked to the back of the bar to slice lemons.

Teela sipped her cocktail and went on. "She used to be cool, like a big sister. Now she's just one more person who has it in for me."

Chelle tsk'd. "She does not. She just don't like you flirting with her man."

Teela rolled her eyes. "I'm so not flirting with Chef Tim."

Andrew snorted. "You so are."

"I'm not! But Tim had my back when Wes started harassing me. He said he'd tell him to back off, while Gigi insisted he was harmless. Well, he clearly wasn't, because someone here killed him."

Gabe spoke without turning around. "You better watch yourself with that kinda talk."

"I don't care who knows. I'm glad Wes is gone. He was giving off a real stalkery vibe."

Chelle nodded in agreement.

"All that talk about me wanting him to be more demonstrative. Where did he get that from? I told Tim I wouldn't keep working here if he didn't get rid of Wes."

Andrew chewed on an orange slice. "And the next day the dude was dead."

An icy hush fell over the bar, and I tried to thaw it. "Why didn't you go to Gigi and say you'd quit if Wes didn't stop harassing you?"

Teela laughed. "I did. I complained about Wes all the time. Nothing ever came from it. I think Gigi was hoping I'd quit. She's been trying to get rid of me since she got pregnant. She says I'm unreliable, but I think it's because Tim doesn't look at her the same way anymore and she blames me."

Gabe turned with anger flashing in his eyes. "Okay. I think you've had enough. Gigi is our boss, and she's in a delicate state."

Gabe has obviously never seen Gigi whack the head off a lobster.

"She deserves some respect and a little latitude. She works sixty hours a week when she should be home resting. And she deserves to be treated a lot better by her abusive husband than to have him flirting with an immature child who can't get her act together."

Teela's eyes shone with unshed tears. "Tim's not her husband."

I told myself to mind my own business, but I was horribly out of practice. "I really don't think Tim is abusive." *Now, Gigi maybe.*

Gabe dropped the lemon he was slicing. "Sorry. It's been a long night, and I have to get up early. Let's just call it until tomorrow."

We slid off the barstools and said our goodbyes. Chelle walked Teela out front to wait for her ride, while I headed towards the kitchen to leave by the back door.

Andrew followed behind me. "Gabe must be having a really bad night. I've never heard him say anything harsh to anyone, and Wes would get under his skin every night."

"How would he do that?"

"By calling him Big Daddy. Gabe did not like that at all. But he does seem more on edge since the guy died."

"I'm sure the murder investigation has been tough on all of you."

Andrew grabbed his coat from the rack. "Honestly, not as tough as Wes hanging around was."

"I heard you decked him good."

Andrew tsk'd. "Don't ever expect anything to be kept a secret here."

He went silent, and the walk to the back door became tense and awkward. "Who locks up?"

"Since Tim left early and it's Tyler's night off, Gabe does. Tim trusts him because he was a Marine."

We stepped out into the night, and I shut the door behind us, wondering how Gabe could lock up without a set of keys.

CHAPTER 29

I returned home to discover that several life-sized light-up carolers had congregated by the front porch. Four extension cords lay in a heap on the side of the steps, creating a nice, festive fire hazard. Gigantic LED snowflakes dripped from the big oak.

I stepped onto the brick pathway, and three animatronic squirrels in Santa hats started to sing "We Wish You a Merry Christmas."

My yard was starting to look like Clark Griswold had run wild. *What happened to understated elegance?*

I stopped in the front parlor to check on my Dickens Christmas village. Apparently, the London strangler was loose, and one of the Victorian carolers lay dead in the snow with her hands clutching at a knit scarf that had been transformed into a noose. I yawned. *That will have to be a problem for tomorrow.*

Joanne had left out a plate of cookies for the guests in the shape of murder weapons. We were going to have to have a talk about this theme. The revolvers were marked gluten-free, so I grabbed one and took a bite. *Lemon. Nice.*

Glittery red feathers from a sequined cardinal lay in tatters on the rug in front of the fireplace. More of Fig's handiwork. I was too tired to deal with it right now. I dragged myself up the stairs.

General Tso was fast asleep on the landing with his head stuck in a small Rubbermaid storage container. His gentle snoring rumbled off the inside of the plastic bowl. I pulled it off his head and gave him a little pat. He blinked and gave me a dog version of a smile, then fell right back to sleep.

Fig met me on the top landing. He let out a low grumble and did a couple of figure eights.

"What's the matter, baby?"

He looked at me expectantly and meowed again. His tail flicked back and forth like a whip.

The velvet rope blocking access to the third floor had been unlatched and was lying limp on the stairs. The hair on my arms sent a wave of goose bumps up to my neck, and I shivered. I stepped up to the landing and looked around.

A soft shuffling sound came from the direction of my bedroom. The door was slightly ajar, and a beam of light bounced around like a drunken firefly. *Who's in my room? And how did they get in?* I touched the engagement ring on my left hand. *Was I so distracted with wedding stuff that I forgot to lock the door?*

Several plans formed at once, fighting for preeminence. Call 911, get the wrought-iron poker from the storage room, get Kenny for backup . . . scratch that—get Aunt Ginny for backup.

I heard the intruder bang into the footboard on my bed and cry out in pain.

Iris.

My first instinct was to throw the door open and scream, "That's it, you're outta here!" But then I'd always be looking over my shoulder, waiting for her to break back in to resume whatever it was that she was doing while we were away. Better to catch her in the act.

I took soft steps towards my room and spied on her through the crack in the door.

Her back was to me, and she was rifling through my dresser. She paused, and I watched as she put the flashlight down and took out my jewelry box. Anger rose through my body. *When will that background check come through?*

She opened the little porcelain container and dug around. Then she shook her head and closed the lid, placing it back where she'd found it.

I had a beautiful ruby-and-diamond ring that my late husband, John, had given me for our twentieth wedding anniversary in that box. Not to mention a set of pearls Aunt Ginny had given me on my wedding day and several pieces of jewelry I'd collected over the years. They were all genuine and worth a few bucks. *She's looking for something specific.*

Iris picked up the flashlight and started to turn around.

I backed away from the door and crept back down a few stairs. I raised my voice loud enough that I knew she could hear me. "Hello, Figaro. Were you a good boy while Momma was away?"

I stepped loudly up the stairs. "Who undid the velvet rope?"

Iris appeared at the top step. "I'm sorry, that was me. I was just about to knock on your door. Is now a good time to talk about the wedding?"

I stared her down until a red blush crept up her neck. The flashlight was gone. Her pockets didn't appear to be full. And my bedroom door was closed. "Do you know what time it is?"

Iris chuckled. "I guess I'm still on European time."

"What do you want, Iris?"

"Nothing. But I am your mother, so I'm sure you'd want me to have my own things if I'd left them here."

"I can think of one thing you left here that you didn't want."

Iris's eyes grew big, and she inched closer to me. "What is it?"

She backed away when she saw my expression. "You know what? I think I am tired after all. Let's talk about it tomorrow." She flew down the stairs, and I heard her bedroom door close behind her.

Fig rubbed against my ankles and started to purr. I picked him up and gave him a snuggle. Peeking into the storage room, I spotted the flashlight sitting on a chest of Fourth of July bunting by the door. I slipped it into the pocket of Aunt Ginny's old sable coat. I wanted to keep an eye on Iris until we could find out what she was up to, but I wasn't about to make it easy for her to ransack my house.

Fig and I went into the bedroom, and I looked around to see if Iris had disturbed anything else. I was pretty sure the photo of John and me on the far bedside table had been moved. It was angled wrong. I picked it up and gave John a smile before replacing it on the table. Then I gave Fig a few kitty treats for being a good watch cat and sat on the love seat.

I was unsettled. Betrayal and violation draped around me like a shawl. I was too antsy to sleep, and it was too late to call anyone, so I watched a few cat videos while Fig stretched across my lap.

I checked the weather app on my phone. Still no snow in the forecast. The weather was determined to ruin my New England postcard experience.

I turned on XM radio on my laptop. Bruce Springsteen started jingling the sleigh bell intro for "Santa Claus Is Coming to Town."

I frowned at the laptop and turned it off.

I flopped onto the bed and lay there. Figaro curled into my neck with his wet face against my arm. In what felt like just a few minutes later, I woke up in the exact same position, only now the sun was coming through the bedroom windows.

I yawned and checked my engagement ring—still gorgeous. I smiled—still ecstatic about it. I turned on the radio—still Bruce Springsteen. "Ugh! Come on!"

An hour later, Fig and I dragged ourselves down the back stairs to make coffee and stare at the birds through the kitchen window. That second one was mostly just Fig. I was stirring stevia into my coffee when I heard a small clatter against the glass.

At first, I thought it was a bird. Then it went, "Pssst, Poppy."

Birds rarely whisper. Or have tufts of cottony white hair on top of their heads. Mrs. Dodson was peering into the kitchen from the side yard.

Figaro was glaring at the window, ears pinned, irritated that his routine was being interrupted for the second time in a few hours.

"What are you doing out there?"

"Is Ginny awake?"

I looked out the window and found her on top of a kitchen step stool. "Not that I know of. Get down from there before you get hurt. Why didn't you just come to the front door?"

"Shh. I need to know what Ginny is making for the Senior Center Bake-Off."

"Are you serious?"

"My reputation is on the line."

Oh, fer Pete's sake . . . "Get down from there this instant!"

The door to Aunt Ginny's bedroom opened, and she called out to me. "Poppy? Who are you talking to?"

"No one."

Mrs. Dodson's eyes widened, and she started to wiggle vigorously. I was very nervous that she would break a hip falling off of that step stool. Suddenly, her head disappeared below the window sash, and I heard her grumble. I opened the side door to see if she was alright and caught sight of her hobbling quickly through the yard to the front, dragging the white metal step stool with her. She reached out her cane and whacked one of the wise men in the nativity scene as she limped by, then disappeared from my view.

"You didn't tell that nosy nellie what I'm making for the bake-off, did you?"

"No. I don't even know what you're making."

"Good. I'd hate to have to mess you up before Christmas." The bedroom door closed again.

Joanne and Kenny both came to work fifteen minutes late, even though one of them only had to come two flights down to get here. I had already put fresh coffee in the dining room, the cinnamon rolls in the oven, and sliced potatoes for home fries, so they joined me at the table while I drank my third cup.

Aunt Ginny clomped into the kitchen, in vintage red T-strap heels, with a sassy look on her face. She was dressed in a 1950s robin's-egg-blue shirtwaist dress with a flared skirt and a tiny little lace apron. "I need you lot to clear out of the kitchen after breakfast."

Kenny's eyes nearly popped out of his head. "Holy Donna Reed, Batman. Where are the pearls?"

Aunt Ginny pulled a strand of pearls from her pocket in a smug flourish. "I need help with the clasp."

I took them and draped them around her neck. "What is this all about?"

"I'm making my secret dessert today after you monkeys clear out. And I have some deliveries I'm expecting, so no peeking if you happen to see the boxes."

Joanne chuckled. "My offer to help with your dessert still stands."

Aunt Ginny flounced her skirt to fan it out. "Don't need it. Got my baking duds on. Got my secret ingredient yesterday. I'm all set to take down Edith's whiskey fudge. Oh, before I forget." She pulled a list out of the kitchen drawer. "Here's what I signed you up for, Poppy."

"What do you mean 'signed me up'? Signed me up for what?"

"You're making some of the food for the Senior Center Christmas party."

I took the list from her hands. "Aunt Ginny! There are five kinds of hors d'oeuvres on this list."

Aunt Ginny took a coffee mug down from the cabinet. "The food at the Senior Center party usually tastes like it comes from a nursing home, and I want to be sure it's good this year. Plus, you need to bring something when you attend."

"Who said I was attending?"

She paused with the carafe over her cup. "Did I forget to mention that part? I signed you up as my date. Royce was tricked into going with his sister, God bless him."

"I don't want to go to the Senior Center Christmas party. I have enough with trying to find out Iris's secret agenda and spying on Tim's staff."

Joanne muttered under her breath. "Don't forget running the B and B."

Aunt Ginny rolled her eyes. "If you don't know who killed that man by now, you're not going to find out by missing my party."

"I'm finding out all kinds of dirt. Last night, I learned that Teela complained to Tim and Gigi that Wes was getting handsy and they did nothing to stop him."

Joanne shook her head. "A well-run H.R. would have the complaint documented in an employee file. Obviously not a fly-by-the-seat-of-your-pants one like they're running, but a professional establishment would."

"Hey. I have everything under control here."

Figaro rocketed through the swinging door and careened through the kitchen with a stuffed chickadee in his mouth, a garland of bells on felt draped over his tail.

Kenny snickered and took a Yoo-hoo from the fridge.

Aunt Ginny put her cup down with a thud. "Poppy Blossom, sometimes you have to take one for the team. I need some ringers in the crowd to vote against Edith."

Joanne and Kenny grinned as they watched me squirm. Then Aunt Ginny waved her hand in their direction. "I signed you both up too, so look sharp Saturday at six. Joanne, here's your list. I want samples of all five cakes before the party, and I'll decide which ones you'll make."

Aunt Ginny gave Joanne a list, and the snicker slid off of her face, making up for some of my frustration.

Georgina burst through the dining room into the kitchen in red slacks and a designer Christmas sweater. "Figaro?"

We all pointed to the exit on the other side of the kitchen.

"That cat had General Tso trapped by the buffet when I tried to straighten the star on the tree and the bells jingled around. You know the rest."

I took a deep inhale and let it out slowly.

Georgina spotted everyone sitting around the table. "What are you all talking about in here? You aren't planning the wedding without me, are you?"

I showed her my list. "Aunt Ginny assigned us a party to cater by tomorrow night."

Georgina's eyebrows took a dip. "What party?"

Aunt Ginny took another list out of the kitchen drawer. "Since you're always reminding us that you're well-to-do, you're bringing champagne for the punch."

Laughter carried through the dining room, and the words

"Did you see the tiny crime-scene tape? What a hoot!" caught my attention.

I lowered my forehead to the table.

Kenny poked me in the side. "Come on. It's not that big a deal. They love it."

Georgina added. "That's true. They all keep saying how awesome that you keep on theme and put out a holiday crime scene."

Aunt Ginny snorted. "And before you ask, no one has confessed."

A knock sounded on the swinging door, and Georgina pushed it open. Iris stood there with a huge grin on her face. "Hello."

"What do you want?"

"I was hoping now was a good time for us to talk about my new life plan."

Is this woman insane?

Iris looked around at our stunned faces. "You can't hide out in the kitchen, eating all day, just to avoid me, like when you were five."

The temperature of the room dropped several degrees.

"Are you calling me fat again?"

"I'm just saying I always knew to find you around the cookies when you were upset."

Aunt Ginny picked up the pepper grinder and threw it at Iris's head. It crashed into the door jamb. "Get out!"

Iris backed out of the kitchen, and the door swung closed.

No one moved, then the door pushed open again, and Aunt Ginny grabbed the saltshaker. This time it was General Tso, and he was carrying the stuffed chickadee. He dropped it at my feet. I gave his head a little pat and tried to steady my voice. "Aww, thanks, buddy."

I set the Christmas ornament on the counter and stared at it. "I caught Iris searching my jewelry box when I came home at midnight. She didn't take anything."

Aunt Ginny's eyes narrowed and slid to the side. "Hmm. Interesting."

Kenny dropped to the banquette. "I really thought I set up a good distraction by leaving a photo album of you in grade school out on the library coffee table."

"Apparently, pictures of the life she missed with me weren't as exciting as rifling through my things."

Georgina's hands flew to her hips. "And you thought I was crazy when I wanted to hire a security guard."

"That *was* crazy."

Joanne shook her head. "I followed her all afternoon yesterday. She must have waited until I left for the day to go snooping."

Aunt Ginny quietly tsk'd. "I think I know what she's looking for."

"What?"

On the other side of the door, the lady with the allergies sneezed a few times. "Look, honey, the lady across the street just added the cutest light-up polar bears you've ever seen to her yard."

Aunt Ginny ran from the kitchen, leaving us looking clueless.

She returned a minute later on her cellphone. "Smitty. I need an igloo."

CHAPTER 30

Some people are infected with chronic stress, and others are carriers. I think you know which one Aunt Ginny is.

Aunt Ginny refused to tell me what she thought Iris was looking for. And after trying to talk her out of whatever harebrained scheme she was devising and double-checking all the locks, I left the house with a sense of impending doom.

Aunt Ginny denied that she was competing with Nell across the street, but when I was leaving home, she was on the phone with the Cape May County Zoo asking if she could borrow some penguins until January.

I pulled out my phone and texted Smitty.

No wildlife!

Nell was in her yard, setting up a sleigh with presents. She did not greet me in her usual friendly manner. And I knew she saw me because I accidentally set off the new roof Santa, who started bellowing "Ho ho ho" when I stepped off the porch and ran into the new yard Santa, who was feeding the light-up reindeer.

I backed the car out of the driveway and made sure to

take the route to the coffee shop that did not pass in front of Nell's house.

La Dolce Vita was packed. Gia had called in Momma's out-of-work sous chef, Marco, as extra holiday help to back up Sierra while we went over to Mia Famiglia to ambush—I mean interview—Jackson Seymour.

Gia gave me a tight grin from behind the espresso machine when I appeared in the dining room. "*Cara mia*, I will be ready in a moment."

Marco was working the register and calling drinks as fast as Gia and Sierra could foam the milk for lattes. "*Buongiorno,* Poppy! Is your arm getting tired from carrying that huge rock around on your hand all day?"

I flashed my engagement ring with a smile. "Never."

Gia brought a red paper cup around the counter and handed it to me with a kiss. "Eggnog latte for my lady."

Sierra groaned. "Eww." She smiled at me before the steam from the espresso machine obscured her from view.

Gia and I walked down the courtyard and around the back of Mia Famiglia, while he ranted about his morning and the newest development in Momma's hostile takeover of our wedding. "She want to have ten kinda pasta for reception. I tell her, Poppy can have no gluten, and she say gluten allergy is no real. Then she want my sister Madalena son to be ring bearer. He shove everything up his nose. We will never see wedding ring again."

I took one of his hands to keep him from whacking the silver bells off the lamppost. "Okay now, calm down."

"*Si!* I am calm!"

"Uh-huh. Well, you're yelling. Plus, your accent gets stronger when you're upset."

Gia stopped at the back door and turned to face me. "You say my accent is sexy."

I ran my free hand down his arm and tried to keep the amusement I was feeling off my face. It was so rare that

Gia was irritated. He was always the calm in the midst of my storm. I guess today it was his turn for a meltdown. "Yes, it's very sexy. I just don't want you getting this worked up about your mother over one day. We'll figure it out. We'll lock Momma in a room with Aunt Ginny, Georgina, and a wedding magazine and wait outside to see who makes it out alive."

Gia chuckled. "Okay, but my money is on Aunt Ginny."

I kissed him and felt the tension leave his shoulders. "Are you ready to go inside now?"

He grinned. "*Si*. Yes. I am ready."

"Okay." I let out a little snicker.

He unlocked the door, and we entered the kitchen that had been shut down since Momma broke her hip. The scent of garlic and rosemary clung to the air like a memory.

"Have you heard from Frankie or Esteban? Did they ever get new jobs when Momma couldn't stay open?" *Or rather, refused to stay open if I were in the kitchen.*

"The last I heard, Frankie was part-time at the Mad Batter, and Esteban is collecting unemployment."

"I'm sorry to hear that."

"This time of year is very hard. No one wants to hire you for a few weeks, only to lay you off after Christmas. At least I can give Marco some hours." Gia went through the dining room, turning on lights and unlocking the front door.

I heard voices and checked the time. *Jackson must be early.*

I crept over to the swinging doors and peeked through one of the windows. Gia was seating Jackson at the farthest table from the kitchen, with his back to the door. *I'll never hear anything.*

My phone buzzed. It was Gia. I looked through the window and saw him put his phone face down on the table. I clicked the answer button and muted my microphone. *Sexy clever man.*

"We currently use Leo Produce, but we want to explore new options."

Jackson passed a paper to Gia. "You'll see that we have very competitive prices for new customers willing to sign a three-year contract."

"Three years is long time for a restaurant. I have never heard such a thing. Leo has one-year commitment."

Jackson nodded and handed Gia another paper. "I could give you a ten-percent discount with a twelve-month contract, if you join our partner network. Everyone in the network has agreed to give the same discount to each other."

Gia took the offered paper and put on his glasses. "You have one of every service. Dairy, florist, linen, bread, seafood. All these companies are with you?"

"They are. I don't have an Italian restaurant yet, and you must agree to offer your products and services to vendor partners at the same discount. Fair is fair, and we want to reward loyalty."

"I am only looking for a produce vendor. What if I do not want to make other changes?"

Jackson nodded. "The only way I can offer you the discount and the contract is if you agree to exclusivity with the entire network."

"But I already have contract with other supplier for meat and seafood."

"You would have to wait until those contracts run out or break them. The savings might be enough to offset any penalties you'd face. Unless . . . Who is your seafood vendor?"

"Deepwater Fisheries."

"Then I'm about to save your business, buddy. You want to stay as far away from them as you can get. No matter how much of a discount they say they are giving you, the hidden fees are not worth it, and the quality is not what they promise. My seafood guy has taken over some of their old clients, and they have horror stories. You should check your contract. There is probably some small print just to take advantage of you financially."

"Maybe I should change. I heard the owner of Deepwater Fisheries was killed. They might not even be in business anymore. Then what would I do?"

"Leave now before they replace Wes. I heard his brother is taking over the company, and the Baileys love a lawsuit. You can save yourself a lot of heartache by joining my team."

"You probably got a lot of new business when the seafood competition shut down."

The phone went silent, and I wondered if the call had dropped. Finally, Jackson said, "Some. But there's enough business in Cape May to go around."

Gia waved the paper at Jackson. "And all of these companies have agreed to this?"

"They have." Jackson reached across the table. "I need that back. Once you sign the contract, I can get you your own copy."

Gia nodded, took his glasses off, and placed them on the table. "Are you sure that what you are doing is legal? You cannot penalize a business for using your competitor."

Jackson shot up from the table and gathered his papers. "We're not penalizing anyone. You just don't get the discount and short-term contract. It's perfectly legal. What Wes Bailey was doing wasn't legal. No one tried to stop him but me!"

Gia stood and glanced my way. He patted the air with his hands trying to calm Jackson down.

Jackson was still hollering on his way towards the door. "If you're worried about morality, you shouldn't be with Deepwater Fisheries. They'll rob you blind, then stab you in the back."

I poked my head out the kitchen door and waited until Jackson had left the building. I met Gia in the dining room.

"I am sorry. I spooked him when I mentioned the law."

"You did wonderful, honey."

"He said he had another meeting he was late for. I did manage to get a business card."

Gia reached into his pocket and pulled out a white card that said SEYMOUR VEG in bold green type, with JACKSON SEYMOUR named underneath. I turned the card over. The very bottom had a tiny smudge of something bright pink. I scratched at it and a little bit flaked off.

"What is it?"

"I think it's paint. And I'm pretty sure the last time I saw this paint, it was sprayed across Wes Bailey's van."

CHAPTER 31

I pulled into the lot between the Villas police station and the library. The brown-brick Teen Center had one lone strand of colored lights hung defiantly over the door. The basketball court and skateboard ramps were deserted, but school let out in a few minutes, so things would get busy soon.

Brenda, the Teen Center's gatekeeper, was pinning notices on the corkboard at the front of the lime-green lobby. Her silver, cat-eye glasses were perched on the end of her nose as she positioned a flyer marked HOLIDAY DANCE for next weekend. "Hey, lady. It's good to see you. The kids have been looking forward to this class for weeks."

I gave her a quick hug. "You dyed your hair red and blond since I was last here. It used to be pink."

Brenda was about ten years older than me, shaped like a beach ball, and full of spunk. The teens loved her, and most of them thought anyone over the age of thirty was a dinosaur. She patted her colorful spikes. "This is my Heat Miser doo for the holidays."

I laughed. "It's perfect."

She reached out and took one of my shopping bags and led me down the hall. "Come on, I'll help you get set up in the kitchen. I heard you found another dead guy."

"This one found me."

"Get outta here. I thought you found him in the freezer of some fancy restaurant."

"A vendor found him. But the killer left a note asking for me by name."

Brenda put the bag on the kitchen counter. "Who did you piss off that they're now addressing victims to you personally?"

"I wish I knew."

She tsk'd and shook her head. "Hang in there. I'm sure at least a couple more murders would have to happen in Cape May before they run you outta town. On the bright side, I do have some good news. Youse won't have to clean up after your class today. I've got someone coming in to do court-ordered community service, and they're going to organize the supply closets for me. Then I'll have them clean the kitchen and do all the dishes after youse guys are done."

"Okay, cool."

Brenda left to go back to her desk out front, while I unloaded my bags and lined up the ingredients for the sugar cookies. I was so busy setting up stations around the kitchen that I hadn't heard anyone come in until Brenda called me.

"Okay, lady, here is your helper for the day. Just tell her what you need."

When I saw who my helper was, I dropped the cookie sheet with a loud clang.

Chelle appeared to be just as stunned as I was. Her eyes narrowed, and her hands went to her full hips. "Are you checking up on me?"

"I thought you were at the hairdresser."

"Community service is supposed to be confidential. If

Gigi told you to spy on me, I'ma kick her little white butt to kingdom come."

Brenda looked at me with wide eyes. "Are you gonna be okay in here, Poppy?"

Oof. Well, code name Mack is out of the bag. A shiver ran up my arms. "Yes. Of course."

If Chelle was violent, they wouldn't let her work with kids, right?

"Why wouldn't she be okay with me? What do you think I'm gonna do?"

Brenda stood her ground. "Ms. Cleveland, if you give me any trouble, I'll cancel your community service at the Teen Center, and you'll go back to your previous assignment."

I stepped towards the two ladies, who were squaring off over the fondant frosting. "We're fine. Everyone's cool. Right, Chelle?"

Chelle gave Brenda a tight nod, and Brenda backed out of the room, holding her eye contact.

The usually cheery hostess dropped to a metal folding chair with her head in her hands. Her face transformed into steel before my eyes. "What do you plan to do with this information?"

I pulled out the folding chair across from her. "I'm just here to teach a baking class."

"Look. I know what you're thinking, but you're wrong. I made a mistake, okay? I was desperate and foolish. And I've learned from my mistakes."

"I'm not thinking anything."

"Yeah, right."

"Do you want to talk about it?"

"Nah, I'm good."

People love to talk to you, Mack. Blah blah blah. So much for Tim's theory. "If you change your mind, you know where to find me."

Chelle rolled her eyes. "Just don't rat me out to Tim

and Gigi, okay? Because Gigi will fire me on the spot. She's fired people for less."

"You don't have to tell me. She's tried to fire me twice, and I'm only a temp."

"Yeah, she don't like you. And you have to stay on Gigi's good side if you want to work there."

"I bet she goes through employees like paper napkins."

Chelle grinned and pulled out her cell phone. "Have you seen the write-up about her on Bad Bosses dot com?"

"What? Nowah. Where is it?"

Chelle pulled up the website on her phone and read some of the reviews past employees had left for Gigi. "Known to have fits of fury and abuse. Here's another—I suspect multiple personalities, and all of them are unpleasant. Verbal attacks served daily."

We both started to giggle.

She held up her phone with another. "I have PTSD from working at Le Bon Gigi. I once saw her throw a roast chicken across the kitchen because the skin wasn't crispy. How can such a small package hold so much rage?"

I snorted in a very unladylike way, and Chelle laughed harder.

Chelle wiped her eyes and put her cell phone back in her pocket. "Look, I'm not the only employee who's been inside."

"How do you know that?"

"Because I've seen my probation officer show up to do a site check, and he wasn't there for me. I'm not proud of what I did, but there were extenuating circumstances. I'm just saying, I'm not the one you need to be worried about."

"Who is?"

Chelle looked away like she didn't hear me.

"Do you know who killed Wes Bailey?"

"Nope. But I'm sure he brought it on himself."

"Why do you say that?"

She looked dead in my eyes. "Because he refused to mind his own business."

I didn't let her see that she rattled me. "Do you know who's been stealing food from the walk-in?"

Chelle shrugged. "I dunno. But Tim said things didn't start to disappear until after we came over from Gigi's. She's convinced the homeless man has been breaking in and raiding the freezer."

"What do you think?"

"I'm worried that Tim's going to get his self into trouble. He and Gigi argue a lot. We all hear them."

"What do they argue about?"

Chelle leaned. "Just between you and me, Tim is doing something that Gigi disapproves of. I don't know what it is, but I'm sure he feels he has to. Tim's a good guy. I would have been fired long ago if it weren't for him."

Kids started filing into the kitchen. Some gave me wary smiles, while others went right to the cookie cutters to lay claim on the ones they wanted.

Chelle pushed back from the table. "Well, let me know when you're ready for me to do the dishes. I'll be over here organizing this pantry and googling Poppy and Cape May."

CHAPTER 32

Chelle gave me a lot of curious glances and a couple stare-downs during my class. She never asked me who Poppy was, but if she'd googled me, she wouldn't need to ask. I was the weirdo Cape May corpse finder. There was nothing on the web about me being a police informant because Amber did a good job of keeping that a secret. The real question was, what would she do once we got back to Maxine's? Would she tell everyone I had death radar?

I was more concerned about her innocence. I liked Chelle. She was fun. But she was holding some dark secrets. You don't get community service for murder, but you don't get it for nothing either. If she found out who I really was, I wouldn't be able to trust anything she told me from now on. She'd be more careful to watch what she said. She was definitely worried about Tim and Gigi finding out she'd been in trouble with the law. I wonder how far she'd go to protect that secret if Wes Bailey had found out.

By the time my class was done, I had enough icing on

my clothes to frost a dozen cookies. No way could I go to Maxine's like this. I had to run to the South Jersey Christmas supply depot—aka Aunt Ginny's house—and change.

As I approached home, Aunt Ginny was on the front porch with Gia's mother, and they were jabbing what looked like a breadbasket back and forth. Georgina was pushing a casserole dish into Teresa's hands and shaking her head no. I rolled the window down and heard, "Poppy isn't here. We didn't invite you to dinner, you whack-adoo!"

I considered hitting the gas and just buying new clothes, but the driver's side door of a little blue car at the curb flew open to block my path, and I had to slam on my brakes to keep from ramming it.

Teresa's husband, Angelo, stepped out of the car, holding a giant metal bowl. He gave me a wave. "*Buona sera*, new sister."

I peered over the steering wheel at the big man, who was pointing in the bowl and mouthing "sa-lad." *What in the world is going on?*

A sedan pulled up behind me, blocking my escape, and two of Gia's sisters got out, each carrying covered dishes. My cell phone pinged a message from Gia.

Do Not go home!
Too late. What is this?
Ambush family dinner.

I looked around the yard at the gathering crowd and sighed.

My phone pinged a new message from Gia.

I am coming over.

Aunt Ginny rapped on my window. "They won't leave. Should I call the cops?"

"No. I'm trying to save the cops for my next death threat."

"I can make a death threat, no problem." She looked around the yard. "But to which one?"

"We're going to be related to these people soon. We might as well invite them in and try to be nice."

Aunt Ginny's hands flew to her hips. "If I have to be nice, then I'd say we're even for that engagement picture in the paper."

"No . . . we're not. And I don't think you can pull it off."

Aunt Ginny loved a challenge almost as much as she loved a good brawl. She looked into my eyes. "Try me."

A white Lincoln Continental stopped in the middle of the street, and Gia's Uncle Alfio stuck his head out the window. "*Ciao*, Poppy. How much vino do you have?"

Not enough for all this.

"Do I need to tell Karla to bring?"

"No, I have some." I turned back to Aunt Ginny. "Okay. Let's see whachu got."

Aunt Ginny turned into Hostess of the Year just to stick it to me. With her arms outstretched, she led Momma and all the Larussos into the house while I parked the Corvette and texted Tim that I would be late.

Georgina met me on the sidewalk to get in some personal complaint time before joining the others. "What are you going to do about that future mother-in-law of yours? You can't have her showing up any time she wants without being invited."

I wanted to ask her how she wasn't choking on hypocrisy right now, but I held my tongue because I needed allies.

Karla pulled in behind the sedan and released Henry, who ran for me and started chattering about his day. "Mary Jane said I have to eat paste if I don't let her sit next to me tomorrow. Do I have to eat paste?"

"No, honey. Of course not. Do you want to sit next to Mary Jane?"

Henry shook his head. "I want to sit with Amelia. She's my friend. She eats bologna."

Karla snickered and ran her hand through his hair. "I'm not sure how those two things are related, buddy."

I squatted down and gave my little guy a hug. "You should sit with your friend, and don't let Mary Jane boss you around."

Henry gave a single nod.

"Why don't you let Georgina take you inside and get you some juice."

Georgina put her hand out. "We have that fruit punch you like."

Henry took her hand and let her begin to lead him. He looked at me over his shoulder. "Are you coming?"

"I'll be there in a minute."

I turned my attention back to Karla. "Figured you'd bring the child as your ticket in?"

"I'm no dummy. Forget the casseroles. You'd never say no to that little boy."

Gia appeared at the end of the driveway in a wool pea-coat and knit cap. A deep frown was etched into his face, and dark circles rested under his eyes. He puffed out his breath like an angry dragon.

Karla took a step back towards the house. "I'll just wait inside where there are witnesses."

Gia closed the distance between us. "I am so sorry about my family."

I took his hand in mine. "I guess it's nice that they want to welcome me. I think."

He snorted. "They want to make sure I will still take care of things after we are married. Since I go where you go, they do not want you to go far."

I leaned against him and let him hold me. "I'm not planning on going anywhere." I spied Momma watching me from the front window. "But out of curiosity . . . If I was . . . where would we go?"

An explosion of light and sound assaulted us in the driveway as a million watts flamed to life all at once, and the three wise men began to belt out "You're a Mean One, Mr. Grinch."

Gia squinted and shielded his eyes. "What in God's name is happening?!"

I sighed. "It must be five o'clock. Aunt Ginny keeps her chaos on a timer now."

Gia started to laugh at the absurdity of my house in all its festive insanity. "I bet they can see it from space."

Cars started to slow down as they drove past to take it all in.

"Do you want to come inside?"

He made a face. "No. But I will for you."

I took his hand, and we walked up the front steps. His family was spread all over the house, holding plates of food. Gia's sisters Daniela, Stefania, and Karla were in the library with Teresa and her husband, Angelo. They waved. "Come join us."

"In a minute. I have to get changed first."

Momma was sitting at the head of the dining-room table with Iris on her left and Georgina on her right. Zio Alfio was at the opposite end of the table, helping himself to a serving of chicken marsala. Aunt Ginny was fluttering around in a frilly apron, offering to refill their wineglasses. She made sure to give me a long, penetrating look as she poured and thanked Oliva Larusso for bringing such a lovely spread.

Kiss up. The best way to get Aunt Ginny to do something is to tell her she can't.

Henry came running into the dining room. "Poppy. Figaro's in the tree!"

Aunt Ginny smiled broadly at Gia's mother. "That's our festive tree cat. He's rearranging the ornaments to surprise us."

Oliva grinned and nodded. No telling how much she understood.

Aunt Ginny put the wine bottle down. "Henry, I have a little surprise for you."

His eyes widened like the ceramic balls Figaro was swatting around the sitting room. "What is it?"

Aunt Ginny reached into her apron pocket and pulled out two glass penguins. "I ordered these on the internets, but they are too small to put in the yard, so I thought you would like them."

Henry reached out and reverently took the tiny figurines. "Thank you."

Iris smiled at the little five-year-old. "What do you want for Christmas, Henry? A bike? Some video games? Action figures?" She looked at me. "I've been reading up on what toys are hot this season."

"Why?"

She grinned. "Oh, you never know. You could have a baby of your own, now that you're getting married."

Aunt Ginny and Georgina were as silent as the morning after an ice storm. Gia gently took my hand.

Henry walked his penguins down the table. "I already told Santa what I wanted."

Iris was too self-absorbed to feel the shift in the room. "What is it?"

"It's a secret," Henry said.

Oliva said something in Italian, but we caught the words, Henry and *Natale*.

Gia translated. "Momma say Henry is in school play tomorrow night. He is a nutcracker."

The ladies aww'd in unison.

Henry looked from his penguins to me. "I signed you up to make two dozen cupcakes for the party."

Gia's hand tensed in mine. "Piccolo! You cannot sign Poppy up without asking her."

Henry's eyebrows knit together, and his glasses slid down his nose. "All the mommies are bringing snacks for the party."

My heart swelled so large it pushed against my rib cage. "Of course, I can make you cupcakes, baby." I smiled at Gia. "I would do anything for my boys."

My phone buzzed. It was a text from Chuck.

911—Tim is ranting about you being late, and Gigi has gone mental. You need to get here now before someone gets hurt.

CHAPTER 33

"Girl, Tim is so pissed at you right now. I thought you were coming in right after the Teen Center." Chelle handed me another ramekin.

I cut my eyes over to the grill, where Tim was scowling. Then I handed Chelle the chocolate-orange crème brûlée I'd just caramelized. "I went home to change and fell into a scene from *The Godfather* with my future mother-in-law." I called up my best Don Corleone impression. "*One day you will need a favor from me, so I ask you today to do this for da family and let my daughters be in your wedding.*"

Chelle laughed. "What'd you tell her?"

I fired another crème brûlée. "I said I was late for work. Then I escaped through the back door and came here."

Gigi emerged from the walk-in freezer, swinging a clipboard like a claymore. "Five! Five tenderloins and two standing rib roasts are missing. I want new security cameras, and I want them now!" She grabbed a frozen pie and threw it across the room. It hit the edge of the sink and shattered.

Chuck held a broom and dustpan at the ready. He swept up the shards and dumped them in the trash.

Gigi had been on a tear through the walk-ins, counting every last shrimp and hurling anything that displeased her—at anyone who displeased her.

Tim took the clipboard from her hands. "Geeg. I think you just miscounted. There's been a lot going on."

She covered her forehead with her hand and rubbed her temple. "I want the hobo gone. Tonight, Tim. Enough is enough."

I handed Chelle another crème brûlée, and she added it to her tray.

She whispered, "If she reaches for a roast chicken, be sure you duck."

I held back a snort and looked away. I picked up the tray of ramekins and carried it towards the walk-in refrigerator, careful not to step in the splattered tomato that Gigi had hurled a few minutes ago when she discovered a bunch of garlic had disappeared from the fridge.

Andrew came in to pick up an order and opened the walk-in for me. "I got it."

"Thanks."

He followed me in and took the tray from my hands. "I just heard the cops were here the other night."

I started moving the crème brûlée to the shelf. "Gigi is determined to get that homeless man arrested."

"Wow. I take one night off, and look at what I missed."

"What did you do on your night off?"

"Don't tell Gigi, but I moonlight as a waiter for Pop-up Bistro."

"What is that?"

"It's an underground restaurant program. You never know who the chef will be or where the dinner will be served, but you have to be ready for anything."

"I didn't know such a thing existed. How do people find out where to go?"

"You have to download the app. It books up months in advance, but you don't know where the bistro will pop up until the day of your reservation."

"That sounds really cool. And you moonlight with them?"

He glanced at the door. "As a waiter every Tuesday night. The tips are great because the food is freakishly expensive. Always some seven-course tasting menu. Different chefs sign up to take turns hosting."

"I'm going to have to look for this app."

Andrew grinned and reached for the handle.

We pushed our way back into the kitchen just as Nikki poked her head in. "Chef Tim. Some lady has questions about gluten. Could you come talk to her, please?"

"Gluten is Mack's territory. Mack, can you . . . ?"

Tim had his hands full with pregnancy hormones and insanity. "Yeah. I'll be right there." I put the baking sheet on the workbench, then followed Andrew out to the dining room.

The place was packed with guests for the dinner rush. Nikki caught my eye, and I followed her over to a table of ladies who matched, from their red sweaters to their White Christmas Martinis to their air of being accustomed to making special requests.

"Hello, I'm the pastry chef tonight. How can I help?"

"Can I get the seafood pasta half gluten-free so we can all share it?"

"No."

"Why not?"

"Because gluten won't respect your boundaries." I was working on my professional attitude, so I only rolled my eyes a little before a ruckus at the front of the house drew my attention away.

Three large men in leather coats surrounded Chelle. One of them had a large face tattoo of a swordfish curling around one eye, the sword piercing across his forehead.

He had grabbed her wrist and was trying to pull her outside.

Nikki followed my eyes to the front. "What the . . . Call Tim."

"Tim nothing. Call the police." I left the table and headed towards the door.

The men had taken Chelle out front, and the one with the swordfish tattoo had her against the building. "You were warned this would happen if you didn't make the deadline."

Chelle had wild eyes. She swung her arms madly to push away from the beast of a man. "I just need more time."

"Get off her. The cops are on their way. They'll be here any second."

The one with a scar across his neck advanced on me. He reached inside his coat. "This doesn't concern you. Just walk away."

Chelle cried out, "Don't hurt her."

Flashing police-car lights blazed through the night, and the men tried to look like three normal guys waiting for a table. They looked as normal as a trio of gorillas in hoop skirts.

Wow, the police arrived really fast.

The cruiser pulled into Maxine's parking lot and drove around the back, followed by a tow truck.

Where are they going? We're right here.

The big man pushed Chelle's head against the building, and it hit the siding with a crack. "Next time, I won't be so gentle." They took off across the street, keeping to the shadows.

Chelle started to tremble and slid down the wall.

I took her arm to help her stand. "What was that all about?"

"Just some nasty business you don't want to know about. You shouldna come out here."

I started to lead Chelle back inside. "If I hadn't come, they might have killed you."

"They won't kill me yet. You can't collect from a dead woman."

Andrew and Nikki met us at the door. "What happened?"

Chelle tried to wave them off. "It was nothing. Misunderstanding about our reservation system. Watch the front for me while I go to the ladies' room and freshen my makeup."

"Chelle . . ." It was no use. She disappeared faster than you could say Blitzen.

Gabe crossed the room from the bar. "What's going on? Why does Chelle look upset?"

Andrew said, "Didn't you see those guys drag her outside?"

Gabe flew to the window. "What guys?" He threw the door open and looked out front.

Nikki drew an arc on her cheek with her fingernail. "Did you see the tattoo on the big one?"

I nodded.

"That's the mark of the swordfish gang. They're into some ugly business."

Andrew looked out the door. "Like what?"

Nikki crossed her arms. "Drugs. Money laundering. Fight fixing. You name it. If you can make money illegally, they're into it. Whatever they want from Chelle, they'll kill her if they don't get it."

Gabe narrowed his eyes and considered her. "How do you know all that?"

Nikki shrugged. "It was on the news."

What has Chelle gotten herself involved in? "The seafood vendor who died here, did he have a swordfish tattoo?"

Nikki flipped her hands up. "I have no idea."

Andrew shook his head. "No. I would have noticed one."

Gabe turned to me. "What did they say to her outside?"

"They threatened her. You'd have to ask Chelle for specifics. If you ever see them again, call the police immediately. I can't believe they got here so fast. Good job, Nikki."

Nikki took a step backwards. "The cops are here?"

"Didn't you call them?"

Nikki wouldn't look me in the eye. "Yeah, of course."

Yellow lights bounced off the front windows, and we looked through the curtains. The tow truck was turning towards the bridge, and it was pulling a pickup truck. "Uh-oh. Someone's getting towed."

Andrew cursed and started for the kitchen. "That's Tyler's truck."

I followed him back, and we pushed through the double doors. Tim and Tyler were arguing with Officer Consuelos.

Ben handed Tyler a slip of paper. "Your truck is being searched for evidence as part of an ongoing investigation. We have a few questions about your movements the night of Wes Bailey's murder. I'm going to need you to come down to the station with me."

"Dude, why do you want me? I have an alibi. I told you I was with my girlfriend all night."

"Your girlfriend changed her statement. She says you left in the middle of the night."

CHAPTER 34

A gentle nudge on my shoulder woke me.

Kenny stood over me in Charlie Brown Christmas pajamas, a finger to his lips.

I checked my phone—two a.m. I raised my eyebrows, and he nodded towards the storage room.

I got out of bed and followed him to the hall, where we peeked through the crack in the door. Iris was going through cardboard boxes at the back of the room under the window.

I rolled my eyes at Kenny.

His lips flattened, and he shook his head in shared disbelief.

I nodded to him and jerked my head towards Iris.

Kenny pointed to himself and vigorously shook his head no. He nodded at me and jerked my head towards Iris.

I bowed my head and silently chastised myself for not fleeing the country when I had the chance.

I frowned.

Kenny put a hand on my shoulder and squeezed. He

disappeared down the hall to his bedroom before I could change my mind.

When he'd closed his door, I flicked on the lights. "What do you think you're doing?"

Iris jumped a mile. "Not here! What?"

"Give me one reason why I shouldn't send you packing right now."

Iris ran her hand through her flyaway hair and looked around the room. "I was just looking for my old Weight Watcher books . . . for you."

This is going to make me really mad, isn't it?

"Since you're getting married soon. I thought you'd want to try to lose a few pounds before the big day."

A vein in my temple throbbed. I rubbed it with my thumb. "At two a.m.? Other than being incredibly rude— I don't believe you at all. What are you really looking for?"

"Nothing."

"It must be pretty important if you've come back after all these years for it. You sure didn't come back for me."

"Whatever are you talking about?" Iris struggled to her feet. She was holding a cigar box. "I told you. I want my old diet books. Look, Petal. Men don't like fat women. He might want to marry you right now because he needs a mother for his son, but eventually he'll grow restless and leave you for a younger, thinner woman. I don't want to see that happen."

I could feel the anger rising up my spine like I was a puppet, and Iris was pulling my strings. "You know, my whole life I've been obsessed with my weight. I wouldn't try out for cheerleading or the school plays because I was nervous about how I would look. I was too afraid to wear a bathing suit in front of people to go swimming with my friends. I even refused to wear a coat in the winter because it added to my size. I chose frostbite over comfort."

I stretched my neck side to side until it popped. "You know how many years I was a chubby anorexic? Ashamed to eat in front of people? How many parties I didn't go to because I didn't have anything to wear that made me look skinny?"

Iris clutched the cigar box closer to her chest.

"I always wondered why it mattered to me so much. Where had the thought begun that I wasn't good enough the way I was?" I took a breath. "It was you. I don't know how or why, but you made me ashamed, and I've lived my whole life feeling ugly."

Iris took a baby step towards me. "I didn't mean to . . ."

"I used to wish I could go back in time and keep you from leaving. Now I wish I could go back and have you leave me with Aunt Ginny sooner, before the damage was done."

A tear rolled down her cheek.

I reached out and took the cigar box from her hands. *I can't wait for that background check any longer.* "You're toxic. And you have no intention of telling me the truth. I want you to leave as soon as possible."

Iris pushed past me, her footsteps receding down the stairs.

I opened the cigar box. Inside was a baby rattle and a hospital bracelet that said Poppy Blossom. My heartbeat thudded in my ears to the tune of regret regret regret.

I was too upset to go back to sleep when I returned to my room, so I picked up the diary and turned to where I'd left off. I couldn't get a straight answer from Iris, but maybe I could get some answers from Grandpa Rooster.

June 30
Oswald invited me for a game of Parcheesi last night. It turned out to be a ruse to match me with his hideous cousin, Elodie. She had nice

trim ankles, but billowed out from there. After accepting an apology cigar and brandy, I made my way home and turned in early.

July 1
The shrew next door has decided to take out her venom on me, even though I was not the one who tittle-tattled around Jackson's Clubhouse that she shaves her upper lip. Not that I remember anyway. It's too hot to throw dice. I'm going night-swimming to keep my sanity.

July 8
Will no one deliver me from this horrible woman? If only she had a husband who could talk some sense into that empty head of hers. Never before has so little thought gone into so many words. No, madame. I will not put on trousers when I am on my private veranda. You and your live-stock can stay in your house or look the other way!

July 11
The shrew across the field said that until I apologize and make amends to her cow, death and destruction will follow me all the days of my life. The woman should be sent to the lu-natic asylum. She believes herself to be a gypsy, or a medium, or some such nonsense. I told her I shall never

apologize for that picayune offense,
which lives only in her imagination.

July 15
It has taken me a couple of days to
process the events from the other
night. The most shocking development
has taken place. I was on my usual
route home from Jackson's Clubhouse,
the shrew be dammed. It is not my
fault she planted melons on the path
to my home. I may have partaken in
a few too many of Breckenridge's new
gin rickeys, and the night air is good
for clearing one's head. I happened
upon a poor soul who had been bru-
tally attacked. One side of his head
had been crushed by a large rock,
and he'd been left on the side of the
road dead. I called for an officer at
once. I must confess, it has nigh
shaken me to my core. I came
straight home and had a restorative
brandy and took to my bed for the
next two days.

CHAPTER 35

I stayed up way too late reading and overslept. Once Grandpa Rooster stumbled on a murder victim, I found I couldn't put the diary down. It wasn't until I heard Georgina scream about out-of-control froth that I was jerked awake and jumped out of bed.

I should probably have changed out of my flannel pajamas before running down the stairs, but that thought didn't hit me until I leapt over General Tso and heard the sisters giggle "Good morning" from their room.

I found the problem in the library. All five of them. "What the heck are you all doing?"

Aunt Ginny and the Biddies had set up a four-tiered silver champagne fountain, and whatever was running through it was foaming like a dishwasher on Dawn.

Mrs. Dodson was hobbling in a wide circle, whacking the foam with her cane. Mother Gibson was praying to Jesus for a miracle, while she scooped out the offending liquid with a six-ounce china teacup and poured it into my ficus. Mrs. Davis was laying a mountain of paper towels on my parquet floor to sop up the overflow. Georgina made herself useful by jumping up and down and giving a blow-by-blow on which side was making the highest amount of froth.

And, of course, Aunt Ginny was doing her usual and supervising from the wing chair. "I warned you not to use Sprite, Edith."

Mrs. Dodson wiped her cane with the corner of her dress. "You said Sprite was the closest to champagne, and we should make sure it worked before wasting money."

Aunt Ginny sniffed. "It doesn't matter whose idea it was. Lila must have turned it up too high. No way it's supposed to shoot out that fast."

Mother Gibson grunted and plunged her tiny cup into the bowl. "You said we didn't need to read the directions first, Ginny."

"Well, I didn't say to put the fountain in turbo mode. Who knew it would churn up this kind of foam?"

I leaned against the desk. "Can't you just turn it off?"

Mrs. Davis whined. "We tried. It has a mind of its own."

Aunt Ginny crossed her legs and picked up a magazine to fan herself. "The machines have finally taken over."

Georgina waved her hands at a mountain of bubbles that threatened to lunge at her. "This fountain is in perfect condition. Smitty replaced the motor just last night."

Well, that mystery's solved. I caught Aunt Ginny's eyes across a quivering peak of foam.

She shook her head. "Good God, Georgina. You know we have a rule in this house that everything Smitty fixes comes with a warning. You should have told us!"

I reached over and pulled the plug. The jet engine whined down to a hum.

Mrs. Davis danced around on the sopping paper towels. "Where's Kenny? Isn't this his job?"

Mrs. Dodson stepped back from the fountain. "I'm going to go find him."

You know, this is a problem these ladies can handle all on their own. They don't need me. I turned to leave them to it and caught the nativity set out of the corner of my eye. Two glass penguins were paying homage to the baby Jesus. I giggled. *Henry*.

Kenny lugged a mop, a bucket, and a scowl as he passed me on my way down the hall to the kitchen. I found Mrs. Dodson bent over the mudroom dryer. "What are you doing?"

She tried to stand up too fast and banged her head inside the drum. "Ow! I was just looking for something."

I looked into the kitchen at Joanne, who was refilling the juice pitcher for breakfast. Her shoulders shook with silent laughter. "Oh yeah? Something like what?"

Her eyes roved back and forth. "Towels. To clean up the Sprite."

I reached out and grabbed two fluffy folded bath towels from the top of the dryer. "You mean like these?"

Her cheeks quivered as she looked at the white Egyptian cotton in my hands. "Those look like good towels. I was looking for old towels." She gave a quick glance at the top of the dryer. "Darn it."

A stack of cleaning rags lay neatly folded in a basket on the washing machine. "Uh-huh. You're looking for Aunt Ginny's secret dessert for the Senior Center, aren't you?"

"I have won first place for my whiskey fudge two years running. Is it too much to ask for a hat trick?"

"A hat trick?"

Her face screwed up in thought. "Did I say it wrong?"

"Not if you mean three goals in a hockey game by the same player."

She blew out her breath and scanned the top of the refrigerator. "Oh good. That's what I thought Neil called it."

"Get away from my kitchen, you sneaky cheater!" Aunt Ginny barreled down the hall shaking her fist. "You'll never find it, so you can quit snooping."

It's not even nine a.m. My cell phone rang, and I

checked the screen. Cape May Historical Society. "Good morning. This is Poppy."

"Hello there. This is Lionel. I work with Albert at the museum here. Thanks for the cookies. I found them at the bottom of the drawer under Albert's journal on the history of the island and his spare teeth."

I tried to say, "Oh." But it came out more like "Eww."

"Yeah. He thinks the teeth will keep me out. Amateur. Anywhoo. I called the place on the bag, and the fella at La Dolce Vita said they were from you, and you'd been looking for some information."

"I was in a couple of days ago to ask about land records on my street."

"A couple days ago? I found your request buried under a stack of donation letters I was supposed to send out last month. Do you still need the information?"

"Yes, I definitely do."

"Well, it seems your ancestor, Callum McAllister, had an arrest record for carousing back in 1880. In fact, he had quite a few run-ins with the police all that same year. Being drunk in public. Disturbing the peace. There's even one here for endangering livestock."

"Is there any information on who made those complaints?"

Lionel chuckled. "Some of the reports list the neighbor at number thirty-two. That's the Crow's Nest B and B today. You familiar with it?"

"I definitely am."

"House was built in 1880. Of course, a few came in from number twenty. Apparently, Callum stole a pie from her windowsill."

Great. That's the Horseshoe Crab. Why is nothing simple?

"In fact, there are quite a few reports like this for ol' Callum's descendants over the decades."

"What do you mean?"

"The McAllisters seem to have had quite the history of unfortunate events when it comes to murder. I'm surprised Albert didn't tell you about that. It's all here in his book. Well . . . He's no spring chicken, and his mind is slipping, so . . ."

"Are you telling me that all my ancestors found murder victims?"

Lionel chuckled. "It seems to skip generations, but they're an unlucky sort. Always at the wrong place wrong time."

What the Frankincense?

"Okay then. Glad I could help. If you need anything else, Albert don't like anything raspberry. He says it tastes like soap. But I love it, if you catch my drift."

"I do indeed."

CHAPTER 36

I pulled out my cell phone and called my ride-or-die best friend. "Sawyer, what are you doing right now?"

"I just finished my third donut, and I'm about to get a fourth. Why?"

"The guy from the Historical Society just gave me a hot lead, and I need to go down to the Crow's Nest. Wanna go with?"

"Anything to get me away from these Boston creams. At the rate I'm going, I won't fit into my car. Meet you in ten?"

"I'll be the one standing next to the baby Jesus, who looks ashamed to be in my yard."

I hung up my cell phone and ran upstairs to change my clothes. Then I headed back down the spiral stairs to greet my guests. The dining room door moved an inch and stopped. I gave it a gentle push and heard something woosh against the floor. I stuck my head through and looked to see the mini-chow flat on his back with all four legs in the air. "Good morning General Tso."

He gave me a little tail wag.

Everyone else gave me pleasant greetings, including one Iris McAllister, whom I had told to vacate the premises. My poker face dropped for a moment, and my eyes narrowed into angry slits.

Iris picked up her juice glass and looked at the little old couple she was sitting next to. "I hear the parade tomorrow night is not to be missed."

Kenny peeked around the wall from the sitting room, the edge of a bucket inching into view. He gave me a droll look and smacked his lips before disappearing again. I walked through the sitting room to check on the champagne-fountain fiasco and caught a glimpse of my festive crime scene. Someone had hit the mayor on the head with an acorn, and he was bleeding out in the snow by Ye Olde Bank.

He was still having a better day than I was.

I grabbed my coat and waited outside by the manger scene for Sawyer to weave her little car through the crowd of gawkers lining the street in front of my house.

She parked in Mr. Winston's driveway and gave him a thumbs-up, which he returned. Then she slowly made her way to the edge of my yard, her eyes scanning Aunt Ginny's handiwork in all its glory, like she was doing a spot-the-difference picture. "What happened?"

"You know what happened."

"Yeah, but how did she get all this by you?"

"She has Smitty add new horrors every time I leave."

Sawyer's mouth hung open. Her eyes roved to the roof, where she audibly gasped at what I can only assume was the spaceship Santa.

A man across the street with two small children called out to me. "Hey, lady. Can you turn on those dancing snowmen?"

I sighed and flung my arm back and forth in front of the motion detector and a trio of jiggling Olafs started swaying side to side to the tune of "Do You Want to Build a Snowman?" while the kids squealed.

I walked down the driveway to rescue my best friend from stage-three retina burn. "Stop looking or you'll see blinking lights all day."

Sawyer rubbed her eyes as we headed towards the Crow's Nest. "Did I see Yoda in the manger, or did I imagine that?"

"Next to Darth Vader Joseph and the Stormtrooper wise men in the space nativity."

"Aunt Ginny's more out of control than usual."

"I blame the Senior Center Christmas party. She's determined to take down Mrs. Dodson at any cost, and the competitiveness is spilling over into other areas."

"Her whiskey fudge is going to be killer to beat."

"Especially with Neil being one of the judges."

We walked down the street until we stood in front of the blue-and-gray bed and breakfast.

The stately Second-Empire–style home had been an inn for as long as I could remember. With dark, silvery-blue siding, ornate gray bric-a-brac, and a bank of tall windows that ran along the front side of the wraparound porch, the three-story square home resembled a stack of presents. A decorative shingle hung from the first-floor eaves, displaying a black crow perched on a bare, gnarled tree branch.

Sawyer rubbed her hands over her arms. "I always thought this house was a little menacing for a beach vacation, don't you think?"

"I think they do really well with tourists who like ghost tours and graveyard walks."

"Mmm. Should we go knock on the door?"

"Yeah."

Neither of us moved.

"I should've peed before we left your house, but the penguin conga line distracted me."

"I almost ran the car into the garage door when I saw Rudolph staring back at me through the window."

We stood for another moment of silence.

Sawyer turned to me. "What are you gonna say to the owner here?"

"I don't know. That's why I brought you. You're the quick-thinking one."

She put a hand over her stomach. "I shouldna ate that fourth doughnut then."

"Maybe we should check out the Horseshoe Crab instead."

The front door opened, and a reedy woman stepped onto the porch. She had a broad smile, with a strong row of off-white teeth and deep wrinkles on either side of her mouth, like parentheses. "Well, are you all gonna stand out there all day or knock?"

Sawyer and I glanced at each other, then headed up the steps together. I put my hand out. "I'm Poppy. We've met a couple times at the innkeepers' meetings."

"I know who you are."

I dropped my hand to my side. "Right."

"I'm surprised we're not having rolling blackouts with all the energy you're consuming at your house."

"Sorry about that. I think my aunt regrets not signing up for the Victorian Homes Tour, like our neighbor across the street."

The woman's lips twitched into a semblance of a smile, and a street map of lines formed around her forehead. "Ginny always did love the spotlight." She put her hand out to Sawyer. "Patricia Morrison."

Sawyer nodded, focused on the woman's giant emerald ring that covered the top of three bony fingers. "Mmm. Nice to meet you."

She led us inside to a front parlor decorated in Wedgewood-blue wallpaper patterned in tiny colorful birds, the bottom half covered in white wainscoting, and took a seat. "Well, what can I do for you?"

I caught myself staring at her eyes. They were like twin pinpoints of intensity, crow's eyes. "I, um . . . We were wondering if you could tell us about your house."

Her lips twitched into a bemused grin. "My house? Whatever for?"

I looked to Sawyer for help.

"Uh . . . we're researching the history of the street."

Patricia chuckled. "After all this time? Why now?"

I'd gone silent for too long, and Sawyer pinched me in the back.

"For my newsletter."

"She's writing a newsletter."

"For my inn."

"The Butterfly Wings. Down the street?"

Patricia lazily crossed her legs and motioned for us to sit on the love seat across from her. "Yes. I'm very aware of your inn, Miss McAllister."

"Sorry."

She showed her teeth again. "Don't worry. I'm sure you'll get the hang of it eventually."

A foursome came down the arched stairway dressed in festive sweaters. They were carrying their coats. Patricia greeted them with practiced grace. "Don't you all look Christmassy. What are your plans for the day?"

They chatted easily about all the events Cape May had to offer for the holidays, while a ginger cat strode into the room and jumped into Patricia's lap and sent me a death glare. Once she'd sent the group on their way to a craft show at a local church, she stroked the cat with her ring hand and turned her eyes back on me. "So, you wanted to know about the history of the Crow's Nest for your newsletter?"

"If you don't mind."

Patricia pursed her lips, and all the little lines came together like a bar code around her mouth. "The house was built in 1879 by Stephen Button." She waved the back of her hand towards a portrait that was hanging over the fireplace. "My grandfather, Richard Noss, bought the house in the 1940s. When my late husband, David, passed—God rest his soul—I decided to turn it into a bed and breakfast to pay the upkeep. Being an innkeeper is a lost art."

I nodded, trying to form a question that wouldn't make me sound crazy.

Patricia stroked the orange cat and tapped her foot like a metronome, keeping time with my heartbeat. "Anything important you ladies want to know?"

I took a breath and dove in. "Do you know anything about Bettina Meier? Or maybe George Meier? He might have been her father or a brother?"

She cocked her head. "There is probably a lot of information about them at the Historical Society. You should check there. I'm surprised you don't know your Cape May history after growing up here. Most families pass that sort of information down one generation to the next. To have one of these wonderful homes and not know more about its origin should make one positively ashamed, don't you think?"

Is she insulting me?

Sawyer jumped in before I could say something we'd regret. "I've lived here my whole life, and there's still a lot I don't know about Cape May history. I'm just excited to find it out now. And it's amazing what Poppy has discovered after being home just a little over a year. She's a marvel at digging up information."

Patricia looked deep into my eyes with that intensity again. "Keep digging. I can't wait to hear what you uncover."

A family came in, looking for her to make them a dinner reservation, so we thanked her for her time, and she showed us out. Once she'd closed the door behind us, we fast-walked down the steps to be out of earshot. Sawyer whispered, "I can't tell if she was really sweet or a little creepy."

"A bit of both." I looked over my shoulder and saw Patricia watching us through the curtains in her front window. "There's the creepy."

She gave us a friendly wave goodbye.

I raised my hand and waved back. "And there's the sweet."

"See. It's really hard to tell."

"Maybe we're just imagining it since she's pretty salty about you having a B and B on the street."

"Hmm. Maybe."

We started the slow walk home. "I have to get to the bottom of this curse, if there is one. Maybe I'm just horribly unlucky. But things have to change. I'm going to be a mom soon. I can't be running into murder victims while taking Henry shoe shopping. Or have poisonous flowers with death threats delivered to the house where he's having playdates. People are already saying mean things."

"Who's saying?"

I shrugged. "Trolls."

Sawyer reached over and squeezed my hand. "Idiots."

"I need to protect him and let him be a child as long as possible. He shouldn't have to think about death and killers."

My cell phone buzzed a text from Tim.

911

What now? I glanced at my best friend. "What are you thinking?"

"Well. I'm thinking two things. One—you love Henry with all your heart, and you'll keep him safe. I'll be here to help you every step of the way."

"What's the second thing?"

"I should've peed at the Crow's Nest."

CHAPTER 37

"I don't actually work for you, Tim. You can't nine-one-one me because you're down a server. And I told you that I'd need time off for prior commitments."

Tim shut the office door behind him and Gigi, barricading me in the tiny room with the three of them, counting the baby. "I understand that, Mack. But Nikki just called out with a sick grandmother, and I could really use your help tonight."

"I'm leaving at six to go to Henry's play. I wouldn't miss it for the world."

Gigi's face went pink. "Tim was there for you when you were arrested, and this is how you repay him?"

"What part of 'I don't work here' are you two having trouble with? Do you actually want me to investigate Wes Bailey's murder? Or are you just looking for part-time help? Because if it's the latter, you can count me out. I've got enough work of my own to deal with at home. My mother showed up with a secret agenda, Aunt Ginny and her friends are planning my wedding without me, and my new mother-in-law has the contacts to have me whacked if I don't convert to Catholicism. Now if your emergency is about the investigation, how about you start helping by answering my questions instead of blowing me off?"

Tim's eyes narrowed. "I don't know what you're talking about. I've told you everything."

"Dude. You've told me nothing. Like what's the deal with the contract dispute between you and the guy who ended up in your freezer?"

Gigi whined. "What did you tell her?"

Tim waved his hand. "That's not relevant."

"And what was going on between the fish guy and Teela? She said she complained to you both that he was stalking her, and you did nothing about it."

The blood drained from Gigi's face. "She's such a drama queen. It was harmless. And she was the one leading him on when she thought he was rich. That's not our fault. If she was uncomfortable, she should have quit."

"Is that what you wanted? Did you encourage Wes to come on stronger so she would leave?"

Gigi lowered herself into the office chair, her breath becoming more ragged. "Where did you hear that?" She glanced at Tim. "I may have offered a little advice, but only because I wanted to see those two crazy kids happy. Besides, it's none of your business. And it has nothing to do with Wes's murder."

"Unless you killed him, you have no idea what does or doesn't have to do with his murder."

Gigi's nostrils flared. "Did you even find out that someone on our staff has a criminal record?"

Tim threw his head back and looked to the heavens. "I can't believe you went there, Geeg! Andrew is a good worker. I don't want to implicate him for Wes's murder and be wrong."

Andrew? "Are you actually saying you want me to convince Amber that Andrew killed Wes?"

Gigi squawked like a stool pigeon. "Yes! Why haven't you done it yet?"

"Arrests are public record, you ninny. Amber would already know if he has a criminal background. And if it was that heinous, he'd be down at the station right now. It doesn't mean he's a killer. If anything, it looks more suspicious that you're trying to throw the blame on him."

Gigi let out a howl that caused me to jump back and collide with Tim. She grabbed her stomach and doubled over.

Tim shoved me aside. It was a gentle shove, but a shove, nonetheless. "Geeg! What is it?"

"The baby's coming!"

"Are you sure? You're not due until January."

I probably should have offered to call the rescue squad or boil water or something. But my mind went straight to calculations. "She got pregnant in April?! Did you even wait for me to choose between you and Gia before you slept with her?"

"Yes, I waited!"

Gigi grabbed the edge of Tim's desk and cried out again. "Is this really the time?"

"You need to take her to the hospital, Tim."

Gigi sniped at me. "Ya think!"

"Come on, Geeg. Let's get you to the car."

Tim helped his baby mama out of the chair, and I kept chefs and servers out of their way so they could get through the door to the parking lot by screaming, "The baby's coming now! Move it, people!"

When the kitchen door shut behind them, I turned to Chuck and Tyler. "I'm still leaving at six tonight. I will not miss Henry's play."

Tyler gave me a nod. "You got it, boss."

Chuck saluted, and I grinned to myself. I'd hate to see them out of work if Maxine's was shut down. But if Tim and Gigi were guilty, there was very little I could do to stop the inevitable. They might not have stabbed Wes

Bailey, but they were about as innocent as a White House politician.

A wave of shame hit me for thinking that way about Tim. I'd known him since we were kids. He wasn't a killer. But then he was also never a cheater, and that was looking real iffy right now.

The kitchen door flew open, and Teela came running through, ripping her coat off. "Where's Tim? Chelle gave Andrew the office party. Reservations are supposed to go in my section. I need those tips. You can't begin to understand how hard it is to pay for my acting classes now that my dad only pays half."

Chelle arrived on the trainwreck's heels. "Girl, you are twenty minutes late. What do you think would have been fair? If I told them to sit there quietly until the princess arrives to fill their water glasses?"

Teela huffed and disappeared down the hall. A moment later, she returned. "Where is he?"

Tyler came out from behind the grill. "Your protector's not here. You're dealing with us tonight."

Teela scanned the kitchen, looking for someone to take her side. "Tim said I could have the groups. It's not my fault that I'm late. My mother hogged the bathroom, and I had to wait to put on my makeup in the good mirror."

Professional Poppy was on a break because I laughed right in front of the girl. My former Ukrainian chambermaid, Victory, had been a better employee.

"It's true! I told her I had to go to work, but she went in there anyway. And where the heck is Nikki?"

Chelle shook her head. "You gotta learn when to shut up."

Chuck cleared his throat. "Nikki called out, so you and Andrew will both need to pick up the slack."

Teela tossed her hair over her shoulder. "Are you serious? I'm a full-time student, and I've worked every night this week. Why does Nikki get a night off?"

Andrew shook his head and snorted. "You mean the acting classes you take at community college three days a week?"

I'd had enough. "Andrew, what's the office party doing?"

"Waiting on bar drinks."

"Go check in with Gabe to see if he needs help. Chelle, go back to your station in case other early birds arrive, and be ready to chip in. Teela, you're doing the back tables tonight. You were late. End of story. You can take it up with Tim when he's back. Everybody, move."

Chelle held my gaze and nodded. "You got it . . . *Mack.*"

"Your hair looks great."

We stared each other down for a beat, then Chelle backed away, while holding my gaze.

The front-end staff left through the dining room, grumbling along the way. Chuck and Tyler gave me a polite round of applause, and I felt the heat rise to my face. "I can try to find you a replacement for Nikki since it's a busy night, but you'll have to pay them."

Tyler grabbed an order slip as it printed off the ticket machine. "Do it. We can't be down a server plus two chefs, and you're leaving early."

I went back to Tim's office and pulled out my cell phone. I dialed Kenny.

"'Sup."

"Hey, you wanna make a little extra money tonight and spy on Tim's staff?"

"Do I have to take my clothes off?"

"No."

There was a pause. "I'll do it anyway. What is it?"

"Come on over to Maxine's, and I'll give you a server's apron."

"Can I get dinner on the house?"

"Absolutely. Chuck and Tyler will hook you up."

"On my way. Just let me lock up the silver and set a diversion for Iris."

Kenny clicked off, and I shoved my phone down in my pocket. I was about to head to the walk-in to see how much crème brûlée was left when I noticed Tim had run out without locking his laptop.

I checked down the hallway, then shut the office door. I had a moment of *maybe I shouldn't be doing this,* that I squashed with a rebuff of *Tim asked me to find the truth.* Whether he meant the whole truth, or just the truth about everyone except for him and Gigi, I was no longer sure about. I just knew that I needed some answers so I could get my life back.

I opened Tim's accounting software, saw the bank balance, and had a moment of panic for the staff. I didn't know when payroll was supposed to run, but they needed a sold-out night tonight if Tim was going to keep the lights on. *That's a lot of overdue bills.*

I checked the vendors tab and clicked on Deepwater Fisheries. The account went back a few years, but there had been a dramatic increase in costs over the past year. Only the totals were listed, no description of what was bought. If the checking account was any indication, Tim wouldn't be able to pay the seafood bill without a Christmas miracle.

Like the owner dying before he could collect.

No. Tim isn't like that.

I moved to the employees tab. Andrew started at the end of April. His name was starred for some reason. Chelle, Gabe, and Teela all had start dates listed on the exact same day in June. That must have been when Tim and Gigi merged restaurants. No other name set off alarm bells quite as loud as the one who wasn't there.

Nikki was missing from the employee file. No start date. No Social Security number, and no paychecks on file.

I heard a clang in the kitchen and froze. Trying to hear over my thumping heart, I waited for someone to come down the hall and catch me.

Ten seconds. Twenty.

Nothing.

I closed the bookkeeping software and moved to the file cabinet. The second drawer was full of employee records. Everyone except Nikki the ghost.

I pulled Teela's file. If Joanne was right, I would find a copy of the complaint Teela made against Wes inside.

Joanne was never right. The folder was empty. Well, not totally empty. It had an application for employment. An application that listed Teela's age as thirty-six. Whoa! I took a moment to let that sink in. She must be a really good actress because she is totally pulling off that help-less twenty-year-old schtick.

Her list of previous employers was as long as my arm, with a reason next to each one for why things didn't work out. Everyone she'd ever worked for had taken advantage of her in some way. One of her bosses fired her for attack-ing her manager. *What the heck was that all about?*

I snapped a picture with my cell phone, shoved the file back in the drawer, and pulled the others.

Chelle either had an impressive résumé of work expe-rience or she had done a significant amount of padding. Maybe she *had* worked for Guy Fieri. Who was I to say? *Snap.*

Andrew was hired as part of a bonding program for ex-cons. No charge was listed, but he had finished a court-ordered anger-management program. *Snap.*

Gabriel's file had something the others didn't have. A dishonorable discharge from the Marines. *Oh.*

That sounded really bad, but maybe it was one of those things that sounds worse than it is. Like that time Mrs. Dodson had congestive heart failure and we thought it meant imminent death, but a diuretic fixed everything, and she was back at bingo the next night.

Then I noticed someone had written "assault" in the margin.

I took more pictures and put the folders away. I found the vendor files in the next drawer. I thumbed through them until I found the Deepwater Fisheries account. It was thick with a capital K. I hoisted it out and laid it on the desk.

Tim had bought a lot of seafood over the years. I leafed through the stack and saw charges for shrimp, mussels, sea bass, tilapia, oysters. Recent invoices looked different. Wes was getting sloppy. One of them had the product name smudged like it had got stuck in the printer.

There was a crumpled invoice shoved in the middle dated from a few weeks ago. Three hundred dollars for shark fin. *Eww. Who's gonna order a plate of shark fin? Gross.*

A bright pink sticky note was stuck to the back scrawled with *You wouldn't want this to go public. Give Gunter's Produce a call and save money!* The handwriting looked familiar. I took a picture. Then I tabbed through my photos to the one I took of the note Teela dropped. They were the same. So . . . the note was from Wes Bailey. But when was it left? And if it was really meant for Teela, why did she lie about it?

I found the contract in the back of the folder. It was set for three years, and Tim had another year left before it was over. The terms were fabulous—if you were Deepwater Fisheries. A base order was listed for weekly deliveries billed at a market rate to be determined by the supplier.

Deepwater Fisheries could raise rates whenever they wanted, and Tim would have to pay, or he'd be in breach of contract. The penalty for being in breach was a lawsuit.

I set the contract on the desk and picked up the Post-it note. Someone was blackmailing Tim, but for what? And what the heck was Tim doing with shark fin? It wasn't on the menu.

I dug through the trash can and found a balled-up wad of paper under some napkins, an empty can of Red Bull, and a used bottle of prenatal vitamins. It was a letter printed on Seymour Veg letterhead appealing to Tim not to break their contract. Jackson had handwritten, "I'm begging you to reconsider your actions. Don't make me do something you'll regret."

I pushed the laptop away from me to smooth out the threat and take a picture of it with my phone. The desk blotter shifted, revealing a corner of a paper hiding underneath. I gave it a tug. It was a one-year contract for seafood delivery with Atlantic Coast Seafood, signed by Gigi. The date was only a few weeks ago. For the past month, Maxine's had two seafood vendors, and the one run by Wes Bailey was threatening to sue.

I wonder if the lawsuit was off now that the owner was dead. *Fat lot of good that would do Tim from jail.*

I was too engrossed in what I was reading. I never heard the footsteps coming down the hall. Or the scrape of the door handle turning.

And then it was too late.

CHAPTER 38

"What are you doing in my office!" Tim was frozen halfway through the door, with his hand still on the doorknob. His eyes went wide, and he jumped into the room and threw the door closed behind him.

"Where's Gigi? I thought she was in labor."

"False alarm. She felt better after we left, so we called her doctor, and he put her on bed rest to be safe." Tim's eyes roved from the look of shock and horror on my face to the papers in my hands. His glare was so hot I worried it would melt my mascara. "Why are you in here?"

"Um." I looked around for a way out. *Can I shimmy through that vent to escape this tiny office? No. Probably not. Wait. Why should I run?* "I'm doing what you asked me to do, Tim. I'm looking for something that casts suspicion on one of your employees."

Tim stared at the Atlantic Coast Seafood contract on the desk. He ran his hands through his hair and looked like he was about to fry up a conniption and serve it with a big side of meltdown. "Where did you get that?"

"It was under the blotter. Did you know about it?"

"Of course, I knew about it."

I held up the signed contract for Deepwater Fisheries. "You know this makes you look guilty. I'm trying my best to give the police another suspect, but I keep finding evidence that casts suspicion on you and Gigi."

Tim's eyes flared with a burst of anger that I hadn't seen since college. "Alright. Yes. Gigi went behind my back and signed a contract with Atlantic Coast Seafood so we could save money. She was trying to rescue Maxine's. She didn't realize I still had a year left on my contract with Deepwater Fisheries and I couldn't afford to buy it out. She only knew we were getting taken advantage of by Wes Bailey."

"You were getting more than taken advantage of, Tim. The terms of this contract are outrageous. You should report him to the Better Business Bureau." *Oh right.* "Well, I guess it's too late for that. But these rates are criminal."

Tim shoved his hands in his pockets and wouldn't look me in the eye. "It's no big deal."

I picked up the smoothed-out letter from Jackson Seymour. "Is that why you tried to break your contract with Seymour Veg? To get a discount from Wes if you switched produce suppliers?"

"It's this economy. Prices are going up everywhere. It's happening with all my vendors."

I tapped the Deepwater Fisheries contract. "This isn't inflation, my friend. This is extortion. Wes Bailey raised your rates by thirty percent over the past year, citing market fluctuations. What does that even mean?"

Tim kicked the trash can. "It means whatever he wants it to mean. He raised my rates by five percent every month when I wouldn't switch all my suppliers to his vendor alliance. I was too embarrassed to tell Gigi that I failed to read the fine print on the penalties. She expects me to have all the answers."

"Sure. I mean, after all, you are her mentor."

Tim threw me a sardonic scowl. "And I didn't want the

police to find out about that contract because it would incriminate her. Gigi didn't kill Wes."

"She did threaten to kill him."

"That isn't the same thing, and you of all people should know that."

I opened the Deepwater Fisheries folder and pulled out a couple of invoices. "What's up with this shark fin? What is that?"

Tim's face went scarlet. "Nothing. You're not a chef, Poppy. Sometimes we experiment in the kitchen with new products."

"Is that what shark fin is? A new product?"

He snatched the invoice from my hand. "Where did you see that?"

"On this weird invoice from Wes Bailey that looks different than the others. And he left a note threatening to expose you."

He ripped the invoice to pieces. "Have you found anything useful that will actually help me?"

"Why are you paying Nikki cash under the table?"

"This again? Why are you so focused on Nikki? I told you it's not a big deal. Nikki works for tips as a 1099. I couldn't verify her Social, and she said she might have written it down wrong. She'll bring in her card as soon as she can find it in a box she hasn't unpacked. Until then, I pay her in cash."

"That's illegal. And it's a great way to get yourself taken advantage of. And what's up with three employees with a history of anger issues? Do you get some kind of kickback for hiring people who assault their coworkers?"

"I asked you to help me clear Gigi's name, not cause a lot of problems. Why don't you stick to questioning the staff about their alibis."

"A killer will lie about their alibi, Tim! You need evidence! Every single person Gigi brought over is waving a big red flag. We already know Wes was blackmailing you for something. What if he was blackmailing one of them too? Any one of them could have snapped and killed him."

"They all have issues that make it hard for them to get hired. I like to give people second chances. But after you, I'm learning to regret it."

"You want to go head-to-head with me on a lifetime of regrets? Bring it on. But quit lying to me and using me as free kitchen labor under the false pretense of wanting help. You know what? That's it. I'm leaving. I wish you and your baby mama success in beating murder charges. You're gonna need it."

CHAPTER 39

I bolted from the office and grabbed my coat and purse without slowing down. Chuck and Tyler silently followed my exodus with wide eyes. I slammed the door in lieu of saying goodbye and left a piece of my soul on the other side. As soon as the door closed, I burst into tears. *Oh Tim, I trusted you. When did you start lying to me?*

I turned the corner to my car and ran into the homeless man. He was up against the building, staring into the side window. "What are you doing up here? You know they'll call the cops on you."

He replied, "Judgment Day is coming. You need to be ready."

Okaaaay. I got in my car and cranked it to life. The radio came on. Bruce Springsteen was midway through "Santa Claus Is Coming to Town," and I spun him off. I laid my forehead against the steering wheel. *Maybe Springsteen owns the radio station.*

A flicker of frustration crossed my mind. *I never got to ask Tyler why he was detained. And I forgot to get the picture of the contract. Well, it's not like it would help anyway. I mean, it would help literally everyone except Tim*

*and Gigi. And what is the homeless man doing staring
into the kitchen? How often does that happen?*

Kenny pulled into Maxine's as I was pulling out. He
stopped and rolled down his window. "Aunt Ginny
thought you'd be gone longer. You might not want to go
home just yet."

"Why?"

He bit his lip. "I'm not allowed to tell you. But I'm
sure you'll hear it from Nell really soon."

I drove home with my heart pounding in my ears, like
thundering reindeer hooves were leading the way.

I heard the mariachis as soon as I turned the corner
onto my street and came to a dead stop. A line of traffic
was backed up to Ocean Drive. It was a slow crawl to my
house.

A slow, foreboding crawl.

Toward flashing lights and dancing snowmen. And
three wise men playing guitar to "Feliz Navidad" blaring
through a loudspeaker at the top of my lawn. Aunt Ginny
was dressed as a very pregnant eighty-year-old Virgin
Mary and was handing out candy canes while a parade of
light-up penguins were sailing around the yard on a track.
Smitty was on one of the chimneys, attaching what looked
like a dancing reindeer in sunglasses.

Nell's beautiful Victorian Christmas Homes Tour that
she'd been preparing for all week was underway across
the street. At least I assumed it was. Her house looked deserted. Everyone was in front of my monstrosity, where
Christmas had thrown up all over my yard.

I slow-rolled past the house and held eye contact with
Aunt Ginny as the opening notes of Run DMC's "Christmas in Hollis" blasted out of the speaker on the front
porch. The virgin knew she'd been made, but she flinched
not.

I took the Corvette around the block and parked at
Mr. Murillo's house behind us. I cut across his yard and

went in through the back door. Figaro was waiting for me, his tail flicking angrily. Something had annoyed his lordship. We had words, then I followed him into the kitchen to fill his bowl. I opened the cabinet where we kept the King Tut wet food and found General Tso face-planting into the side of the bag of Gourmet Kitty Krunchies, sound asleep.

Figaro hissed at the pouf.

I gave the mini chow chow a little nudge. "Now you've gone too far, my friend."

He turned his head in my direction and blinked his tiny eyes. A blue tongue shot out and licked my hand. I was able to coax him out of the cabinet and gave him a bowl of fresh water. Figaro ate his tuna-and-lobster feast with one eye trained on the tiny bear-dog.

I started my espresso machine and went to the refrigerator for oat milk. There was a note held on the door with a somewhat naughty fireman magnet.

Ginny, I made five sample cakes. Which four do you want for the Christmas Party? PS—We ran out of regular flour, so I had to use Poppy's gluten-free blend, so don't blame me if they taste like crap. We'll need to buy more of both ASAP.

Under that, Aunt Ginny had scrawled. *I have no idea, Joanne. I like them all. Poppy, what do you think?*

Under that, a printed photo of Mrs. Dodson peeking in the mudroom door with the words "Beware of sneaky peepers" written in red Sharpie across the top.

I looked around the kitchen for remnants of cake. Five Post-it notes were lined up on the banquette, but only four mini cakes remained. They were covered in plastic, each one labeled.

White cake with raspberry filling and whipped cream.

Coconut cake with lemon curd.

Chocolate cake with peanut-butter ganache.

Carrot cake with brandy cream cheese.

The vanilla-bean cake with mocha buttercream and chocolate espresso beans was missing.

I looked at Fig. "Is this heaven? Did I finally have that stroke?"

I made my cappuccino and sat at the table. Each cake was the size of a cereal bowl and had already suffered a direct attack from Aunt Ginny. I tasted all four. Then I ate half the raspberry whipped cream cake, taking out my anger and frustration in every bite. I made myself stop before it got embarrassing. Okay, after it got embarrassing, but before it got shameful.

It may have been a little bit shameful.

I was ashamed.

I left a note on the paper that the raspberry was my favorite and wrapped up the cakes that I hadn't demolished, then headed up the hidden stairs to my bedroom. The neon lights from the Vegas strip in my yard bounced around my room like a disco. I pulled the shades and turned on some holiday jazz to try and drown out the Christmas on crack soundtrack that was playing the obnoxious hippopotamus song in my front yard.

I sent Amber the pictures I'd taken at Maxine's. Then I grabbed my laptop and did a deep dive on Deepwater Fisheries, checking review and complaint sites. If I was hoping for a lot of unhappy customers, I was sorely disappointed. They had stellar reviews. Mostly five stars, with just a few outliers complaining that Wes sold them farmed blue crabs and illegally charged them for wild-caught. *I don't know how you would be able to tell the difference.*

I tried different search terms, like "Wes Bailey and sexual harassment." Then "Deepwater Fisheries and extortion." Nothing. I was at the end of the internet and couldn't find anything accusatory. Until I found a report on the Better Business Bureau site from Harry K. The names were replaced with asterisks, but I knew who it was. "W***** sold me counterfeit seafood and threatened to ruin me if I didn't pay his exorbitant penalties and switch all my contracts to his vendors."

I did a search for NOAA, Office of Law Enforcement. I called the twenty-four-hour hotline—because apparently people have fish emergencies at three a.m.—to ask a few questions about Deepwater Fisheries and what shark fin was used for.

Within a few minutes, the very nice lady was asking more questions of me than I was asking of her.

"Where are you calling from, hon?"

"Cape May."

"Are you aware of any local establishment selling counterfeit fish or shellfish?"

"Um . . . possibly. I think there may have been an unscrupulous fisherman down here."

"Hold, please."

She disappeared for a bit, then returned to the line. "Do you happen to have any documentation that you could send me? Product labels? Invoices? Photographs?"

"I was really just looking for the information."

"Yes, I understand. It's against the law for seafood to be improperly labeled by a wholesaler or reseller. Are you aware of anyone buying or selling shark fin?"

A curl of fear unwound in my chest. "Shark fin? Why?"

"Shark fin is commonly used in scallop fraud."

I felt my mouth go dry. "Oh. I didn't know that."

"They cut the fin with a metal round and sell it as sea scallops. Sometimes they use skate or surimi. It's a felony to mislabel seafood. Which establishment did you say you were calling from?"

I never once said anything about Tim or Maxine's. "I'm not calling from anywhere . . . I'm just doing research . . . for a blog. The Mommies Blog."

"Uh-huh."

Apparently, mislabeling seafood for profit is a big fat illegal deal. For both the distributor and the restaurant. My stomach gave a sick little quiver. How many times had I eaten scallops from Tim's restaurant? Surely, they weren't shark fin cutouts. Tim wouldn't do that. *Would he?*

"Okay, hon. Well, you need to let us know if you're aware of anyone who might be involved. Seafood fraud is very serious. There are several investigations ongoing in your area, especially for counterfeit scallops. You don't want to be found complicit by withholding information."

"No ma'am. I'll call you back if I have any further questions. For the blog."

I got off the phone as quickly as possible. Tim had been buying illegal seafood—by accident or intentionally I didn't know. And he couldn't report Wes because he was threatening to take Tim down with him.

Wes was an extortioner. I wondered how many of his customers found themselves dangling at the end of an unethical contract that they couldn't get out of for fear of being reported to NOAA. They wouldn't even have to have ordered illegal seafood. Wes would only need to falsify invoices for them to look guilty.

I didn't know how Tim got himself involved in fish fraud, or how deep the conspiracy went, but that was surely the leverage Wes Bailey was using to keep Tim on the hook.

And once again, all evidence pointed to Tim and Gigi.

CHAPTER 40

There was a light rapping on my bedroom door. I expected it to be Iris, checking to see if she could ransack my room again, so I ignored it.

"*Bella*, are you ready to go?"

I threw the door open to find Gia grinning. He was devilishly handsome in black jeans, a black T-shirt, and a slim brown leather jacket. My breath caught in my throat.

"What time is it?"

He kissed me. "Time for Henry's play. You were supposed to meet me at the coffee shop. What happened?"

"Tim and I had a fight, and I walked out. I was doing research on the guy who died, and I fell down a rabbit hole. I just need to get dressed."

"I will wait." He sat on the love seat, giving me a mischievous grin.

I sashayed to the bathroom door. "Joke's on you. My dress is in here."

He sucked his teeth and playfully sighed.

I went into the bathroom and changed into a rust-colored sweater dress and a black leather jacket. I came out and pulled on tall black leather boots.

Gia whistled appreciatively. "This play better be really good to compete with that."

I giggled and grabbed my purse. "Follow me."

I led Gia to the hidden staircase by Kenny's room and beckoned him to follow me down.

"What in the world is this? Did you know that naughty picture was on the wall there?"

"That's one of my great-uncle's mistresses, and he hid it in here to get back at my aunt for not letting him go to the casino."

We arrived in the pantry and popped out into the kitchen.

Aunt Ginny was sitting at the table dressed in her Virgin Mary regalia, eating an Italian hoagie during her break. "Geez Louise, you scared the salami out of me."

I swept my hand in an arc like a tour director. "And here we have the original mother of Jesus, who doesn't look a day over eighty due to her liberal use of Noxzema cold cream."

Aunt Ginny stuck her tongue out, and Gia snorted.

I grabbed the box of dairy-free cupcakes for my little man and swept through the kitchen out to the hall. Henry was lying on the floor by the grand staircase, giggling uncontrollably, as General Tso stood on his chest and licked his face.

"Look, Poppy, it's a bear."

"That's a puppy." I snapped my fingers. "General Tso. Take five. Come, Piccolo. We don't want to be late to get into costume."

Henry popped up to follow, and Gia snickered, not so silently, beside me. "This is one of my favorite days ever."

After depositing the cupcakes in the party room and Henry with his teacher for his "nutcracker transformation," we took our seats, and I filled Gia in on my fight with Tim.

"*Bella*, I know you don't want to believe it, but is it possible that Tim is guilty?"

"Then why would he ask me to question his staff?"

"Maybe he thought he'd look more innocent if he invited Cape May's Jessica Fletcher to look around."

The house lights went down, and prerecorded music started to play through the speakers. The next hour was awesome. The play was horrible. We weren't even sure what the story was. It seemed to be about a bunch of toys on Christmas Eve. Every time a kid forgot a line or mugged the audience, looking for his parents, it was pure gold.

Henry marched out as a nutcracker in his thick glasses and scanned the crowd. When he spotted us, he grinned and held up a plastic stick. "Look, Daddy, I have a sword."

The teacher frantically waved her hands for him to keep going, but once the audience had started laughing, it went straight to his head, and he hammed it up even more.

He goose-stepped across the stage and brandished his sword at Raggedy Ann and a dancing dreidel. A pretty little ballerina pranced onto the stage, and Henry took her by the hand. He led her around in a big arc. He was so busy grinning at us instead of watching where he was going that he led her right into a giant book of nursery rhymes who loudly complained, "Watch it, Henry!"

I was laughing so hard I'd wiped half the mascara off my eyes.

When the cast took their bows, we gave a very rousing round of applause and waited for Henry in the party room. He skipped across the floor and made a beeline for my side, still in costume but sans sword—smart teacher—and chatted nonstop.

"Did you see me? I saved the ballerina from the evil sheeps and took her to Santa."

Gia's eyebrows dipped together. "Are you sure that was the story?"

Henry nodded excitedly. "Uh-huh. And the ballerina is my best friend, Amelia." He put his hand out to me. "Com'ere. I want to show you. She just moved here from Florida, but that's a secret."

I put my hand in his and let him lead me across the room to meet his little friend.

"Amelia, this is my new mommy."

The little brunette with big green eyes took my hand in both of hers. "Hello, Henry's mom. It's very nice to meet you. This is my mom. Mom!"

The woman being beckoned to was in conversation with the teacher. She turned at the sound of Amelia's voice. "Just a minute, baby."

The woman froze like a statue, with the words barely out of her mouth as we stared each other down.

Amelia pulled her mother's hand. "Mommy. This is Henry's new mom that I told you about."

I lifted my hand in a weak wave. "Hello, Nikki."

Nikki pulled Amelia to her side.

"How's your grandmother?" I asked. "Was she able to come to the play?"

Amelia's little face screwed up in confusion. "Grannie lives in Florida. She lives too far away to drive."

Nikki kept her eyes on mine, but I saw a gentle nudge of her foot against Amelia's.

Amelia's eyes shifted from me to Henry to her mother.

Nikki kept her voice light and breezy. She gave a lilting little chuckle. "No, silly, Granma Betty. The one we live with that we take care of. You know."

Amelia's gaze shifted to my boots. "Oh yeah. We moved from New York to take care of my Granma Betty, and she's really sick, and Mom has to take care of her every day."

Henry was oblivious to her deception. "I thought you lived next to Mickey."

Nikki chuckled. "Those were Disney vacations, honey."

Amelia dropped her attention to her ballet shoe. "Sorry, Henry."

Henry shrugged it off. "That's okay. Can Amelia come over and play during Christmas break? We can make cookies."

Gia and I looked at each other to suss out the other's thoughts on a playdate. Gia gave Nikki a nod. "It would be fine with me."

I watched Nikki's face very closely. "We could do it at my house. My aunt has everything possible in the yard that lights up or sings a song. It's not Disney World, but Amelia might get a kick out of it."

Amelia tugged Nikki's hand. "Can I, Mommy? Can I?"

Nikki put her loose hand over the one holding Amelia's, and the child grew quiet. "We'll have to wait and see."

I pulled out my cell phone. "Should I text you?"

Nikki shrugged. "Sorry. My phone is dead."

Amelia looked into her mother's face. "No, it isn't, Mommy. You just got a call from your work before the play. The mean lady wanted you to come in."

Nikki's eyelids fluttered, and she breathed out a chuckle. "Amelia, why don't you and Henry go enjoy the party. Didn't you say Henry's mom made him special cupcakes?"

Amelia took Henry's hand. "Come on, Henry. Let's be manatees."

"Stay where I can see you."

"Yes, Mommy."

They skipped off to play, and Nikki turned to me with eyes that were dark as coal. "It's hard enough to get a job that lets me work around my grandmother's medical needs. I don't want my employer knowing I'm a single mom. I'd appreciate it if you kept this to yourself."

"My lips are sealed."

"I know you tell Tim everything, but this is important. And especially keep it from Gigi. I'm already on thin ice for taking off last week when Amelia had strep. I told her my grandmother had pneumonia."

"Gigi's about to have a baby of her own. She's bound to be more understanding of your circumstances."

Nikki ran her long fingernails through her dark hair. "I wouldn't count on it. She doesn't like it when you rock the boat. That restaurant comes before everything else, even Tim. She nearly fired Teela for being rude to the fish guy because she was concerned he'd raise his rates again."

"I was under the impression Teela was being harassed by Wes."

Nikki scanned the room for Amelia. "She brought that on herself. But Gigi refused to step in because she said it was bad for business to be rude to the vendors, and Teela should just get another job if she was so worried about it."

"And Teela didn't want to do that?"

"I think she's burned a lot of bridges, and Tim is her last hope."

"So I gather you don't stay after for cocktails because you have to get home to Amelia?"

Nikki craned her head to look through the crowd of kids playing with the shepherd crooks. "I get so little time with her since she started school. I don't want to waste it sitting in a bar, drinking with people I barely know. She's my everything. Amelia! I'm sorry. I have to go find her."

Nikki pushed through the parents and disappeared into the crowd.

I looked at Gia. "That was weird, right?"

He was still looking across the room after where she'd gone. "Mmm. I bet there is no grandmother."

"That seems kinda extreme just to hide that you're a single mom."

Gia nodded. "And why does she think you tell Tim everything?"

"I don't know, but I have a bad feeling that someone at Maxine's has been blabbing."

CHAPTER 41

"No one wants to eat Christmas crime-scene cookies, Joanne."

Kenny took another peppermint candlestick from the tray and popped it in his mouth. "Speak for yourself."

Joanne put the finishing touches on her noose cookie. "That's where you're wrong; they absolutely love it. Those new guests from Tennessee checked in last night, and they already left a five-star review about the cookies and the Dickens serial-killer village. Hashtag murder house owns it."

Georgina walked in carrying a cake plate. "Found this in the hall outside Iris's bedroom."

Joanne shook her head and sighed. "That explains the missing vanilla-bean cake Poppy didn't get to try."

Georgina put the plate in the sink. "We might need to start locking up food at night if she's going to come in here and help herself." She grabbed a cup of coffee and a festive noose cookie and left through the dining room.

I spooned another dollop of cheesy dough onto my cookie sheet. "I keep expecting to hear that she's wanted by Interpol for international fraud."

Joanne snorted. "She was on the phone with her lawyer yesterday, so maybe she knows that's coming."

I put the third tray of cheese puffs in the top oven and hollered for Aunt Ginny. "Did you arrange for someone to pick up the hors d'oeuvres for the Senior Center?"

A loud metal clang came from the pantry. Aunt Ginny shrieked. "That was just my girdle. You stay out of here while I set this dessert on my mother's good cake plate. And just worry about your own self. We're leaving at two thirty to get down to the beach for the Christmas Sandman Competition."

"Aunt Ginny, I don't have time for that."

Something that sounded like a tower of metal lids fell over. "Geez Louise, who put those there. No excuses! I told you weeks ago we were going to the annual event together. It's a big charity doo, and you're part of the community now, so we're going to attend."

"What about the food for the Senior Center party?"

"I got my dance instructor coming to help me load Lila's van when we get back."

"You're gonna trust Mr. Shake Your Boom Boom Ricardo with something as important as that secret dessert entry?"

Kenny did a quick cha-cha move. "I'll be here to help the pensioners load the goods. Don't worry."

Another loud bang came from the pantry. "Crackers!"

Joanne put some silver sprinkles on a knife cookie. "Are you okay in there?"

"Stay out!"

I sniffed the air. "Do you smell that?"

Joanne lifted her head. "Is it almond?"

I sniffed again. "No. It's not almond. I don't know what it is. I'm not sure I've ever smelled anything like it."

Aunt Ginny banged on the door. "You two stop that sniffing. You'll see my dessert when I unveil it tonight. Joanne, did you finish those cakes yet? I told you the peanut butter is my top priority."

Joanne kept right on decorating her murder weapons with festive little flourishes. "You know I did. Except for the raspberry one that Figaro knocked off the counter."

I cut circles in my puff-pastry dough for the cranberry-Brie bites. "Aww. I liked that one."

"So did General Tso."

Kenny handed Joanne the bloodred frosting. "There was an incident with Figaro and the stuffed blue jay. Neither the blue jay nor the cake made it."

The pantry door slowly creaked open, and Aunt Ginny carried a domed cake stand covered with a red-and-green tea towel gingerly to the mudroom. She locked the door and pointed a finger at each of us. "Don't anyone go in there. And keep your eyes peeled for that sneak, Edith."

She disappeared down the hall, and we immediately started talking about her.

Joanne took a batch of lemon revolvers out of the bottom oven and set them on a rack to cool. "She is not gonna handle it well if she loses tonight."

Kenny snorted. "Yeah, but what can she do? I mean, she won't try to burn the place down or anything, will she?"

We all grew quiet for a moment as we worried about Aunt Ginny's lust for retribution.

"I have a box of Amaretto truffles I've been saving in case Edith wins again. They're in the cabinet, hiding inside a box of quinoa, in case you need them in an emergency."

Kenny nodded. "Duly noted."

Figaro slunk into the kitchen, covered in glitter with something clamped in his mouth, and skirted the perimeter. General Tso was on his heels licking his chops looking for some quid pro quo. They were followed by Georgina, who was holding a shredded bag of sorts. She frantically looked around the room, waving the tattered plastic. "That cat and his new partner in crime stole four of Smitty's presents from under my tree and shredded them open."

I stared at the bag in Georgina's hand. "Which tree do you think is yours?"

"That isn't important. Those two ate an entire bag of Wagyu beef jerky. It's twenty-two dollars an ounce."

I cornered my naughty cat by the dishwasher. He had an entire piece of jerky in his mouth, and he made a preemptive swat in the mini chow's direction when I picked him up. "What have you done? Kenny, please take the jerky packaging to the sisters and tell them what happened. Make sure there is nothing in there that will make General Tso sick. And you, Sir Figaro Newton. You are out of control."

Figaro was trying to chomp the jerky down as fast as possible, but I wrangled it away from him.

"You are going on a diet right after the holidays, mister."

Figaro's ears flattened, and he tried to wriggle out of my grasp. I took him out on the deck and held him up above my head to let the wind blow the glitter out of his cottony fur.

Kenny appeared in the doorway and sang out a ridiculous version of the opening of "Circle of Life" from *The Lion King*. "Naaaan ingonyama bagiti baba."

I busted out laughing. Until Aunt Ginny ran back into the kitchen, yelling, "You will not believe what she's done now."

Kenny and I hauled butt to get back in there and see what drama was unfolding.

Aunt Ginny was pacing. "That Nell knows she can't compete with my Christmas display, so she added five grapevine reindeer to her sled. One of them has a red nose. Can you believe it? A red nose!"

I cast my eyes from Aunt Ginny to Kenny, then Joanne, then Georgina, and then realized I was still holding Fig up in the air. He started to purr. Fig had grown immune to Aunt Ginny's tirades long ago. Plus, he was drunk on jerky.

Aunt Ginny picked up the phone. "People are starting to pass my house to look across the street. I need to call Smitty to add . . ."

"No!" We all yelled in unison.

Figaro objected and squirmed until I put him down. "We're going to need to take out a loan to pay for the electric bill as it is now."

Kenny gently backed me up. "You may be the reason it hasn't snowed. The heat coming off this house from your million light bulbs is melting it before it hits the ground."

I added, "And our roof wasn't built to hold three Santas and a spaceship. If you add anything else, it's going to collapse."

Aunt Ginny's lips flattened down until her cheeks puffed out. "Oh, it is not." She thought for a minute. "What about one of those air-dancer things like they have at grand openings? They don't weigh much."

Joanne handed Aunt Ginny a plate of finished Christmas weaponry. "Here, why don't you go put these out and take a picture for Instagram. I bet Nell doesn't have murder-weapon cookies at her house."

Aunt Ginny held the plate aloft and slid her eyes to Joanne. She gave an evil little grin. "I bet you're right."

Georgina took out her cell phone. "Come on. I'll help you post it. I'm getting pretty good at the gram."

They left through the dining room door, and Aunt Ginny randomly hollered, "Shut up, Iris. No one cares."

The front door opened, and Amber came around the corner. I fantasized that the international background check had arrived and Iris McAllister was wanted by MI6.

"You know the constable's head is stuck in a bucket in front of the Dickens church."

"Yeah. He was waterboarded. I think the baker's wife finally got even for her husband being shot."

Amber picked up a frosted lead pipe. "Festive. Hello, Joanne. Kenny. Where'd you all get the tiny crime-scene tape?"

They both shrugged. Joanne said, "We don't know who's doing it or where they came from. It's just a different murder every day."

The timer went off, and I removed my cheese puffs and put in the tray of Brie bites. "Well, if it's that sweet little old couple, today will be the last day because they check out at eleven."

Amber looked on top of the fridge. "What do you have today?"

"I have my dad's peanut-butter fudge." I reached for a tin can and pulled off the lid.

Amber inhaled deeply. "Oh yeah." She took a large square and bit it in half. "That's the stuff."

"It's his secret recipe, which was probably on the can of sweetened condensed milk in the seventies." I put the tin aside so she could help herself. "What's up?"

Her words came out garbled through the mouthful of fudge. "Need an update."

"Want to go in the sunroom?"

She nodded and picked up the can to take it along. We sat in white-leather wing chairs across from each other in the pewter-colored room, the fudge between us on the coffee table. The pink-and-maroon Victorian tree in the tower sparkled under the glow of white lights and frosted glass balls. The Biddies had done a lovely job of decorating it. The lace and pearls were expertly draped, although I suspected Aunt Ginny may have moved them around after everyone had left since there were none on the top third of the tree.

I nudged the can closer to Amber. "Why'd you impound Tyler's truck?"

"We got a tip to check the security camera at the marina. The footage clocked him entering the parking lot just before two a.m. last Friday."

"Tip from who?"

"I don't know, but someone's watching out for us."

"Or setting Tyler up to take the fall."

"They impounded the truck to check for evidence. And he lied about his alibi."

"I can't believe Tyler would kill anyone. For what motive?"

"He's had pretty severe financial problems in the past. Four years ago, he lost his restaurant, Devon's Steaks and Seafood. Deepwater Fisheries was his fish supplier. Maybe there's a connection."

"But Tyler knows I'm investigating. He's been helping me."

"Doesn't mean he's been telling the truth. Maybe he's been throwing you off."

"I don't buy it. Tyler has worked for Tim for almost a year, and he'd seen Wes deliver every day. Why would he wait until now to get revenge?"

Amber nudged the lid on the can and took another square of fudge. "Maybe he was waiting for the perfect opportunity."

"Stabbing is deeply passionate. I can't imagine bottling that kind of hate for four years, and then, one random day, you snap."

Amber leaned back in the wing chair. "I'd have to agree with you."

"What about Jackson Seymour and that pink paint on Wes's van?"

"It's definitely a match. But it's not evidence of murder."

"Did you look into the vendor-alliance scheme I told you about?"

She nodded. "Deepwater Fisheries had been manipulating customers for a couple of years, requiring them to join their supplier mafia or get stuck with heavy fines if they used a competitor. It was so clearly illegal that I can't figure out why no one reported them. People just kept paying and breaking contracts all over town."

"Jackson Seymour tried to report Wes to the Chamber of Commerce and the Better Business Bureau. He even wrote a letter to the local paper. No one listened. And he was threatening Tim with a lawsuit if he bailed on him."

Amber picked another piece of fudge. "And now he's started his own vendor alliance to compete. He doesn't have the same threatening language or heavy penalties, but very few people have joined him. What's missing?"

"Probably the blackmail."

CHAPTER 42

"That's it. I'm done." I put the last batch of honey-mustard ham biscuits in the aluminum chafing dish for the Senior Center. "It's up to you to see that the hors d'oeuvres get reheated in time for the party."

Aunt Ginny blew her hair out of her eyes. Her hands were covered in melted marshmallow from a hot-cocoa mishap. "Don't worry about me. You just get there before the judging starts."

"Gia and I will be sure to cast our votes for your pistachio cake."

"Nope."

"Almond-chess pie."

"No again."

I'd been trying all morning to guess what Aunt Ginny's secret dessert could be. She had me completely stumped, and I was getting concerned that one could stroke out from gloating.

The front door chimed, and General Tso barked and flew to the kitchen to alert me to prowlers. Figaro also did his part, with a cursory glance and a lick of his paw from his perch in the window. A bunch of giggling and tap-tap-

tapping from a cane down the hall let me know the Biddies had arrived. Mrs. Dodson stopped in front of Aunt Ginny, and the two faced off like rival queens having a border dispute.

"Virginia."

"Edith."

Mother Gibson unwound a mile of crocheted scarf from around her head and neck. "Now you two play nice. No matter who wins tonight, I'm sure both entries will be delicious."

I handed Aunt Ginny a wet washcloth. "I'm going to grab my coat, and I'll be ready to walk down to the board-walk."

Aunt Ginny kept her eyes on Mrs. Dodson while she scrubbed her hands. "Hurry back. The cocoa won't stay hot forever."

I took the spiral stairs in the pantry up to the third floor. Along the way, I gave another deep sniff. *What is that smell? Is it a spice? A fruit?* I was racking my brain to try to place it.

I popped out into the hall and found Iris sitting on the bed in the "haunted Siobhan room." She was staring out the window. "What are you doing in here?"

She turned to face me, her eyes puffy and red. "I'm so sorry. Please don't send me away. I've paid through to-morrow. I promise I'll be good."

Did she have a redheaded voodoo doll she was poking in the heart? I owed this woman nothing and somehow my insides cringed. *Was compassion a side effect of DNA? Or was I just too soft?*

"I never meant to hurt you by saying you needed to lose weight. I think you are absolutely lovely. Your experience won't be my experience."

"What is that supposed to mean?"

"It means Gia will always love you, no matter what, and I should not have projected my fears onto you."

I stood silently, waiting for more.

She turned her head and looked back out the window.

"What is it you've been looking for?"

Silence.

"And where have you been for thirty-five years?"

"Around."

I started to step into the room and ask her for a better explanation when Aunt Ginny hollered at me from the bottom of the steps.

"Poppy! What is taking you so long? We were supposed to be on the beach at one o'clock sharp to claim our spot."

I bet Patricia doesn't holler up the steps at the Crow's Nest.

I went to my room and grabbed my coat and sunglasses, making sure to lock my door behind me. *Won't be fooled again.* Then I joined Aunt Ginny and the Biddies on the front porch. Mrs. Davis handed me a tote bag full of costume pieces. "What's this for?"

"We're dressing your sandman up as a flapper from the twenties."

"What do you mean *my* sandman? I thought just businesses were competing."

Mrs. Dodson shook her head like I was dimwitted. "The Butterfly Wings is a business."

"I didn't sign up . . ." I looked at Aunt Ginny, who was suddenly a fresh shade of caught red-handed.

"Did I not mention that I entered you?" She pushed her rose-gold sunglasses up on her nose. "Step lively. We're late."

The short trek down the block to Beach Drive was like taking a preschool class to the circus. The Biddies wanted to stop and look at everything, talk to everyone, buy soft pretzels and popcorn on the boardwalk. "Ladies, this is a timed event."

Mother Gibson blew me off. "You got plenty of time. They have cinnamon and sugar today."

"How about I meet you down there?"

They were already gone. Once they smelled the roasted almonds, they forgot all about me and the fact that I was lugging a giant bag of beaded fringe. I checked in with the event manager and got a number and a map.

I passed the Chalfonte team and the Bagel Time Café competitors. Hot Sauce Louie's people were wearing reindeer antlers, and the Blue Pig team came dressed as elves.

Was I supposed to dress up for this? How does Aunt Ginny get me roped into these things? I wound through the competitors in search of my designated area. It looked like I had a prime spot next to the judges' table with a mountain of extra sand. *Who did Aunt Ginny pay off to put us there?*

I wasn't paying attention and rammed into the back of the man in front of me. "Oh, I am so sorry."

He was just as surprised as I was when he turned to face me. It was Jackson Seymour. He was wearing a number on his chest, with the business name SEYMOUR VEG splashed above it. He grimaced and muttered an apology.

I asked the Chambers Mansion Spa team to trade spots with me so I could park it right next to him. When they saw my prime placement, they willingly swapped numbers and thanked me for my generosity.

I pinned the number to my coat and smiled at a wary-looking Jackson. "Hey there."

His beard rustled in the wind. "Hello again."

"I'm sorry I almost knocked you over."

"I should have been paying attention."

"Is this your first time at the Christmas Sandman Competition?"

"I compete every year." He sniffed and looked around.

"It's for charity. I'm surprised the police have time to enter. Especially with a murderer walking free."

Hm. Had not thought about that. "Like you said, it's for charity. Besides, I'm here representing my aunt's bed and breakfast—The Butterfly Wings."

Jackson eyed the feather boa blowing out of my bag. "Oh. I see. Any leads on who might have killed Wes Bailey?"

I shoved the boa down. "It's an ongoing investigation."

A silver-haired lady in a blue ski suit called through a megaphone, laying out the rules of the event along with the time limit. Then a loud blast on the air horn sounded, and everyone started building their sand snowmen.

I dropped to my knees and pulled wet sand into a pile with the little trowel Aunt Ginny had put in the bag and started to form the bottom round of my flapper. "I saw the letter you wrote to the paper about Deepwater Fisheries."

Jackson fumbled the bucket of sand he was scooping and crushed the ball he'd formed. "That was ages ago."

"It sounds like you were trying to warn the business community. Did anything ever come from it? Did anyone investigate Wes Bailey to see if what he was doing was illegal?"

Jackson's face softened, and little crinkles formed at the corners of his eyes. "Nothing. I couldn't get anyone to take me seriously. Wes was steamrolling my clients into terrible contracts where they were forced to leave me and sign three-year deals with Gunter's Produce."

"And Gunter's Produce was on board with this?"

"Of course, they were. They were raking in new clients left and right. They weren't just taking mine, but Frank's Produce and Westfield Farm's customers too. We were all losing business so people could avoid Wes's outrageous penalties."

"Did Tim tell you he was switching to Gunter's?"

Jackson shrugged. "No. We were good."

"So Maxine's wasn't going anywhere?"

"Why? What did they tell you?"

"That you threatened repercussions if they broke their contract."

Jackson grunted. "Tim assured me they weren't leaving. He said they had another way planned."

"Another way like what?"

"I dunno. You'd have to ask Tim."

I dumped another bucket of wet sand and tried to pat it into some sort of ball. One of the judges came by to observe the proceedings. I waited for him to move on before asking, "Why'd you paint 'thief' across the side of Wes's van?"

Jackson eyed me, like he was trying to determine if this was entrapment. "*If* I painted thief on Wes's van, it would have been because I lost thirty percent of my business when he started his vendor alliance. He had prices that no one could compete with. He was undercutting everyone's rates by twenty percent. My friend at Finn's Fish said he couldn't make payroll at those prices. He declared bankruptcy a year ago."

"Maybe Wes was giving quantity discounts, like those big-box stores that buy cheap goods and resell them for pennies."

Jackson took a trowel to his design. "If he was, he didn't pass on the savings for long. Wes got people in for bargain-basement prices, but once they signed the contract, he'd slowly start to raise their rates and tack on hidden fees."

"Why did people stay with him?

"He made it too expensive to leave."

"And no one wanted to report him to the authorities?"

Jackson's hands flew out to his sides. "You think I didn't try that?" He counted off on his fingers. "I reported him to the Better Business Bureau, the Chamber of Commerce, the FTC. I even called a lawyer. They told me what Wes was doing was called torturous interference, and it wasn't a federal crime; it was a civil issue. My business was already circling the drain. I couldn't afford a lawsuit."

I gathered another bucket of sand and forced myself not to giggle at his mispronunciation. *Torturous interference.* "So you started your own vendor alliance. If you can't beat 'em, join 'em, right?"

Jackson cut into his sand with his trowel like beach Michelangelo. "I had tried everything else. No one would help me."

I stepped back and considered how to get sand boobs to stick. "You aren't worried about your own tortious interference?"

He shrugged, but a slight pink appeared on the apples of his cheeks. "It's business. And I'm not price gouging or tacking on fees when people don't switch to my partners. I'm just offering incentives for those who do. Everyone with me has been burned by Wes. Heck, a couple of them used to be *with* Wes. You know what happens to those discounts after you sign the contract? They go bye-bye. Then he gets a personal kickback for marketing like he's the kingpin of Cape May. Some of my people left his alliance at great cost when the rumors started."

"What rumors?"

He quickly looked away and scraped into his creation to add a dimple on the top. "I wasn't one of his customers, so I have no idea if they're true, but word on the street is don't order the scallops."

"Are we talking about seafood fraud?"

Jackson stopped troweling and peered at me over his creation. "I'm just saying people need to pay attention to what's delivered to make sure it's what they ordered."

"So Wes was doing a bait and switch with the products, so to speak."

"That's what it sounds like."

I ran my hands over my sand lady to round her head more before adding the black wig. She was looking a little bit like a hunchback in a flapper dress.

Jackson added a pair of enormous plastic sunglasses to what had turned into a giant peach with legs. "A lot of people have been hurt by Wes. I reported him to three different agencies, called the news, and yes, even painted 'thief' on his van to warn people. But at the end of the day, it's just money. I wouldn't kill a man over it."

"Well, someone did. If not for money, then why?"

Jackson threw down his trowel and surveyed his peach lady. "That's a question you should be asking those who had a lot more to lose than just a few clients."

CHAPTER 43

The legs of my jeans were soaked, and the cold cut right through to my bones. My teeth chattered during the whole walk home while my sand-lady building skills were critiqued. Aunt Ginny and the Biddies were less than enthused with my flapper, even though they conveniently showed up five minutes before the buzzer and didn't have time to help me with it.

Mrs. Dodson tsk'd. "I can't believe you didn't even place, Poppy. What happened?"

"Probably because I've never done it before, and I didn't have any time to prepare since I had no idea I was competing until two hours ago."

Mrs. Davis wrapped her pink coat tighter around her. "What happened to her boobies? They were two different sizes."

"Same thing that happened to yours. Gravity."

"That man on the other side of you didn't have any trouble. His boobies were perfect."

"Well, he looked like he had a lot more experience with them than I have . . . And please stop saying boobies."

Mother Gibson shook her head. "Haven't you ever seen a flapper on TV? They're rail thin, honey."

"Well, snowmen aren't. I assumed sand women would be the same. Three balls and a carrot."

Mrs. Davis snickered.

"Don't be ridiculous." Aunt Ginny had a cinnamon pretzel hanging off each wrist. "Why weren't you in front of the judge's booth where I put you? Do you know what hoops I had to jump through to get you that spot? I have to help Louella clean up after her stupid pottery class for the next eight weeks."

"What difference does it make where my entry was?"

"It mattered."

Hmm. The Chambers Mansion Spa team did take first place. I cut my eyes to Aunt Ginny. "What did you do?"

Aunt Ginny took a bite off one wrist pretzel. "The less you know, the better."

We arrived home, and I went up to my room to shower and change for the parade. I pulled on fleece-lined black leggings and Uggs, and a long green sweater. I put my hair up in side ponytails, then put on my white hat and scarf that Mother Gibson had made me.

I grabbed my coat on the way out the door. Aunt Ginny handed me a printout from the internet of a professional sand-sculpted mermaid with big boobs. "Practice this for next year."

Next year I'll be in Belize. I folded the paper and shoved it in my back pocket. "I'll see you at the party."

"Don't be late."

I passed the Crow's Nest on my walk to La Dolce Vita. Patricia was out front, sweeping leaves off the porch. "Hello there."

She stopped sweeping and leaned on her broom. "Well, look at you in your pigtails. Aren't you just something."

"Thank you." *I think?*

Patricia was hard to read. Was she aggressively sweet or seething with condescension? Had I done something to offend her at an innkeepers meeting? Or was I just telegraphing my fears after a year of being involved with nice people who turned out to be murderers? I gave her a wave that she returned with an icy stare. "You should go talk to your aunt."

I looked back at my house. It did look like a Nightmare Before Christmas theme park from here. "Sorry."

The Washington Street Mall was packed as people jostled for position to wait for the parade.

I went in the back door of La Dolce Vita to greet my boys before we went out to join the crowd. The front of the store was stuffed to the rafters as people enjoyed their last bit of warmth and caffeine before heading out to watch the Cape May High marching band lead off the Christmas Parade.

Gia watched, grinning from his station behind the espresso machine, as Henry ran for me to launch into a hug. "Poppy! A package arrived for you."

I hugged him tightly. "A package? Where?"

Karla was working the milk frother. "It's under the counter."

I looked across the room to Gia, who held up a large manilla envelope with the name Poppy written on it.

Marco was filling the pastry case with the peppermint brownies I'd made the other day. "Some kid, he bring it by little while ago on his bike."

I took the envelope from Gia. "A kid on a bike? Did you get his name?"

The men shrugged and shook their heads.

A woman would have gotten a name. I opened the envelope and pulled out a stack of eight-by-ten photographs of Teela and Gabe. They appeared to have been taken from the front of the restaurant because the bridge was in the background. It was dark, but you could just see their faces in the dim streetlight. Teela had one hand on Gabe's arm, and she was tucking her hair behind her ear with the other. In the next photo, Gabe had his arms out like he was about to wrap the strawberry-blonde in a hug. In the final shot, Gabe was looking over his shoulder like he was afraid they were being watched.

Henry pushed his glasses onto the bridge of his nose and wiggled through my arms to see the pictures. "Who is it, Poppy?"

"Some people I work with." I turned the photos over. On the back of one was written a date. That was the night Wes Bailey was killed.

"Why did they send them to you, *bella*?"

"Someone wants me to know Gabe and Teela are closer than they appear."

Gia looked over his shoulder at the pictures. "She is flirting with him."

I nodded and flipped a picture over. "It has December third written on it."

Karla glanced our way. "That doesn't prove anything. That might just be when someone wants you to think they were taken."

Marco handed his customer a chocolate muffin. "*Si.* You could write da year 2078 on da photo, and dat no mean the photo travel in time."

I took a picture of the front and back of each photo with my phone and sent them to Amber. Then I slid the photos back into the envelope. "True. It's more curious that someone would go out of their way to get these to me. Are they trying to help, or shift suspicion off themselves?"

"Supsission for what?" Henry asked.

I kissed him on the forehead. "People do all kinds of naughty things and try to get away with them. You just need to keep being good, and we won't have to worry about that."

Henry gave me a serious nod. "I will. Santa is watching."

Gia tousled Henry's hair. "More important, Piccolo, God is watching. Santa is just a man."

Henry's eyes were the size of quarters through his thick glasses, but they narrowed as he gave that some thought. "Does Santa know how to find you if you move?"

"Of course, honey. Don't you worry. Santa will find you, even if we live with Aunt Ginny."

Henry snuggled into me.

Gia handed me a latte and nodded towards the manilla envelope. "Who would be in the best position to take that shot?"

I blew on the foam. "Anyone who works at the front of the house. The hostess and the other servers."

Karla pulled two pumps of vanilla syrup into a paper cup. "I can't blame the girl for going after the hot bartender."

Gia bristled. "There is a hot bartender?"

I chuckled to myself. "Yeah. He could give you a run for your money."

Gia's eyes narrowed, and he muttered something I didn't catch, but Karla laughed. "Settle down. Poppy is only interested in you, you big idiot."

Gia worked his lower lip with his teeth, and I took his hand. "Do you have any idea how ridiculous this is?"

"What? I can be jealous. You are beautiful woman. You could be with anyone."

Where was that attitude from boys when I was in high school? "Well, I only want you. Besides, who else would help me investigate Seymour Veg and Deepwater Fisheries?"

Gia grinned and gave me a quick peck. "Piccolo, go get your coat. It is time."

Henry jumped off my lap and ran to the back of the shop.

Marco handed a mocha to the last customer at the counter. "Don't tell me you are using dat fish scoundrel."

I sipped my latte. "The what now?"

Marco crossed his arms over his chest. "Chef Oliva would never use da Deepwater Fisheries. She call dem da fish scoundrel."

"Why?"

"Because-a dey cheat. Dey came by once and try to sell her short fin mako and pass it off as swordfish, but she know da difference. Chef Oliva, she is no dummy."

"Short fin mako, as in shark?"

"*Si*. Is no good."

I blew the foam on my latte. "Have any of you heard of the swordfish gang?"

Marco shrugged.

Gia pulled out his cell phone and started typing. "Members of the swordfish gang can be recognized by the swordfish tattoo over the right eye. Based in Miami, the local gang is spreading operations up the East Coast. Known for drug trafficking, illegal gambling, money laundering, and violent crime."

I looked at Gia. "Wow."

He kept reading. "It says here they are also known for their rivalry with the CKs."

"Who's that?"

"Cuban Kings. Rival gang distinguishable by a tattoo on the right hand."

Gia turned his phone around to show me a tattoo of a skull wearing a crown.

"Hmm. Interesting."

"Why do you want to know?"

"Some men came into Maxine's the other night with swordfish tattoos on their faces."

Henry ran through the dining room like a tornado, with one arm shoved in his coat, the other sleeve dragging the floor. "I'm ready."

I snickered and helped him find his other armhole. We joined the throng on the Washington Street Mall and jostled to get a good spot down the main thoroughfare to watch the parade, just as the high school marching band passed playing "God Rest Ye Merry Gentlemen."

Henry squealed when they threw a handful of candy at his feet. Gia held out the bag he'd brought to hold the loot as Henry gathered Smarties and Dum Dums as fast as he could.

Gia leaned his head towards mine. "Are you sure you want us to spend the night Christmas Eve? You see how much excitement we get for a parade."

"Absolutely. I want you there on Christmas morning. Holiday pajamas and hot chocolate and Henry getting his presents from under the tree, if Figaro hasn't totally destroyed it yet."

"Hey! You there."

I turned to the sharp command fighting over the sound of Middle Township's drum corps. It was the Grinch from the Horseshoe Crab a couple doors down. "Are you talking to me?"

The Grinch came closer and pointed to my chest. "You know I am, missy. You need to tell Ginny to turn down that racket. My people didn't settle on an island to put up with that three-ring circus you've brought to our street."

Gia flinched and started to step towards my neighbor. I put my hand on his arm. "I'm so sorry it's been disturbing you. I don't want anything to harm the relationship between our families. You know what I mean?"

The neighbor noticed Gia, and his bristles retracted.

"Whatever. Just tell her there ain't no acceptable music this time of year other than Bing Crosby. If she's not gonna play that, she should just keep her noise to herself."

"Oookay. Just so long as we're not feuding, you and me. I want our families to be friends. Alright?"

His bushy eyebrows twisted together. "I don't know what you're goin' on about. Just keep it down. And while you're at it, tell that cop lady to lay off my godson. He's a good boy. He didn't hurt no one."

He spun away from us, and I reached out and grabbed his shoulder. "Wait!"

He jumped and came down with karate hands like he was going to strike me or break a board. "Whoa! You can't just grab a man on the Washington Street Mall. Don't you got no class, girlie?"

"I'm sorry. I didn't mean to startle you."

He raised his shoulders and cracked his neck to the side. His hands relaxed. "I could have killed you just now." He quickly looked at Gia. "Not that I would, of course."

"What did you say a minute ago about your godson?"

"Tell your cop friend she's barking up the wrong tree. Tyler's got a good heart. He's always tryin' a help people. I gotta get outta this noise. Those ruffians look like they could snap and run wild any moment."

I wanted to get more information, but he disappeared into the crowd. The ruffians in question were the Sunshine Babes, the kindergarten tap class from Miss Kristi's School of Dance.

Gia nodded after the man. "Who was that?"

"That was Willie. Of the Horseshoe Crab Willies."

Henry grabbed my hand as a very aggressive tapper came over to demand he take her Smarties.

"Mary Jane, I presume?"

Henry gave me a very serious nod.

Sawyer ran up behind us, out of breath. "I'm so stinking tired. I think I just passed my Christmas sales record from 2014. Did I miss the corgis?"

I nodded down the parade route. "Coming now."

Sawyer squealed.

Henry squatted down to talk face-to-face with a corgi dressed in a reindeer costume. "You're so cute, you little guy." He reached out and patted the dog on the head.

The owner grinned at me. "Your son's adorable."

My chest expanded so much it hurt. "I know he is." I held up a little dog biscuit I'd brought for this moment, and the owner nodded. I handed it to Henry, who squealed with glee when the little reindeer took it from his hands with his velvety snoot.

Gia took my hand in his. "You're so good to him."

My little guy was lit up like a parade float as he greeted another corgi dressed as a snowman. "Hi. Hi there."

"I love him. I would do anything for Henry. I think I could lift a car to save him, I love him so much. We might need to move away if I keep stumbling upon poor souls who've met an untimely end. His safety means more to me than my own happiness."

Gia squeezed my hand. "I don't think it will come to that, *cara mia*. As long as we have you, we have everything we need."

A ruckus down the block started to crest like a wave. I couldn't see what all the fuss was about yet, but it was getting a lot of cheers. I stretched to look around the crowd. "Something exciting is coming."

Sawyer linked her arm in mine. "I hope it gets here soon. I need a snack."

I handed her a pack of Smarties.

A giant gingerbread-house float rolled around the corner to the sound of cheerful little bells and a hauntingly familiar voice crowing out Mariah Carey's holiday anthem.

Oh. Dear. God.

Gia sucked in a mouthful of air.

Sawyer coughed and spit her sweet tart into her hand. "Is that . . . ?"

Aunt Ginny was singing lead vocals to "All I Want for Christmas Is You" while doing the twist in a red spandex cat suit with white-fur fringe around the neck. The Biddies were performing a well-choreographed backup routine in red-velvet mini dresses, and Royce sat upon the white-leather wing chair from my sunroom and tossed candy to the cheering crowd.

I sighed. "How is her life so much more exciting than ours?"

Iggy and Fiona were driving the pickup truck towing the float. Iggy gave a quick double tap on the horn and a wave as they passed by, and I noticed the banner on the side of the float said BUTTERFLY WINGS BED AND BREAKFAST.

Followed by the smaller subtitle WHERE ONLY *ONE* PERSON WAS MURDERED. I groaned and pulled my hat lower over my face.

Gia let go of my hand and put his arm around my shoulders.

Henry shouted, "Hi, Aunt Ginny!" and waved to the eighty-year-old, who was dancing dangerously close to the edge of the second-story stage.

Aunt Ginny blew Henry a kiss.

It took three marching bands, the high school majorette squad, and the troupe from the East Lynne Theater Company before I could talk again.

I turned to ask Sawyer if she was going to the Christmas party and found her eating a turkey leg. "Where'd you get that?"

She pointed over her shoulder. "Some guy."

"Like in a store?"

She shook her head no and took another gnaw of the meat.

A foreboding tinkle of the piano keys, followed by the menacing shake of jingle bells, started to blare through the sound system.

"Oh no."

Gia looked down the street. "What is wrong now? Aunt Ginny is not doing another lap, is she?"

The spoken intro about it being cold on the beach and the wind whipping down the boardwalk was like a choke-hold.

"I don't think I can do it again."

Sawyer yawned. "Do what?"

Sure enough. Santa's sleigh rounded the corner to the South Jersey holiday mantra. People started to cheer as Bruce Springsteen's "Santa Claus Is Coming to Town" played for the millionth time that week.

Henry squealed and grabbed my free hand. "Look, Poppy, it's Santa! He's here!"

I nodded and smiled at him. "I know, right?" *Maybe now Bruce Springsteen can lay the heck off.*

As the sleigh began to pass us, Santa held out a bucket and shook it. One of the elves took it from him and tossed a pile of Smarties at my feet.

CHAPTER 44

"Never underestimate how sneaky Aunt Ginny is."
Gia pulled into the Senior Center parking lot and found a spot in the back. "I just want to know how she gets so much past you."

"First of all, she plays the old lady card a lot. Don't fall for it. Plus, she takes advantage of all the time I'm stuck in dark alleys with . . . suspects." I glanced over my shoulder at Henry. He was grilling me, hanging on every word. I gave him a grin.

He gave me a cheesy smile back. "Is there food here?"

I unbuckled him from his car seat. "Yes, I made sure there will be dairy-free snacks that are safe for you." We walked hand in hand into the building and were greeted by the Senior Center director.

Neil was dressed in a tuxedo and giving out candy canes. "Merry Christmas, everyone. Thank you for coming. Be sure to check out the dessert competition table."

The sounds and smells of the season were on full display: the seniors dressed to the nines, Nat King Cole singing "Chestnuts" overhead, the scent of roasted meats and puff pastry wafting invitingly through the air, and Aunt Ginny screeching my name from the dining hall. "Poppy Blossom! Gia! The judging is in here! Watch out for Edith. She tripped Irma Fieldman on the way in."

Somewhere in the background, Mrs. Dodson hollered. "I did not! She stumbled."

Gia and I looked into each other's eyes. "Ah, the holidays."

We followed the voice of Cape May's very own Songbird Supreme as she bellowed directions to us like we were the three blind mice and had never been here before. As soon as we hit the dining hall, she shoved paper ballots into our hands and grabbed me by the wrist. "I'm number ten. Right there. See it?"

In the middle of a long, cloth-covered banquet table, nestled on an antique cake pedestal, sat a fragrant golden-brown bundt. The card in front read: BLACK WALNUT CAKE.

Aunt Ginny smiled proudly. "That's your winner right there. My secret ingredient is black walnut bitters."

"Black walnut." I leaned in closer to sniff it. "I don't think I've ever had black walnut anything. It smells very interesting."

Gia reached for the cake knife, and Aunt Ginny smacked his hand. "What are you doing?"

"What? You want me to try it, no?"

"No, I don't want you to try it. I want you to vote for it."

Gia stared the crazy lady in the face. "How can I vote for it if I do not know how it tastes?"

Aunt Ginny craned her neck and stared back at the six-foot-two, gorgeous Italian. She did not break eye contact until he wrote the number 10 on his slip of paper.

Henry screwed up his face and nudged his glasses back. "How do you spell walnut?"

Aunt Ginny took the pencil from him. "Don't worry about that, honey. I'll put the number on your ballot, and you just put it in the box."

We shoved our totally unsolicited votes into the ballot box, and Aunt Ginny went to harass the next pawn in her game of take-Edith-down.

Gia snickered at her retreating form. "Has she ever run for office?"

"Please don't give her any ideas."

We went to the head of the buffet table and got our plates. I picked safe foods for Henry to eat, and the seniors made over him like he was royalty.

Ivey Spisak cornered us by the ham biscuits. "Aren't you handsome? Poppy, is this your new son?"

I couldn't keep the grin off my face. "He sure is."

"You're a lucky fella to have a mom who can cook. These biscuits are fabulous, Poppy. So much better than what we usually have."

Henry reached up and linked his pinky with mine.

Mrs. Spisak lowered her voice and leaned in closer. "Such a shame what happened over at that restaurant."

"Hmm. True. Gia, honey, why don't you take Henry and get seats somewhere. I'll come find you."

Gia gave me a knowing look and a nod. "Come, Piccolo. We will find a table."

"But I want to know what happened at the restaurant."

"*Si*, I know. That is why we are finding a table."

They disappeared into the dining room, and I turned my attention back to the little woman in the white chiffon. "It was very sad. I'm sure his family is devastated."

She patted my hand. "You know, my cleaning girl, Inez, told me that there's a fella what works there who killed a man. I bet he's the police prime suspect."

Say what now? "Did Inez give you a name?"

"George, I think. Or maybe it was Greg. It started with a G."

"Gabriel?"

"No, that's not it. It'll come to me. The boy did two

years in prison for manslaughter. I hear he got out early on parole."

"Manslaughter?"

She dipped her ham biscuit in the honey mustard and nodded. "Killed someone while drunk driving. I'll go ask Reggie what the boy's name is."

She flitted away, and I circled the buffet. Joanne's cakes were on a table marked AUCTION DONATIONS COURTESY THE BUTTERFLY HOUSE BED AND BREAKFAST. There was a sign-up sheet filled with silent bids.

Wowza! *I wonder if Neil knows he's running a silent auction.* I'd better make sure this isn't another grift of Aunt Ginny's.

I went back over to browse the competition table. The entries ran the gamut. There were some fancy cream puffs made with Tahitian vanilla beans, something called a dump cake, a tiered dessert called Death by Chocolate, and a few pies and layer cakes. I made my way down to Aunt Ginny's cake. Quite a few slices were missing. I took a tiny corner and sniffed it.

"It's a strange one, isn't it, *bubala*?"

I followed the voice to my neighbor, Mrs. Sheinberg. "The black walnut cake?"

"Yeah. We used to make a black-walnut rugelach at the bakery when I was just a girl. Oh, they were so good. Ginny's outdone herself with that cake. It's delish. I think she made it for me and Sol one year for Christmas. Or maybe it was Passovah. Sol! When did Ginny make us that cake?"

Mr. Sheinberg shuffled over to join his wife. "The what?"

"The cake! The cake! When did Ginny make us that black walnut cake?"

"Oh." Mr. Sheinberg shrugged. "I think it was 1977."

Mrs. Sheinberg tsk'd and shook her head. "He don't know. I think it was Passovah. Anyway, I hope she wins."

"We all hope that, Mrs. Sheinberg."

Mother Gibson sidled up to the table with a grin on her face. She looked around, then plucked a piece of whiskey fudge from the three-tiered stand and added it to her plate. "Don't you tell Ginny."

Ivey Spisak rushed across the room, cradling a cream puff in her hand. "Andrew. His name is Andrew. There's no G. I don't know who I was thinking about."

Poor Andrew. Manslaughter. What a terrible thing to go through so young.

Mrs. Sheinberg reached across Mrs. Spisak and took her own piece of whiskey fudge. "You talking about that mess ovah at Maxine's?"

Mrs. Spisak nodded, her mouth full of cream puff. "Manslaughter."

Mrs. Sheinberg waved her hand. "Yeah, yeah. I don't think he killed the guy, though. I heard the boy's been scared straight. His sistah does my hair and she says he hasn't had a drop of likah since. Now fightin'. That's anotha story. The boy has a hair trigger. He beat up this one fella so bad for scratching his car that he has court-ordered anger management he hasta do now."

We all nodded as we let that sink in.

Mother Gibson chewed thoughtfully. "I heard Teela Kerr works at that restaurant."

"Do you know her?"

She shook her head. "Not anymore. She was in my Sunday school class when she was a little-un, but that's a long time ago. She still crave the spotlight?"

"I would say yes. Yes, she does."

Mrs. Sheinberg blew a raspberry. "That girl is a train wreck. Her poor mother can't do a thing with her. Almost forty, and she still lives at home, wants to be an actress now. Pish."

Mrs. Spisak tut-tutted. "She's been fired from a dozen

jobs, but it's never her fault." She flicked her hand out like she was shooing away a gnat. "She's one of them people who thinks the world is out to get them because everything isn't handed to her on a silver platter."

Mr. Sheinberg took a cream puff off Mother Gibson's plate and darted his eyes around the circle to see if anyone noticed. "These kids today are allergic to hard work. They want to be . . . what is that foolish thing we saw in that movie?"

Mrs. Sheinberg gave him an assist. "An influencer."

"Yeah. An influencer. What a buncha hooey. I heard she tried to sue her last boss for firing her."

Mrs. Sheinberg cut in. "Yeah, yeah. And she was callin' out sick at least once a week so she could sneak off to them cockamamie acting classes. Her poor father's paid a fortune in tuition already."

I lowered my voice, the universal signal that I was about to gossip. "I heard she attacked her manager."

Mrs. Sheinberg shrugged and rolled her eyes. "If you wanna call puttin' a buncha mean stuff out on the Twitter an attack, then sure."

Mrs. Spisak eyed the tier of fudge. "Does anyone know what a GoFundMe is?"

Everyone else in our little circle stared at her like she'd spoken Mandarin, so I answered. "It's an online program to raise money for people in need."

Mrs. Spisak snorted. "Well, she's got herself one."

I pulled out my phone and did a quick search. Teela had a GoFundMe set up to *rehome a starving actress while she focuses on her craft and works her way through college.* She'd collected twenty dollars. I scrolled down to the words of support. There was one comment by Wes Bailey, who'd left the only donation. "You can live with me rent free."

Mr. Sheinberg looked around the circle and popped the

cream puff into his mouth when no one called him out for pinching it. Mother Gibson gave him some side-eye, but kept silent.

A hunched-over little man with a mop of fluffy white hair pushed his walker up next to me. "Wanna dance, cookie?"

"I'm sorry. I'm here with my fiancé. I should really get back to him."

The man leaned on his walker. "In that case, pass me a piece of that whiskey fudge."

I picked up a piece with the silver tongs and prepared to place it on his plate.

"Poppy!"

Aunt Ginny caught me fudge-handed, and the others scattered like they were on the FBI's most wanted list.

"How could you do this to me. You know what's at stake tonight."

"It's not mine. I was holding it for a friend. I voted for your cake." I pointed over her shoulder. "Look, it's Kenny and Joanne. Did they vote yet?"

Aunt Ginny gave herself whiplash to grab the new-comers before they wandered away. "Joanne. Let me get you a ballot."

I took off in search of Gia and Henry and found them at a table with two old men who were deep in conversation. Gia made a face that either meant run for your life or join him immediately.

"Poppy, do you know Barney Spisak and Irving Collazo?"

Apparently, it was the latter. I pulled out the chair next to Gia. "We've met a few times, in passing."

Gia put his arm across my shoulders. "They were just telling us about one of your neighbors."

Mr. Spisak was chewing on a toothpick. "I think his family's one of the oldest on the island."

Mr. Collazo leaned back in his chair and patted his

belly. "I'm surprised Ginny didn't tell you about him. They had to have grown up together. Both their families are original owners, all the way back to the fire."

Gia made a face and nudged me.

"Who are we talking about?"

Henry yawned. "Someone really old."

Mr. Collazo chuckled. "True enough. Willy can be a bit prickly about tourist season. So, in his mind, Ginny's now part of the problem, what with havin' a B and B and all."

"Maybe I'll take him some cookies later. Do you know anything about the Crow's Nest?"

Mr. Spisak took the toothpick out of his mouth. "The Crow's Nest?"

"Yes. The other end of the street."

"I'm not familiar with the history there. I hear the lady who runs it's an odd duck."

I tried to hide my disappointment.

Mr. Collazo scratched his chin. "Of course, you could just ask Albert over at the Historical Society."

"I've been there." I had so many questions and only one really good reason not to ask them right now. And she was stomping this way.

"The judging is fixed. That whole contest was a sham!"

Aunt Ginny was shaking a second-place ribbon like she was showing it who was boss. "My cake was delicious."

Mrs. Dodson was keeping pace, even with her cane and Aunt Ginny's indignation. She furrowed her brow and held out her own second-place ribbon. "What a crock!"

Aunt Ginny slapped her ribbon on the table next to me. "We were robbed."

"Both of you?"

Aunt Ginny crossed her arms in front of her chest and tapped her foot furiously. "I made a scratch cake with the finest ingredients. You would not believe what has taken first place."

Mrs. Dodson huffed and looked around the room. "Where is the traitor?"

I followed Mrs. Dodson's gaze and spotted a very chagrined Mrs. Davis holding a first-place ribbon, trying to disappear behind a skinny Christmas tree. "What dessert won?"

Mrs. Dodson shook her head. "Thelma has skunked us both with her Death by Chocolate nonsense. It doesn't even contain alcohol. I blame the Heath Bars."

Aunt Ginny's cheeks flamed. "Boxed brownies, instant pudding, and Cool Whip! At a baking competition. Of all the culinary atrocities, this is the worst."

CHAPTER 45

Gia and I had taken our cue to leave when the music changed, and the seniors took to the dance floor. Our presence wasn't required after Aunt Ginny's shakedown was over, and it was safer to get out of the whiskey-fudge-fueled hot zone before things livened up. We had driven around for a while, listening to Christmas music and looking at lights before taking Henry home for a bedtime story tuck-in. By the time my head hit the pillow, I had already been asleep for half a dream.

The alarm jarred me, and for a moment, I had trouble figuring out what day it was. *Sunday. Iris McAllister's check-out day.* I smiled to myself and rolled over onto a lump and pulled out a wet stuffed blue jay from under my back. "Figaro! I'm buying you a shock collar!"

Fig gave me a lazy yawn and an unconcerned squint.

"These are family heirlooms, Fig. For Christmas you're getting a bill for a box of new birds."

I checked the clock and saw that I had a few minutes for Grandpa Rooster's woes before heading downstairs into my own.

July 22
That damnable woman has caused no end to my suffering. She all but convinced the constable that I had killed the wretched man I stumbled upon by the road. With her mouth full of deceit, and a grin of malevolence, she insists she saw me strike him with the rock. If it were not for Mrs. Abernathy across the way to uphold my good name, I don't know what would have become of me last night. I will forever be in debt to the old woman for putting her cat out at exactly the right time to observe my return home.

July 26
As I sit here in my study, I am waiting for the constable to arrive with another complaint from the shrew. It seems someone stomped upon all her melons in the middle of the night. What a pity that must be for her. I do not know who would do such a treacherous thing. I shall have to send over a message of sympathy after I wash the honeydew from my boots.

July 26, later
My sympathies were not well received. I believe the woman to need a tincture for hysteria, and I said as much. She did not agree with my assessment on the matter.

July 31
I won sixteen dollars at a delightful game of cribbage last night. With my winnings I bought a goat. I'm very excited.

August 2
What a horrible mistake. I have returned the goat to its former owner. Now I understand why it was only sixteen dollars.

August 9
I could not bring myself to stay home after the horrific calamity of this morning. On my way to the market square, I stumbled upon a live chicken seller. The chickens were live. The seller, alas, was not. From the knife in his back, I do not believe it to be suicide.

August 20
The wretched woman is taking perverse delight in my misfortune. Is it any wonder that no reasonable man will have her? For the better part of the past two weeks, I have been questioned no less than five times over the death of the poultry man. The constable seems to be a man of decency who will listen to reason. The sergeant, however, appears to have the wits of a dim child and a head full of pudding.

Been there, done that. If the curse skips generations, what switches it on?

I sprang out of bed and stretched around in a few yoga moves, but I was way too excited about Christmas shopping with Sawyer today to focus on breathing. Especially for breathing through Figaro. "Why is yoga so fascinating that you want to be right under my face when I do it?"

I slid Fig to the side and resumed my downward dog. We were going off the island to the mall in Vineland this morning after the guests checked out. I had a few ideas for Gia and too many for Henry. I had to contain myself. It would be no good to set the bar that high my first Christmas. What if I couldn't afford a pony every year?

Figaro did some figure eights through my hair, then bit me on the ankle. "Alright, stop it. You win."

I showered and dressed quickly so I could be the first to the kitchen. I was planning chocolate-orange scones for breakfast. I hit the pantry and heard voices on the other side of the door. I pushed it a crack and spotted Aunt Ginny sitting at the table with Iris.

Aunt Ginny looked peeved. She had a cup of tea sitting off to the side. "I know what you're looking for, but I want to know why."

"It's mine, Ginny."

"You left it here."

"I never intended to leave it forever. I still want it."

"It's been thirty-five years. Why do you want it now?"

"I just do. Like I said, it's mine."

"It should go to Poppy."

"Shouldn't that be my decision? I am her mother."

"Is that supposed to be starting now? She's been waiting her whole life for you to remember that."

"I'm desperate, Ginny."

"That makes me very nervous, Iris. Desperate people do foolish things they regret later. Like leave their children."

Figaro, the Lord of Persistence, let out a very rude meow to signal his impatience with the door not being opened into his breakfast kingdom. Iris turned her head and looked my way. I had no choice but to enter the kitchen like I had just arrived.

Aunt Ginny gave me a look that she knew better. "I didn't make the coffee yet because I found Iris rifling around the kitchen."

Iris huffed. "I told you, I was making us tea."

I can't wait to hear what she was looking for. I cut my eyes to Aunt Ginny. "Sure. Aunt Ginny loves tea." I started the kettle to make coffee, and my cell phone buzzed. I looked at the screen. A text from Tim came in.

HELP Then one from Chuck.

Can you come in? Now?

Then one from a number I didn't recognize.

What did you do!?

Then one from Tim again.

Why is NOAA all over Maxine's investigating me?

My mind raced back to my call with the fish police. Did I tell them anything incriminating? I don't think I even gave them my name. I'm sure they have a record of my cell number, but how did they link me to Maxine's?

Iris sipped her tea. "Why don't you make us some of those eggs benedict we had the other day?"

Aunt Ginny was watching me from across the room. "Poppy? What is it? You're white as a sheet."

I turned the kettle off. "You'll have to make breakfast without me."

CHAPTER 46

I kicked myself all the way to Maxine's for not adding *and you can check Iris out before I get home*. I had no doubt she'd try to weasel her way into staying longer so she could keep looking for whatever she'd left behind. *I was left behind. She sure isn't looking for me.*

A gremlin of worry was gnawing on my stomach like a parasite. Surely my call to NOAA had nothing to do with this. Coincidences happen every day—right? *Life-changing, jail-threatening coincidences.*

A blue van was parked in Maxine's lot next to a couple of official-looking cars with the NOAA logo on them.

Chuck and Tyler were standing outside the back door, drinking out of paper hot cups. Chuck breathed a sigh of relief. "Thank God you're here."

Tyler stepped towards me quickly. "Trust me when I say it's not safe to go inside right now."

"Why? Is Gigi here?"

Chuck bit his lips and shook his head no.

I tried to look brave. "Then how bad can it be?"

Tim bellowed from inside the kitchen. "That better be a flighty redhead that I hear!"

Chuck and Tyler's eyes grew wide to mirror mine.

Tyler tossed the rest of his coffee. "The fish police got a hot tip that Tim has been serving counterfeit scallops. They're searching the premises."

My mouth was suddenly so dry. "What would give them that idea?"

Tyler gave me a shrug. "Someone must have reported him."

Chuck sighed. "We just found out Deepwater Fisheries was under investigation for fish fraud with NOAA. So all the restaurants Wes supplied to are on their radar. For some reason, they've moved our search to the top."

The back door flew open, and Tim roared. "I need to see you inside."

I gave a final look to the sous chefs that I hoped would be interpreted as *send in a search party if you don't hear from me in thirty minutes* and followed Tim through the kitchen. The scent of half-cooked bacon hung limply in the air, and every workstation had something abandoned mid-chop, -sauté, or -whisk. Officers in jackets that said FEDERAL AGENT across the back were combing every inch of the place. They were in both walk-ins and the storage room. Their voices were coming from Tim's office, where I caught a glimpse of a woman holding a cardboard evidence box.

I followed Tim out to the dining room, where I expected a frontal assault, but we passed the rest of the staff gathered around the bar as he led me to the empty fireplace room, which was set up for champagne brunch. Tim grabbed my shoulders and looked into my face, his eyes glassy. "Mack, please tell me you didn't do this. You didn't report me to NOAA, did you?"

I put my hand on my heart. "I would never."

The wrinkles in his forehead relaxed.

"But . . ."

His hands tensed. "But?"

"I did call them to ask questions about Wes. I never told them who I was or mentioned you or Maxine's." I sucked in my breath, waiting to see if the verbal machine guns would come out.

Tim dropped down to one of the dining chairs. "Oh, Poppy."

"Maybe they did some kind of Google search for me and found you. I guess that's possible."

He closed his eyes and rubbed his forehead with his hand. "It took me twenty years to build my restaurant from the ground up, and you destroyed it with one phone call."

I tried to keep my voice even. "If you'd been honest with me, I would never have stumbled upon NOAA in the first place."

Tim's eyes held a new sheen. Less sorrow and more ice. "I asked you to help find out who killed Wes to clear my name. Not go through my files and call the Feds."

"Everything I've done has been to help you. You asked me to find evidence that someone else killed Wes other than you and Gigi. I didn't know you were going to fight me every step of the way."

An official woman in a polyester suit came around the corner. "Mr. Maxwell, we're ready for you." She turned her eyes to me. "Ma'am, we're asking everyone who works here to give a statement."

I nodded, too nervous to trust my voice.

I drifted out to the bar, where the rest of the staff were brooding over drinks and cornbread. They all had cocktails with fancy straws or umbrellas. Teela and Chelle had a few empty glasses in front of them.

Gabe poured something golden from a cocktail shaker and passed it to Nikki, but his eyes were on me. "What are you doing here?"

"Tim asked me to come." *Asked. Demanded. It's a fine*

line. "I was expecting to see Gigi. I'm pretty sure she texted me also."

Andrew played with the straw in his drink. "Gigi's on bed rest. She's not supposed to be back until after the baby comes."

Teela snickered. "Christmas came early."

Gabe picked up a mule mug and polished it. "That isn't nice. She's been through a lot. It can't be good for the baby."

Nikki huffed. "Take it easy, Gabe. She's not your baby mama."

Chelle looked through her eyelashes at the gorgeous man. "She would be so lucky."

I took a seat at the bar. "Do you have kids, Gabriel?"

He dropped the copper mug, and it hit the counter with a clang. Without a word, he walked out of the bar, headed for the back.

I thought it was a friendly conversation starter, but everyone looked at me like I'd asked him if he eats babies for lunch. "Did I say something wrong?" *As per usual.*

Chelle shrugged and gave a wistful sigh. "Honestly, I have no idea. Gabriel's always been really touchy about Gigi and her pregnancy."

Teela snorted. "Oh my God, what if the baby is his?"

Nikki rolled her eyes. "Well, if it is, she won't be able to hide it for long once it's born."

Chuck and Tyler ambled over to the bar. Chuck poured himself an orange juice. "The Feds are finished with both walk-ins. Now they're questioning the staff."

Chelle pointed a lime wedge at Tyler. "This is your second time being questioned this week, Big T. Did you ever find out why the cops took your truck?"

Nikki pushed her cornbread away from her and reached for the cocktail Gabe had abandoned. "Probably just more government overreach. I wouldn't read into it."

Tyler added a shot of vodka to his orange juice. "They gave me some song and dance about showing up on a security camera down at the marina."

I passed him a long-handled spoon. "They'd only care if you showed up during the window when they think Wes was killed. What time did they clock you?"

He spun the spoon lazily through his drink. "I dunno, like two."

Teela wrapped her hair into a twist and stuck a swizzle stick through it. "In the morning! What were you doing here so late?"

"My buddy has a fishing boat down there. He lets me use it when I have insomnia and feel like night fishing before work. It's no big deal. I do it all the time."

Chuck pushed his glasses up with his knuckle. "Since when?"

Tyler shrugged. "Since always."

"You've never mentioned it before."

"I don't tell you everything, Chuck."

Chuck glanced at me, then picked up his juice and headed back to the kitchen.

I reached across the bar and poured myself a ginger ale. "I thought you were home in bed with your girlfriend all night."

Tyler chuckled. "I was wrong. I am not good with details that early in the morning. I went out on the boat for a couple of hours, not thinking I'd be hauled in here to face a stiff in the freezer and Cape May's blue line at the butt crack of dawn. Thank God, my buddy can back me up."

Teela reached across Andrew and took another piece of cornbread. "It does look suspicious, Tyler."

Chelle's lips flattened. "Girl, you best be quiet before someone wants to talk about all the questionable life choices you make."

Teela grunted. "Like what?"

Andrew chewed on a piece of ice. "How about those hundred-dollar tips Mr. Goatee leaves you for a fifteen-dollar salad."

Teela's face turned crimson. "What are you implying?"

Andrew smirked. "He seems way too grateful for extra croutons and dressing on the side."

Chelle trilled. "Alright now. Truth."

Teela sent a venomous glare to Chelle. "Really? You hand out *all* the tips lately, Chelle? And those goons who were here the other day, I suppose they were selling Girl Scout cookies?"

Chelle flicked her fingers up and leaned away from the bar. "Least I didn't run to Tim for special treatment. I dealt with the situation my own self."

Teela's lip curled. "Oh please. If it weren't for Tim, you'd all have been fired a long time ago. He goes above and beyond what any boss of mine has ever done for me. He's been paying Nikki under the table for weeks."

Nikki coughed and put her drink on the bar. She slid off the stool. "You all wonder why I don't hang out after work. It's crap like this. No one knows how to mind their own business." She moved into the other room.

Andrew called after her, "Aw, come on, Nikki. Don't pay any attention to her. You know she's bitter that Tim is with Gigi."

Teela reached for Tyler. "You know I'm right, don't you, Tyler?"

Tyler spun away from Teela's touch. "I know no one likes a whiner."

I was so wrapped up in watching the drama unfold that I jumped when my phone buzzed a text from Sawyer.

Where U at?

Maxine's

How long U gonna be?

IDK. Maybe shop later?

Sure. No prob. What time will you be done?

At least another hour.

K.

Andrew hopped down from his barstool. "I'll be out front if Ressler and Keen want me."

Teela huffed. "You all suck. My anxiety can't take this vibe. I'm getting tired of always being made out to be the bad guy. I'm going to sit in my brother's car away from this negative energy."

She walked out the front door, and it was down to Tyler, me, and Chelle. I gave Chelle and Tyler a tiny smile, hoping the cascade of aggression I seemed to have started was over.

Tyler chuckled under his breath. "What a day."

"I heard you used to have your own restaurant. How did I not know that about you?"

Tyler shrugged. "It was another lifetime, and one of many failed restaurants that year."

"What happened?"

He put his arm lazily on the bar and shook the ice in his glass. "You name it. Bad location, no parking, and I could not balance my overhead with the quality I wanted to put out."

"Did you come work for Tim right after that?"

He shook his head. "No. I worked at Kailanni's for three years. She was good to me. A real class act. But my girlfriend wanted to move down the shore, and I followed."

"Do you think you'll ever want your own place again?"

He gave a little shoulder nudge. "Maybe. Have to see where life takes me."

An agent came out of the back and scanned the room until his eyes landed on Tyler. "We're ready for you."

Tyler left to give his statement, and it was down to me and Chelle. She sighed, lost in her memories. "That murder has made this an unhappy work environment."

"Murder will do that."

"We all used to be so close."

"How so?"

Chelle got off the barstool and headed to the back of the bar. "We had these great staff dinners before the doors opened. We'd hang out and talk about our day."

She reached for a four-by-six photograph thumbtacked on the back wall. "No one is saying it, but we're all afraid we're gonna lose our jobs. And right before Christmas too. It's like everyone's been avoiding each other since Wes died, afraid they're gonna find out one of their friends is a killer."

She handed me the picture. "This was just a few weeks ago."

Everyone was laughing and smiling. Chelle was grinning up at Gabe, clearly flirting with him. He was smiling back, but looked more reserved. Brotherly? Maybe slightly embarrassed. Andrew was staring adoringly at Nikki like the sun shines out of her butt, but Nikki was laughing at Tyler, who was grinning back at her like they were sharing a private joke. Teela had her hand on Tim's arm, and she was leaning way too close to him, while Gigi was scowling at Teela like she wanted to rip her to pieces. Off to the side was Chuck. Alone. Eating a plate of pasta. Watching the fun, but not a part of it. They may have felt closer a few weeks ago, but there were clear signs that things were starting to crack. When Chelle went behind the bar to get the wine, I took a quick snap of the photo with my phone. I scrolled through my pictures to show her the photo of Teela and Gabe together.

Chelle didn't flinch. "Where did you get that?"

"I stumbled across it earlier. Do you know what's happening here?"

She shook her head. "No, but Gabriel is kinda like the staff dad. He's the guy you go to when you need advice or a shoulder to cry on. And Teela does love to cry on a shoulder."

"So you don't think Gabe is flirting with her?"

"Naw. I bet this was after that incident with Wes getting all gropey with her here at the bar. She was really shaken up that night. This might be when Andrew went off after him."

"Then who took the picture?"

Chelle shrugged. "I don't know. That is weird."

The front door opened, and a beautiful light-skinned black woman stepped in and looked around.

Chelle called to her, "Sorry, we're closed. Staff emergency."

The woman took a step towards the bar. "I'm looking for someone. Captain Johnson."

The room hushed, silent as a prayer, as Chelle and I stared at her and tried to decipher her words.

She spun the bracelet on her arm with a flick of her wrist. "I'm sorry. Gabriel. I heard he works here."

Chelle's smile plummeted like the barometer. "Oh."

I shoved my phone in my pocket. "I'll see if he's in the back. Hold on."

"Tell him Darlene is looking for him."

I found Gabe sitting in the storage room. He frowned when he saw me.

"I'm sorry I upset you. I was just trying to make conversation."

His face softened. "I can be too sensitive sometimes." He held out his hand. "Truce."

I took his hand in mine. "Truce. Can I show you something?"

I pulled the picture of him and Teela up on my cell phone.

Gabe frowned. "Where'd you get this?"

"Someone sent it to me."

"Who?"

"I don't know. They didn't leave a name. When was it taken?"

"I think this was the first time Teela's father told her she had to move out and get her own place."

"Oh? How long ago was that?"

"Pssh. Before Halloween."

"So not last weekend?"

Gabe's eyebrows dropped. "What? No. Who told you that?"

The date on the back. Someone's lying. "Like I said, I don't know who sent it."

"That's not even the whole picture. We were outside getting ready for a staff photo shoot for social media." He took out his phone and pulled up a picture on Facebook. He and Teela were wearing the same clothes as in the other shot, and the background and lighting were the same, but just about everyone else was in the photo. They were posed in front of Maxine's, and the caption said, *Maxine's is ready to serve you the finest in South Jersey dining.*

"Why isn't Nikki in the picture?"

Gabe shrugged. "I think she had to leave early because her grandmother was sick."

I considered the photo that had been delivered. Was someone trying to throw me off, or were they trying to point me in the right direction? "I only came back here to let you know someone was looking for you. For Captain Johnson, actually."

His whole body tensed. "I don't ever want to hear that name again."

"I'm sorry. I didn't realize the Marines were a bad time for you."

Gabe looked away. "My military history is none of your business."

"Well, anyway. A lovely woman named Darlene is here to see you."

Gabe shot up like a rocket. "She's here?"

I nodded.

He looked around and wiped his hands down the front of his black jeans. Then he started back to the dining room.

I closed the app and put my phone back in my pocket while I followed him out.

He stopped about twenty feet away from the woman. "What are you doing here, Lena?"

The woman flicked her wrist. "Hello, Gabriel. I need to talk to you."

The front door opened, and Andrew came back inside, rubbing his arms. "It's flippin' freezing out there."

Gabe walked to the woman, put one hand on her arm, and led her through the door. "Outside."

The door shut behind them, and Andrew rejoined us at the bar. He went around the back and refilled his glass with Coke.

Chelle kept her eyes on the front door. "What do you suppose that was about?"

I looked back at the photograph on the bar. I didn't want to hurt Chelle, but Gabe was not giving off the same vibe that she was in that picture. "Maybe it was his sister? I've made that mistake before."

"Hmm. Maybe."

One of the Feds came into the dining room. "Rochelle Cleveland?"

Chelle hopped off the stool and muttered, "Tim has been very good to me. He's not going down on my watch."

The agent led her through the kitchen door.

Andrew clinked his glass against mine. We each took a sip.

"How long have you been sober?"

"Four years."

"That's amazing."

He shrugged. "Hitting bottom will do that."

"I may have heard through the grapevine that you were in a serious accident a few years ago."

Andrew's face remained impassive, but he swallowed hard. "Are people still talking about that?"

"That's the trouble with small towns and long memories. It's why I left twenty-five years ago."

He watched a bead of condensation roll down his glass. "I was eighteen and wasted out of my mind. I got into an accident on prom night and killed a lady coming off the night shift at the hospital. It was the worst day of my life."

"Oh Andrew, I'm so sorry."

"I was sure my life was ruined. When I got out, Tim gave me a job and a fresh start. I would do anything for him."

"How far does anything go?"

Andrew's eyes met mine. "I wouldn't kill for him, but I'd help him hide the body if he needed me to. And he's never asked for my help."

The kitchen door banged against the wall, and Gigi cast a wide shadow into the dining room. "Tim asked you to help us, and this is how you repay him? You report him to NOAA?!"

Teela was right on Gigi's heels. "Whoa!"

Chelle appeared in the doorway, clumped behind them. "Mack, you didn't?!"

Andrew started to cuss me out, but Nikki had heard the door bang and came to see what was going on. "You hypocrite! You've been strutting around here looking down on everyone, like you're better than us. Asking nosy questions about where we were when Wes died, and the whole time, you're just a narc for the Feds?"

"I'm not. I didn't."

Gigi picked up a tray from the server's station and winged it at me. It hit my ginger ale glass and shattered it. "You've made everything worse. Get out! Get out! Get out!"

CHAPTER 47

I went out the front door because no way was I going to walk past Gigi while she was melting down. The door banged shut behind me, and I nearly ran into the homeless man lurking at the front windows.

He looked me in the eye, then looked away. "The rats are on to you. Time is running out."

"Duly noted."

I should have asked him to elaborate, but I was afraid a lynch mob was forming inside, so I speed-walked past him to my car. Gabe and Darlene were crying in the parking lot. I was too angry to eavesdrop, and that was unusual for me.

Someone had taped a threat to my window. It wasn't a threat against me, mind you. It was a cheap printed photograph on photo paper of a roadside-cleanup detail. Across the top in marker it said, *Do the right thing and let Tim and Gigi know or I'll turn you in myself.* It was signed *W*.

I ripped it off the window and climbed into Bessie. It took me a minute to realize the person in the unflattering orange jumpsuit was Chelle. Her hair was frizzed out, and she had a wild look in her eye and a trash poker in her hand. She was looking belligerently at the camera, like a B-list celebrity whose embarrassing mugshot was the only fame they'd had in months. Wes was blackmailing Tim. He was blackmailing Chelle. Who else was he blackmailing?

I cranked the car to life and peeled out of the parking lot in time to see Gabe's mystery lady crying and running to a little red Jeep.

Not my problem. None of this is my problem. I can't help people who won't let me help them. And no matter how much I like a person, it never keeps them from lying to me or from me believing them. Why do I trust anyone? Aunt Ginny is right. Everyone is hiding something.

I drove the few blocks down to my street. A ton of cars were parked in front of my house. *Victorian Christmas Week. I should have put the cone out.* I parked at the end of my driveway, blocking someone in. Too angry to deal with it now.

I needed to get out of here. I dialed Sawyer and got out of the car.

"Hello?"

"You ready to go shopping?"

Sawyer had a ruckus in the background. She had to practically yell for me to hear her. "Uh . . . where are you . . . Poppy?"

"Dear God, woman. Turn the TV down. I'm at my house." I threw the front door open and caught just about everyone I knew hanging pink streamers and blowing up gold balloons. Sawyer stood in the middle of the sitting room, tying ribbons to an umbrella, her phone tucked between her chin and her shoulder. "What's going on here?"

Sawyer dropped her cell phone into her hand. "Surprise. It's your bridal shower!"

So this is when I have that aneurysm I've been expecting.

Sawyer's grin dropped ten stories. "Are you disappointed?"

"What? No." I looked around. All the Biddies. Georgina. My high school friends Kim and Connie. Kenny. Joanne. Aunt Ginny. Even Royce's sister, Fiona. They were all frozen in place in the middle of hanging up decorations and setting out food. They couldn't know I'd just had the morning from hell and received one or two death threats. I mean, those odds were always in my favor, but they couldn't know for sure.

I pasted a smile on my face. They deserved at least that. "I'm just stunned. I can't believe you've all done this. And to think, I've only been engaged for a week." *Are they afraid I'm going to skip town and elope or something?*

I started around the room, hugging and thanking each of them.

Iris crept in behind Aunt Ginny and put her arms out to me. I deflected her. "Not you."

Sawyer handed the umbrella to Kim and wrapped me in her arms. "I was supposed to keep you busy all morning, but when you were called into Maxine's, we had to come up with a plan B. We didn't expect you back this early."

Aunt Ginny's eyes narrowed. "Why *are* you home so early?"

"Gigi threw me out."

She tsk'd.

"She has a split personality. Sometimes she's filled with desperation for my help, and other times it's seething resentment that I exist."

Aunt Ginny's shoulder twitched. "It sounds like she's afraid. She worked hard to steal Tim away from you. When you work that hard to take a man, you have to work even harder to keep him."

"Well, she can have him. He's been a total jerk this whole time."

Aunt Ginny led me to a wing chair and pushed me

down. "I thought we were going to have to call Tim and tell him the FBI was here to talk to you."

Mrs. Davis tied a black balloon around my ankle with white string. "We told her that was too close to home and maybe just say the house was on fire instead."

"Yeah. I can see how that could be too believable. What exactly are you doing?"

She glanced up at me. "That's your ball and chain. Don't let anyone pop it."

"Or what?"

Mrs. Dodson, topped with a new silver bouffant doo, placed a bingo card in my hand. The squares were filled with names of small appliances and household goods. "Or you lose, silly. Here's your card for Wedding Gift Bingo. Don't set it down. Fiona has that win-at-all-cost gleam in her eye."

Fiona craned her neck to read my card from the love seat and grinned a full set of dentures. I tilted the card protectively against my chest.

The doorbell rang, and Sawyer floated away to answer it. Gia's mother and sisters marched in two by two, spotted me, and launched into a heated complaint that ended with my best friend pointing to the sitting room and yelling. "She's early! Now just take a seat and shut it, or I'll make sure she serves boxed spaghetti and Ragu at the reception."

The sisters promptly took seats in a row of folding chairs behind the couch, while Momma was led to one of the wing chairs of honor next to me.

Kim and Connie were rearranging a pile of presents and watching me expectantly. I was trying hard to pivot my thoughts from the morning. *Who tipped off the fish police that Tim might have fake scallops? Was it me? How did they find out that I knew him? Why is sexy lingerie hanging all over the sitting room like this is a Victorian bordello?*

And who strung up my Dickens caroler to the lamppost with a garter?

Fig galloped around the corner sideways, his foot caught in the straps of a red bra. Kim swooped him up with one hand. "I've hung this bra on the bookcase twice now. Just stay out of it."

Fig's ears flattened, and he swatted at the feather earrings in Kim's ears before she extracted him from the underwear and put him down.

Sawyer clinked a knife against a champagne glass. "Okay, ladies. Let me officially welcome you to Poppy's bridal shower."

The women cheered like I was the underdog in a last-place beauty pageant and they were just happy I hadn't fallen up the stairs. While Sawyer gave a rundown of the order of the event, my eye caught movement in the library across the hall. The doors were pulled to a crack, but I could see someone creeping around by the desk through the gap.

The bridal shower guests headed en masse to the dining room to fill their plates with finger sandwiches and chocolate-dipped strawberries, but I tried to duck across the foyer. Connie grabbed my arm. "Where do you think you're going? You're the guest of honor."

I whispered and nodded to the intruder. "I'll be right back."

Connie followed my gaze. She narrowed her eyes and let me go. I crept into the library and stood behind Iris McAllister, who was on her hands and knees, her derrière sticking straight up in the air. She was digging through the bottom drawer of my antique rolltop desk.

"I thought I told you to stop snooping around my house."

Iris jumped and banged her head against the center drawer. "No. I was just . . ."

"Quit lying."

Iris dropped to her butt onto the oriental rug. "I haven't even started lying."

Aunt Ginny answered from behind me. "We know a lie was coming because your lips were moving."

Iris's face pinked, and she looked back at the open drawer she'd been digging through.

I looked across the hall to the people who loved me— and Gia's family—and I felt more sadness than anger for the woman who gave birth to me. "I'm your only daughter, and this is my bridal shower. Instead of trying to sneak in to be a part of my big day, you're using it as a cover to pilfer my house."

Aunt Ginny tsk'd. "Tell her what you're looking for, Iris, or I will."

A fat tear rolled down Iris's cheek. "I need my engagement ring."

That was definitely not what I expected. "What?"

"When your father proposed, he gave me a two-carat, square-cut sapphire that had been passed down from his grandmother. When I told his mother that I was checking myself into a facility until I could get my head straight, she made me leave it with her."

Aunt Ginny's words sliced through the air with the precision of a Ginsu knife in a tin can. "My sister was no dummy. She knew you couldn't be trusted any farther than we could throw you. That ring is to stay in the family and pass to Poppy." Aunt Ginny jabbed her thumb in Iris's direction. "She's been searching the house ever since she arrived. This whole visit has been a ruse to find that ring."

Iris shook her head. "No. That's not true. I also wanted to see my daughter."

"Why? For real this time."

Iris's voice trembled. "I need your help."

Aunt Ginny threw her arms in the air. "What is it, Iris? Gambling debts? Drugs? Why do you need that ring so bad?"

"And why do you want it now?"

Iris looked from me to Aunt Ginny. Lines deepened around her eyes the harder she thought. "Because I want the money to pay for an adoption."

Aunt Ginny made a choking sound. "For what?"

The hamster in my brain fell off her treadmill. "Like, as in adopting a puppy?"

Iris shook her head. "I want to adopt a baby. I didn't get to be a mother to you. I missed out on so much. I've applied to a very reputable agency, and my turn is coming up. The agency wants immediate family to sign character references. I came here to ask you to write me a letter of recommendation. Don't you see? I need you to tell them that I'd be a good mother."

Neither Aunt Ginny nor I moved until Sawyer called that we had to come eat. Aunt Ginny's lips clamped down, and she faced me with a raise of her eyebrow. I nodded. Together we pointed to the front door. "Get out."

Iris tried to make a plea to be allowed to stay, but we were done. We corralled her to the front door and then through it. Aunt Ginny had Kenny go fetch her purse and keys. "We'll pack your bag and call you when it's ready, but right now, we're going to enjoy your only daughter's happy event."

Iris stormed off the porch, complaining that she never got a chance to explain herself and it wasn't fair that we would keep this opportunity from her. "If I can't have the ring, can you at least write me the recommendation?"

"Goodbye, Iris."

I stood with my arms crossed over my chest, my eyes burning, while watching her speed away. Aunt Ginny's hand on my back brought me some small comfort. I wiped my cheek and spotted a padded envelope sitting on the rocking chair on the porch. It had my name written on it. I picked it up and looked inside. There was a cell phone and a Post-it note with a six-digit code. I plugged in the code, and the phone opened to a background wallpaper of Wes Bailey holding a giant swordfish and grinning. *Oh. My. Lord. Why can't I just get one of those fruit bouquets for a change? Or a nut tower. I could do a lot with a nut tower. I could make brittle.*

I knew I needed to call Amber, but I also knew once I did, I'd never see the phone again. I pulled out my own cell phone and called Gia. "Can your brother-in-law transfer the data off one phone onto another?"

"Probably."

"How soon can you get him over here?"

Gia's voice was muffled for a beat, then he returned to the phone. "He wants to finish his cheesesteak first because Teresa has him on a diet for the wedding. How is fifteen minutes?"

"The sooner the better."

There was a loud pop behind me. I turned and spotted Fiona grinning at my busted balloon.

"What was that?" Gia asked.

"I forgot to protect my ball and chain."

CHAPTER 48

If you're going to play bridal-shower bingo with a bunch of old ladies, make sure you have a crock-pot square on your bingo card. I got four of them, along with a spirited argument from the Biddies and Fiona as to which one of them had called dibs on giving me the slow cooker.

Gia's sisters had all given me steak knives—that was a bad omen—and his mother seemed to think I was going to do the dance of the seven veils on my wedding night because she gave me the trashiest piece of lingerie I'd ever seen.

The doorbell rang, and I excused myself to let in Gia and Angelo while the ladies carried on with the festivities.

Angelo held up a burner phone. "Hello, new sister. I am here to clone your phone."

I shushed him and handed him the cell from the padded envelope. "Thank you. Make sure you don't delete anything from the original." I'd been dying to look at it since it arrived, but I couldn't let Sawyer down. She'd put a lot of effort into planning my shower.

Gia eyed my headpiece as he kissed my cheek but had

the good sense not to comment on the paper-plate hat covered in ribbons and bows.

"It's a wedding veil."

He narrowed his eyes and nodded. "Do you have to wear it in the actual wedding?"

"Definitely not."

"Okay, then it is cute."

I gave him a grin. "I'm happy to find out this early in the game that you are one bad liar."

Gia leaned in and kissed me, to much raucous hooting from the bridal-shower ladies. "Are you having fun?"

I cut my eyes to where Sawyer and Aunt Ginny were passing out newspaper for the ladies to play a party game. "I'm trying to. I had a really rough morning. Tim is being investigated by NOAA, and it might be my fault."

"How would that be your fault?"

"I called them anonymously to ask questions about Deepwater Fisheries."

"Did you mention Maxine's?"

"No."

"Did you call from Maxine's?"

"No."

"Did you give them your name?"

"No. But maybe they traced my number and found a link between me and Tim."

Gia chuckled. "They are not Homeland Security. It sounds like coincidence."

"Someone said they were tipped off."

"The timing is very convenient. Everyone there is murder suspect. I bet your killer called in this NOAA to deflect attention from the investigation."

Angelo waved me into the library. "I have a connection now, but it will take time to move all the data."

Sawyer made eyes at me from the sitting room. She was elbow deep in a ham-and-cheese hoagie. She nodded to where Gia's sisters were wrapping Kim and Connie in newspaper. Georgina and Kenny were making a veil for Joanne. "I need you to come judge the best wedding dress when they're finished."

"I'll be there before they finish the bouquets."

She nodded and took a chomp on a dill spear.

Angelo looked longingly across the hall. "Can I get one of those hoagies without Teresa noticing?"

Teresa was overheard from the sitting room. "Does anyone else smell grilled onions?"

Angelo shook his head. "Never mind. It's too risky."

While the data was being transferred, I went back to the party and ate a finger sandwich. I gave hints as to what I wanted my wedding dress to look like, what kind of veil, long train or short. Mostly I rattled off random adjectives, while the women tried to catch each other using the words "bride," "groom," or "wedding." I thought Momma had an unfair advantage since no one could understand anything that came out of her mouth but her daughters.

Aunt Ginny watched me closely. She knew my heart was divided, and I was tamping down emotions over Iris's slap in the face. She suggested we put on some Christmas music. I tried to stop her, but I was weighed down with my mouth full of strawberry. As soon as she hit the button, Bruce Springsteen ho-ho-hoed at my bridal shower. I told Aunt Ginny that I'd converted to Judaism so I would never have to hear that song again. *Hanukkah doesn't have to put up with this.*

Gia appeared in the doorway and made small talk with the ladies. His mother said something that made him blush, but he wouldn't tell me what it was. He made a face that I interpreted as they were ready, so I grabbed a couple cookies and excused myself for a minute.

I placed the contraband on a napkin on the coffee table and surreptitiously slid it towards Angelo, who quickly palmed and pocketed them. He in turn slid Wes's phone across the table to me.

I turned it on and saw Wes holding the giant swordfish. "Nice work, Angelo." I scrolled through Wes's text messages. Everything recent was business as usual except for some nude shots a woman had sent him a couple of months ago. "You lying little . . ."

Gia leaned over my shoulder. "What is it?"

"These are from Teela. Her face is reflected in the shower door in this one."

Gia frowned. "I thought she said Wes was harassing her?"

"Well, she obviously fed his interest. But what was she trying to accomplish?"

Angelo sneaked a cookie out of his pocket and nibbled it. "Sugar daddy?"

Laughter erupted from the sitting room, and Sawyer poked her head around the corner. She mouthed *five minutes* before biting into a giant cookie.

I checked Wes's call log. The last calls he made were to a Florida number in the afternoon and to a local number at seven p.m. That was the day before his body was found in Tim's freezer. The last call he received was at one forty the morning he died.

Fear gripped my chest and threatened to bring up my sandwich. "I think I know that number." I took out my cell phone and dialed.

The call connected, and a recording played on the line. "Thank you for calling Maxine's." I hung up and sighed. I sat there for a minute, weighing my options.

Gia took my hand in his. "Do you want me to call Amber, so you don't have to be the one?"

I brushed a tear before it could fall and nodded. "I can't put it off any longer. The list of people who could be in that office at one in the morning is very small."

I went back to the party while Gia made the call. Amber arrived in a squad car twenty minutes later, just as Sawyer had me cut a gluten-free cake shaped like a stork.

Amber took one look around the sitting room, and her voice took on a hard edge. "Let's make this quick so you can get back to your shower."

I grabbed the stork's beak holding the baby and led her across the hall. "The bridal shower was a surprise, Amber. I had nothing to do with the guest list."

Amber sniffed and pulled out her notebook. "I'm sure."

I held out the piece of cake to her. "I would have invited you if I'd known."

Amber eyed the cake and flicked her eyes to mine. She reached for the plate. "I guess I'll have to take your word for it."

"Thank you." I showed her the envelope and what had come inside it. "I found this on the porch."

"Who sent it?"

"I don't know, but it came fully charged, and they sent along the code to unlock it. It's Wes Bailey's phone."

Amber had a mouthful of chocolate icing. "Gia said Wes received a call at one forty?"

I pulled up the call log to show her. "From someone in the office at Maxine's. It lasted three minutes."

"Awesome. I've been waiting for that subpoena to get Maxine's phone records for a week. I'll run a trace on these last two calls Wes made as well."

"We, um . . . we did call them. From Angelo's phone. The Florida one is out of service, and the local number has been no answer so far."

Amber licked frosting off the side of her fork. "Okay. I'll get IT on it. The coroner just confirmed that Wes had been frozen for four to six hours, putting time of death between midnight and two a.m. Since we know he received a call at one forty from Maxine's, I think it's safe to say the time of death was two a.m. Jackson Seymour was at a Christmas party in North Wildwood with his wife until one. It's not impossible that he dropped his wife at home, waited for her to fall asleep, then met up with Wes and killed him by two a.m., but it would be tight."

"I don't think he has it in him to kill Wes anyway. He turned his anger towards public outcry and building his own vendor alliance instead of murder."

Amber looked towards the bridal shower. "There is one other thing I need to tell you, but I don't want to ruin your big day here."

"What is it?"

"Kieran just arrested Tim. He's charging him with Wes's murder."

CHAPTER 49

Sawyer and I stood in the doorway, waving goodbye to Karla and the sisters.

"Thank you for coming."

"And thank you for the gifts. I'm sure Gia and I will . . . eat a lot of steak."

The six sisters waved as they gawked around my yard. "Goodbye now."

"See you on Christmas Eve." I closed the front door. "How did that happen?"

Sawyer led me into the library and flopped on the couch. "You let the one called Francesca talk you into having them all come to the Christmas party."

I bent over the fireplace and lit a match to set the logs on fire. "I need to register for a backbone."

Sawyer yawned. "Let's see if we can find a two-for-one special. Ben told his mother we'd come for Christmas dinner, and before I knew what I was saying, I agreed to it."

"When did we become such people pleasers?"

"Girl Scouts."

"That sounds right." I flopped onto the couch next to

her and put her feet in my lap. "Gia and Henry are coming for the Christmas Eve party and spending the night. I want to buy matching pajamas."

"Your first Christmas as a family. Ben asked for the night off to come to the party, but he probably won't get it. The crime rate goes up over the holidays, but I don't have to tell you that." Sawyer grinned, then her eyes went soft. "Are you doing okay?"

"I'm trying to stay distracted."

"If Tim is innocent, you'll find a way to prove it."

"I hope you're right."

Kenny popped into the library. "All four crock-pot are in your room, along with your naughty nighties and the fruit-roll-up underwear Mrs. Davis bought you."

"Oh goody."

Sawyer snickered. "When are you gonna make that sexy pasta you got from Aunt Ginny?"

"I'm saving it for a special occasion. Maybe I'll use it in a pasta salad for a PTA meeting. That'll get people to stop talking about Henry's mother, the Murder Magnet, and they can just call me a pervert instead."

The doorbell rang, and Figaro galloped to the foyer to assume the position of Lord of the Manor. A pink ribbon from one of my shower presents was caught around his foot. He tried to shake it off, but it rattled against the wood floor and spooked him. He dove under the couch to escape it.

Kenny peeked out the window around the front door. "It's just the new guests for the Purple Emperor Suite. Last guests of the year."

He led a couple from Virginia past the library to the registration desk. The woman remarked. "Your house is the most decorated one for Christmas that I've ever seen."

I waited till she was out of earshot to say, "She's never seen South Jersey competitive rage decorating before."

Sawyer snickered. "Aunt Ginny may have invented a new sport."

I put my feet up on the coffee table. "Honey, thank you for today. It was a beautiful bridal shower."

"I know you're still caught in the middle at Maxine's, but I needed to get it done before Gia's sisters pulled a fast one. I can tell they have it in them to Ocean's Eleven your entire wedding before anyone figures out what they're up to."

"You are not wrong. I'm expecting Momma to show up on the plane with her suitcase packed for the honeymoon."

Sawyer giggled and yawned again. "I'm sorry I'm so tired. The bookstore has been crazy this Christmas. I'm wiped out every night. Ben says I need to lie down more often, but when am I supposed to get anything done if I do that? I barely have time to make a sandwich for dinner as it is."

My cell phone rang, and I checked the screen. It was that number that texted me this morning. "Hello?"

"Poppy, it's Gigi."

I hit the disconnect button and put the phone back on the couch. "Hey, have you ever heard of Pop-up Bistro?"

"No. What is that?"

My cell phone rang again. Same number. "You won't believe who's calling me."

"Who?"

I answered by hitting the speaker button. "Poppy, don't hang up. It's Gigi. I need your help."

Sawyer's eyebrows shot up.

I hit disconnect and silenced my phone. "Apparently it's this moving, one-night-only, exclusive guest-chef restaurant scheme."

Sawyer pulled out her phone. "Cool. Pop-up Bistro?"

My cell phone started vibrating against the couch. "Andrew works as a waiter for them every Tuesday night.

He says they never know where they're going or who the chef will be until the app tells them."

Sawyer held up her phone. "I found it. Downloading now." She picked up my phone and answered it. "Stop calling, you crazy witch. You kicked her out, and all she's tried to do is help you."

She hung up and put the phone back on the couch.

"Does the app show a record of guest chefs who participate?"

She thumbed through the list. "Only after the event. Some of the chefs have photos and links to their websites."

"Can you see who the chef was last Wednesday?"

"Mmm. Chef Devon at a warehouse in Wildwood. He got five stars."

"Any pictures?"

Sawyer shook her head. "No."

Aunt Ginny came around the corner, carrying the cordless phone from her bedroom about eight inches away from her ear.

Gigi's voice sobbed through the speaker. "I know he didn't do it because the police said someone called Wes from our office phone at one forty, and Tim and I were having a fight from our separate apartments at the time. I deleted the texts. Now the cops don't believe me, and they want to hold Tim until they can get the transcript from our cell provider. That could take weeks. If you ever loved Tim, you can make up for everything by helping him now."

Aunt Ginny held the phone out to me. "It's for you."

I rolled my eyes so hard I pulled a muscle in my forehead.

Gigi croaked, "Please, Poppy. I'll never ask you for anything ever again."

I took the phone from Aunt Ginny. "What is wrong with you?"

"I'm eight months pregnant and desperate. There are things Tim didn't want you to know that I can tell you."

You stupid, crazy . . . "I want all access."

"You got it."

"You'll answer all my questions truthfully, no matter what?"

"I promise."

"If you give me any attitude or throw a chicken, I'm walking."

"You have my word."

I had a choice to make. Either hurl the phone into the fireplace or buy Tim some cigarettes and chocolate bars to trade for favors in prison. I guess going into Maxine's was also a choice, but right now it felt like a fool's choice.

Tim was there for me when I was in jail . . .

Aunt Ginny raised one eyebrow. "Should I hold dinner for you?"

I huffed. "I'll be there as soon as I can." I hung up and handed the phone back to her. "What's for dinner?"

"Whatever you feel like making."

"I'm cooking?"

"I vote for turkey pot pie."

"So I'm not really involved in this decision at all."

"I want you to feel included."

I looked to Sawyer for moral support. She was sound asleep.

CHAPTER 50

All the way over to Maxine's, I felt like an idiot. How many times would I let these people kick me and go back for more? I put my hand on the radio and paused. Surely, it would be different this time. Twelve days to Christmas—they must be diversifying the playlist by now. I would even take that obnoxious hippo song. I turned the knob and held my breath. It was a new holiday song by a singer I didn't recognize. *Thank goodness.*

I took the curve on Washington to cross the bridge; the song faded into the wind whipping down the boardwalk, and Bruce Springsteen punched me right in the face.

I spun the knob hard to the left and considered ripping the radio out of the dash and throwing it into the marina. I pulled into the parking lot and did a one-eighty to face the road for a quick escape, spraying broken clamshells across the expanse.

The homeless man was down by the marina, looking at the water and talking to himself. He turned and spotted me, then transformed. He shoved his hands in his pockets and hunched over. *Weird.*

I went through the kitchen and found it abandoned. "Gigi! I'm here." *Come out, come out, you obnoxious little elf.*

Her quivery voice answered from the dining room. "In here."

I expected Gigi to be alone.

No. Strike that.

I expected Gigi to have a meat cleaver and jump out to attack me as soon as I crossed the threshold. What I did not expect was to see everyone on staff sitting around the long table, looking bored and irritated.

"Why are you all still here?"

Andrew flicked his eyes to mine. "We've been called back."

Chelle sighed. "Mandatory staff meeting."

Teela crossed her arms over her chest and tsk'd. "I better be getting paid for this. I've given enough to charity this Christmas. That mall Santa made two dollars off me when I was shopping for new boots."

Gigi sat in the middle, like Jesus at the last supper. "I think we need to talk about our plan moving forward. Poppy is here with some ideas."

Gabe's irritation was soft as a prickly powder puff. "Aren't you supposed to be on bed rest?"

Gigi snapped at him. "No. That's just a precaution. Maybe we need some food for the meeting. Chuck, go whip up some of that mushroom Parmesan risotto I like."

Chuck pushed his glasses up the bridge of his nose while giving Gigi some side-eye. "You want me to make risotto, right now?"

Tyler sounded bored. "The Feds shut us down, Gigi. We should all go home."

Murmurs of agreement did the wave around the room.

"It's not like we're serving it to customers." Gigi shrugged. "If not the risotto, how about some carbonara?"

She called them in because she doesn't want to be alone. "Why do you think Wes was killed in your kitchen, Gigi?"

All eyes popped to attention on me.

Gigi had promised to be civil. Her face pinked from the exertion. "I've said all along I think that homeless man has been breaking in to rob me. I think Wes caught him in the act and he killed him. He seems mental."

"Why would Wes be here at midnight? And why would he care if you were being robbed?"

Gigi shrugged. "Well, I have no idea."

Teela let out a breath, long and slow. "If the homeless man was stealing from you, he'd take money. And booze. Not frozen meat."

Nikki nodded, but kept silent.

Gigi threw her arms out to the sides. "Even with the new locks he got in again last Wednesday."

I pulled out a chair to sit across from her. "Why do you think it was Wednesday?"

She shook her blond curls. "I did the inventory myself Thursday afternoon."

"You discovered the meat was missing on Thursday, but it was probably taken overnight on Tuesday. It's probably always taken on Tuesday."

"How do you know that?"

Everyone's eyes fell on me like tiny little fire pokers. I looked around to see who would look away. "Let me ask you this instead. How would the homeless man store and cook two tenderloins and a bunch of steaks out there in a pop-up tent, and eat it all in one night? There's no meat lying around back there. And the animals would be stalking him if he had a tent full of prime rib."

Gigi huffed. "I don't know. He doesn't have to eat it all the same night. I don't trust him. I think he's the reason business has been so bad these past few months."

Chuck stared at the table. "He's only been out there for a few weeks."

I tried to keep my voice even. "Do you think maybe meat was going missing before he got here, and no one noticed?"

Gabriel pushed out his chair. "I'm gonna go check that tent and talk to him."

Gigi dropped her head in her hands. "I just don't know. Everything is a mess, and I can't control it. Contracts, vendors, inventory, now an investigation. I thought once I'd reported Wes to NOAA that they'd shut him down and all our problems would go away." Her lip trembled. "I never imagined that it would come back on us."

The employees started murmuring.

Nikki's eyes were narrowed to slits. "When you called NOAA, did you give them your name?"

She removed her hands from across her face. "No. I did it all anonymously."

Andrew added, "Did you do it from the back-office phone?"

Gigi nodded. "Yeah, but I didn't tell them Maxine's or anything."

Everyone without pregnancy brain groaned.

Gigi was still clueless. "What?"

Teela huffed. "Have you never heard of caller ID?"

Gabriel walked back through the dining room. "There is no evidence he's been cooking anything down there in the few weeks he's been here. And that homeless man hasn't been homeless very long."

"How do you know?"

"His nails are too short. And his teeth are too white. I worked with a homeless shelter in Philly for a while, and this guy is too well groomed to have been living rough for months."

Gigi pointed. "See! I've been telling you he's suspicious."

"Who's suspicious?" Tim's voice boomed across the dining room, the light from the kitchen casting his shadow across the linen-covered table.

CHAPTER 51

Gigi launched herself into his arms, knocking the wind out of him. "How did you get out?"

"They let me go. One minute I'm being formally charged, and the next thing I knew, they said I could leave. Apparently, I've been released pending further inquiries." Tim pulled out a chair and joined everyone around the table.

Gigi kissed him like he'd been narrowly saved from some cult sacrifice. "You can all go home now."

You didn't have to tell them twice. Everyone shot out of the dining room before she could remember the purpose of the meeting and make them stay. Everyone except Andrew, who lingered, eyeing me questioningly while inching towards the kitchen.

I pulled out my cell phone and texted Amber.

Why'd you let Tim go?

Tim managed to extract himself from Gigi's claw-like embrace. "What are you doing here, Mack?"

"Your baby mama begged me to come."

Amber texted me back.

Kieran got a call from up the food chain. Tim has friends in high places.

Tim gave a stunned glance to Gigi. "Why?"

Gigi sounded exasperated in a way that every woman understands. "You were arrested, boo. If anyone can get through to that policewoman, it's your ex here."

I don't know about that. "I was told you were ready to answer my questions."

Tim sighed. "Go ahead."

"Where were you two the night of the murder?"

Tim cut his eyes to Gigi, as if looking for permission. As promised, she spilled the tea and told me everything. "We were fighting. Merging our restaurants hasn't been the experience I'd hoped for. Tim seems to think I work *for* him."

Been there, girl.

Gigi reached into a large pink tote bag at her feet and pulled out a bag of almonds. "I gave up everything to come here. I mortgaged Le Bon Gigi to pay Maxine's bills, but I didn't realize the money was mismanaged or that the contract with Wes was horrifying. I didn't know what Wes was up to, and I tried to take matters into my own hands when Tim wouldn't deal with it."

Tim crossed his arms. "That's not fair, Geeg. And you made everything so much worse when you signed an agreement with Atlantic Coast Seafood. Now we're on the hook with two fish vendors."

Gigi snorted. "If you had just told me what was going on, I wouldn't have done it. I thought we could pay Deepwater's penalty to get out early. I had no idea you had agreed to those shameful fees or that Wes had something on you."

"So you each went to your own apartments, and then what?"

Tim's tone was icy. "She complained about me all night through texts."

Gigi's jaw dropped. "You're a brilliant chef, and yet you served shark fin to our customers and told them it was scallops, Tim. And what's worse, you kept it from me. We could lose everything."

Maybe it's not entirely his fault. "Under what circumstances could you ever be persuaded to serve shark fin and pass it off as scallops?"

Tim's words had a biting edge to them. "Under the circumstances of being over-tired, over-stressed, and over-trusting. I admit that I should have been more careful to check my deliveries and keep up with my paperwork. I didn't know Wes was cheating me. I knew something was off, but my invoice said scallops."

Okay, so thirty percent at fault.

"When I said, 'Dude, what the heck is this?' he told me it must have been a clerical error at the docks. It was too late to replace the order without a huge up-charge, and I should just serve them because no one would know. He said it happens all the time that restaurants charge for an expensive dish and sub in a cheaper fish. Diners can't tell the difference."

Fifty percent at fault? "And you refused?"

The biting edge was back to his words. "You saw my bank statement. And scallops are one of our best-selling items."

Nope. One hundred percent at fault.

Gigi got up from the table and disappeared for a minute. She came back with a bag of butter cookies.

"When did the shark fin show up on the invoice?"

Tim let out a sigh that ended with a frustrated groan. "A few weeks later, when I told Wes that Gigi was bringing her own fish vendor from Le Bon Gigi. He said he didn't want to report me for serving shark fin as scallops. When I said it was my word against his, he said he'd been hanging out at my bar every night for weeks and we had never had shark fin on the menu. And he'd been substituting shark fin for scallops for months. He sent a copy of an invoice that listed shark fin as if I'd ordered it. You saw it. My signature was on it."

"Was it forged?"

"I don't know. Things had just ended with you and me." He paused for a moment, and Gigi shoved an entire cookie into her mouth. "I was merging businesses with Geeg, and she found fault with how I ran everything. I was trying to be super-chef to make her happy, but it was burning me out. That's why I gave Wes a key in the first place. I'm too old to work twenty hours a day anymore. I had no idea he was slipping me counterfeit shellfish until it was too late."

Gigi turned the cookie bag upside down. Nothing came out, so she got up and left the room again.

"Is it safe to assume this was all going on while Wes was pressuring you to join his vendor alliance?"

"Pressure turned to blackmail overnight. He made it very clear that if I didn't agree to exclusivity with his dedicated vendors, he would take it public that I was involved in fish fraud."

"Why would he gamble with his business too?"

Tim laughed bitterly. "He made sure he was clean. It's not against the law to sell shark fin. It's just against the law to call them scallops. My business would have been destroyed, my reputation ruined."

Gigi returned with chips and salsa and a bottled protein drink.

"I don't get it, though. Why go to such lengths to force his vendor alliance on people?"

"He was building a monopoly. Forcing everyone outside the alliance to go under. If you're in food service on the island, he'd control every aspect of your business in just a few years. He could charge any price he wanted."

"There were probably a lot of other vendors who wanted to see him gone, but he was killed here—in your kitchen. After someone called his cell phone from your office."

Gigi chomped on a fistful of chips. "Right. And we were home, texting each other."

Tim said wryly. "You were doing most of the texting."

"There has to be a connection to your staff. Do you remember what time you closed that night?"

Tim and Gigi looked at each other and shrugged. Gigi answered between sips of her liquid grass. "The usual time. Midnight."

"Were you the last to leave?"

They nodded.

"Who locked up?"

Tim pointed to himself. "I did."

Gigi had a mouthful of chips. "We already told all of this to the police."

"Wes met someone here after hours. Either they were able to get in, stab him, then Houdini him into the locked freezer without touching his keys . . . or someone has a key that you don't know about."

Gigi pulled out a candy bar and ripped off the wrapper. "You'd have to ask your boyfriend here. He gave out lots of keys."

Tim sighed.

"Are you sure there are only four copies?"

"I gave one to Jackson, one to Wes, and one to Gigi."

"Why not Chuck or Tyler?"

Tim shrugged. "They use mine when they lock up."

Gigi's eyes narrowed at Tim as she chugged her protein drink.

"How often does that happen?"

"Lots. They had keys to the back door before Gigi came over."

Gigi sighed. "That's why I said we'd only have walk-in

keys for the two of us moving forward. And those keys can't be copied. They're security keys."

"What about your other deliveries? Meats and linens and soda? How do they get in?"

Tim sat back and crossed one leg over the other. "They come in the afternoon."

"How does Gabe lock up on nights you leave early?"

Tim cleared his throat and glanced at Gigi. She had her eyes frozen on him. A fistful of chips held at the ready. "I leave him my key."

Gigi sputtered.

Tim sat forward, his palms turned up. "What! We only put the locks on the walk-ins because you're obsessed with the homeless man."

Gigi crushed the chips she was holding. "Why didn't you just give the homeless man a set of keys, Tim?"

I brushed some of the tortilla dust off my sweater. "Is it safe to assume you didn't track inventory before the homeless man started hanging around?"

Tim looked affronted. "I take inventory. But a couple steaks go missing here and there, and I just figured I counted wrong. Chalk it up to stress. Or the guys made them for their dinner on nights I was off and forgot to mark the shortage board. No big deal." He gave a pointed look at Gigi. "Even now, it's not like it's thousands of dollars a week that disappears."

Gigi pulled a sandwich out of one of the pockets from her voluminous dress. "It's hundreds Tim. Every time it happens, which is at least once a week, it's hundreds."

"I think the theft is being committed by someone on staff, and you didn't notice it until the homeless man showed up. The question is, did Wes know? Wes Bailey was dealing in secrets, and he liked to blackmail those with something to hide. Was stealing meat a secret so awful that the thief had to silence him rather than be exposed?"

I took out my cell phone and showed them the picture of Teela and Gabe out front. "Do you recognize this?"

They both looked and shook their heads.

Gigi narrowed her eyes. "I think that's when we were setting up the group shot for our Facebook page."

"Did you send me these, dated December third?"

Gigi shook her head. "No."

Tim added. "Those were taken for our Octoberfest event."

I pulled up the picture of Chelle working off her community service on my phone. "How about this one?"

Gigi glanced at the picture, and a blush crept up her cheeks. She looked away.

Tim squinted at my phone. "Yeah. I've seen it."

"Did Wes show it to you?"

Tim nodded. "A few weeks back. He thought I'd fire Chelle, but she's a really good hostess. And who hasn't made mistakes?"

Gigi smacked Tim on the arm. "You knew!"

I turned to the perky momster. "You taped this to my car window, didn't you?"

Gigi huffed. "Well, you're not looking at anyone to be guilty but me and Tim. I paid Wes two thousand dollars not to post that on our social media and tell everyone we hire ex-cons."

Tim sighed. "Geeg. Half the restaurants in America would shut down if nobody hired ex-cons. You gotta give people a chance."

A knock sounded on the front door, and we all jumped. A woman's face appeared, and I recognized her as the woman Gabe had been arguing with this afternoon.

Gigi hollered, "We're closed!" and pulled a pack of cheese and crackers from inside her dress.

I stood up. "I'll get it." I crossed the room and opened the door. "Hi. Darlene, is it?"

The woman nodded as she tried to look around me towards the bar. She was holding a baby on her hip. "Is Gabriel here? I thought you didn't close until ten."

"Change of plans today. And who is this beautiful girl?"

The woman shifted her weight. "This is Gabrielle. Gabby, for short."

"What a pretty name."

The baby gave me a shy smile. She had Gabe's piercing blue eyes. *She looks just like him.* "Does Gabe know?"

Darlene gave me a searching look and nodded. "He knows, but he's never met her."

I let the baby wrap her chubby hand around my finger. "Hello there. How old is she?"

"Nine months. Gabriel and I have been apart for a year. I didn't leave my husband until after Gabby was born."

I nodded. "Are you a Marine also?"

"Not anymore. Jason is still active duty. My service ended six months ago. Jason made sure of that." She shifted the baby's weight on her hip. "It's hard to leave your husband when you can't go anywhere without being charged for desertion."

I nodded and gave her a sympathetic smile. "You must have felt terribly trapped."

"My ex is abusive, but he was smart about it. He knows how to hurt without leaving evidence, so I could never get him charged for anything. When he found out I'd been having an affair, he hurt me so bad I almost lost the baby. He made me report that I'd tripped over the laundry basket and fallen down the stairs."

"Oh, Darlene. I'm so sorry."

She swallowed and changed her attention to the baby. "I don't know why I'm telling you all this. I love Gabriel. I let him down when I didn't leave Jason after I got pregnant."

"How did he get the dishonorable discharge for assault?"

She hugged the baby closer. "I'm surprised he told anyone about that. Gabriel was a lifer. A dishonorable discharge is as shameful to him as committing treason." Darlene fussed with the baby's dress while she fought back her tears. "He broke Jason's nose after he found out what he'd done to me. Gabriel can't stand to see a woman being hurt. He has no tolerance for abusive men."

"How did that result in a court martial?"

"Jason was our commanding officer, and that made him untouchable. He taunted Gabriel, saying that he would never see his baby, and if he told anyone he was the father, he'd make sure I paid the price for it. Gabriel could have fought it, but he took the assault charge to keep me from being court-martialed for adultery."

"Did anything ever happen to your ex? Did you ever report Jason for abuse?"

"I filed a formal complaint right after I was discharged." Darlene gave me a flat look. "He's about to be promoted to lieutenant colonel."

"That sucks."

"Can you get a message to Gabe for me?"

"I'll do what I can."

A tear rolled to the corner of her eye, and she blinked it away. "Tell him I'm sorry for everything, but I'm here for Gabby. She needs to know her daddy. No matter what he's done, we forgive him."

The baby giggled in her arms, making me smile. "I'll make sure he knows."

I shut the door behind her. Gigi was eating a pack of Skittles. "Who was that?"

"That was one of those secrets Wes Bailey had in his pocket."

CHAPTER 52

I left Maxine's so Tim could take Gigi home. Tim's business was in free fall, and his life was following right behind. Many of his problems came from trying to look like he had it all together instead of asking for help. I wondered how different things would have been in our relationship if he'd confided in me earlier too.

I turned the corner onto Lafayette and spotted the Seymour Veg box truck making a delivery. I pulled into the parking lot and blocked him in.

He was in the back, getting a crate of peppers. "I'll only be a minute, lady."

"Actually, I wanted to ask you a question."

Jackson looked over his peppers, his shaggy hair covering his prickly eyebrows. "What is it now?"

"Can I see your keys again?"

He paused a minute. Maybe he was thinking of demanding a search warrant, like they do on cop shows on TV. Maybe he was just thinking of telling me to shove off. Then he put down the peppers and pulled out a giant ring of keys and handed them to me.

"There are too many here for me to know what I'm looking at. Just give me the ones for Maxine's."

He wiggled his fingers, and I placed the metal clump on his beefy palm. He rifled through them and took off two keys.

"Can I keep these for a couple of days?"

He pulled an iPad from a bin of cucumbers and tapped it awake. "My next delivery for Maxine's should be Wednesday morning. I'll need someone to let me in."

"I'll make sure Tim knows." *If he's not back in jail by then.*

"Do I get a receipt that the police have taken the keys?"

I scrawled a note on the back of a Seymour Veg invoice and signed my name. He seemed mollified by that. I went back to my car, pulled out my phone, and searched for locksmiths. There was only one on the island. The listing said twenty-four-seven emergency service. I gave them a call.

"Hi. I've done something really silly and locked myself out of the house. I don't want to break one of my two-hundred-year-old windows to get in. Can you help me?"

The voice on the phone took my address and said they'd be right over. I quickly drove home and locked the front door. I texted Aunt Ginny.

Don't come outside. I'm testing something.

Then I waited on the porch, warmed by the glow of a million little flashing lights.

A white van with a giant red key painted across the side pulled up to the curb. A short woman in overalls climbed down from the cab and marched up the walkway, carrying a red tackle box.

"You're locked out, eh?"

"I don't know what I was thinking when I left. I guess—*I have less than two weeks for Christmas shopping, ahh!*"

She nodded. "There's a lot of that going around. Lots of keys locked in cars at the mall this time of year."

"Do you have lock picks?"

She placed the tackle box at her feet and examined the lock. "Don't need 'em." She pulled out a long metal key with zigzaggy teeth running down one side and a black rubber stopper at the head. She slid it into the lock.

"What's that?"

"This here's a bump key." She took out a small mallet and tapped the key in the lock about ten times until the handle turned. The door swung open on a whiff of rum. "There ya go."

Figaro appeared in the doorway, wearing reindeer antlers, and gave her a peeved look. Followed by Aunt Ginny, with an almost identical look. "Who the heck is making all that noise?" She looked from the locksmith over to me, then called over her shoulder. "It's just Poppy and some farmer."

Georgina called from inside, "Let them come in. We need another tashte tesht . . . teshter."

I took a whiff. "Why does it smell like a distillery?"

"We're making rum balls. Did you see the cat?" Aunt Ginny cackled.

The locksmith glanced at me wide-eyed. "Didn't you check to see if anyone was home?"

"I guess they didn't hear me knock." *Or check their texts.*

"That'll be a hundred dollars."

Holy crap, I'm closing the bed and breakfast and becoming a locksmith! I pulled out the security key that Jackson Seymour gave me. "While I have you here, can you make me a copy of this key?"

She took the key from my hand and turned it over. "I could, but I won't."

"What do you mean?"

Aunt Ginny sidled up next to me to be at a better vantage to be nosy.

"There's no law preventing you from making a copy of a 'do not duplicate' key; it's just not worth the headache. That's why the local hardware store won't do it."

"I thought a 'do not duplicate' key was illegal to copy."

"Nope. It's not a patented security key, so that stamp is meaningless. It's like putting out a 'beware of dog' sign in your yard when you don't actually have a dog. I got enough stress in my life than to have some business owner come after me 'cause you robbed them with a key that I copied. So I won't make 'em."

"What if I want to buy a bump key. Where can I get one of those?"

"You can get them on the internet."

"Really?" I pulled out my phone and looked for bump keys on Amazon.

"Yep."

"Wow. There they are."

"'Course, they're illegal if you're not a locksmith, and you go to jail for eighteen months and face a ten-thousand-dollar fine if you're caught using one tied to illegal activity."

Aunt Ginny was also scrolling on her phone. I snatched it out of her hand. "Absolutely not!"

She gave me her best hurt look, which meant she was definitely doing something sneaky. "What? I'm just Christmas shopping."

I looked at her screen. She had a bump key set in her Amazon shopping cart. I deleted it. "Don't vex me, woman."

I handed the locksmith my credit card.

She ran it through an attachment on her cell phone. "Thanks. I like the skeleton dressed in the Santa coat by the mailbox. Very cute."

I glanced at the mailbox, then narrowed my eyes at

Aunt Ginny. She gave me a cheesy grin and took a step backwards into the foyer.

The locksmith handed my card back. "You know, you can usually tell when an amateur uses a bump key because they forget to use a rebound ring."

"How would you know?"

"They damage the lock. It would be scratched and possibly dinged around the face."

"Thanks. And I'm sorry about that farmer remark."

Aunt Ginny handled the faux pas with her usual grace. "You don't usually see overalls on a woman your age. Want some rum balls?"

The locksmith declined and went on her way.

Aunt Ginny shrugged. "More for us."

I gave her my best chastising look as we went into the house.

I took out my cell phone and called Amber.

"What's up, McAllister? You calling to say you need a police escort to your elopement?"

"Ha-ha. Very funny. I need to see a couple of the crime-scene photos."

"You know I can't do that . . . *officially.*"

I powered up my laptop at the registration desk. "I don't need photos of the victim. I need all the pictures you have of those brand-new locks on the walk-ins."

I heard clacking in the background. "Why?"

"Because I have a theory."

Figaro peeked halfway around the wall from the sunroom and watched me. *Weirdo.*

"I've been thinking. Wes was blackmailing half the town, but whoever killed him clearly had no idea what they were doing. They cleaned up the crime scene, but stashed the body in the freezer. What was the point of that? The marina was just a few feet away. They should have thrown him in the ocean. And I get wiping off the murder weapon, but wiping off all the fingerprints on the freezer when you were already hiding in plain sight? Not to mention the kitchen is full of rubber gloves. They could have just reached over and slid a pair on. I think they were panicking."

"Possibly."

"And then to use the office phone to call the victim at one forty in the morning. Now why would they do that? Everyone knows there's going to be a record of those calls. I think the killer called Wes's cell phone after he was dead because they wanted to throw off the time of death and conveniently put Tim and Gigi in the frame. And Tim and Gigi would be easy to frame because they fight daily, they fight loudly, and they fight about Wes."

Figaro disappeared behind the wall, and I knew he was up to something.

"I don't think the murder was planned. I think Wes lured someone to Maxine's to shake them down over something he discovered, and they snapped. And once they'd killed him, they freaked out and did a lot of weird crap for damage control."

The clacking stopped. "Coming your way."

"And that note. You don't go to all the trouble of trying to cover your tracks, and then stick a note on the victim to find someone who works with the police. I think there's more than one person involved."

"You think the killer had an accomplice?"

"I think the killer phoned a friend for help after the fact."

I checked my email. Nothing yet. "Gabe's a Marine. He could have killed Wes a dozen different ways without a weapon, and you'd never find the body, so it seems unlikely that he would make such a mess of it. But he might help Gigi if she called on him to stash an extortionist in the freezer. He'd probably have her put her feet up while he mopped the kitchen."

"I bet he would have cleaned it a lot better too."

"With precision." I heard the tinkle of bells from the sitting room and knew that Fig had taken advantage of my distraction to climb that tree again. "Jackson's a stretch. Not only is the timing wrong, but he could have killed Wes anywhere. Why at Tim's restaurant? Plus, he put up such a campaign to take Wes down through the proper channels, and when that failed, he started his own alliance scheme."

"Then who is likely?"

"I'm pretty sure Chelle has a gambling addiction, and she owes money to some dangerous people. She could be desperate enough to kill."

A loud crash came from down the hall, and my heart sank to my ankles. A moment later, Aunt Ginny and Kenny were shouting, and a damp Figaro slinked down the hall on his belly, dragging a wet ribbon of sleigh bells.

"Teela might have gotten in over her head by leading him on. She was giving mixed signals, and he might have cornered her. She could have killed him out of self-defense. I did find that note he left for someone to meet him after closing. It was in her order pad, but someone could have planted it. In any case, Wes was there because he was expecting someone."

"Nikki was not usually around when Wes hung out, but she's been scamming Tim for months. Getting paid under the table, taking off time for a grandmother who might not exist. A secret child she doesn't want anyone to know about."

"I didn't know about a child. And the ID she gave me was a fake."

"Andrew has anger issues, but he's already done time for taking a life. And it's left such a deep scar on him, I don't think he would ever kill out of vengeance."

"How are you so sure the killer isn't Tim or Gigi?"

"Because they should have killed Wes months ago when the blackmail started. Not waited until now, after the damage was done. Not to mention that no chef would treat their knives like that. If he'd been bludgeoned with a frozen chicken, I'd say Gigi hands down."

Amber's email arrived, and I clicked the icon and opened the attached photos. I had to enlarge them to see the details. The lock was set, and it indeed was scratched and dinged, and there was even a little dent from someone hitting it. The refrigerator lock was perfectly shiny. This was no homeless man. This was a broke chef who'd been stealing meat to use during his Pop-up Bistro nights. "Well, that sucks."

Kenny walked past me, dragging the shop vac. "Don't go in the sitting room."

A moment later, Aunt Ginny brought me a plate of high-octane chocolates that were putting off fumes strong enough to curl my eyelashes. "These are gluten-free. Eat a few of them as soon as possible."

Amber sounded bemused. "What's going on over there?"

"Figaro trashed the bird tree." I closed the pictures.

"Did the photos help?"

"I think Tyler's been robbing Tim's freezer—probably for months—to try and revive his own restaurant career. Maybe Wes found out and was threatening to expose him."

"Tyler can't be the killer. Security cameras at the marina caught him arriving at two a.m. Thirty minutes later, he was on a boat, heading out to sea with his buddy. He didn't have enough time to kill to Wes and clean up the crime scene."

"No, but thirty minutes is plenty of time to help the killer stash the body, then hoof it across the street to hop on a friend's boat for a convenient alibi. I bet if you check his phone, there's a record of an incoming call after midnight."

Amber was quiet for a minute. "So who was he helping?"

"I don't know. But he's known the whole time what I've been doing, so whoever he helped has just been putting on a good show and lying to me through their teeth."

Amber's radio squawked. "On my way. I have a 10-70 to respond to, McAllister. I'll subpoena Tyler's phone records. Keep me posted."

I hung up from Amber and closed my laptop. If Tyler had been helping the killer, then who'd been helping me?

Someone had wanted me to be involved in this case from the start. Wes's phone showed up at my house with the lock code cracked. Who at Maxine's has that kind of skill set? The same person who left the note on the body? Was I sent the phone just so I'd see the call history, or was there something incriminating that I'd missed?

I pulled out the cloned phone and took a deeper look at Wes's calls. He called an 800 number on the morning he died. The call lasted nearly ten minutes. Then he called a trackphone around seven p.m. that lasted two minutes. He received his last call from Maxine's office at one forty a.m., and I believe he was already dead.

I checked his email and his text messages. Nothing interesting, other than one of his customers complaining about their contract a few weeks back. I remembered what Andrew had said about Wes and his fishing videos and opened his YouTube history. He was paused halfway through a fishing video about a huge catch.

I scrolled the video back a minute. The presenter introduced a man who caught a seven-hundred-pound tuna on one of his fishing excursions. The man gave an impassioned plea for help from subscribers to find his missing daughter, who'd been kidnapped by her mother. I stared into the face of the little brunette with the big green eyes, and there was no mistaking that I'd met that girl before. Then a picture of her mother flashed up on the screen, along with a reward for ten thousand dollars and an 800 number to call if you'd seen either of them. It was the same number Wes had called the day he died.

Wes had fallen upon a Moby Dick–sized secret, and no doubt he'd planned to reel it in to his fullest advantage.

"Aunt Ginny!"

She came around the corner carrying a roll of paper towels. "What?"

"Let me see your phone a minute."

She pulled her cell phone from the pocket of her Thug Life hoodie and handed it to me before heading back to the sitting room. I used it to dial the trackphone. It was answered on the third ring, with a very nervous sounding "Hello."

"Hi, Nikki. We need to talk."

CHAPTER 53

"You don't understand."

"Tell me what I don't understand, Nikki."

"Please . . . It's not what you think."

"Uh-huh." *Has anyone ever not said that?*

"It was self-defense, I swear. Look, I'm turning myself in."

"When is that happening?"

"I'm at Maxine's now, waiting for the police." She started to cry. "What will happen to Amelia? My poor baby."

I could hear sirens in the background.

"Can't you leave her with your grandmother?"

Nikki cried harder. "There is no grandmother. I made her up. I have no one."

"I'm sure the police will send a family liaison to help you."

"Please, Poppy. Tim says you are a good person. And Amelia has told me such nice things about you through Henry. Could you please come watch her until Social Services sends someone? I don't want her to see me taken out in handcuffs. And I can't stand the thought of her sitting alone in the police station."

Amelia's little face appeared in my mind. Then I thought of how Henry would feel if he knew his best friend was hurting and I could have helped and didn't. My heart pulled against my head until I felt like I would be ripped apart.

Nikki made a strangled sob.

The sirens were getting closer. I pulled the phone away from my ear to make sure they were coming from the phone and not rolling down my street to arrest me for crimes against Christmas. Once I was satisfied that they were heading to Maxine's, I agreed to meet. "Fine. I'll be there in ten. If I don't see police cars, I'm leaving."

"Poppy, I'm sorry." The phone went dead. I shoved it in my pocket and grabbed my keys.

I shielded my eyes from the sitting room so I couldn't see the carnage from Sir Figaro, the mighty Styrofoam-bird hunter. "I have to run out to Maxine's. Nikki killed Wes Bailey to keep him from exposing that she kidnapped her daughter. It's all there on Wes's YouTube video. I'm going to get her daughter while she turns herself in."

I could hear the snark in Kenny's tone. "You're walking into an empty restaurant at night to meet the killer? That's the plot of a hundred horror movies. You're gonna get shanked."

"The cops are probably already there. Amber got the call when we were talking."

Aunt Ginny didn't sound convinced. "Oh-kaay. Just be careful. And maybe pick up some Thai food on the way home. You're not going to want to make those pot pies after all this."

"Fig really did a number on the tree, huh?"

Kenny answered. "Just don't look."

I need to get that cat in commercials, so he can start

paying for all of my things he's broken. I climbed into Bessie and headed for the bridge. When this was all over, I could get my life back. Maybe I would make a gingerbread house with Henry this weekend.

I was even willing to listen to Bruce Springsteen. I turned the radio on, and Nat King Cole was singing the coziest holiday song ever written, and I could feel the stress floating off my shoulders. I drove into the clamshell parking lot and parked the car.

The lot was empty. *No one's here yet.*

The only other person around was the homeless man lying in his tent; a small orange glow reflected his silhouette inside the nylon dome.

Where is Amber? I heard at least two police cars on the phone.

I sat in my car and stared at the back of Maxine's. The lights were on, but there was no movement in the windows. The only car in the parking lot was a little black Honda. I waited a minute and listened. All was quiet. Too quiet. Something was wrong.

Well, I'm not about to get shanked.

I reached for the ignition to start Bessie and get the heck out of there when someone tapped on my window. I found myself looking down the barrel of a very large gun.

"Get out of the car."

Now, every time I see something like this in a movie I think, *What are you, stupid? Do your mirrors not work? You can't see someone walking towards you out in the open like that?* I might need to write an apology to the Screen Actors Guild, because apparently when someone doesn't want to be seen, they know how to creep up on you. *Where did this guy come from?*

I considered reaching for my keys anyway.

The man tapped the window again. "Get inside . . . now. I don't want to shoot you out here and mess up this car. The fifty-eight Corvette is a classic."

I ran through a few scenarios in my mind for how to escape. In all of them, I looked like Winnie the Pooh trying to run away from the Woozles with arms and legs that don't bend. I reluctantly climbed out, and he herded me inside to Maxine's dining room. I couldn't see him, but I never stopped being aware of the gun at my back or the sweat trickling down the side of my face.

Nikki was zip-tied to a chair; the man from the video who caught the giant tuna was sitting lazily across from her, one ankle resting on his opposite leg, a handgun pointed at Nikki balanced on his other knee. He had close-cropped dark hair and tattoos running up both arms.

Nikki's hair was matted on one side of her head, and a trickle of blood ran down to her cheek. Her eyes were wild. One of them was red and swelling shut, and her lip was cracked and bleeding.

The man from the video looked my way. "It's about time. Is this the one who helped you take my daughter and run away from me?" He pointed the gun at me and then at the chair next to Nikki. "Sit." He looked at the thug who'd forced me inside. "Zip-tie her."

The Woozle jerked my hands together behind the chair and roughly yanked a plastic band until it cut into my wrists.

Nikki shook her head wildly. "Please, Roman. She's nobody. She don't even know who you are. I told you— she works here as a chef. That's all."

Roman lunged at Nikki and hit her on the temple with the gun. "Shut up! How stupid do you think I am? I told you what would happen if you tried to leave me. And I know she's been helping you hide my kid. Now, where is Amelia?"

Kenny was right, I deserve to get shanked. Please God, Aunt Ginny knows I'm here. How long until she gets worried enough to call Amber? Or hungry enough to track me down to see when dinner is coming?

Nikki doubled over at the waist and let out a stream of obscenities.

I steadied my breath and played along. "How did you find us?"

"I got a tip on my hotline from a YouTube video. Some greedy fool called me and said he knew where my ex was and asked about the reward. We were supposed to meet up two days ago, but he never showed. We were trying to track him down, and what do you know? We find out my little wife here has killed him."

"What makes you think Nikki killed him? There is a dangerous vagrant out back."

Nikki had a moment of bravery or hysteria. "Don't tell him anything, Poppy. My husband's an extremely dangerous man, and he controls dangerous people. He'll kill us both as soon as he finds out where Amelia is."

Roman raised his hand to strike her again.

I was much calmer than I had a right to be, possibly a contact chill from rum-ball fumes. "Wes would probably have double-crossed you as soon as you paid him."

Roman snorted. "I wasn't gonna pay him. You think I don't know greed when I hear it? He wanted to make a big show of turning Nikki in to impress a woman."

"You should probably get out of here. I heard sirens when I spoke to Nikki earlier. The police are on the way."

Nikki's voice trembled. "I'm sorry, Poppy."

Roman held up his cell phone and hit a button. Sirens started to play through the speaker. "Another YouTube video. My ads are on fire this month."

The goon who forced me inside chuckled.

Nikki struggled to get free from her chair. "I'm not going back to that life, Roman. I told you I want out. I want my daughter to be safe."

Roman raised his fist to strike her, but at that moment, Bruce Springsteen started singing "Santa Claus Is Coming to Town" from my back pocket. *I see Aunt Ginny changed my ringtone for her again.* I couldn't reach my cell, so it had to play through.

The thug bobbed his head along with the music. "I love this song."

Roman was not amused. His voice turned hard and dark. "Where's Amelia, Nikki! I'm gonna kill your friend here, and then I'm gonna start taking your fingers one at a time."

Nikki spat at him and screamed. "If I don't come home tonight, I have someone who will disappear with her, and you'll never find her!"

Roman raised his gun to Nikki's head and revealed a tattoo on his hand of a skull wearing a crown. "That's always been the problem with you. You underestimate my intelligence. I know all about your little friend, Tyler. I'll deal with him as soon as we're done here."

I kicked my foot out and hit his wrist. The gun went off, and his partner behind him dropped to the floor, a pool of blood oozing from under his back.

Roman looked at his gun, then at his henchman behind him. "What the . . ."

The homeless man was standing four feet away with a handgun aimed at Roman. He was bleeding from the temple. "FBI! Roman Martinez, you're under arrest."

Roman looked from the lifeless body on the floor to the scruffy FBI agent towering over him and raised his hands. Sirens cut through the quiet, and this time it wasn't Roman's phone.

The agent took Roman's gun, flicked the safety, and slipped it into the back of his waistband. Then he cuffed Roman's hands in front of him, while Nikki and I watched in stunned silence. "Agent Michael Spielman, Organized Crime Division. Are you ladies okay?"

Nikki and I nodded, mutely.

He pulled out a cell phone and made a call. "We got him. I need an ambulance." He disconnected the phone and looked like he might come release us, but the front door splintered off its hinges and a loud primal scream cut through the room like a death-metal reunion tour.

The Biddies flanked Aunt Ginny like Charlie's geriatric angels. Aunt Ginny had done some kind of karate on Tim's front door that I'm sure we'd have to pay for. Mrs. Dodson spun her cane like a Ninja wielding a staff, and Mother Gibson held her Bible in one hand and a taser in the other. "Aaaah!"

The FBI agent let out a strangled cry. "Stop!"

Nikki and I tried to intervene. "No! He's FBI!"

Mother Gibson hit him in the chest with the taser, and he dropped to the ground like a sack of flour.

Roman scrambled to get the agent's gun out of his hand. I tried to kick him over, and Nikki lunged at him, but we were still tied to the chairs. He extracted the gun and pointed it at Aunt Ginny.

A shot rang out, and I saw my life flash before my eyes. Nikki wouldn't have to worry about Amelia because I was going to rip her gangster husband's head clean off his shoulders. Roman Martinez flew backwards and lay unconscious, bleeding from the chest.

Aunt Ginny was still standing and looking more than a little confused. "Who is the bad guy?"

A police radio beeped, and Amber spoke into the receiver on her shoulder, her Glock still aimed at Roman Martinez. "Backup and rescue to Maxine's Bistro on 109."

The FBI agent was starting to rouse, and Aunt Ginny and the Biddies rushed him to help him sit up.

"Gah!" He tried to crab-walk away from them.

Amber held her gun down by her side and collected the FBI agent's piece from the floor next to Roman. "Mrs. Frankowski! I should arrest you right now for stealing my police car."

Aunt Ginny had one hand on the FBI agent's elbow

and the other on his back. "We had no choice, Amber. Poppy had Bessie, and Ethel couldn't get her van out of the driveway because one of the reindeer flew off the roof onto the hood."

"That is absolutely no excuse. When will you ladies learn to let the authorities do their jobs?"

Mrs. Davis was a little pouty. "That's hardly fair, Amber Michelle. You wouldn't even have known Poppy was here if Ginny hadn't called and told you about that video for the missing child."

Amber spoke through gritted teeth. "I was on my way to Ginny's house because one of her neighbors reported it was on fire."

Aunt Ginny nodded. "Yeah, it's a lot of lights."

The FBI agent rubbed his head. "Will you all please just shut up!"

Amber groaned. "What is going on here, McAllister?"

With my foot, I pointed to Nikki's husband. "That's Roman Martinez. He's trying to kill everyone. And that over there is his henchman."

Nikki nodded towards the lump on the floor. "Brother, actually."

"Oh really?"

She nodded at me. "Yeah."

I considered their size difference. "Not much of a family resemblance is there?"

Nikki half-shrugged. "Roman takes after his mother. She's more petite. That's where Amelia gets it."

Amber reverted to her cheerleader voice. "Ladies, please! Who is that?"

She was looking warily at the man we'd thought was a homeless man.

"He's an FBI agent. Apparently, he's been undercover ever since Nikki arrived, trying to catch her husband."

Amber threw her free hand up to her hip. "Why? Who is he?"

Aunt Ginny and the Biddies had managed to convince the agent that they were not a terrorist cell of old women, and he struggled to his feet. "He's Roman Martinez, leader of the Cuban Kings in Central Florida, and he's wanted for too many crimes to list right now, while all I can taste is metal and my head is buzzing."

Officers Birkwell and Consuelos arrived with the paramedics, and they began securing the scene and treating Agent Spielman's injuries. Amber relaxed enough to put her gun away after two FBI agents took Roman out in handcuffs to a waiting ambulance. Now she was busy scolding Aunt Ginny and her geriatric swat team on the dangers of vigilante justice.

Nikki and I sat alone, waiting. I'd seen this happen about a dozen times now. The accused always looks sad, sometimes hopeless, sometimes angry. Nikki just looked relieved.

She leaned back against the dining-room chair and took a deep breath. "I'm so sorry I put you in danger. When you called my burner phone, Roman was convinced that you'd been helping us and you knew where Amelia was."

"No wonder you were in hiding."

Her lips flattened, and she gave me a sad look. "I can only imagine what you think of me. When Wes discovered who I was, he threatened to call my husband and tell him where we were if I didn't give him ten thousand dollars. I don't have that kind of money. I barely make enough here to survive. I've had Tim paying me under the table to keep off the grid so Roman couldn't track us."

"That explains why you wiped the fingerprints from the walk-ins. You didn't want to show up in the system and give your location away."

A tear rolled down her cheek, and she wiped it away with her shoulder. "I had to protect my daughter. We've been on the run for months. Wes Bailey was about to turn us in to my abusive husband for a cheap reward. Even if I had paid him, he would have called Roman before I'd driven away. I saw Amelia being trapped in a life of drugs and violence, and it made me furious that this ugly, greedy man would do that to her. I didn't think—I just reacted. I grabbed a knife off the counter and plunged it in his chest as hard as I could."

Another ambulance arrived, and I knew it would be for Nikki. Officers Consuelos and Birkwell were starting to cordon off the dining room with crime-scene tape. She'd be taken into custody soon.

"You freaked out and called Tyler for help, didn't you? Is he the one who told you who I was?"

Nikki closed her eyes. "Tyler said to avoid talking to you at all costs, because you figure things out for the police, and no one knows how you do it. I tried to stay away from you, but you just kept digging. Every time I turned around, you were asking more questions. I was going to take Amelia and head up to Canada to start over, but I knew I'd look suspicious if we left before the police made an arrest."

Amber was giving instructions to Officer Birkwell over by the bar and nodded to the chairs where Nikki and I were sitting. She had that look in her eye like I was in trouble for going rogue again. "I was only here to prove that Tim and Gigi weren't killers. Well . . . mostly Tim. Just how involved is Tyler?"

"He's not. He's been a good friend to me and Amelia, and he shouldn't pay the price for what I've done."

"He will if the police think he helped you kill Wes."

Nikki shook her head. "He didn't. He tried to warn me Wes was a dirtbag, and I shouldn't meet with him. Tyler only came after, to open the freezer and help me move the body. He said we had to throw off the time of death. He had me call Wes's cell from the office phone, so it would look like Gigi had called to meet about their contract. Then he told me to wipe down the things that I'd touched."

"But why did you put the 'Get Poppy' note on the body?"

"I didn't."

"Then how did it get there?"

Nikki shook her head. "I have no idea. Tyler is convinced it was Tim."

Birkwell crossed the room. He gave me a sad smile and put his hand on her elbow. "Let's go, ma'am."

He helped her to her feet, and they started for the door. Nikki paused and turned to look at me over her shoulder. She had a tear running down her cheek. "Please, don't remember me as a monster. I did it to save my kid."

I felt sorry for her. What a terrible series of events her life had taken. "We're all just one bad decision away from destroying our lives, Nikki."

Birkwell took her through the door and out to the waiting ambulance.

Aunt Ginny came to watch over me while the Biddies compared weaponry with the agents. She rubbed my back like she'd done when I was sick as a child to calm me.

My shoulders were on fire, and my head was starting to throb. As I watched law enforcement work the scene, I realized that an FBI agent would have had access that even the local police lacked.

Agent Spielman stepped back into the restaurant with his head and hand bandaged and scanned the room. He spotted me and walked over. "How are you holding up, Poppy?"

"I'd like to go home."

He looked for Amber and waved her over. "They're just about done here. I'm sure you can give your statement later."

"Can I ask you something?"

He nodded.

"Did you place the 'Get Poppy' note and send me the cell phone?"

Spielman grinned. "I was wondering if you'd figure that out."

"But why?"

Amber gave the agent a hard look. "You compromised my crime scene. It had better be for a good reason."

He took a chair from a nearby table and dropped into it. "I've been after Roman Martinez for three years. We've come near to catching him a few times, but he always manages to slip through our fingers like he's made of Teflon. When Nikki arrived in Cape May a few weeks ago, we knew it was a matter of time before he tracked her here. So we set up two points of surveillance. One across from her home, and one here where she works. We figured Roman was getting desperate to find her when he started making reckless pleas on social media. We knew he'd gotten a tip and was on the move when he took his hotline number down a week ago."

I rolled my head to the side to stretch my neck. "That must be when Wes called him, looking for that reward."

"Exactly." Spielman leaned forward in his seat. "And then the whole operation went to hell when Wes Bailey walked in here at midnight and never came out. I heard the altercation, but my orders were not to engage unless Roman Martinez showed his face."

Amber took out her notebook. "Did you see anything?"

Spielman shook his head. "There was a lot of suspicious activity, but my view was obstructed by the Deepwater Fisheries van. I knew Nikki was here, and I knew one of the men she worked with had arrived shortly after her, but I didn't know which one."

He cut his gaze to Amber. "The problem with the police in this town . . ."

Amber rolled her eyes and flipped her notebook shut.

"Is that they are so short-staffed and overrun with tourists, sometimes they rush to judgment. They want the case closed and tidied up quickly. That meant one of the owners would most likely be arrested within forty-eight hours and the investigation closed. Do you deny that, Officer Fenton?"

Amber looked my way and cleared her throat. "Not if I had anything to do with it."

Spielman grinned. "We knew NOAA was investigating Deepwater Fisheries for seafood fraud. It didn't take a big leap to figure out Tim Maxwell and his partner would be on their radar as having a solid motive to kill Wes Bailey. I knew the minute you made an arrest, Nikki would be in the wind, and so would my chance to catch Roman Martinez. Who knows when another opportunity would have come along? And I almost lost that chance when you arrested Tim Maxwell this morning. If I hadn't called in a favor to have you release him, Nikki would be halfway to Canada by now."

Aunt Ginny huffed. "Well, that's all fine and dandy, but when did you put 'Get Poppy' on the dead guy? The cops had her out of the house first thing in the morning, before the stiff had time to thaw."

Spielman nodded, and Amber took her notebook back out. "Once Nikki and her friend left the premises, I called my partner and told her Nikki was on the move. I waited for the van to move. When it was clear something was wrong, I did a walkthrough. That's when I found Wes Bailey, dead in the freezer and his cell phone in the trash. I couldn't call it in myself because my cell would be pinged, but I knew the produce delivery was scheduled for a couple hours later. I preserved the evidence that would have been lost to the garbage collectors by the time police arrived on the scene. And left the note to get Poppy in hopes of slowing down the investigation to keep Nikki in town."

I wasn't sure if I should be offended or not. "What do you mean I would slow it down?"

Spielman chuckled. "I knew you and Officer Fenton would be thorough, considering all angles, no matter how long it took. Bringing you in bought me time to get Roman in place while we waited for the lab to run forensics. We're sending Chief Kieran Dunne a copy of our findings, now that Roman is in custody."

I wasn't entirely mollified by that answer, but I let it go. "But how did you get inside the locked freezer?"

Agent Spielman leaned back in his chair and grinned. "Lockpick tools. We have the best in the business."

Aunt Ginny pulled out her cell phone. "What's your opinion on this bump-key set I'm . . ." She saw my expression and clammed up. Then she shoved her phone back in her pocket. "I mean, how does the FBI even know about Poppy?"

Amber craned her neck to stare the agent down. "I'd like to know that too."

He chuckled and looked my way again. "Ma'am, you've found ten murder victims in a year. Your record is better than our cadaver dogs. Even though your handler here keeps your name out of the official reports, we hear the chatter. Do you really think the FBI doesn't know who you are?"

I could feel the heat rising up my neck. "Okay, that's fair. There is one more thing."

Agent Spielman nodded. "Anything."

"Do you think someone could unzip my hands and get me out of this chair now?"

CHAPTER 54

The door of La Dolce Vita opened in a cinnamon burst of Christmas spirit. The air was heavy with the scent of oranges and brown sugar, while Frank Sinatra sang "Hark! The Herald Angels Sing." Gia's face split into a grin from behind the espresso machine, and my heart lifted. This is what it feels like to be home.

Gia came around the bar, so Marco and Sierra could take over pulling the shots for the line winding back to the door. He took me in his arms and kissed me a little indecently, but I didn't complain. "*Cara mia*, I have missed you."

I giggled. "We were on the phone until two a.m."

"It is not the same as holding you in my arms." He kissed me again. "Should we go for a walk?"

"I'll go with you anywhere."

He took my hand and led me onto the brick pathway to stroll down the lane. "Is everything finished with the investigation?"

"My part is. Tim called this morning. He's having some kind of I'm not going to jail slash Christmas celebration he wants us to come to."

"Does Gigi know we are invited?"

I snickered. "I dunno. She was pretty excited to hear they weren't getting fined by NOAA. Apparently, when Tim had to destroy everything in his freezer because a body was discovered, he got rid of everything Deepwater Fisheries had sold him."

"What about all the paperwork?"

"Gigi set it on fire after I found it in their office. There wasn't a shred of evidence left on the property that Tim had been involved in anything illegal with Wes by the time NOAA arrived."

Gia chuckled. "They were so lucky. And when is this celebration?"

"Tonight. But we don't have to go if you don't want to."

"Of course, I want to spend the evening with your ex-fiancé, who held you hostage for the week that I barely saw you."

I gave him a crooked smile. "If we get cornered and want to leave, the code word is frosty."

"I will find a way to work that into the conversation."

We came to the end of the lane and circled around the block to go past Rotary Park and headed for the gazebo. It was covered in white lights and had boughs of greenery tied in red bows around the frame.

I took a seat on the bench inside, and Gia wrapped his arm around my shoulders. "Are you having fun planning the wedding?"

I thought about putting a brave face on things, but Gia was one of very few people in my life with whom I knew I could be totally honest and totally myself. "Not really."

"Why not?"

"I feel like it's been hijacked. Between Georgina, and Aunt Ginny, and, of course, the Biddies—all of whom I love."

He kissed the back of my hand. "Not to mention Oliva Larusso and her desperate bridesmaids."

"They have grand plans for this to be a big flashy event, but none of it is what I want. I already had the big wedding with John. I didn't know anyone there."

He nodded. "Mmm. I had it with Alex. Her father paid a fortune, and then we lived in a one-room studio apartment over a deli and nearly killed each other."

"I want something simple and romantic."

He tucked a loose tendril of hair behind my ear. "You don't think two hundred Italians from the old country dancing you around on a chair will be romantic?"

A lump formed in my throat, and all I could do was blink.

He laughed.

"I just want our closest friends and family to hear how much I love you and Henry, and that I want to spend the rest of my life with you. If we don't stop everyone, our wedding will become the spring version of Aunt Ginny's Christmas decorations." *That wiped the smile off his face.*

Gia leaned in and kissed me. "Do you trust me?"

"Completely."

"Then I will take care of everything."

CHAPTER 55

I returned home to the Nightmare before Christmas.
Mr. Winston was hooking up a lone electronic plastic
snowman in his front yard. It glowed to life and raised its
stick arm to a top hat and tipped it in greeting, making me
smile. There's your understated elegance.

"My yard was feeling a little underdressed over here,
so I thought I'd join the fun."

"The glow from my house doesn't keep you awake at
night, does it?"

He chuckled. "I don't sleep much these days anyhow. I
heard you been talking to the Meiers. Finally putting that
feud to rest, are you?"

"What?"

His bushy eyebrows shot up to his blue wool cap. "Did
I get that wrong? I thought your family was the one
Albert said his kin had been holding a grudge with all
these years."

"Albert from the Historical Society?"

Mr. Winston scratched his head. "Maybe it was Nell he
was talking about. I can't remember anymore. I used to
work at the museum a ways back before my ears went.

Couldn't hear the chime on the front door anymore. Left a whole room of tourists waiting for an hour while I licked stamps in the back office. I was sad when I had to give it up."

"Yes, that's very sad. But what did Albert say about a feud?"

"Oh, he said it was long before his time, but his family hands the story down from one generation to the next."

"Which house is Albert's?"

Mr. Winston nodded slowly. "The Crow's Nest. Just over yonder. Been in his family for generations. Back to George Meier and his daughters."

"Then who is Patricia?"

"Albert's sister. She's been running it as a B and B just like yours."

Not according to her it isn't. "And Albert said there's a family curse?"

"I was sure he said Ginny, 'cause when he said they were waiting for an apology, I thought—well, that'll be the day. But now . . . maybe it was Clara. Her husband's people have been here that long. 'Course, their son has moved away . . ."

"Thank you, Mr. Winston." I left him to his memories and ran into my house to get to the diary.

I didn't get far. The tree in the sitting room was a bedraggled mess, and I stopped for a moment to mourn its demise. A few of the branches were broken, and only six birds remained. Aunt Ginny had filled in the bare spots with ornaments that I'd made as a child—macaroni angels and felt snowmen. They were horrible, but it warmed my heart that she'd kept them.

Due to his level of shame over the destruction of so many of my precious birds, Sir Figaro Newton was curled up in the middle of the Dickens Christmas village snoozing comfortably, with his head on the skating rink and one foot in the spice-shop window. The yellow tape around the butcher shop was undisturbed. "Really. That's where you draw the line? You went scorched earth on my tree, but the crime scene is hallowed ground."

Fig opened one eye, looked at me, and closed it again.

A redheaded Barbie in a gold sweater dress and stilettos stood next to Ebenezer Scrooge's house with a magnifying glass in her hand. *That's supposed to be me. I wish I could wear stilettos.* The fish monger lay dead in the snow, his eyes exed out with electrical tape, a bottle of poison discarded next to a flounder. "Well, I don't know how much detecting is necessary here, Poppy-Barbie. The skull and crossbones on the bottle gives it away."

Who did this? Everyone was gone. All the guests who were here when the police tape started appearing had checked out. Iris had finally been told where to go. Even the Biddies hadn't been here today because they were doing their post-investigation tour around town, filling everyone in on the details of their daring rescue at Maxine's last night, where they took down an FBI agent.

That curly-haired Barbie looked vintage. I only knew one person who collected vintage Barbies, and they had to be taught a lesson. I pulled out my cell phone and texted Connie, asking to borrow something appropriate from eight-year-old Emmilee's collection. It was time to give someone a taste of their own poison.

I heard Joanne and Kenny in the kitchen, arguing over where to frost the holiday sprig of holly on the Grim Reaper. I crept up the main staircase to my room to finish Grandpa Rooster's diary before they discovered I was home.

I couldn't believe that, all this time, Albert and Patricia were brother and sister. And why did neither of them just tell me there was a feud? Whether there's a curse or not, if you're holding a grudge against me, at least give me a chance to apologize. And yet Aunt Ginny and I had never heard boo before we found the diary. Maybe there was more to it. I curled up on my love seat in the tower and opened the fragile pages.

August 29

I had some business to attend to in Philadelphia yesterday and was looking forward to the pleasant journey on the train. Upon my return, my good humor was broken as I discovered a tramp, dead behind the rail station. I do not believe it to be murder as such. I believe the drink to have been the culprit. I confess I was quite shaken up by the sad ordeal and turned to a hot toddy and a female companion for some comfort.

September 2

It is dreadful the state of discord that enters one's life when death comes unbidden to one's door. The constable was less inclined to believe my innocence upon the third occurrence of my discovery of malfeasance. Oswald, on the other hand, has been telling everyone who deigns to listen my tales of woe for the low price of one brandy sour.

September 5

Breckenridge fancies himself to be Mark Twain for naming a drink in my honor. It is only egg nog, but made with whiskey instead of rum. He calls it a Mad Cow. I dread to think what will happen when the horrid woman hears about this.

September 7
The shrew across the field has discovered the dubious honor bestowed upon me, and she is mad as a March Hare. Word of the woman's rancor has spread all over town. Oswald warns that I should not provoke her, as I have had a spate of bad luck lately inasmuch as I have had the misfortune of stumbling upon three corpses in a half a year. He does tell the truth on occasion.

September 9
I do not know how I got home last night. The throbbing ache in my head reminds me of a few too many Mad Cows. They do grow on you.

September 11
That infernal woman has bought two pigs and placed their pen on the border edge of my property. The putrescence is beyond acceptable. I have informed the witch that she has the option of relocating them or joining me in a ham dinner. I dare not repeat her words to me. She is demanding an apology if I want her to lift her curse. Never! The woman is deranged.

September 14
I have found another. There is talk of amends with the woman, either by duel or by marriage. The duel is the more favorable option.

September 18
In way of making peace to the cow and her offended livestock, I intend to offer the woman an emerald ring that I won at the tables last night on a black straight. I refuse to utter one word of mea culpa, for I have done no wrong. While I feel I would much more enjoy keeping the prize to myself and a future bride, should fate so incline, if it is the price of blissful silence, then I welcome it wholeheartedly.

September 20
The shrew accepted the ring, but still demands I abase myself with witnesses. Foul witch! She can curse as many generations of my progeny as she likes. It is nothing to me. I wash my hands of her. I will not speak of it again.

Maybe if he had spoken of it, earlier generations of McAllisters could have nipped this in the bud years ago. That was the last entry in the diary. I returned it to my nightstand and called Sawyer. "I have to go to Patricia's house and apologize that my ancestor offended her ancestor's cow. Would you like to come along as backup?"

Sawyer was silent for a moment. "Did you say he offended her cow?"

"Yes."

"This I gotta see."

I went to the kitchen to look for a gift that says *I'm sorry my great-grandpa said your relative was crazy, and could you please remove this curse? Also, please don't make fun of me if there is no curse.* I loaded up a tin with Aunt Ginny's rum balls, then went to the foyer and shrugged on my coat to walk down to the Crow's Nest.

I had just passed Patricia's mailbox at the end of the block when Sawyer popped out of her little car. "Gia loaned me Marco to cover the bookstore, so I've got Italian cookbooks on sale for the next hour. What's the plan?"

We stood in front of the blue-and-gray Victorian, waiting for courage to bolster our nerves.

The menacing crow blew in the wind, and the iron screeched a warning to turn back. "I'm going to be direct."

Sawyer sucked in some air through her teeth.

"What?"

"That's just . . . not really your forte."

"What do you mean?"

"You're more the beat-around-the-bush type."

"True. But I'm told I don't have the luxury of time on my side."

The front door opened, and Albert leaned against the door jamb, crossing his arms in front of his chest. "Well, you better come in then."

Sawyer and I silently marched up the steps and into the grand foyer. I handed Albert the tin. "Aunt Ginny's rum balls."

He took the tin and lifted the lid. "Whoo! Better not keep these by the fire." He replaced the lid and led us down the hall into a dark-paneled library. A warm fire blazed in the hearth, and two glasses of wine were waiting on a Queen Anne cherry table. Patricia was sitting on a green-silk tufted chair, with the orange cat in her lap. "Well, look who's back."

Albert held up the can. "She brought rum balls."

"How nice."

She doesn't sound like she believes it's nice at all. "May we sit?"

Patricia waved her hand at a matching green-silk sofa behind the table, her emerald ring reflecting the firelight.

Both she and her brother watched me expectantly.

"Why didn't you tell me you were Bettina Meier's descendants? You said your grandfather, Richard Noss, bought the house from the original owner."

Patricia smiled sweetly. "He did. Richard Noss Meier bought the house from his brother, who had inherited it from their father, George Meier the third."

Sawyer jabbed me in the side.

"And, Albert, I came to you for help. Why didn't you just tell me who you were and what had happened so we could straighten things out?"

Albert shrugged. "You said you wanted to share the history of your home with guests. Not apologize for a great wrong that Callum McAllister had done."

I hardly think it was a great wrong. Insulting, maybe. "I didn't even know what he'd done. If you'd told me, I could have come much sooner."

Albert chuckled. "Dear, there is so much more to it than you know."

Patricia smiled condescendingly. "I did tell you to speak to your aunt."

"I thought that was about the yard."

Sawyer jabbed me in the side again.

"What?" I hissed.

She nudged her head towards the fireplace and hissed back. "The painting."

I followed her eyes to see what she was going on about. A portrait of a dark-haired woman standing by the ocean hung over the hearth. The layers of her blue-and-green silk robes billowed in the ocean breeze.

"Why do you have a portrait of Madame Zolda?"

Patricia reached for her glass of wine and took a delicate sip. "I don't know who you mean."

Albert crossed the room to the fireplace. "That's Bettina Meier. Our fifth-generation great-aunt. She was one of three daughters to move here with their father. She never married."

Sawyer snorted. "She looks just like the hinky psychic who first cursed Poppy because an owl flew into her sign."

I gave Sawyer a death stare.

She lowered her voice. "How's it going around those bushes, babe?"

I took a breath and dove in. "I understand that my quadruple-great-grandfather said some hurtful things to Bettina Meier, and he refused to apologize. It is believed that she put a generational curse on him to . . ."

Patricia stroked the cat. "Be followed by death, dear. I believe you are familiar with it."

"Yes. Well, I think the curse may have transferred to me, and I'd like to apologize now for his actions and make amends."

Sawyer whispered, "And for the cow."

"And I apologize that he offended Bettina's cow and might have scared it half to death with his fireworks."

Sawyer nodded. "Naturally."

Albert's eyebrows raised, and his lips cracked into a sort of a smile. "How wonderful. After all the years of waiting. No one has ever come to apologize before."

Probably because they didn't know anything about it.

Albert crossed his arms over his chest. "Our family

was sworn to secrecy from ever confronting one of yours about the curse. It was said that we'd recognize genuine humility when one of you finally took it upon yourself to find out the truth. I had hoped that's what you were after when you came to the museum."

Patricia put the cat on the floor. "Holding a grudge is what your family is known for. It used to be said on the island that anyone who crossed a McAllister knew they'd never hear the words 'I'm sorry' touch their ears."

"Well, I'd like to change that."

Albert held out his hand for me to shake. "Apology accepted."

I shook it and offered my hand to Patricia. She looked at it like it was a hoof. "You are still a disaster of an innkeeper."

"I can only get better."

She took my hand and limply nudged it.

Sawyer jabbed me again. "The curse?"

I swallowed my pride, feeling terribly foolish. "Does this mean the curse is lifted from me and I can stop finding murder victims? Or is there something else I need to do, like buy you a new cow or put an ad in the paper or something?"

Patricia and Albert looked at each other and laughed. Albert shook his head, and his fluffy white hair danced in all directions. "Silly girl."

Patricia took another sip of her wine. "If your ancestor's curse has been passed to you, it's because his sins have passed to you as well."

"I don't know what you're talking about. I haven't trampled anyone's melons."

Sawyer snickered, and I banged my knee into hers.

Albert poked the fire. "All I know is that old Callum caused his own problems when he let his pride prevent him from apologizing to Bettina. Every generation given to pride and unforgiveness would be cursed with the same fate. You need to figure out where your pride is getting in the way of your relationships."

At least I'm not carrying a grudge for a hundred years. And why isn't Aunt Ginny surrounded by dead people? This was feeling more ridiculous.

Albert popped a rum ball in his mouth. "Whoo wee!" He passed the can to me, and I shook my head. Sawyer reached for a rum ball, and Patricia snatched the can away. "Not in your condition, dear."

"Since when can't you have rum because of menopause?"

Patricia grinned. "You're not in menopause."

Sawyer snickered. "Yes, I am. I haven't had a period in three months."

Patricia's eyes fluttered. "And what else can cause that?"

Albert chuckled. "My sister is never wrong. Second sight runs in the family."

Sawyer blinked. Then her eyes went big, and her smile followed. "I mean . . . it's possible, but I'm forty-four. Isn't it too late?"

Patricia lifted both of her palms. "I guess you'll both have to wait and see if I speak the truth."

I looked back at the portrait of Madame Zolda and a shiver ran up my neck. I could have sworn she was frowning a minute ago.

CHAPTER 56

Gia and I stood hand in hand outside of Maxine's. The tent was gone, and all evidence of the homeless man had vanished overnight. Club music thumped from inside the restaurant, and the windows rattled slightly from the pulsing beat.

Gia sighed. "We are a long way away from Dean Martin."

I squeezed his hand. "I know. But then you are a forty-year-old man with a ninety-year-old soul."

The door opened, and Chuck beckoned us inside. "Everyone is waiting for you."

Gia gave me a sexy grin and led the way.

A buffet of cold seafood and salads had been laid out on the kitchen worktable. The portable carving station had a prime rib set up, and hot sides waited under the warming lights. "Tim and Gigi spared no expense for this celebration."

"We are just so excited it's over, Mack." Tim stood in the doorway from the dining room. His eyes were on Gia, and his smile was forced, but he was clearly trying to be civil.

Gia held out his hand in peace. "I am really glad it all worked out for you."

Tim clasped his hand. "Mack cleared my name, like I knew she would."

Gia offered me a warm smile. "She is gifted at reading people."

This is not awkward at all.

Tim looked away. "Well, get some food and go on in. Gabe has made some Christmas cocktails, and I know everyone wants to thank Poppy." He turned to me. "And I'll catch up with you in bit. My new fish guy needs an order before six." He left us and headed down the hall towards his office.

"Well, some things never change. Should we go say hello?"

"*Si.* I cannot wait to greet the missus."

We entered the dining room, and everyone whooped a greeting like I was Norm from *Cheers*. I introduced Gia to everyone, then Teela made a beeline to shake his hand. He said it was nice to meet her and pulled me closer to his side.

Gigi was working her way through a seafood tower for four. She expressed her gratitude by cracking a crab, while her eyes stayed on me. She glanced at Gia and grinned like a cat who just discovered the dog is on a leash.

Chelle crossed the room and wrapped me in a hug. "Can I call you Poppy now? Once I saw who you really were, I knew you would figure out who had killed Wes. And I didn't tell anyone, girl. I've never kept a secret for so long in my life. It was like three whole days." She cut her eyes to Gia. "And, girl . . . your man is fine. Look at you go."

I introduced Gia to Gabriel so they could swap hot-guy bartending stories, and I picked up a mulled wine to make my rounds catching up with everyone. A lot had happened in twenty-four hours, and I was behind in my gossip.

Andrew and Chelle had made themselves a mini buffet from the raw bar, and they were camped in front of the fireplace. Andrew waved a jumbo shrimp. "Where's your food?"

"I'll get some in a minute. Any word from Tyler?"

Andrew dunked his shrimp in cocktail sauce. "He was arrested last night, trying to escape on his friend's boat."

Chelle chuckled. "Apparently, his friend had given the alibi based on info from Tyler as to what time he'd arrived the night Wes was killed. He wasn't even home."

"What are they charging him with?"

Andrew picked up another shrimp. "Accessory after the fact."

"Oof." I took the shrimp that Andrew offered. "What about Tim and Gigi? Are they pressing charges for all the meat Tyler stole?"

Chelle looked at me under her fake eyelashes. "They fought about it all morning. Gigi wants to nail his butt to the wall with a criminal suit—and then a civil suit—making him pay back every dime by garnishing his wages."

"What does Tim want to do?"

Andrew chuckled. "Nothing. He wants it to go away."

Chelle tsk'd. "The poor thing is so hurt. He said he can't believe Tyler would do that after he gave him a job when Devon's closed. Tim is too kindhearted for his own good."

Chuck snuck up behind me and gave me a hug. "Tim also sucks at inventory, so he has no idea how much meat was taken and for how long, but don't tell him I said that."

The front door opened, and a blast of cold made the flames in the fireplace sputter. Darlene entered, with Gabby on her hip. Gabe came out from behind the bar and crossed the room. He took Gabby in his arms and kissed Darlene, then led her over to the bar.

Darlene perched on a barstool, scanned the room, and caught my eye. She smiled brightly and waved.

"Why is she here?" Chelle made a face like she'd sucked on a lemon.

"I hate to tell you this, but that's Gabe's girlfriend."

Darlene flashed her left hand to Gia, who smiled and nodded, then toasted her.

"Sorry. I think that might be fiancée now."

Chelle's shoulders slumped. "I really need some good luck for a change. Nope. I take it back. In Gamblers Anonymous, there is no such thing as luck. I make my own fortune in life by hard work."

Andrew raised his glass to her "One day at a time." Chuck and I lifted our glasses to join them.

Teela brought over a plate of prime rib and mashed potatoes and pulled out a chair the next table over. "Guess what I just heard from my friend at the Boat Club? Deepwater Fisheries was shut down by NOAA. Wes's brother was totally blindsided. He didn't know anything about the fraud or blackmail Wes was involved in. When Wes died, all their clients bailed immediately, and his brother had to hire a bankruptcy lawyer. My God, that guy was such a loser."

I took another shrimp from the platter. "Then why'd you lead him on?"

Teela gave me a look like she couldn't believe I was asking her that. "Because I thought he was rich. He was always bragging about how successful he was. I let him take me out to dinner after work one night, and you know where he took me? The bowling alley snack bar."

Chelle laughed. "Uh-uh. No way."

Teela nodded. "I need to find someone to take care of me while I'm still hot. I don't want to live with my parents one day longer than I have to."

The front door opened again, and an attractive man scanned the room. He was clean-shaven, his hair was styled, and he was wearing a sharp designer suit. He spotted me and beckoned for me to join him.

I pointed to my chest, and he grinned. I realized the man was Agent Spielman.

"I'll be right back." I crossed the room and shook his hand. "Wow, look at you."

He smiled. "Can I just tell you how much I love hot showers."

I laughed. "How are the headaches after my aunt and her friends tazed you?"

He chuckled. "My ears have stopped ringing, but I'll never live it down. The bureau is threatening to bring those ladies into the academy for training exercises."

"You laugh, but those ladies could teach new recruits a thing or two. What can I do for you?"

"First, I brought your tent back. And I wanted to thank you for your kindness while I was undercover."

"I'm glad I could help in some small way. I wish I could have done more than just feed you."

He covered his lean stomach with his hand. "I did have a team bringing me things on the regular. And the owner of the marina was working with the investigation, so I had his facilities at my disposal. Besides, the pregnant lady would never have allowed it."

Both of us glanced at Gigi. Her eyes had followed me across the room. The tower of seafood in front of her was all shells.

"No, you're right. If she'd caught me, you'd have been busting in to save me sooner."

He laughed. "Most likely."

"I've been wondering, what took you so long to get in there last night? I saw you in your tent. Roman had Nikki held at gunpoint for a while before I arrived."

"While I was shadowing Roman, his brother got the drop on me. When I came to, I immediately called for backup."

"I'm glad he didn't kill you."

His expression grew serious. "If he'd known I was FBI, he would have. In fact, I'm here now on official business."

"Oh?"

"Even though we were technically working different cases . . ."

I chuckled. "That's generous."

He grinned. "I thought you'd like to know that Nikki disappeared from police custody overnight."

"What!"

He shrugged, but there was a slight quirk to his lips that belied his concern. "She and her daughter have completely vanished. She gave us enough evidence to put Roman away for the rest of his life. I'm sure we'll track her down in time to testify before the grand jury, although I expect she'll disappear for good after that. The police are furious, of course."

"Of course. How will they prosecute Tyler for accessory without a murder charge?"

"Without Nikki to testify, that will be a challenge. There's a good chance Tyler will walk free. There is one other thing. I tracked down that information you wanted for your friend. If she's willing to work with the agents assigned to the swordfish gang, they're willing to make a deal."

"Can they keep her safe?"

"It's a big country."

I thanked Agent Spielman and introduced him to Chelle.

She made sure she got an eyeful of him before taking his card and leading him to a snug to talk in private. "If I'd a known you looked like this under all that grunge, I would a brought you some shrimp and grits myself."

I turned around to find Tim and Gigi lurking behind me.

Gigi's face was clearly warring with her emotions. A scowl was on the edge of winning the battle. "I wanted to thank you for your help these past few days, and whenever you want to bring your husband here for dinner, it's on the house."

I admit that I did smile, but I want the points for not laughing out loud. "What if I want to come alone?"

"Don't even think about coming here by yourself."

"Geeg!" Tim's eyes bugged out with shock and exasperation.

I gave Gigi a nod. "I hear you."

"Good." She tossed her perky blond curls and waddled to the dessert table.

Tim and I were alone. He chuckled nervously.

I looked across the room at Gia. He felt my gaze and gave me a warm smile before turning his attention back to Andrew and Chuck, who had settled at the bar.

Tim cleared his throat and rubbed his palms on his chef pants. "I, ah . . . can we sit?"

We went to the side room and took a table by the fireplace.

Tim took a deep breath and steadied his voice. "I want to apologize for the way I acted. The evasiveness, the lying, just all of it."

"Go on . . ."

He met my gaze, and there was sadness in his eyes. "I've been so ashamed of what I let Wes talk me into. It's no excuse—I went along with it out of desperation. I didn't want you to find out because I didn't want you to think less of me. You'd already chosen to end our relationship for another guy. Again. And I didn't want you to think you dodged a bullet."

"Why would you care what I think? You've clearly moved on. You have a baby coming."

He sighed. "Things happened with Gigi at the wrong time and for all the wrong reasons. Pretty much hours after you broke my heart. I was hurt. And a little bitter.

And Gigi was . . . what my ego wanted. I wasn't looking for a relationship. And I definitely wasn't looking for a baby. And now here we are."

I nodded. *Been there.*

"I wanted you to know that now I understand the decision you had to make twenty-five years ago, and I'm sorry I wasn't there for you. I spent all those years angry and hurt and never realized what it had cost you. The way your life changed, the dreams and plans you had to let go of. I was only thinking about how your decision had affected me."

My eyes started to sting, and I felt years of burden melting away.

"Then you were suddenly in my life again. I never gave my heart to you fully. I knew I was holding something back, but I didn't know how to stop. So I don't blame you for choosing Gia. I let my own bitterness from the past get in the way of what we could have had, and I only hurt myself because you didn't even know about it."

I took a breath to steady my voice. "I'm sorry things ended the way they did. Both times. I've never wanted to hurt you, Tim. And I forgive you for the past few days. I know you've been under a lot of pressure both here and at home. It's all going to be okay. My relationship with John started out a lot like yours with Gigi, but we had a really good marriage. I hope you and Gigi will be just as happy."

Tim's voice was tight with emotion as he pushed his chair back. "Thanks, Mack." He patted my hand and left the room.

I watched the fire until I got my emotions under control. Then I went out to the bar and put my hand in Gia's. "That martini looks frosty."

"Goodnight, everyone." Gia slid off the barstool, then ushered me out the back door. "Did Tim say something to hurt you?"

"No. Nothing like that. We just finally healed some old wounds. I had to get out of there before I started crying. And now I realize what Albert and Patricia were talking about with not letting your pride get in the way of your relationships."

He opened the car door for me. "Does that mean what I think it does?"

"It means I have to have a talk with my mother."

CHAPTER 57

"**Y**ou can do this, *cara mia*. You are the kindest, most loving person I know."

I snuggled into Gia on my front porch, not wanting to say goodbye, but knowing I had to do this on my own. "I think your opinion of me is greater than it should be."

He chuckled, his breath warming my neck. "And you have never seen just how beautiful you really are. You are not forgiving Iris because she deserves it. You are doing it because you deserve to be free."

"I'll keep telling myself that. I want to let go of this resentment that's been dragging me down my whole life."

It was a very tender moment between us, despite the caroling squirrels, dancing chipmunks, and roof spaceship that was programmed to the local radio station now that the neighbors, aka Willie of the Horseshoe Crab Willies, had complained to the cops about the noise.

A car slowed down in front of the house, and we heard the heavy-metal version of the "Dance of the Sugar Plum Fairy" coming through the car speakers. Across the street, Nell's house looked like the cover of *Victorian Christmas*

Monthly. Hers was as beautiful as mine was a five-year-old's fever dream.

I kissed Gia one more time. "I'll call you when it's done."

He walked down the sidewalk to his car, and I went inside, shutting the door to blissful silence. I gathered the reservation book and looked up Iris's phone number. She answered on the first ring.

"Helloooo?"

"It's Poppy. When would be a good time for you to come over so we could talk?"

She replied instantly. "Now. I can come now. Is that okay?"

"I'll be waiting."

I hung up, but my hands and stomach were quivering like jellyfish.

Figaro took tentative steps over to my desk and rubbed against my legs. I picked him up and snuggled him under my chin, making him purr. "You're still on my list, mister."

I noticed a box from Connie addressed to me sitting on the corner. *It's here!* I cut it open and took out the vintage redheaded Ken doll. Kenny Love was about to get his comeuppance.

Figaro followed me into the sitting room, where I started a fire. No new damage had been done to the tree. Apparently, knocking it over had spooked the last drop of fearlessness out of him.

As I waited for Iris to arrive, I changed the Ken doll into all white and hung him upside down by his ankles from the Dickens church steeple. Then I took out the Robin Hood archer and glued one of his arrows to Ken's chest. I placed the redheaded Barbie in the tufted cotton snow and gave her Robin Hood's bow and arrow, pointed in the right direction. Then I circled all the townsfolk around to watch. Finally, I moved the Christmas pudding vendor and placed her in position to sell snacks for those watching the chambermaid get his due.

I giggled, knowing Kenny would be shocked to find himself in the scene for a change. Then the front door opened, and my stomach thought it was Iris.

Sawyer came around the corner, holding a plastic bag from the drugstore, a sheepish look on her face. "I didn't want to do it by myself."

"You don't have to explain—I get it."

She looked down at the Christmas village and laughed out loud. "That's Kenny, isn't it?"

"Yep."

"Who's doing this?"

"It's been Kenny, but I did this one."

"That's awesome. How did you figure out it was him?"

I pointed to the redheaded vintage Barbie.

Sawyer grinned broadly. "I wish I could see his face when he finds this."

A knock on the front door sounded, and she clutched the bag to her chest. "Is that your guests?"

I gave her a look. "That would be Iris. We're about to have a talk, and I'm going to try to forgive her."

Sawyer searched my face for signs of sarcasm or stroke. She raised one eyebrow.

"No, really."

"You're more generous than I am, but I'm here for you. Just not here—here. I'll be in the kitchen eating all your fudge."

"I would do the same for you."

Sawyer disappeared through the dining room, and I opened the front door. "Come in."

Iris skipped into the sitting room and took a seat on one of the wing chairs. "I'm so glad you called. I've been craving your cherry cookies."

"It's time for total honesty—no judgment."

Iris nodded. "Total honesty."

"Why did you leave me?"

"What happened to your tree?"

"It doesn't matter."

She blew out her breath. Then she reached into her pocket and pulled out her cell phone. "Wait, I think I'm getting a call."

"Iris!"

Her eyes drooped, and she set the phone on the table. "Fine."

She took a quivery breath. "Your father was the love of my life. When he died, I wanted to die with him. I didn't know who I was anymore. I was so lost and alone." She took a minute to stare out the bay window before continuing. "You may not remember this, but I didn't get out of bed for three months. Your grandmother came to stay with us, just so we didn't starve."

"I vaguely remember."

She clenched her hands together. "When they found me wandering around Kmart, confused and hallucinating, it's because I had taken something. I just wanted the pain to stop. It was your grandma Emmy who suggested the facility. I couldn't be a good mother to you, but I knew your grandmother would love you like I couldn't. So I brought you here and checked myself into a psychiatric hospital."

I handed Iris a box of Kleenex. "How long were you there?"

Iris wiped the tears from her eyes. "Three months. I don't like to remember it. The things they did to me. No TV. And they took away my cigarettes. Most of the time, I was bored to the point of being numb. Nurses would taunt me to snap out of it, but I couldn't snap out of it. It was like someone had dropped me in a dark hole and there was no way to climb out."

"That sounds horrible."

"It was. And I missed you, but I knew you were better off without me in your life."

She waited, as if expecting me to rebuff that idea, but how could I? "I'm with you so far."

She shrugged and pressed on. "I wasn't getting the level of care I knew I needed. No one seemed to understand how hurt and lonely I was. I decided I had to find myself before I came for you. So I took the life insurance money and started to travel. I took up yoga, meditation, tai chi, and journaling."

"For thirty-five years?"

Iris wouldn't look me in the eye. "I liked traveling and meeting people. Doing my own thing. Getting up when I wanted and going where I wanted. I told myself you were doing fine, and every day it got easier to believe that I wasn't cut out to be a mother."

It was like a gut punch. One that you see coming a mile away, but don't have the sense to dodge. "So you just started over without me."

She had the courtesy to look ashamed when she nodded.

"Why come back now? I get that you want money and a reference, but how did you even know I'd be here?"

"I saw you on *Paranormal Pathfinders* when they ghost-hunted the house."

Darn it. I knew that was a bad idea.

"And I saw how well you were doing. Memories flooded back to me. Of you being a baby and a toddler."

"And the ring."

"Well, yes. And the ring. But also, how much I loved you." Her voice broke, and she struggled to speak through the tears. "And how ashamed your father would be to see that I had abandoned you to be raised by your grandmother."

Well, we agree on that.

"And I wanted a second chance."

"And by a second chance, you mean with a new baby through adoption?"

Iris nodded. "Our relationship will never be what it could have been. I ruined your life."

"That's not true. Aunt Ginny and Grandma Emmy loved me. They taught me how to be kind, and generous, and faithful. Aunt Ginny helped me pick up the pieces after my husband died and showed me how to take my life back. I don't know where I would be without her. There were so many wonderful things waiting me for that I would have missed out on if I'd given up. And Gia and Henry fill my heart with more love than I thought possible. Aunt Ginny's friends are like a crazy pack of grandmothers. Even Georgina has become like a mother to me. My life is full of joy."

Figaro sensed that he was left off the list and climbed out from under the couch. He patted me on the leg and meowed. Then he jumped on my lap and gave me a vibrating massage for some brownie points while he settled down.

Iris's face brightened. She dabbed her cheeks with the tissue and blew her nose. "I'm so happy for you. Really. You've had a second chance at life, and that's all I want. I have always loved you."

Yeah, but you love yourself just a little bit more.

"Iris, I want you to know that I forgive you for leaving me. You were going through unspeakable pain. I understand. I don't agree with your choices—I wouldn't have made the same ones—but they were yours to make. And I was loved and cared for. I wish I could go back in time and tell my nine-year-old self that it wasn't her fault and that you weren't coming back, so I could stop agonizing over your return. But those experiences made me who I am today. And I like who I am."

Iris reached for my hand, and for the first time since she arrived, I didn't recoil. "Since you're doing so well, do you think you could write the reference for me? My heart aches to be a mother."

I sighed. "I can't write you that letter. I'm sorry, but I don't know you. And the little I do know can't recommend you for motherhood. But I wish you well. And once the adoption goes through, you should bring my little brother or sister around to meet the rest of the family."

Iris looked a little taken aback. "Oh. And what about my engagement ring?"

"That's not mine to give you. I don't think I've ever seen it. What about the money my father left you? You said you were well off."

She deflated. "Traveling the world is expensive."

"I bet. Can you get a job?"

Iris stood and looked forlornly around the room. "I'm sure I can. But I don't want to be a working mom. I want to be a stay-at-home mom, like I was with you."

I stood and patted her on the shoulder. "You'll figure it out." I led her to the front door and opened it to see her off. "Goodbye, Iris. Take care of yourself."

She gave me a sad little wave and walked down the front path into the night. I wondered if I'd ever see her again. It was a slightly disappointing encounter—like thinking you have a chocolate-chip cookie, then biting into a raisin—but I felt like a great ache was gone. I wasn't rejected because of me. Her issues were her own. I forgave her, and I'm moving forward without the anchor of bitterness weighing me down. *Surely, with that, the curse is lifted. And since I'm the last McAllister, it ends here.*

"Is she gone?" Sawyer leaned out of the kitchen, looking down the hall.

"Yeah. She's gone."

"How'd it go?"

"It's moments like this that I'm reminded of words from Aunt Ginny. 'You can't make people be who you want them to be. You can only choose whether to let them into your life or not.'"

"I'm sorry." Sawyer made a pouty face.

"Don't be. I have the best family in the world."

She pulled a pregnancy test stick out of her pocket. "Are you ready to see if it's about to get bigger?"

CHAPTER 58

A pattering on my window woke me. The mid-morning sunlight was streaming through with glistening expectation. I hadn't slept this late since we opened the B and B. Figaro was snuggled into my side, purring. "It's Christmas Eve, Fig. I want you on your best behavior for the party tonight. So don't go all Rambo on another tree or try to steal the roast. You can torment Kenny, though." I giggled. "He's still trying to outdo my Christmas crime scene after we powned him." He'd nearly lost his mind with laughter when he saw what I had done.

He told me, "I was afraid you'd be mad at me when you found out I was behind it, but then I couldn't stop myself. Everyone loved them so much."

The patter happened again. "What is that?"

"Well, you'd better get up and see." Aunt Ginny scared the bejeezus out of me, standing over me dressed in her fancy Sunday church clothes.

"What is happening? And where are you going?"

"Just go look out your window."

My heart was way ahead of my brain, and it started to

pick up speed. I jumped out of bed and threw open the window.

Gia was standing in the yard below, looking illicitly sexy in a black tuxedo. He raised his palm and beckoned me outside.

"Are we getting married?!"

He smiled a devilish smile. "Surprise!"

I screamed and shut the window.

Aunt Ginny threw open my bedroom door. "Come on! She's finally up!" And a team of fancily dressed Biddies bustled into my room and went to work putting Cinderella's mice to shame. Aunt Ginny sent me into the bathroom for a five-minute shower, then handed me some beautiful silk undergarments that I definitely did not receive at my bridal shower.

Then the Biddies went to work doing my hair and makeup. "Do you all know what you're doing? Please don't make me look like Betty Boop."

Mrs. Davis tsk'd. "Girl, we've been doing this since long before you were born."

Mother Gibson had the hair dryer going over my hair while Mrs. Dodson put my feet in stockings and white, lace-up kidskin boots. "That's an interesting choice."

She rolled her eyes at the other Biddies, and they all snickered.

Georgina brought in the wedding dress I'd pinned to my board. "I'm glad you picked this one. It's the one I wanted for you."

"How did you know? It was on the back of that awful cupcake-liner dress that would make me look like a beach ball on top of a circus tent."

Aunt Ginny did up the zipper in the back. "Please. We know what looks good on you."

"Then why all the hideous options?"

Mother Gibson chuckled as she applied a burgundy

gloss to my lips. "Cause you got to think you picked it out on your own."

Georgina wrapped my hair into a fancy braided bun at my neck, and Mrs. Davis clipped a stunning diamond hairpiece along the side. "I wore this when I came out as a deb. It's very old, but now they call it vintage."

She applied half a can of hairspray, then the ladies stood back and admired their handiwork, nodding to themselves—and tearing up, in the case of Mother Gibson.

Aunt Ginny sniffled and pulled a square-cut sapphire from her pocket and placed it on my right ring finger. "Something blue your grandma always wanted you to have. I wish she were here to see you now."

Georgina added her diamond drop earrings to my ears. "Something borrowed." Her voice broke. She turned away and wiped her eyes.

Sawyer's voice called to me from the hall. "Where is the bride?"

I giggled. "In here."

She stopped dead in her tracks, and her eyes traveled the length of me. "Oh wow. You are stunning."

"So are you."

Sawyer did a little curtsy in her floor-length burgundy velvet. The tiniest baby bump was starting to show.

The ladies said they would meet me at the front door and tell Gia I was on my way. They tittered all the way down the stairs.

I had Sawyer give me a twirl. "It's perfect. How did you all pull this off?"

"Gia said you turned it over to him and you didn't want to wait."

"He was right. I feel like I'm eloping."

"We're all eloping with you." Sawyer was glowing. She was going to be a mom. And I was going to be an aunt. Henry was already telling everyone he was going to have a new baby cousin. We were supposed to wait ten minutes before reading the pregnancy test, but that second line had appeared so fast we had no doubt.

I grabbed her hand. "How are you feeling?"

"A little scared. No morning sickness, but I'm high-risk because this is my first baby and I'm in my forties. The doctor is already using the words 'bed rest,' and I've just started my second trimester."

"Don't be scared. I'll be with you every step of the way. I promise I'll never leave you."

She wrapped her arms around me. "Ditto."

Kenny was waiting at the bottom of the stairs in a black tuxedo with a burgundy velvet cummerbund. He handed me a stunning bouquet of cream cabbage roses, scarlet anemones and ranunculus, eucalyptus and frosted pinecones. "Your bouquet, madame."

"It's beautiful."

He gave me a mischievous look. "You should probably use a better password for your Pinterest account than FigNewton."

"I thought this looked familiar."

He slid his eyes to the Dickens village and grinned. I craned my neck to see into the sitting room. He'd set up a wedding in front of the church with the redheaded Barbie bride and . . . "Is that groom . . ."

Kenny nodded, pleased with himself. "Yep. Desi Arnaz. That was the closest I could get to your hunky Italian."

"I love it."

Joanne came down the hall, wiping her hands on a tea towel. "Hey, not bad."

"Wow, Joanne, I've never seen you wear a dress."

"I've never had a reason to. But tricking you into picking that raspberry whipped-cream wedding cake seemed like the right time. And just so you know, I made Gia the mocha grooms' cake, and his is not gluten-free. This is a classy event."

Figaro galloped across the hall from the library to the sitting room. He was wearing a white bow tie and tuxedo jacket. He slid into the tree skirt, then galloped in place for a couple seconds before heading back across to the library.

"Hold the fort, Fig. And stay outta the tree."

Aunt Ginny draped a white fur cape around my shoulders. "Are you ready?"

"I've never been more ready for anything."

Georgina opened the front door, and I spotted the love of my life as his jaw hit the ground.

Gia said a string of something in Italian that—I got the gist—meant he approved. Two black stallions pulling a white carriage had stopped in front of the house. He put his hand out, and I took it. "Your sleigh, m'lady." He helped me ascend and whispered in my ear. "Do not worry. We are not going far."

"I don't care. I'd go with you anywhere."

The carriage pulled away from the house, and a few light snow flurries swirled around us.

Gia took my hand. "Do you have any idea how much I love you, *Bella*?"

My cheeks were starting to hurt from smiling, but I couldn't stop. "I love you too."

Mother Gibson's church van drove past us, followed by Itty Bitty Smitty driving Georgina's car, then Gia's sister Karla in his car, and Kenny and Joanne in her pickup truck. We turned the corner, and the horses trotted down towards the ocean.

The wind whipped at my hair and my dress, and I had to protect my bouquet, but a little greenhouse had been erected on the beach.

"Okay, now I understand the boots."

The greenhouse was full of roses and candles. The day was overcast, but the salt tickled my nose while the waves crashed on the shore just a few yards away through the mullioned windows.

As soon as I stepped inside, Vivaldi's "Winter" began to play.

Aunt Ginny, Georgina, Joanne, and the Biddies were already seated next to Amber and Kieran—who, I noticed, were holding hands—watching eagerly for my entrance.

Gia's mother and siblings filled up the other side of the aisle, but some of them were looking a little sour about the turn of events.

Henry was waiting at the front next to Kenny and Ben. Connie and Kim were bouncing with excitement in their burgundy-velvet bridesmaid dresses on the other side of the aisle. Gia walked around to the front of the greenhouse and gave me a dazzling smile.

Sawyer removed my fur cape and draped it over a chair. "Are you ready for this?"

"You know it."

She squeezed my hand, took her bouquet, and walked down the aisle ahead of me. Vivaldi's "Winter" hit a crescendo and everyone stood up. Smitty was dressed in tails and a top hat—Georgina's doing, I'm sure—and offered me his arm and wiggled his eyebrows. "Come on, kid. Let's get this parade on. That groom of yours can't take much more waiting."

I linked my arm in his so he could walk me down a carpet covered in scarlet rose petals. He handed me off to Gia at the front, and I don't think I'd ever been happier in my life.

Henry edged closer and linked his pinky in mine, and we both giggled. I whispered to him, "We're getting married today."

The minister said a few words, then we began our vows.

I handed my bouquet to Sawyer, and Gia took my hand.

"Poppy, I have loved you from the moment we met, and there has never been a day that I did not want you to be my wife. I promise my love for you will only grow stronger through the years. We will have good times and bad, but I will be your strength. I will never give up on us, no matter what life throws our way."

Henry passed Gia the wedding band, and he placed it on my finger and gave me a smile filled with pure joy.

"Giampaolo, I felt like I was only half a person when we met, and you've made me whole. The tear in my heart is healed. You've taken my loneliness and filled me with love. You are the kindest man I've ever known. I promise to always love you. You will never be lonely again. I'll be your best friend, and your port in every storm." I turned my eyes to Henry. "I will try to be the best mom. I will be there for you and promise to keep you safe. You will always know that you are loved."

Henry passed me the band, and I placed it on Gia's finger, and we became a family, surrounded by everyone we loved.

When Gia kissed me, he was so excited to be married that he lifted me right off my feet.

Everyone wanted to congratulate us, so they swarmed the platform with hugs and well wishes.

Aunt Ginny whispered in my ear. "I told the minister to remove that part about speak now or forever hold your peace because of you know who."

I followed her eyes over to Momma, who was looking a little cross. "Mmm. Smart."

Aunt Ginny tapped the side of her nose.

Amber sidled up to me and handed me an envelope. "I realize now is not the best time for this, but I thought you'd want the results of your mother's background check before you leave for your honeymoon."

Gia was busy with his mother giving him what I assumed were wedding night instructions, judging from the scarlet glow of shock on his face. So I slipped my finger through the seal, pulled out the folded document, and gave it a scan. "Are you serious about this? This is for real?"

Amber bit her lip and nodded. "No criminal history, but your mother's loaded. She's got it all stashed away in the First National Bank of Belgium."

Of all the . . . What a . . . I ran my thumb along the underside of the sapphire my grandmother left for me. "All that talk about wanting to be a good mother and adopt, and it wasn't even important enough to her to spend her own money to do it."

Amber placed her hand on my arm. "I'm sorry. But just look at the family you've made for yourself."

I looked around the little greenhouse at Aunt Ginny and Georgina and the Biddies. All laughing and dancing, celebrating with me. My Henry, who was glued to my side. Kenny and Joanne and friends new and old. Even a couple of Gia's sisters were already talking about the coffee dates and shopping we were going to do. Amber was right, my life couldn't be more full of love if we all shared the same DNA.

I was overcome with emotion, and before I could reason with myself, I reached out and pulled Amber into a hug. She resisted only for a moment—I like to think it's because she was stunned—then she gave in and hugged me tighter.

"And girl, what is the deal with you and Kieran?"

Amber blushed. "We'll talk about that when you get back from Italy."

Aunt Ginny announced that everyone was invited back to our house for a champagne-brunch reception. I had a moment of terror that they were going to hook up that fountain again. Then it didn't matter, because we were together. I turned to Gia and whispered, "Do you take this Aunt Ginny, to corral and restrain, as long as chaos doth transpire?"

He kissed me. "I do."

We ran down the aisle through a shower of rose petals, and Henry joined us in the carriage for the ride home. As we were pulling away from the curb, a line of police cars turned on their lights and whoop-whooped their sirens to escort us around the block.

Gia told the carriage driver to take a victory lap so we could have a few moments alone before the reception. Henry linked his pinky with mine and snuggled into my side. "This is what I wanted for Christmas. A mom."

EPILOGUE

I clutched Gia's chest as he wound the Ducati through the streets of Rome. We'd spent the morning in a side-walk café overlooking the Roman Forum, and we were eager to get back to the hotel room.

Christmas had been a beautiful, wonderful adjustment. Waking up with a man in my bed, and a five-year-old jumping up and down, yelling that he wanted to open presents. We had our matching pajamas and our dairy-free hot cocoa in front of the fire, while the whole house joined us in the excitement of our first Christmas together.

Smitty and Georgina snuggled on the couch. Kenny passed a tray of cocoa and croissants to Sawyer and Ben.

Aunt Ginny glowed with pleasure, watching Henry open his gifts. I hadn't considered that not only was he the only child I'd ever have, but he was also the only grandchild she'd know.

Henry belly-laughed when Figaro gave me a box of new birds with an apology for destroying all the others and then immediately attacked the blue jay on top.

Henry had made me a picture frame out of popsicle

sticks and glitter. Letters made out of purple felt spelled FAMILY, and a photograph of the three of us together was nestled inside.

Aunt Ginny gave me a fancy lotion set from the mall, then asked if she could borrow it.

There was no snow. The tree was destroyed. Bruce Springsteen played a hundred times on the radio. But it was perfect.

The Biddies all came for brunch before going off for dinner with their families. As we sat around the dining room table, finishing coffee and listening to the sound of Henry playing with his new game doohickey in the other room and explaining it to Figaro, I asked something that had been weighing on my mind for weeks. "Aunt Ginny, if Grandpa Rooster's curse skipped generations, and was activated by pride and unforgiveness, why haven't you ever stumbled upon a murder victim?"

Aunt Ginny and the Biddies went dead silent. Their faces blank, stoic masks.

I chuckled nervously. "What is happening?"

Then the Biddies all cut their eyes to Aunt Ginny.

She picked up her coffee cup, but kept her eyes straight ahead. "That's a secret for another day, dear."

And that's how we left it.

Now Gia and I were on our honeymoon. This week Rome, next week Tuscany, then two nights in Venice. We tried sightseeing, but there were more interesting things to see and do in the hotel.

We pulled the motorcycle up to the curb, and Gia handed the valet the keys. The concierge greeted us with a huge grin as we tried not to run through the opulent lobby to the elevator. "*Buona sera*, honeymooners."

I giggled, "*Buona sera*." It was hard to be dignified with Gia's hands already on me before the elevator closed. He kissed me and said something very naughty that made me race down the hall to the room when the elevator opened.

As soon as I got to the door, he had me against the wall, fumbling for the key with his lips on mine.

He threw the door open and nudged me into the dark suite, his lips on my neck, his hands in more places than I thought possible. My foot caught on something, and I tripped. I landed on a pile of laundry.

Gia muttered. "Sloppy housekeepers." He flicked on the lights.

There, on the floor next to an opened suitcase and an overturned bucket of melting ice, the housekeeper lay facedown with a dagger in her back.

I jumped to my feet. "Are you freakin' kidding me? The curse is back! Whatdowedo?"

Gia covered his mouth and stared. "No. It is coincidence. That is all."

"We can run for it. I made the mistake of hanging around too long the first time. Won't do that again."

Gia took my hand and pulled me close. "*Bella*, we need to call the *carabiniere*. It will be okay. I am here with you."

My heartbeat slowed down a fraction. I looked back at the housekeeper on the floor and sighed. "How is this possible? Who else have I pissed off?"

Gia took my hand and pulled me close. "I can call Zio Vincenzo. He could make us disappear."

The housekeeper started to giggle. Three nosy Biddies popped up on the other side of the bed and yelled, "*Abbondanza!*"

The housekeeper rolled to her side, revealing that she was a very sneaky redhead who was supposed to be in America watching the bed and breakfast. "Gotcha!"

I turned to my husband. "Make the call."

Cherry-Coconut Balls

Yield: 3 dozen balls

This is my mother's Christmas cookie recipe. I don't remember a Christmas without these buttery little cookies. Now they're my husband's favorite. He says it isn't Christmas until I make them. My mother's are lighter and puffier than mine because she uses butter-flavor Crisco instead of real butter. I can't bring myself to do that, but I will admit that hers are a little softer than mine.

Ingredients
1 cup sugar
¾ cup butter
1 egg
1 tsp vanilla
2 cups sifted gluten-free flour blend with xanthan
    gum
½ tsp baking powder
½ tsp salt
½ cup chopped maraschino cherries
½ cup grated coconut
½ cup toasted pecans (optional)
2 Tbsp juice reserved from maraschino cherries
1 cup powdered sugar

Instructions
Preheat oven to 325°F.

Cream the butter and sugar with a mixer. Blend in the egg and vanilla.

Sift the dry ingredients together, then add them to the creamed butter.

Fold in the cherries, coconut, and pecans.

Drop small, rounded mounds by teaspoons on a lightly

greased cookie sheet or a cookie sheet lined with parchment paper.

Bake for 8–10 minutes until the cookies are just beginning to brown on the edges; you don't want them to brown on top.

Let them cool on the pan before moving them to a wire rack or sheets of parchment paper.

Make your frosting by slowly adding the powdered sugar to the cherry juice. You want the fondant to be thick enough to spread. If it is too runny, it will melt down over the top of the cookies.

When your cookies are cool, frost them with the pink fondant. I like to leave a few unfrosted to show off the cherries.

Dad's Peanut-Butter Fudge

Yield: 1 bread-pan-sized block

This was my father's favorite Christmas fudge, and he made it every year. It's not fudge in the truest sense, but I think it's even better.

Ingredients
1 bag semisweet chocolate chips
1 can sweetened condensed milk
1½ cups smooth Jif Peanut Butter

Instructions
Line a bread pan with parchment paper.

Melt the chocolate chips in the sweetened condensed milk—either on top of the stove on low heat or in the microwave. Stir together until smooth.

Add in the peanut butter. Mix thoroughly.

Spread the mixture in the bread pan, and let it cool until set.

Pull out the block using the parchment paper. Cut into squares and hide from the family. My daughter and mother will each eat an entire pan of this over the holidays.

Gluten-free Gingerbread Biscotti

Yield: around 16 biscotti

Ingredients

$\frac{1}{2}$ cup unsalted butter, room temperature
$\frac{1}{2}$ cup sugar
$\frac{1}{2}$ cup packed brown sugar
2 large eggs
$\frac{1}{2}$ cup almond meal
$1\frac{1}{2}$ cups gluten-free flour blend
1 teaspoon xanthan gum, if not included in your
    gluten-free flour
2 tsp baking powder
2 tsp baking powder
1 tsp ground cinnamon
1 tsp ground ginger
$\frac{1}{4}$ tsp ground cloves
$\frac{1}{4}$ tsp ground nutmeg
$\frac{1}{4}$ tsp sea salt
$\frac{1}{2}$ cup crystallized ginger, diced fine
$\frac{1}{2}$ cup chopped almonds
1 bag white chocolate chips for melting and dip-
    ping after baking

Instructions

Preheat oven to 325°F (300°F convection). Mix butter and sugars together until light and fluffy. Add eggs.

In a separate bowl, combine the almond meal, gluten-free flour, xanthan gum if needed, baking powder, baking soda, spices, and sea salt. Whisk together.

Add the dry ingredients to the butter and sugar mixture, and beat until smooth. Fold in the diced crystallized ginger and chopped almonds.

Transfer the dough to a piece of parchment paper, and form into a log. Flatten the log into the size and shape you want your finished biscotti slices to be. Roll the log up into the parchment paper to prevent the dough from spreading all over the pan. It will bake into this shape, so be sure it is as long and flat as you want your cookies to be when you slice them.

Bake for 45 minutes. Remove from the oven. Gently and carefully unwrap the dough from the parchment. Return to the oven and bake for 10–15 minutes longer, until it is dry and firm to the touch. Remove to cool on a wire rack.

Once the dough is cooled, use a serrated knife to carefully slice the log into 1-inch-thick biscotti. The dough won't be cooperative—don't worry. You can mash any broken pieces together for toasting, and they'll stay together.

Place the slices on a parchment-lined baking sheet and bake for another 15–20 minutes until slightly crispy. I like to gently touch them to see if they are dry. They will get crunchier as they cool.

Melt white-chocolate chips in a microwave-safe bowl on high, about 1 minute or 1 minute, 30 seconds. Dip each cooled biscotti in white chocolate and place on parchment paper to set. You can either dip the tops, like you're frosting them, or you can dip one half. It's up to you. I love the way the white chocolate gets all melty when I dip my biscotti into my coffee, so I dip the entire top edge.

Joanne's Gluten-free Christmas Stollen

Yield: 2 loaves

Ingredients
1 cup whole milk heated to lukewarm
4 tsp instant action yeast
2 Tbsp sugar
1½ cups raisins
¾ cup candied orange peel, finely chopped
¾ cup candied lemon peel, finely chopped
½ cup apple juice
4 cups gluten-free flour
1 teaspoon xanthan gum if it is not already in your flour
½ cup sugar
1 Tbsp baking powder
1 tsp salt
1 tsp ground cardamom
¾ tsp ground mace (or nutmeg, if you can't find mace)
½ tsp ground cinnamon
½ tsp ground cloves
Zest of 1 lemon
Zest of 1 orange
¾ cup (1½ sticks) unsalted butter, softened
1 egg
2 egg yolks
2 tsp vanilla
1 cup blanched almonds, chopped
2 7-oz tubes marzipan or almond paste

For the glaze
1 stick butter, melted
½ cup powdered sugar for coating

Instructions

Make sure to take out the butter to soften.

Heat your milk in the microwave for 30 seconds or on top of the stove until it is lukewarm. Lukewarm is cooler than you'd think. Your body is 98°F. Lukewarm is slightly cool to the touch but not cold. If you make the milk too hot, let it sit until it cools down or it will kill the yeast.

Once the milk is just right, add the 4 teaspoons of yeast and the 2 tablespoons of sugar. Stir, then let sit while you do everything else. It should get nice and frothy. If it doesn't, throw it away and start over. If it still doesn't, you need new yeast.

In a microwave-safe mixing bowl, add the raisins and chopped peels. Pour ½ cup rum over the mixture. Microwave for 2 minutes. Cover the bowl with plastic wrap, and set aside.

In the bowl of your stand mixer (or a large mixing bowl), add the gluten-free flour, xanthan gum if you used it, sugar, baking powder, salt, spices, zests, butter, egg, egg yolks, and vanilla. Add the milk-and-yeast mixture. Turn the mixer on low, and beat the dough until all the ingredients are fully incorporated and form a nice ball of dough that pulls away from the sides of the bowl and holds together on the beater. Turn off the mixer.

Drain the fruits in case there is rum that did not get absorbed. Add the rehydrated fruits to the mixing bowl, along with the blanched almonds. Turn the mixer back on and mix until the fruit and nuts are fully incorporated into the dough.

Turn the dough out onto a floured countertop or a larger piece of parchment paper. You may need a little flour for your hands to keep them from sticking. Form the dough into a nice ball in which the fruits are well distributed. Cut the ball in half, and move half to the side. Form the remaining half into a log about 9 inches long. With your rolling pin—or using your hands—flatten the dough into an oblong disc roughly 12 inches long.

Roll the marzipan into a rope a little shorter than the dough. Place the marzipan in the middle of the dough and roll the short sides up to cover the ends of the marzipan. Roll the dough back into a log. Place the log on a clean piece of parchment on a baking sheet, and set it someplace cozy to rise. Repeat the process with the other ball of dough and other tube of marzipan.

Cover with a light tea towel or cheesecloth, and leave in a warm place to rise for 1½–2 hours, until risen and puffy. This is your only rise. Gluten-free breads don't get a punch down and second rise.

Preheat the oven to 325°F and bake for 70 minutes—or until a probe thermometer reads 195–200°F in the center of the stollen. Remove from the oven, brush with melted butter, and dust with icing sugar. Let it cool, then dust with icing sugar again. Serve cool.

Candied Gingerbread Muffins

Yield: 12–14 muffins

Ingredients
¾ cup unsalted butter
¾ cup dark molasses
2⅔ cups gluten-free flour
1½ tsp baking soda
¼ tsp salt
1½ tsp ground cinnamon
1¼ tsp ground ginger
½ tsp ground cloves
½ cup dark brown sugar, packed
1 large egg, at room temperature
½ cup heavy cream
1 cup white-chocolate chips
½ cup chopped candied ginger
Sanding sugar for decorating (optional)

Instructions
Preheat oven to 425°F. Line a muffin pan with paper liners. Set aside.

In a large, microwave-safe bowl, heat the butter and molasses together in the microwave on high for about 1 minute. Stir until thoroughly mixed together. Set aside to cool.

Put your egg—in the shell—into a cup of very warm water so it warms up.

Whisk the flour, baking soda, salt, cinnamon, ginger, and cloves together.

Into the molasses/butter mixture, whisk the brown sugar, egg, and cream until all wet ingredients are combined. Pour wet ingredients into dry ingredients, and mix until just combined. Do not overmix. The batter will be thick and a little lumpy.

Fold in white-chocolate chips and chopped candied ginger.

Divide the batter among the sections of the prepared muffin pan, filling them all the way to the top. Sprinkle with coarse sugar, if desired.

Bake at 425°F for 5 minutes, then reduce the oven temperature to 350°F and continue to bake for 15–16 minutes until a toothpick comes out clean. Allow to cool before serving.

Aunt Ginny's Second Place Because She Was Robbed Black Walnut Cake

Yield: a 1-pound cake

Ingredients
3 cups sugar
¾ cup butter
½ cup shortening or refined coconut oil
2 tsp black walnut extract (buy on the internets)
2 tsp black walnut bitters
5 extra-large eggs
3 cups gluten-free flour blend with xanthan gum
1 tsp baking powder
½ tsp salt
1 cup milk
1 cup black walnuts, chopped

Instructions
Preheat oven to 325°F. Grease and flour a bundt or tube pan. Set aside.

Cream together sugar, butter, and shortening. Add the extract and bitters.

Add the eggs one at a time. Mix well. Combine the gluten-free flour. baking powder, and salt in another bowl. Add half to the butter and egg mixture. Add half the milk.

Add the other half of the dry ingredients. Add the other half of the milk. Fold in the nuts.

Bake for 1 hour until golden-brown and the top springs back when pressed. Test with a toothpick to be sure it's done.

Chocolate-Orange Scones

Yield: 12 scones

Ingredients

3 cups gluten-free flour
1 Tbsp baking powder
1 tsp salt
$\frac{1}{2}$ cup sugar
Zest of 1 orange
8 Tbsp cold butter
$1\frac{1}{2}$ tsp vanilla extract
$1\frac{1}{4}$ cups heavy whipping cream
6 oz dark chocolate, roughly chopped

For the orange glaze

1 cup powdered sugar
Juice from 1/2 of the orange

Instructions

Preheat oven to 425°F. Line a baking sheet with parchment.

Into a food processor bowl, combine gluten-free flour, baking powder, salt, sugar, and orange zest. Pulse until well combined.

Add cold butter by the tablespoon, and pulse until combined.

Add the vanilla extract to the heavy cream. Pour in a little at a time while pulsing. Add in $\frac{3}{4}$ of the chopped chocolate pieces. I like to reserve the smaller pieces to add after the dough is made.

You should form a lovely cohesive dough—not sticky, but no flour left in the bottom of the bowl either. Lightly dust your counter with gluten-free flour. Turn the dough out, and let it rest for a minute.

Form the dough into a ball, and flatten it with your

hands. Press it into the remaining $\frac{1}{4}$ of chopped chocolate pieces. Roll out to a thickness of about $\frac{3}{4}$-inch thick. Cut into rounds with a biscuit cutter.

Place rounds on prepared baking sheet close together, but not touching. As they rise, they will help each other rise.

Brush the tops with heavy cream.

Bake for 15 minutes and check for doneness. If they need a little more time, put the pan back in the oven for 5 minutes. If the tops are getting too brown, turn the oven down to 350°F for the last 5 minutes.

Remove from the oven and let cool. Make your glaze by putting the powdered sugar in a small mixing bowl. Add the orange juice a little at a time and stir, until you have a thick paste that will still run off a spoon. Drizzle the glaze over the top of the cool scones.

ACKNOWLEDGMENTS

Please come find me online at libbykleinbooks.com, and sign up for my newsletter to get all my goings-on, plus gluten-free recipes and Figaro's advice column.

Special thanks to Elizabeth Butcher for sharing her devious Dickens village crime-scene prank.

Visit our website at
KensingtonBooks.com
to sign up for our newsletters, read
more from your favorite authors, see
books by series, view reading group
guides, and more!

Become a Part of Our
Between the Chapters Book Club
Community and Join the Conversation

Betweenthechapters.net

Submit your book review for a chance to win exclusive
Between the Chapters swag you can't get anywhere else!
https://www.kensingtonbooks.com/pages/review/